"Readers who enjoy a wel... ...with *Death by Fire*."

Cyril H. W......, ..., ..., Author of *Cause of Death*

"*Death by Fire* is a genuine page-turner, with excitement and tension in every chapter."

Michael Bowen, Author of *Corruptly Procured*

"Chris Davis' *Death by Fire* is a Clancy-esque tour de force of what readers will demand in all future suspense novels. Davis has interwoven terrorism with technology, creating a scenario far too real to call it 'fiction.' Death by Fire is a must read for those who enjoy a non-stop, full-tilt 'page turner.' I applaud his first novel and eagerly await future efforts."

Walt Brown, Author of *People v. Lee Harvey Oswald* and *JFK Assassination Quizbook*

"With thunderous authenticity, *Death by Fire* throbs with frighteningly realistic possibilities. Out of Chris Davis' wildly imaginative and creative mind comes a plot that could happen."

Gaeton Fonzi, Author of *The Last Investigation*

"The plot of this book is just crazy enough to compute!"

Laura Hockaday, *Kansas City Star*

"…the perfect 'cyber-thriller'."

Charles Ferruzza, *The Sun Newspapers*

"Move over Tom Clancy. Chris Davis has taken the war game thriller to a new crypto-clearance level. Combining historically accurate facts with cutting edge technology and James Bond plots and counter plots. Too real to put down."

Michael Canfield, Author of *Coup d'Etat in America*

"*Death By Fire* takes your breath away, wowing us with its hardware and scaring the daylights out of us with its plot."

Andrew Tomb, *Kansas State Collegian*

Death by
FIRE

Chris Davis

BZ Books

To Cheryl . . .

UNITED STATES DEPARTMENT OF JUSTICE

FEDERAL BUREAU OF INVESTIGATION

WASHINGTON, D.C. 20535

August 29, 1977

Miss Jean Cuff

Dear Miss Cuff:

I have known Mr. Christopher D. Davis since 1961, and his family well before that. He is a fine young man, intelligent and responsible. His father and I attended college together and have remained friends throughout the years. His mother is a splendid lady and his sister a girl to be proud of. I know nothing derogatory to any of the family and highly recommend Chris for a position for which he is qualified. I would hire him were he to apply to me.

My recommendation of Chris should in no way be construed as an endorsement of the FBI, nor has any check been made of our files with regard to any members of the Davis family.

Sincerely yours,

Clarence M. Kelley
Director

TOP TEN US INFRASTRUCTURE TARGETS:

1. Culpeper Switch - in Culpeper, Virginia, this electronic switch handles all federal funds transfers and transactions.

2. Alaska Pipeline - carries ten percent of domestic oil for the US.

3. Electronic Switching System (ESS) - manages all telephony.

4. Internet - the communications backbone of science and industry.

5. Time Distribution System - all major systems depend upon accurate time.

6. Panama Canal - still immensely important in the transport of oil and goods.

7. Worldwide Military Command and Control System (WWMCCS) - particularly susceptible to soft attack.

8. Big Blue Cube - just off Moffett Field in Mountain View, California, this is the Pacific clearing house for satellite reconnaissance.

9. Malaccan Straits, Singapore - the maritime link between Europe-Arabia and the Western Pacific.

10. National Photographic Interpretation Center (NPIC) - a ten-minute walk from the US Capitol, this is the repository and processing facility for all of the government's photographic intelligence.

Most of the men and women who create policy in government are not of the computer generation. They don't understand code, or the fundamental value of data, or the inherently "soft" way the world works. No one is planning for the grand scale attack. No one is planning for the grand scale defense. No one is planning for the "soft kill."

That attack will come. That defense will be necessary.

...Peter Black,
WIRED Magazine
July/August 1993.

Introduction

At 2:38 a.m. on January 17, 1991, Colonel Hussein Kamil Hasan al-Majid was awakened from his sleep by the ringing of a red telephone which was on the makeshift night stand next to his cot. He had been sleeping eighty feet underground in a concrete-fortified bunker attached to Factory 10, a top-secret centrifuge production unit in Taji, 50 kilometers northwest of Baghdad which, as chief of the State Organization for Technical Industries, Kamil had been responsible for creating. His call abruptly informed him that several radar sites in Iraq's western border had just stopped functioning, and that it was believed that the allied attack had begun, which, in fact, was true, since a squadron of Apache helicopters had just destroyed the sites with laser-guided Hellfire missiles, followed by clusters of Hydra rockets.

As Hussein Kamil spoke on the telephone, nearly 700 aircraft of the coalition forces slipped undetected through the "radar-black" corridor, including the 415th Squadron of the U.S. 37th Tactical Fighter Wing, consisting of six subsonic F-117A Stealth attack planes, each armed with a single, 2,000-pound, laser-guided smart bomb. The 415th flew in a tight formation under a blank new moon with only the beavertail plumes of their exhaust showing underneath the stars. If detected in daylight the F-117A's were no match for an enemy fighter with a maximum speed below Mach 1, but by night they were all but invisible.

The only warning the platoon of sentries guarding the Taji Complex had before the plant was hit was the unusual high-pitched whine of the approaching F-117As' General Electric F404-F1D2 turbofan engines. In his bunker below ground Hussein Kamil felt each bomb hit its target in succession. The 415th's final target was Factory 10, and the force of the explosions was enough to cause Kamil's ears to ring for days afterwards, destroying in a moment hundreds of gas centrifuges, spinning lathes, spinning machines, vacuum pumps, and custom valves, all of which he had spent years in acquiring. An hour later, the 416th "Ghostriders" Tactical Fighter Squadron repeated the same bombing pattern, reducing the shattered remains of Taji Complex to flaming rubble and Iraq's nuclear weapons program with it.

By dawn the allied bombing had stopped and Colonel Kamil decided to leave the safety of his German-built bunker. A two-foot-thick steel-reinforced concrete slab which separated the three underground levels from the concrete stairwells leading to the basement of the complex had collapsed under the impact of the bombing, so after Kamil had rounded up a few key members of his staff and ordered them to don nuclear protective gear, he had them follow him along a special exit tunnel which surfaced about a hundred yards from Factory 10. Even though he knew only too well that an allied bombing attack had taken place, the Iraqi colonel was not emotionally prepared for the landscape filled with smoking wreckage which he saw for the first time through his visor.

Destroyed! Years of work destroyed overnight by the air forces of the very same countries who had been his suppliers!

His staff members watched in horror as Kamil fell to his knees and sobbed silently inside his protective suit.

☆ ☆ ☆

Hussein Kamil had begun his career as an errand boy, fielding packages on shopping trips made by the presidential family to Oxford Street when they went to London. Allowed to talk to the women, since he also happened to be Saddam's cousin, Kamil wasted no time in asking the president's permission to marry his eldest daughter, Ragha. After single-handedly stopping an assassin from killing his future father-in-law, Lieutenant Kamil was promoted to full colonel and was granted permission to marry Ragha. The war with Iran found him touring the front lines, side by side with his father-in-law Saddam in the official photographs. In fact, they looked more like brothers than in-laws, having the same dark mustaches, full jaws, and dark skins. In 1986 Kamil was given his first real responsibility, when Saddam Hussein put him in charge of the State Organization for Technical Industries (SOTI), the agency responsible for procuring nuclear weapons technology.

Through dummy companies set up all over Europe, Colonel Kamil had purchased enough equipment so that by the time the war with the United States had begun, Iraq was simultaneously manufacturing weapons-grade fuel using all four of the presently available processes in secret facilities spaced throughout the country. Only the chance appearance of a defector, coming over to the U.S. Marines in June 1991, revealed the existence of five buried plants which had been untouched during the war. In September 1991, after the war was over, Defense Intelligence Agency analysts drastically revised their prewar estimates of how close Iraq was to obtaining the bomb, from five to ten years, down to six months.

☆ ☆ ☆

Almost two years after the allied air attack early in the morning of November 4, 1992, Colonel Kamil heard a pounding on the door of his home in Baghdad and was welcomed by a pair of colonels from Saddam Hussein's elite Republican Guards who ordered him to get dressed and come with them. They raced along the Military Canal past the bombed-out communications center, swerved suddenly into a side street and slammed to a stop in front of a nondescript two-story restaurant with two sentries holding automatics at port arms stationed at the door.

The dining room was empty, save for three men at the center table: Saddam Hussein, the President of Iraq; Sabawi Hussein, Saddam's half-brother and long-time head of Iraqi intelligence; and a German nuclear physicist, Dr. Karl Stemmler, who had supervised Iraq's development of gas centrifuge plants to make nuclear bombs. It had turned into a celebratory dinner as the early evening election returns from America showed Bill Clinton a clear winner over George Bush for the office of President of the United States.

"He lost! The bastard lost!"

Saddam Hussein rose from the table and clasped Kamil's hand, then motioned for him to sit down next to him.

For a man who had only two years ago suffered a humiliating military defeat of immeasurable proportions and whose country was presently overrun with UN inspection teams, Saddam Hussein seemed to Colonel Kamil to be in astonishingly good spirits. The Colonel also couldn't help but notice the barely disguised look of satisfaction on the face of the normally taciturn Sabawi Hussein. Kamil asked himself what difference did it make to them whether it was Bush or Clinton? The war had already been lost, and the country's nuclear weapons program still lay in ruins…Only the German, Stemmler, seemed unaffected by it all, maintaining the same skeptical expression he had when the Colonel had shown him the stolen blueprints for building uranium gas centrifuges at the Rashid Hotel almost a dozen years ago.

In many ways the German scientist was the opposite of the volatile Kamil, who had to be officially reprimanded by his father-in-law for his extravagances during his buying efforts in Europe. Intellectually arrogant and a ruthless manager of his own self-interest, Stemmler resembled nothing so much as a harmless retiree in his battered felt fedora and wrinkled sports coat. Stemmler's saving grace was that at bottom, like many scientists, he was relatively apolitical, which made it easier for him to switch sides if the need arose.

Now seventy-five years old, Stemmler had begun his scientific career in ballistic missile manufacture at Hitler's Nordhausen Rocket Works under the aegis of General Walter Dornberger. Dornberger, a career German artillery officer, had recognized two decades before the war that even though the Treaty of Versailles prevented Germany from manufacturing

most conventional weaponry, it had not banned the building
of rockets, which Dornberger began to add to the Nazi arsenal
in 1932. When Stemmler joined Dornberger's staff in 1943,
battalions of slave laborers from the nearby Dora concentration camp had just been directed by the SS to hack a
square-mile hole out of an abandoned salt mine to begin
Nordhausen's construction.

By the time the plant was liberated by American troops in
April 1945 over twenty thousand prisoners had been systemat-
ically starved and worked to death, their bodies finally piling
up everywhere in the last months of the Reich, since the ovens
were too busy. Far from being charged with war crimes for
having been honorary members of the SS and having set production schedules responsible for working thousands of men
to death, the talents of Dornberger and his scientific staff were
fought over by the Russians and Americans for use in one or
the other side's own military research projects.

But the day before the Americans' arrival Herr Doktor Karl
Stemmler left the plant to avoid being swept up in either
Project Overcast or Operation Paperclip, the secret programs
which were responsible for bringing 765 former Nazi scientists, engineers and technicians to the United States. Eluding
American patrols, Stemmler was passed along a ratline run by
former Abwehr officers and escaped to Syria. From there he
moved to Cairo and worked for Nasser, until the Mossad
found him out and he escaped to Brazil, where he continued
his work for that government's ballistic research missile
program. Later, Stemmler was asked by the Brazilian National
Intelligence Service to become involved in Brazil's nascent
secret nuclear weapons program, which was run by its Navy.
Since the 1950s, Brazilian scientists had been working with
ultracentrifuge technology, the same used in the Manhattan
Project by the Americans, to separate the rare bomb-grade
isotope from regular uranium, which the Brazilians had in
large supply in their local mines. The head of the Brazilian
nuclear program was another former Third Reich scientist,

Wilhelm Hoth, a man of mixed allegiances, who became Stemmler's mentor and fast friend.

When Saddam Hussein signed the top secret ten-year nuclear cooperation agreement with Brazil, Stemmler was instructed by his superior, Hoth, to move to Iraq and become his special representative in Baghdad. There Stemmler oversaw Brazilian shipments of natural and low-enriched uranium, reactor technology, and, more importantly, a special centrifuge project to enrich ordinary uranium to bomb-grade fuel at the Iraqis' first nuclear reactor site in Osirak. After signing the Franco-Iraqi Nuclear Cooperation Treaty, the French, insisting nuclear technology was a question of "national sovereignty," had agreed to export a breeder reactor and a so-called "research reactor" to Iraq and train six hundred Iraqi nuclear technicians. Visiting members of the French Atomic Energy Commission were surprised by the arrival of Brazilian nuclear physicists in the spring of 1981, but were told by Dr. Stemmler to keep quiet or they would be declared *persona non grata* and sent back to France.

But three of the French physicists didn't take kindly to being ordered about by an arrogant old man they suspected was a former Nazi, and upon returning to France, complained to President Mitterand that Saddam Hussein was planning to make a bomb. In Israel, Prime Minister Menachem Begin's chief of staff, General Rafael Eitan, was informed of the French physicists' report by Mossad, who also informed Eitan that the Iraqis' Osirak plant was almost a carbon copy of Israel's own bomb plant at Dimona.

On June 7, 1981, Dr. Karl Stemmler suffered his first major reversal in Iraq, when Israeli F-16s crossed Saudi, then Jordanian, airspace and attacked Osirak with precision-guided missiles and 2000-pound "dumb" bombs in Operation Babylon. After the years spent rebuilding the shattered ruins of Saddam Hussein's nuclear weapons program, for Karl Stemmler at his advanced age, the American attack in January

1991 was the final straw. The message sent by George Bush and the coalition couldn't have been clearer: it was fine for Iraq to buy uranium gas centrifuges from Brazil and Germany; nuclear reactor cores from the French; and plutonium hot cells and laboratories from the Italians—but if these discrete components were ever assembled by the Iraqis to create an atom bomb, they would be destroyed or dismantled.

The second participant, Sabawi Hussein, Saddam Hussein's middle half brother, had replaced one of the dictator's cousins to become acting head of the General Intelligence Department (or Mukhabarat) at the end of 1989. While police forces in many third-world countries are often poorly staffed and inefficient, Iraq's employed more than one hundred fifty thousand people in its various security services. The Mukhabarat had representatives in over a score of Iraqi embassies abroad, who had been responsible for the elimination of exiled Iraqi dissidents in France, Lebanon, Sweden, England, Egypt, and the United States.

Born in the same dirt-poor village of Tikrit as his brother Saddam, Sabawi had been chosen specifically because of the dictator's belief in the family as the key to power. His predecessor, Dr. Radhil al-Barak, had drastically reorganized the department, replacing political favorites with trained professionals, so that by the time Sabawi took it over, the Mukhabarat was quite capable of running successful foreign operations. Under no illusions as to who held the true authority in Iraq and shrewder than many of his other relatives, Sabawi Hussein believed he, more than anyone, understood his half brother's deep-rooted desire to avenge himself for his humiliating defeat at the hands of the Americans and their allies.

☆ ☆ ☆

Saddam Hussein returned to his seat at the table and surveyed his three guests. Each man knew better than to initiate a conversation in his leader's presence so he merely returned his gaze, asking no questions.

The dictator now began a long, rambling monologue, citing instance after instance of treachery and betrayal he had suffered at the hands of his previously faithful armaments suppliers, most of whom hadn't hesitated to join the United Nations coalition arrayed against Iraq in the Gulf War. Carefully and methodically he listed plant after plant which had been destroyed in the massive air attacks, stripping the country of its strategic weapons. His three guests glanced down at the floor in shame, their faces growing longer with each recitation.

"Hussein Kamil Hasan al-Majid!" Saddam began, "you know I am always the first to admit I've made a mistake!"

"Yes, sir," replied Kamil, now fearing for his life, since Saddam's mistakes had often been rectified in the past by drastic changes in strategy and summary executions.

"And Sabawi Hussein al-Tikriti," Saddam continued, turning to his half brother, "your loyalty has never been in doubt throughout this whole ordeal." Then turning to the German, "Nor yours, Dr. Stemmler. Without your help, Iraq could never have come as far as she did…"

Stemmler silently nodded in appreciation.

"But we must simply face the facts—we have taken too many blows to be able to recover, plus it's now impossible for us to start again. Our previous suppliers are now our enemies, and even if they weren't, it would take us years to get where we were before the war. Of course, there will always be the Chinese and the Pakistanis and the North Koreans — if they last that long — but all of you have made it clear to me in the past that they alone were not enough."

Saddam's three guests had informed him early on in the development of Iraq's nuclear weapons program that reliance on only those countries which had not signed the Nuclear

Non-Proliferation Treaty, e.g., China, North Korea, France and Pakistan, would not be sufficient. Iraq would also have to approach the various signatories to acquire all the components necessary to construct a nuclear device. Now, to go back to Germany for centrifuges, Italy for plutonium cells, France for a new reactor, or the United States for replacement equipment was out of the question.

Although each of his three invitees knew this, none dared to interrupt.

"I believed before the war, and I believe now, that my two primary aims in attempting to liberate Kuwait were sound: first, to acquire and control Kuwait's oil capacity, and, second, by doing so, to help relieve our enormous debts by reducing their output, thereby raising world oil prices when it suited us. I don't have to tell you how many times we tried to reason with them and the Saudis over this to no avail, while they continued to defy us and ran their wells flat out...

"Now we have American troops directly across our border, plants overrun with I.A.E.A. inspection teams, and the Saudis and the Kuwaitis laughing in our faces—a state of affairs for which I accept the total blame. What was my mistake? My mistake was to confront our enemies too courageously, too arrogantly on their own terms—and because I made that mistake we lost.

"But after talking to one of you, it's now clear to me that there is another way of accomplishing these same objectives— that there always was another way—which was right under our noses if I had only seriously considered it. The Libyans gave us a hint of it over Lockerbie. It is simply this, gentlemen, to use the enemy's own nuclear forces against himself."

Kamil and Stemmler looked at each other in horror, each knowing the dictator well enough to have understood exactly the ramifications of what he had just said, guessing immediately that the dictator's half brother, Sabawi, whose face continued to remain impassive, had a surprise in store for them.

"But how can we implement such a plan?" interrupted Dr. Stemmler, suspecting encroachment on his territory.

"A method exists, I assure you, gentlemen," replied Saddam. "But what I want to know now is if I have your approval to go forward with this new strategy?"

Dr. Stemmler and Colonel Kamil quickly exchanged glances. They each knew that the one who protested at this point would not live out the day.

"*Na'am*," Kamil answered in affirmation.

"*M'leeh*." Good, replied Saddam. "Dr. Stemmler?"

The former honorary SS *Sturmbannfuhrer* nodded silently in affirmation.

Then, for the first time that day Sabawi Hussein began to speak: "President Hussein has agreed with me that it is of the utmost importance that what I am about to tell you will never leave this room." The chief of the Mukhabarat then paused and rested his gaze on both Stemmler and Colonel Kamil, who again nodded their agreement.

"On the day after the American invasion, a certain Lebanese-American, who I hereafter will refer to as GERALD, walked uninvited into our United Nations Mission in New York."

GERALD was an obscure systems designer who worked in La Jolla, California, at a software engineering firm whose sole business was a classified contract to update the U.S. military's Worldwide Military Command and Control System (WWMCCS).

"Wimex", as it was pronounced at the Pentagon, was the main circuit cable which ran straight from the White House Situation Room to the State Department's Operations Center, the National Military Command Center at the Pentagon, as well as several alternate war rooms, plus NSA's own early warning site, the Defense Special Missile and Astronautics Center (DESFMAC)

*and the North American Air Defense Command (NORAD)
Headquarters hidden in Colorado's Cheyenne Mountain. In case
of nuclear war, the President and the Secretary of Defense would
issue their orders over the WWMCCS network to the three legs of
America's nuclear defense triad: submarines, strategic bombers,
and the hardened silos containing ICBMs.*

Colonel Kamil turned to Saddam Hussein with a look of
absolute bewilderment, but the dictator only nodded his head,
motioning to his son-in-law to continue to pay attention to
Sabawi's story, which, when he heard the rest of it, sent a shiver
down his spine.

"Being a scientist, he avoided political discussion, but
because he was a Lebanese, I had immediately suspected him
of being strenuously opposed to the American war effort,
though I never said anything about it.

"GERALD predicted that the Americans, after taking all
our money, would never let us really have the atom bomb, and
that either they or the Israelis would betray us.

"Naively, I protested. I told him how close we were, that we
were using all four processes at once and that Hussein Kamil
had solved the problem of the capacitors, but he just laughed.

"'Eventually they will destroy you,' he told me, and before
I could protest, he grabbed my arm and told me this story:"

*On his first visit with Sabawi, GERALD slipped a folder from
his jacket, whose contents consisted of a thick sheaf of paper filled
with rows and rows of three-digit codes and handed it to the Iraqi
secret service chief.*

No one spoke as Sabawi Hussein then handed his cousin,
Colonel Kamil, a paper-bound book whose title read,
*Emergency Action Messages—Single Integrated Operating Plan—
SIOP.*

Emergency Action Messages (EAMs) were a special set of
codes used by the American military's Worldwide Military
Command and Control System (WWMCCS) to initiate a

nuclear attack.

Colonel Kamil leafed through the bland-looking book in shock—each page was filled with row after row of three-digit numbers which corresponded to a specific preset target for one of the United States' thirty thousand nuclear warheads. True, to be effective, Kamil knew before it was sent over the Worldwide Military Command and Control System any EAM would have to be both properly encoded and issued by the National Command Authority.

Now in a daze, Kamil realized his cousin was still talking.

On the second visit, Sabawi had instructed GERALD to meet him at the Iraqi United Nations Mission in Vienna, far from the prying eyes of the FBI.

Once in Austria GERALD told Sabawi what he already knew—America's combat systems had all become computerized, since only computers could handle the data loads involved in modern electronic warfare. Communications satellites, radars, jet fighters, SSBNs, naval cruisers — the computers ran them all, hands-free, from target detection to weapons launch.

America's new high command was the operating software deep in the center of each of its battle systems computers—a program that could dispatch thousands of orders in a second. Whoever controlled the operating system software could easily control the hardware; GERALD painted scenario after scenario for his stunned Iraqi host: missiles fired from warships which failed to reach their targets, exploding harmlessly in midair instead; fighter planes whose communications systems totally collapsed in the midst of dogfights; and destroyers which suddenly lost their communications links with fleet command.

Each situation could easily be accomplished by the insertion of a few extra lines of software, a tiny subroutine added to the operating system, known as a Trojan Horse. GERALD could drop a Trojan Horse through a trap door in the operating system, circumventing the security controls, so that no one would even know of its existence.

But GERALD had hardly come all the way to Europe to offer Sabawi a half-dozen malfunctioning missiles or a couple of incommunicado F-15s, he had a much more active imagination than that. He was offering the secret service chief the whole ball of wax, a major rewrite of Wimex, the ultimate national security network.

After Sabawi finished, Colonel Kamil turned towards Saddam with a pained expression on his face. "Mr. President, we have no way to even begin to confirm that this, this GERALD is telling us the truth!"

"Excuse me," Sabawi interrupted, "I never said we had no way to confirm GERALD's bona fides."

Kamil leaned forward in his chair, now letting his full exasperation with his cousin show. "You have absolutely no way of proving it—unless the operation is— "

"May I?" Sabawi softly spoke, pulling out a case of cigarettes and casually lighting one, breaking Colonel Kamil's concentration.

"I don't profess to be a computer expert," Sabawi explained, exhaling a puff of smoke, "but I would never be so stupid as to pay for something like this sight unseen."

"Don't be ridiculous!" protest Kamil. "There's no way to show it works, short of shooting off a missile—which for us even to be discussing is nonsense!"

Sabawi Hussein only raised his eyebrows and looked to Saddam Hussein for support, who held up his hand to silence his son-in-law.

"Naturally, any buyer would want to see some evidence that what he was purchasing wasn't just a hollow claim," Sabawi sighed, "and dutifully honoring our President's wishes in this matter, I so far have advanced only a small down payment to GERALD, the remainder subject to a small demonstration."

Saddam Hussein glanced at his son-in-law for a response, but Kamil was silent. It was obvious Sabawi was now in full control.

Sabawi coolly continued, "I believe the U.S. Air Force is now patrolling the so-called no-fly zone with F-15Cs, correct?"

"Of course, everyone knows that," snapped Colonel Kamil, "but—47"

"While our most advanced fighter is the MiG-29, correct?"

"This is information you can get from the newspaper!"

"And the newspaper has also told anyone who's interested that the coalition's air superiority depends to a great extent on the support the U.S. Air Force's F-15 and F/A-18 fighters receive from the E-3 AWACS and E-2C Hawkeyes, warning them well in advance of the appearance of any of our aircraft into the no-fly zone.

"And I believe the F-15Cs of the Air Force 1st and 33rd Tactical Fighter Wings are armed with Sparrow missiles, while F/A-18s from the *Saratoga* carry both Sparrow and Sidewinder missiles—"

"Please!" shouted Colonel Kamil, shooting a look of incredulity towards Saddam. "We already know all this—"

"GERALD's prepared, against his better judgment, to give us a single, small demonstration of his good faith. Then, afterwards, if we like, we can discuss his terms.

"Mr. President?"

Colonel Kamil looked helplessly towards Saddam Hussein, who, much to his surprise, immediately gave Sabawi the order to send up a MiG-29 Fulcrum, Iraq's most advanced jet fighter, as soon as the proper moment presented itself.

Assessment of Computer Attack
on WWMCCS Information System

Parts I & II

Chapter 1

During the last month of the Bush administration, Saddam Hussein surprised allied communications and decided to test the will of the U.N. forces remaining in the region by ordering several planes to fly into the Western-imposed no-fly zone over southern Iraq and launch a series of daring forays into Kuwait. In one case Iraqi commandos made off with several crates of Silkworm surface-to-surface missiles. Finally, after the U.S. shot down an Iraqi fighter, Hussein upped the stakes and defiantly deployed several SA-3 mobile surface-to-air missiles inside the zone.

George Bush, who had finally had enough of Saddam Hussein's provocations, ordered Generals Chuck Horner and Buster Glosson in Riyadh to conduct two retaliatory strikes against Iraq. Allied air forces subsequently struck four SA-3 missile sites on January 13, followed by a second strike on January 17. The second raid included forty Tomahawk missiles fired from two destroyers, the USS *Hewit* and the USS *Stump*, and one cruiser, the USS *Cowpens*, all stationed in the Persian Gulf. One of the Tomahawks crashed into the courtyard of Baghdad's Al-Rashid Hotel while an Islamic conference was in progress. Another, however, faithfully following the Iraqi terrain with its tiny internal radar preprogrammed by analysts at the Defense Mapping Agency in Washington, located and destroyed a much more strategic target along the banks of the Tigris River, south of Baghdad.

An Iraqi defector who had recently passed through allied lines had informed military intelligence about an untouched network of twenty underground buildings at Tarmiya known as Djilah Park. Djilah Park, the plant which had just been obliterated by the Tomahawk, manufactured calutrons, machines used to enrich uranium, and was Colonel Kamil's last hope of Iraq maintaining its own nuclear weapons program.

Within twenty-four hours of the second air strike, Air Force

Generals Horner and Glosson received word from the White House to launch a third attack, targeting three Iraqi air defense centers and three mobile missile batteries which the allies had missed in the January 13 raid. At dawn on Monday both generals were in the basement of the Royal Saudi Air Force Headquarters building in Riyadh, watching an oversized display originating from a Boeing E-3 AWACS flying lazy 8s just south of the Saudi border. The borders of Iraq, Iran, Jordan, Israel, Saudi Arabia and Kuwait appeared as dotted green lines glowing on the television screen, a much smaller version of which the radar controller of the AWACS was monitoring while he sat at a tiny desk inside the Boeing.

An aide handed General Horner the handset to the special telephone known as HAMMER RICK, the secure communications line to the Pentagon. Twenty-four-hour wall clocks in the background gave the time in Washington, D.C., Greenwich, England, and Riyadh-Baghdad as Horner received the final OK to launch the third attack.

"F-4G package up," the AWACS controller's disembodied voice echoed throughout the auditorium.

"F-111B package up."

The room in Riyadh was ominously silent, since the strike force's orders prohibited any plane-to-plane communication.

"EF-111s activated." Six contiguous radial cones blinked on and off—the electronics-jammers from Torrejon AFB in Spain had arrived.

"F-15C Four-ship One up."

Now, sixty-nine glowing tracks illuminated the display screen, as each of the fighter-bombers sped across the desert in broad daylight to unleash its payload on a preprogrammed target.

☆ ☆ ☆

Far away from Riyadh, inside a nondescript two-story building off Torrey Pines Road in the hills of La Jolla, north of San Diego, California, rows of analysts sat at smaller desks before an identical display screen, which had the words "SITUATION ROOM" printed above it.

Twenty-four-hour wall clocks gave the time on San Diego, Washington, D.C., Greenwich, and Riyadh-Baghdad. Five minutes before midnight Pacific Standard Time the display came alive with the same sixty-nine tracks as displayed on the screen in the Saudi Royal Air Force Building in Riyadh. Unbeknownst to the American public who would read about the air attack in the next day's papers, the American and British fighter-bombers (but not the French) were participating in a RAINBOW-clearance simulation of a strategic nuclear strike on Iraq, known as Operation ARCHANGEL. Each fighter-bomber's battle systems computer had been preprogrammed to fly the plane to target and unleash its conventional payload on automatic pilot as a test of the Worldwide Military Command Control Communications System for strategic nuclear war, Wimex.

"F-111B package up," repeated the AWACS controller's voice.

A line of sweat beads formed across the brow of the analyst whose job it was to monitor the F-111B fighter-bomber squadron's battle systems software. Victor Saleh knew that a simple programming error could cause the F-111's on-board tactical electronic warfare system computer to malfunction, rendering it suddenly and irreversibly impotent in the midst of a bombing mission.

Before the mission had begun, each pilot had been handed an encrypted card, which he inserted into his firepower control computer. Firepower control was segregated electronically from the F-111's other two avionics systems, penetration aids and MTC (Mission and Traffic Control), in order to prevent an enemy who was sophisticated in electronic warfare and computer hacking from sabotaging the mission while the aircraft was in flight.

"APQ-110 TFR activated," silently scrolled across Saleh's CRT screen.

The F-111B's pilot had just switched on his Texas Instruments automatic-terrain-following computer, freezing his and the WSO's sticks and pushing the F-111B into an automatic dive. The aircraft's inertial navigation system, which had been preprogrammed by the Defense Mapping Agency in Washington, was now flying the plane on autopilot, guiding it just a few hundred feet above ground level, where it bobbed over each slope and dipped into each valley.

"BCU activated." The F-111B's navigation-attack system had just informed its ballistics computer unit that it was just about to arrive at the designated targets.

Saleh's display window switched automatically, copying the F-111 pilot's main radar display. The moment the aircraft's BCU aligned the approaching target inside the cross-hairs, the light representing the target began to blink on and off on his CRT screen. Two 2000-pound GBU-24 glide-bombs had just dropped correctly over target, destroying a previously untouched nuclear processing plant in Tarimiya and causing yet another setback to Colonel Kamil's program.

Now the direction of the F-111B package's tracks was reversed, and the digital readouts on the display screen showed it rapidly regaining altitude, climbing in a matter of minutes from slightly above ground level to a prearranged ceiling of 20,000 feet. Traveling at Mach 1.2 it would return to Saudi airspace in almost fifteen minutes.

"Texaco 21, pop-up contact, H-5," the AWACS controller's voice interrupted the silent room.

The AWACS had just informed a nearby F-15 squadron leader that an unidentified aircraft had appeared in their midst. The circling AWACS was being protected by a four-ship of American F-15s, whose squadron leader was in the midst of topping up his tanks from a KC-135 refueling tanker.

Saleh's stomach tightened. H-5 was the Iraqi field at al-Tagaddum, so any Iraqi interceptors which had been launched from there would only be two hundred miles from the returning F-111Bs.

The unidentified aircraft and the F-111Bs were converging on each other at over 2,000 miles per hour, only twenty-five miles apart, while the F-15s racing towards them from the opposite direction were approaching at 45 degrees to the left. Saleh was riveted to the screen, watching the nine different glowing tracks converge.

"Pop-up contact. Two hundred miles north of target."

The squadron leader of the F-15s heard the message over his intercom, noticing he had picked up a single contact on his radar. He wondered what had prompted the Iraqis to launch a single aircraft after the recent demonstration of allied air supremacy just a few days before.

"Two same," replied his wing man.

"No I.D. contact," the AWACS controller's voice echoed over the formation's intercoms.

"Three same," repeated the pilot of the third F-15.

Beads of sweat broke out across the squadron leader's forehead — the unidentified aircraft was approaching his position at Mach 2, cutting through 22,000 feet of airspace every second. Modern air combat tactics necessarily called for each pilot on either side to launch his stand-off missiles well before a visual ID (V.I.D.) was made by either pilot, but the maximum range of the F-15C's Sparrow missile was less than twenty-five miles.

"Target 450 for fifty."

The pilot of the MiG-29 flipped the Delta-H switch of his No-193 pulse-Doppler radar to the number two position for attack from below, and the radar-warning receivers in the AWACS and in all four of the F-15Cs were suddenly activated, as the MiG-29's radar computer automatically illuminated all five targets.

"Hostile! Hostile!" warned the AWACS controller's voice over the American intercoms.

Inside the MiG's cockpit, the five targets were now arrayed in threat-priority order on the Plexiglas head-up display. The Iraqi pilot next flipped on the master arm switch in the upper right-hand corner of the instrument panel, arming his Alamo missile circuit, then squeezed his gun trigger and checked its response on the HUD. The flashing of the rings of the multi-colored threat lights was mixed with a high-pitched squeal from the SPO-15 radar warning receiver, indicating the MiG was being swept by several enemy radars at once.

☆ ☆ ☆

"Target 330 for forty."

In the basement of the Royal Saudi Air Force Headquarters building a small crowd had gathered around the large display screen which was relaying the battle situation from the AWACS near the Saudi border. The oversized television showed everything in the air over most of the Middle East, but all eyes were riveted on the attacking MiG which appeared to be on a suicide mission against the far superior combination of an AWACS and the four F-15Cs.

"Target 210 for thirty."

"He's approaching them dead-on…he's crazy!" muttered General Horner to himself.

The digits next to MiG's cursor flipped rapidly, indicating its altitude had dropped in a matter of seconds from 13,500 to 2,000 feet.

"Target 100 for twenty-five," confirmed the controller in the AWACS.

"Hot right!" the American squadron leader's voice screamed over the public address speaker.

The lead F-15 and his wing man suddenly jinked to the right to get a better lock on their attacker. Closing speed between the two opposing fighters was now at Mach 4, about 45,000 feet per second.

"Lock fifteen miles, 2,000."

"Two same."

"V.I.D. Hostile!"

"Fox one." The squadron leader had just fired a radar-guided Sparrow.

"Fox from two." The wing man had just fired his.

General Horner watched the screen in amazement as the MiG's cursor refused to drop off the screen.

☆ ☆ ☆

At 600 feet above the deck, the MiG's pilot pushed the throttles to ninety percent, his airspeed now at five hundred knots. The two Sparrows just fired by the squadron leader and his wing man had sailed right past him, failing to find their target. A target block composed of all four F-15Cs and the AWACS lit up his HUD, its rectangular radar cursor dancing mechanically from one to the other. Straining against the force of his steep climb, the MiG pilot clicked the white button on his inner throttle knob to activate his Alamo missile's radar-seeking computer.

"*Pusk razrayshon*," a synthesized voice responded in Russian. Launch approved. The Iraqis hadn't had the time to reprogram the Russian woman's voice recorded in the warning system.

The pilot immediately armed the missile trigger, launching two B-27 Alamos at once in order to keep his load balanced.

"*Rubege odin*," the computer responded. Lock-on target.

"Jesus Christ!" General Horner had just seen both the squadron leader's and the wing man's F-15Cs disappear from the Air Force Headquarters display screen.

"Hostile! Hostile! Hostile!" the AWACS controller's voice echoed throughout the basement room, now filled with solemn faces.

Horner watched in horror as the first of the remaining two F-15s dove in a split S, rushing towards the ground, while the second banked in a diving roll in the opposite direction in a desperate effort to let the MiG rush through the hole.

☆ ☆ ☆

The MiG's pilot flipped his battle computer from "radar" to "combat infrared", switching his HUD's imagery to its Infrared Search and Track System (IRST). He banked hard left to acquire the third F-15, fighting to lock him into the narrow pair of vertical lines in the center of his display. The moment the dark splotch of the third F-15 fell between the ladder, his headset buzzed, and he pressed the trigger, launching an R-73 heat-seeking Archer missile.

In seconds, the missile's logic system told it to turn inside its target's flight path, sending it straight up the F-15's tailpipe, so its small warhead exploded inside the fighter's Pratt and Whitney engine. At a higher altitude, its pilot could possibly have survived and bailed out, but at only 1,500 feet he lost control of the aircraft and smashed into the ground.

The last remaining F-15 whizzed by the MiG, beginning a high-G arcing turn at medium throttle to keep his radius tight enough to escape the MiG's sharp angle of attack.

☆ ☆ ☆

"Hostile! Hostile! Hostile!"

General Horner watched in astonishment as the fourth F-15 disappeared from the basement screen. Something was drastically wrong—the MiG-29 had just chewed up a whole four-ship of F-15s; there was literally nothing to stop the victorious MiG from crossing the Saudi border and shooting down the AWACS. The nearest support was a package of F-16s one hundred miles west at 30,000 feet.

At FHI Systems' auditorium in San Diego, as the tracks of the four F-111Bs crossed into the safety of Saudi territory, everyone except Victor Saleh was asking himself what in the world had just happened. The superior numbers of the F-15 four-ship seemed to count for nothing, as the lone MiG downed each of the American fighter jets one after the other.

In another fortified bunker deep under Baghdad, Saddam Hussein, Sabawi Hussein, Colonel Kamil, and Dr. Stemmler were seated in front of a set of display screens similar to those inside the Saudi Royal Air Force building in Riyadh.

"Gentlemen," proclaimed a triumphant Sabawi Hussein, "I think we have just received adequate demonstration of GERALD's abilities,"

Saddam Hussein grinned slowly in response, glancing in his brother-in-law's direction. Colonel Kamil knew better than to protest.

"What's his price? What does he want?" Dr. Stemmler demanded.

"Ten million dollars. Paid in Zurich," replied Sabawi.

Colonel Kamil and Dr. Stemmler both unconsciously turned to Saddam, who uttered only two words.

"Buy it."

Chapter 2

"The computer looks for pattern recognition, and when it finds a fit it gives us a signal," the instructor, David Woodring, intoned, noticing the watch team seemed to be already half-asleep. Woodring was the FBI's recently appointed Assistant

Director of Counterintelligence, the Bureau's chief spycatcher, whose chief present worry was that his men no longer believed there were any important spies left to catch. Tall, blond and lanky, Woodring was only thirty-five years old when he was posted to the Manhattan office, he had been a major force in helping the bureau construct its case against John Gotti, the capo of the Gambino crime family. The new FBI Director, Hubert Myers, had specifically chosen Woodring to lead the FBI's counterintelligence department in the new, less than clear-cut era.

Woodring was on the eleventh floor of the FBI's Los Angeles regional headquarters, a Kafkaesque-looking high-rise on Wilshire Boulevard not far from UCLA. The eleventh-floor bullpen was headquarters of CI-5, the only division of the FBI on the West Coast whose members could boast of possessing a "sensitive compartmentalized information" clearance, that is, a clearance one level higher than "top secret," giving them the power to investigate not only foreign agents, but also errant members of any of the domestic intelligence services, including both the CIA and NSA.

It had been a fast-paced game, chasing men like Christopher Boyce to the former Soviet Embassy in Mexico City, but now much of the crack counterintelligence unit's enthusiasm was gone, since no one believed that their old adversary, the Russians, still posed that much of a threat. But, as they were about to find out, today's subject was a different matter.

"Pentagon started up audio recog on the German border back in the seventies," continued Woodring, pointing his swagger stick at the chalk box labeled AUDIO on the blackboard. "Military boys got real good at telling the difference between Warsaw Pact tanks and trucks and NATO stuff coming over bridges and whatnot. Over the years sophistication level was increased. *Billboard's* Top 40 is done the same way—guy in Kansas City's computers listen to every station in the country and pick out how many times a song is played.

"But today," Woodring paused, slapping a second box labeled VIDEO which woke up half the class, "today, gentlemen, we are gonna talk about *video*."

Now the whole class was listening.

"Two years ago CI discreetly began a program to re-ID all government personnel with restricted access status. Unfortunately, as we all know, the boys at CI found that included about everyone in the greybook, so at the same time, they have been chopping away at the access lists. Anyway, the new IDs are holographic, stored on both CD and videotape for flexibility, depending on the resolution fit.

"Next, CI personnel went around to all their favorite hotspots and retrofitted all the watchstations with new camera technology," Woodring explained, then motioned for someone in the audience to douse the lights.

"The list of camera locations is top secret, but I bet you boys can guess where a lot of them might be," Woodring grinned.

Members of Counterintelligence Division 5 saw a slide photo of a generic-looking television camera appear upon the screen.

"Admittedly, it's not much to look at," Woodring apologized. "But, gentlemen, this is only *the antenna* of a two-billion dollar piece of hardware, the rest of which is in the basement of this building.

"One nice thing about the system is that it can tell us if an RA individual is making multiple visits to unrelated locations, a thing that we always had a problem with before." At that moment a slide appeared of a slim, balding man making his way through a snow-filled parking lot. The next slide showed the same individual in various locations, some foreign, others late at night, which were difficult to make out.

"This is RABBIT," Woodring's voice informed them in the

darkness. "We named him that because he likes to hop around, especially on vacations. One of RABBIT's trips to Europe could burn up more guys than we've got available worldwide. The interesting thing is that before we got the system up and running, CI would have probably never noticed this individual, since he's never been to the same location more than once," Woodring admitted in a respectful tone.

"Anyway, unfortunately for you guys, you don't get to chase RABBIT all over Europe, you're gonna hippety-hop after him right here in your own backyard," Woodring informed them while the lights turned back on.

"Where does RABBIT work?" Special Agent Johnson, a tall black man, asked.

"FHI Systems, San Diego. He's a design engineer in charge of battle systems software. Worked for AT&T before that."

The mere mention of RABBIT's job was enough to bring the membership of the watch team alive. Each agent knew FHI Systems was responsible for updating the telecommunications of America's national security computer network, the Worldwide Military Command and Control System (WWMCCS).

"Why hasn't RABBIT been picked up?" asked another agent.

"Because Mr. RABBIT isn't retailing anything as far as we can tell, he's just picking up real big chunks of change," replied Woodring.

"How big?" another agent asked.

"Last I heard, he was looking to buy a Mercedes."

"A Mercedes!" Johnson exclaimed. *Even the Sovs never paid that much,* thought the Special Agent.

"Who's he working for?" someone demanded next.

"We have no idea," Woodring replied, "no idea at all."

Woodring's assistant, who had been quietly sitting in the

back row during the presentation, left the room before the lights came back on to wait for Woodring in a nearby office.

"We just got a call from CI-4 in New York," his assistant told him when Woodring appeared. He handed Woodring a donut with one hand and a cup of coffee with the other.

"What's wrong?"

"They won't say on the phone, but they want you up there."

"When?"

"Right now. FBI jet's fueled and waiting to pick you up at LAX."

"They want me that fast? *Why?*"

His assistant raised his hand, as if to say, *don't ask me, it wasn't my idea.*

"Thanks for the coffee," Woodring replied, then left the room.

Chapter 3

A week later, the same pair of colonels who had picked up Colonel Kamil the night of the American election arrived to fetch him at his hastily rebuilt office on Anter Square. Fully aware that the penalty for failure in the President's eyes was death, Kamil was filled with foreboding that he was being summoned by Saddam in order to explain the loss of the plant at Tarmiyah. The driver said nothing during the whole trip, but followed the Military Canal to the outskirts of the city, finally stopping at the gates of a quiet villa surrounded by a high wall.

Two sentries at the wooden gate immediately waved them through, and Kamil noticed the grounds were more heavily patrolled than usual, even for the protection of Saddam Hussein.

At the villa's front door, a second pair of sentries checked

Kamil's papers, then let him through the doors, telling him to go to the dining room on the right.

Seated around a large lacquered table were Saddam Hussein, his middle half brother, Sabawi, and Dr. Stemmler.

"*Hussein Kamil Hassan al-Majid! Keef halahk!*" Saddam greeted the Colonel with the same joviality he had shown him on the night of November 2nd, slapping his son-in-law on the shoulder.

"*M'leeh, shookran.*"

"Good! Good!"

Saddam motioned for Kamil to join the others at the table, then sat down and let his brother, Sabawi, open up the meeting. "Sabawi has brought us good news from Zurich."

"*Shookran*, Mr. President. TRAPDOOR is ours." Sabawi carefully handed a slim folder to Colonel Kamil, who, in turn, passed it to his father-in-law, Saddam.

Without opening the file, Iraq's president handed it back to his son-in-law, Hussein Kamil. ...*it couldn't be possible*, thought the colonel, finding himself now holding the separate, plain-white sheet of paper in his hand with the two code groups written on it.

"This is the trigger? For the Trojan Horse?"

"*Na'am*," Yes, Sabawi whispered.

"So," resumed President Hussein, "we need someone with the expertise to break into the American nuclear arsenal, launch one of their missiles at the target, yet leave no trace of our involvement."

"The target?" gasped Colonel Kamil, realizing for the first time how far things had gone.

"The target," emphasized Saddam. "Sabawi tells me Dr. Saleh has already preprogrammed it for us."

Colonel Kamil looked at first one man then another, afraid to ask the question.

"Warren Air Force Base," whispered Sabawi. "It's a missile base in Wyoming with 150 Minutemen III and fifty Peacemakers."

It was madness! Sheer madness! thought the Iraqi physicist. But at the same time there was a compelling element to Sabawi's plan: if the attack were successful, the American military would be disgraced, and demands from its opponents for further disarmament would turn into a chorus. In addition, once the damage had been done, the ensuing chaos would leave the governments of the coalition members too weak to respond to any future Iraqi aggression.

"Surely, gentlemen, amongst ourselves we will be able to locate someone whom we can trust, but who is unknown, to carry on the struggle for us and to help us finally accomplish what we set out to do originally. And it absolutely can't be anyone we've used before, anyone we've been sheltering here like the Abu Nidal Organization," Saddam continued. "Sending him out again would be tantamount to leaving my signature on the event, and, besides, he's not even competent enough for what I want. No, I want to use someone who isn't known to Western security services, but on the face of it would have nothing to do with us — this is the problem, isn't it? We all know what happened after Lockerbie — Palestinians and Jordanians were running across Europe like a bunch of cockroaches on a kitchen floor!"

"An absolute professional, then," murmured Kamil, playing along until he could find out exactly how much further things had gone. "But — " began Colonel Kamil.

"— if he fails?" Stemmler laughed. "He won't have had any tie to us then, will he?"

"So you can see now, gentlemen," Saddam almost whispered, "there can be no question of taking this matter before the party, even to the Revolutionary Command Council which has over sixty members — besides, I've already learned my lesson once in this regard — no, the only way this will work is if we keep it amongst the four of us in this room. I think you can all see that."

The moment Colonel Kamil saw his cousin extract three folders from his carryall, it immediately dawned on him that the candidates had already been selected — the sole purpose of the meeting was to make the final choice.

"Sabawi?"

"Yes, Mr. President, as you requested, without mentioning a word of this to anyone at the Mukhabarat, I selected the following three candidates myself from our files."

The secret service chief started to hand all three of the thin manila folders to Saddam Hussein, who made a circle with his right hand. "Just give one to each of us, then we'll pass them around."

"Yes, Mr. President."

"Meanwhile why don't you tell us about the first candidate," Saddam ordered, folding his file open on the table in front of him.

His half-brother glanced quickly at the title of the dossier he had just handed Saddam Hussein, then cleared his throat before he began: "Stefano Sinagra, Sicilian. Worked for 'Toto' Riina, the *capo di tutti capi* of the Sicilian Mafia, and until Riina's arrest by the Italian military, Sinagra was his top enforcer. Sinagra was a contract killer who was never part of the organization, but answered directly to Riina, himself."

"What's he done outside of Sicily?" Stemmler questioned.

"Needless to say, these things aren't easy to document, but we think Riina sent him to New York to take care of a couple of wayward lieutenants."

"Is that all we know about him?" pressed Colonel Kamil.

"Men in this line of work tend to be rather circumspect, especially ones who have never been caught."

"Good point," muttered Saddam. "Who's next?"

Colonel Kamil made a show of handing his folder to President Hussein, saying the name under his breath for the benefit of Sabawi Hussein.

"Vitaly Chavchavadze, former *spetsnaz* commando, recently demobilized from the 5th Division of the old Soviet Strategic Rocket Forces. Chavchavadze was stationed at several tactical nuclear sites in Eastern Europe, also he was trained as a marksman at Zheltyye Vody, the *spetsnaz* camp."

"What's he doing now?" asked Saddam.

"Enforcer for Vladimir Kumarin, one of the four top mafiosi in St. Petersburg."

"How's his English?"

"Only passable."

"Passable may not be enough," grunted Stemmler to Sabawi Hussein's annoyance.

"The third candidate is an American, whose name listed on your folder is probably an alias, according to our branch in New York. I've saved him until last for the simple reason that he's my favorite. Working on his own for a South American client, he shut down a CIA narcotics smuggling ring known as "Operation BUNCIN" that that agency operated in cooperation with the American Drug Enforcement Administration.

"In BUNCIN the CIA used American drug smugglers as sources and exempted them from prosecution by the DEA — the project was monitored by the CIA's Office of Security. BUNCIN was important enough to be operated out of Homestead Air Force Base in Florida, where classified AFCT planes picked up the results and hand-delivered them to the CIA at Langley."

"The CIA doesn't know his face? How is this possible?" objected Stemmler.

"Because every last person in the operation the American came into contact with, he liquidated himself."

Sabawi couldn't help but notice the small grin that passed across Saddam's face. A man who was ruthless enough to eliminate every possible threat, and in addition wasn't threatened by the CIA…

Chapter 4

The morning's light splashed across the sea of windshields and polished hubcaps, creating a wave of reflections that were distinctly visible to the pilot of a tiny single-engine plane, which was flying directly over United States Interstate 15. But the pilot's eye wasn't focused on the two-acre lot, lined with row after row of gunmetal gray German sedans, but on a tiny flyspeck of a Toyota, which seemed to be moving on a predetermined path towards the entrance of Aristocrat Motors at the Grand Avenue exit. And no one was surprised when the Toyota's driver left the interstate, took the exit, and drove under the weatherbeaten archway which led to the showroom floor.

As Dr. Victor Saleh carefully shut the door of his battered blue Corolla, he debated only for a second whether it was necessary to lock his car door in the midst of so much luxury. The mere thought of this precaution seemed to dent his vanity, and he removed his delicate hand from the old Toyota's door handle as if it were contaminated.

"Dr. Saleh, am I right?" asked the black salesman, flashing a row of white perfect teeth as he extended a large, calloused hand.

"Yes. You must be Mr. Johnson," replied the Lebanese professor replied, somewhat intimidated by the looming bulk of the black man whose voice had seemed so officious on the telephone.

"Ready to go for a spin?"

The pilot of a single-engine Cessna yawned, had another sip of coffee, and banked his plane over Lake Hodges, a silver pool below.

"...taking a black 190D northbound onto Bear Valley Parkway..." a voice crackled over the Cessna's surveillance radio.

☆ ☆ ☆

The pilot set down his cup of coffee, banked the Cessna towards the Interstate, and spied the tiny black Mercedes, now hemmed in a box formed by several of the Bureau's automotive fleet. And if anyone were to look upwards from the ground, at the altitude its pilot had been directed to maintain, the little Cessna would only have appeared as a dark speck, or even nothing at all, to the unaided eye.

"...it's either gonna' be the north or south exit on I-15..." a different voice predicted over the Cessna's radio. "Charlie, you awake up there?"

"No, I'm on autopilot."

"O.K., just let us know which way he goes."

"Roger," the pilot yawned, keeping a firm eye on the new Mercedes below him.

☆ ☆ ☆

"Handles like a dream, huh?" Johnson asked Dr. Saleh, who was driving the 190D.

"Very well. Very well, thank you," Dr. Saleh responded.

Saleh saw the exit sign for I-15 North and casually swung the Mercedes onto the ramp, as a team of facemen rushed past in an assortment of various automobiles.

Johnson's eyes never strayed near the rearview mirror, but somehow he felt the second team jockey into place and confirmed his suspicions as he saw a familiar Buick 88 speed ahead in the passing lane. *Over twenty agents had been recruited for this little farce*, Johnson thought. *Twenty men had abandoned their watch posts to go car shopping all across San Diego. RABBIT lives in Claremont, but, of course, he had to take the Interstate all the way across town to Escondido. Last weekend it had been Chula Vista,* Johnson remembered and visibly frowned.

"Have I been out too long?" Dr. Saleh asked solicitously, having just seen the cloud pass across the salesman's face.

"No! No!"

"You're sure?"

"Sorry, I got a little stomach acid this morning — gotta' stop drinking so much coffee," the FBI agent lied.

"I think I want to buy it," Dr. Saleh announced without warning. "Is it possible to pay with a money order?"

"Money order?"

"That's not acceptable?"

"Hey, sure, boss'll take American Express, Visa, cash, check — you name it, whatever makes you happy."

Dr. Saleh nodded his head in appreciation, and Agent Johnson noticed the smile of satisfaction which appeared on the professor's face.

Chapter 5

While David Woodring's men followed Dr. Saleh in his Mercedes, a handsome American with steel-gray eyes exited his apartment on 62nd Street, walked to Park Avenue, and caught a southbound taxi, giving the driver a downtown address. It was early February and a light snow had begun to coat the streets, mottling the sounds of horns in its mist.

Trinity Church hovered like a ghost ship on lower Broadway, where the driver turned on Wall, pulling over to the curb two blocks later as instructed. If anyone had been watching that morning, which they weren't, they would have noticed a rather tall man pull a slip of paper from his jacket pocket, obviously double-checking an address before he discarded it into a nearby trash container.

Fourteen Wall was a tall, soot-covered, stone building with a granite facade and two brass-plated revolving doors. The stranger entered the lobby, checked the directory which indicated Room 1514 did indeed belong to Digitel Long Distance Services, the same name his Colombian contact had given him, then walked into the crowded first-floor cafeteria past a row of booths towards the rear, finally sitting across from an overweight woman reading a copy of *W* and wearing a pair of glasses with transparent frames. One look at her and he guessed she had previously either worked for AT&T or one of its subsidiaries.

"I'm glad you're here, I was getting hungry."

"Let's order."

A harried-looking waitress appeared at their side, holding a pad and pencil in her hand.

"What'll it be?"

"I'd like a double hamburger with everything, fries, and a chocolate shake."

The waitress shifted her glance immediately to her male companion.

"A BLT and a Coke'll be fine."

The waitress reread their orders to them then went to the next table.

The stranger began:

"I don't know if Luiz told you what I wanted — "

"He explained it, alright."

The stranger blinked. "You sure you can get into the computer?"

"Look, let me tell you something. You don't exactly have to be Mata Hari to get into the military's machines — " the stranger furrowed his brow and the hacker hesitated a moment, taking a sip of Coke. "I know, you've heard they've got passwords, authorization ladders, secret codes, et cetera, et cetera. You gotta understand if everything goes right, none of that really makes any difference."

The stranger still looked doubtful, when the waitress returned with their food, slapping the dishes on the table like they were heavy poker chips. The hacker waited until she left to reply.

"Look, this is hard to explain to an outsider, but the software, the software the military uses isn't exactly airtight. There's holes in it, holes that if you know they're there you can access and essentially take over the whole machine. For instance, you take the Trivial File Transfer Protocol in Unix — " The stranger held up his hand, and the hacker immediately rolled a french fry in the blob of ketchup she'd put on her plate, then stuffed it in her mouth.

"What if you get caught?"

"Look, you saw the company name, right? We're long distance resellers, as in telephone. That's where I used to work. New York Tel, the old Ma Bell. I know my way around the network like an IRT conductor knows the stops on the Red Line — " The stranger frowned again, he knew nothing about New York Telephone long distance switching network. "What I mean is, it's no trouble for me to grab a bunch of numbers and leave no trace that I was even there. I can go over satellite and downlink into Tymnet, and then through a couple of cutouts hook into Milnet — that's what all the bases use — " she stopped to take a large bite out of her hamburger. "They all run on Unix — that's AT&T software — like I said, it's got enough holes in it it's not that hard to become a superuser and collect people's passwords. You just need to give me the files you want."

"Here." The stranger pulled a single notepad-sized sheet of paper from his shirt pocket and slid it across the table. The hacker scooped it up and stuffed it in her pocket without looking at it.

"I work late all the time. I've got nothing better to do.

Come back here tonight and tell the guard you want to see me. That all right with you?"

Her visitor nodded affirmatively.

"Luiz told me you don't want to use your own name. When you come back tell the guard you're Fred Daniels — he used to work here before they switched security services, OK?"

The stranger nodded a second time, finished his BLT, and left.

☆ ☆ ☆

That evening, just as she had told him, there was a single guard on duty who readily accepted that he was Fred Daniels and notified the hacker, who told the guard that Daniels was expected.

The stranger took the elevator to the fifteenth floor and found himself in a deserted lobby, lit by humming fluorescent lights and carpeted in a faded corporate gray. To the right a door was open and he walked in, finding the hacker in the middle of a row of otherwise empty offices, sitting in front of a computer terminal with a fresh soft drink in her hand.

"This one took a while," confessed the hacker. "No one logged onto the department you gave me until an hour ago."

"Could you tell who it was?" the stranger pressed, humorless.

"Couldn't follow him upstream," she replied, typing in a command. "He didn't leave a trail. Used a funny password though."

The stranger looked over the hacker's shoulders as she typed in the base's name, C-H-I-N-A L-A-K-E.

The China Lake Naval Weapons Center is a huge, 1,122,177-acre missile testing base located at Ridgecrest, California, lying between the Sierra Nevada on the west and the Panamint Range on the east. Airspace over its 1,800-square-mile area is restricted exclusively for military use all the way past 20,000 feet. The base principally functions as the Navy's center for research, development, testing, and evaluation for air warfare and missile weapons systems and takes its name from an expanse of dry lakebed which was named after the coolies who worked the local mines in the 1880s.

But in the middle of the southern half of the base lies a separate facility, not guarded by Marines like the rest of the base, but surrounded by a special contingent of Federal Protective Service bluejackets rotated out of Camp Glynco, Georgia. This base within a base, the China Lake Special Operations Weapons Center, reports directly to the Director CIA without going through any military channels; its budget isn't recorded in any official governmental department; and for practical purposes, it doesn't exist. To anyone who knows of its existence the reason for all the secrecy is simple: its residents manufacture devices designed to be used in the most sensitive of special operations: miniature telescope infrared night-vision scopes designed specifically for assassination; makeup kits especially designed to avoid close inspection; tiny cryptoanalytic computers for breaking both foreign and domestic codes; spread-spectrum field communications equipment, like the type used by the various special forces; finally, devices which could either trigger or short-circuit various types of nuclear weapons, both U.S. and foreign.

The stranger also knew that any user logging onto the Special Operations Center's computers ran the risk of being monitored and traced if he were found to be using a significant amount of computer time. But fortunately for him, his friends from Bogota had already given him a name.

"OK, you said you didn't want to be in here long — you gonna give me the name?" the hacker asked.

"Bailey. Edwin D. Bailey."

"Just a minute."

"Restricted File — Veil Classification Required," her screen replied.

The stranger winced. He knew if the hacker failed to give the right password to climb the next rung in the authorization ladder, alarm bells at the base's computer center would immediately be set off.

"Don't worry. I've got the next stage down, too. Thanks to MR. BUNCIN, whoever he was," the hacker breezily informed him. "Seems as if your friend just got out of jail."

"BUNCIN asked for Bailey's file?"

"Not asked for — he updated it. I watched him as he did it."

Bailey's unusual curriculum vitae scrolled vertically across the CRT screen, then froze still, its most recent entry silently blinking as its text cooked upon the printout.

Feb. 5, 1992: Released from USP Marion, Illinois. Last Known Residence: Memphis.

The stranger lifted Bailey's three-page resume from the tray and read it carefully. The hacker had already printed out her own copy when she caught BUNCIN logging earlier in the afternoon, using the CIA's highest clearance, Veil, to access it. What she had read was so frightening she immediately set her copy on fire in the bathroom, then flushed the ashes down the toilet.

"Now ask it for Bailey's key," the stranger requested, still looking at the printout.

"His key?"

"His code key. You'll find it in there somewhere. It's a 56-bit-long binary number, but it could be expressed either way — in decimal form or 1's and 0's. I'll know it when I see it."

"Whatever," sighed the hacker, her fingers dancing on the keyboard, asking for more files.

Chapter 6

The slide photo of a swarthy-looking man with a moustache

filled a screen in the darkened room.

"This is 'Abdul'," a voice explained, slapping the screen with a swagger stick. "Just got on a plane last week and went to Vienna. Didn't say goodbye to anybody."

The next slide was of a younger man with short, curly hair.

"This is 'Hassan', Abdul's partner. He left yesterday for Athens."

"How many others like this?"

"About ten."

"*Ten?*"

"They've all left the United States?"

"That's right."

"They just knocked off," repeated the division chief, McDonald.

"What do you mean they just knocked off?" demanded Woodring.

"Just what I said — they're not following the UNSCOM people anymore," McDonald replied.

He was on the eighth floor of the FBI's district office in New York City, which housed the CI-4 counterintelligence unit, a unit analogous to CI-5 in Los Angeles.

Since the termination of the Gulf War, a considerable portion of the New York field office's manpower had been dedicated to following local Iraqi intelligence agents, who were, in turn, following members of the U.N.'s Special Commission on Iraqi weapons, UNSCOM.

The U.N. Security Council formed the Special Commission after the Gulf War to investigate Iraq's three most dangerous weapons programs: nuclear, biological and chemical. Post-war nuclear inspections, which had begun in May, 1991, were delegated by UNSCOM to the International Atomic Energy Agency (I.A.E.A.) a branch of the U.N. based in Vienna. The I.A.E.A. had the contradictory mission of fostering the use of atomic energy while simultaneously limiting the spread of nuclear weapons technology. Twice-yearly visits by I.A.E.A. inspectors to Iraq for the decade preceding the war had resulted in a complete failure on their part to recognize that Saddam Hussein had been running four separate programs for manufacturing weapons-grade nuclear fuel during the same period. Unfortunately, since many of the I.A.E.A.'s inspectors had been hired from smaller countries, several of them had never seen a nuclear weapons part in their lives.

But the intelligence agencies of the coalition members, America's CIA, the British MI6, the French DGSE, and the Russian ISS, weren't so easily misled, and each agency now fed the results of its own analysis directly to the Special Commission in New York, which, in turn, would assign specific sites for surprise inspection by I.A.E.A. employees in Iraq.

In Baghdad Sabawi Hussein had been quick to react to these new pressures, realizing the best way to outwit the local I.A.E.A. teams was to intercept the flow of strategic data from the secret services to the twenty-one Special Commission members in New York before it reached I.A.E.A. headquarters in Vienna. As a result, he instructed his intelligence operatives at the Iraqi Mission to the United Nations to follow the twenty-one commission members and to steal whenever possible any documents they could find, even if it included breaking into a member's private residence.

The Finnish representative to the Special Commission, Marjatta Rautio, had recently come out of her bathroom to find a man rifling the contents of her desk, whom she later identified to agents of the CI-4 Division as a member of the Iraqi Mission. Afterwards, Woodring ordered an increase in CI-4's surveillance of the Iraqi Mission, sending reinforcements from the CI-3 Division in Washington, D.C. and additional Arab-language speaking agents from other field offices.

Now, Woodring couldn't believe his ears. It was only a

month after the January airstrikes, which had been successful in knocking out the previously untouched nuclear fabricating plant in Tarmiya, which, in theory, had put additional pressure on Saddam Hussein to protect whatever secret nuclear processing plants remained. Instead, McDonald was telling him that Iraqi intelligence in New York had just halved the number of agents they had dedicated to surveilling the UNSCOM people.

Meanwhile, Woodring had a potential spy at the major WWMCCS contractor in San Diego.

Chapter 7

The next day the handsome American who had visited the hacker on Wall Street presented a false passport to the Royal Jordan Airlines desk at Schwechat International Airport in Vienna. He was confirming his seat for the 3:30 p.m. flight which would arrive in Amman, Jordan at 7:30 that evening local time.

"*Ich mochte meine Fahrkarte fur Amman.*"

"*Herr Kluge?*" asked the attendant, folding open the passport and double-checking its photograph with his customer's face. All appeared to be in order, so the Jordanian handed Herr Kluge his tickets.

"*Danke.*"

The first inkling of the Iraqis' interest in his services had come from his previous employers in Colombia. An Iraqi intelligence agent had flown to Medellin, discreetly asking the Colombians about the gringo who had worked for them on Operation BUNCIN. Their visitor exhibited his bona fides by providing his Colombian hosts a crate of Silkworm missiles. The narcotraficantes had refused, of course, to confirm or deny the existence of such a man and had politely shown their Iraqi guest the door.

But the next day, the insistent ringing of a certain telephone inside the American's flat alerted him that his previous client was on the line, because, at the moment, only the Colombians possessed its number. A 9,600-bits-per-second, 30,000-Hertz-range, public-key spread-spectrum scrambler modem and multiplexer, the device had been issued by the CIA to one of the operatives in Operation BUNCIN, and was written off at the news of his disappearance.

Designed to operate over the 1435-1540 megahertz test-band frequency of the KH-14A reconnaissance satellite, the special telephone broadcast its signal via spread spectrum over a 5 megahertz-wide band, which, since the bandwidth of the transmission was so wide, would only sound like noise to someone who picked it up. For the same reason the special telephone's signal was hard to jam or intercept, since it intentionally used a much wider band to transmit than was required by the information being sent.

When the call from Bogota arrived, he told his Colombian clients to tell the Iraqis he would agree to an initial meeting with one of their representatives, as long as it was somewhere in South America where they would be far from the eyes of the allied secret services, who, he knew, were following the Iraqis' movements in certain cities. Shortly thereafter, a pleasant luncheon was arranged on the open roof restaurant of the Caesar Park Hotel on Ipanema Beach in Rio de Janeiro, where he was given a suggested itinerary by a very nervous functionary from the tourist bureau of the local Iraqi consulate.

That evening, using his special telephone far from his hotel room, he called the Colombians back from an open-air bar on the summit of Corcovado, resetting the date and time of his arrival into Baghdad.

Upon his arrival in Amman, the American, whose only baggage was a thin Asprey carryall, found a taxi driver who was more than willing, once he heard the price, to drive his humor-less-looking passenger all 520 miles to Baghdad across the Iraqi border with no questions asked. Eight hours later, upon his

arrival in the Iraqi capital, the American told the driver to drop
him off at the junction of the railroad tracks and Haifa street,
where he walked the remaining half-mile to the recently
damaged Al-Rashid Hotel.

After making a one-word telephone call to a number he had
been given in Rio de Janeiro, the American was picked up at
the door by a plainclothesman in a nondescript Brazilian
Volkswagen Passat sedan, who took him to the same villa
where Kamil had just been summoned.

A pair of plainclothesmen at the gate waved the Passat
through and radioed ahead that the special guest had arrived.

Sabawi Hussein appeared immediately at the door and
whisked his special guest across a hand-woven rug into a well
appointed salon, where the Colonel Kamil, Doctor Stemmler,
and Saddam Hussein were seated in high-backed chairs.
President Hussein motioned casually with a flick of the hand
for Sabawi and the American to seat themselves into the two
remaining empty chairs.

Once he sat down, Sabawi Hussein warily eyed the guest
whose candidacy he had promoted, inventorying his physical
traits. Unlike Colonel Kamil and Dr. Stemmler, Sabawi
Hussein hadn't travelled extensively throughout Europe or
America and didn't have the same feel for Anglo-Saxons as the
others, but, as head of the Mukhabarat, he had learned quickly
to become a good judge of men. The American sitting calmly
before him was just under six feet tall, possessing an athletic
build without seeming "built-up", and was attractive without
having looks that would call undue attention to himself. He
also gave no hint of nervousness or panic from being in the
presence of Saddam Hussein on his own ground, but remained
coolly in his seat, saying nothing and waiting for his hosts to
make the first move.

"I am Sabawi Hussein, this is my brother, Saddam, my
cousin Kamil, and Dr. Stemmler, the head of our nuclear
research program. I — "

"You are the chief of the Mukhabarat and Colonel Kamil runs the Ministry of Industry and Military Industrialization, 'MIMI', I believe it's called by the CIA."

"A cigarette?" offered Dr. Stemmler.

"No thanks, I don't smoke."

"You are well informed," Sabawi Hussein replied, raising his eyebrows when he caught his half brother's gaze.

"I have to be in my business, but then I doubt you asked me to come here to find out information, since you possess much greater resources for that than I do."

An awkward silence reigned in the room, since none of the Iraqis had ever been addressed in such an abrupt manner in the presence of Saddam Hussein. At the same time, each man in the room was aware that no other type of man would have a chance of accomplishing the mission they were about to propose to their guest.

Therefore, without further delay Sabawi Hussein rose from his chair, approached the American and offered him a thick paperbound U.S. government-issue book.

The American took it and read the title without comment.

"Have you ever seen one of these books before?"

"No."

"Do you know what it is?"

"If it's what I think it is, these are the target codes for the U.S. nuclear strategic forces — they're relatively useless unless the sender can authenticate them."

"Exactly," Dr. Stemmler spoke for the first time. "The sender must convince the person who receives an Emergency Action Message that something terrible has happened."

"Good luck," snapped the American. "I think it would be nothing short of impossible to knock out all of the States' command and control networks, which is what you'd need to do in order to fool the people in the field.

"Look, if this is why you brought me here," the American frowned, getting up from his chair, "I think we can end the meeting now. There's no way — "

"No way a submarine in the middle of the ocean couldn't be made to think that Washington's communications network has been knocked out by a sudden nuclear terrorist attack?" Stemmler asked, holding a single, white sheet of paper in his hand.

The American now stood in the center of the room with all eyes upon him. He knew enough about computers to understand immediately what Dr. Stemmler was suggesting.

"You are the commander of an American SSBN. You are far away from everyone, underwater for months at a time," Stemmler whispered, still holding the sheet of paper in his hand.

"Every tour of duty you engage in war games, communicating with Washington over essentially three different communications networks: ELF, VLF, and blue-green laser.

"ELF waves can penetrate the deepest, down to 300 feet, but because their frequency is so low, this system can only broadcast a single bit of information in a minute. A properly encoded and authenticated emergency action message, containing an order for your submarine to launch one warhead would have to contain a minimum of 40 characters, or 250 bits — which, unfortunately, would take over five hours to transmit.

"Thus, in a crisis, ELF transmissions are limited to simple three-letter code groups signifying things like, 'Sub No. 18: ascend to laser depth to receive next message via SSIX.'

"You are the commander. You, in fact, have just received such a message. You have heard nothing from Washington to indicate to you that any crisis exists, but then your communications room tells you the ELF transmitter which it continuously monitors has suddenly gone off the air.

"You have just lost touch with your command authority and you only have so much time. You then decide to surface, to surface just high enough to confirm your orders with the SSIX satellite that's always overhead.

"Trying to stay as deep as possible, you rise to 225 feet, hoping the SSIX satellite's blue-green laser transmission will tell you it's all just been a big mistake. You wait five minutes, and you receive nothing. Your communications room then tells you your sub's photovoltaic sensors are in perfect working order.

"Now you go above 50 feet, releasing your antenna, desperately trying to contact the TACAMO over VLF — very low frequency. The E-6A is the last link in the chain between the airborne emergency command post and the national command authority.

"To your horror the TACAMO sends you a succinct Emergency Action Message which, when it's decoded, orders you to launch a single missile towards a target in the Middle East. You have already spent twenty minutes since you received the FLASH-priority message over the ELF. Now you have only ninety minutes left until you must launch. Ninety minutes.

"You radio back to the pilot in the TACAMO and demand to be patched through to Washington. Then you get the final shock — the E-6A tells you he can't reach any of the National Military Command Centers over Wimex — the NCA is dead.

"Now you have eighty minutes left until launch. You quickly review all the possibilities in your head. Has Washington been knocked out by a nuclear terrorist attack? Or are you a victim of sabotage? Has someone somehow gotten control of your communications system's software, stolen the codes, and hijacked TACAMO as part of a massive deception? What if there has been an error, a gigantic miscalculation, leaving you responsible for possibly initiating the Third World War?

"At great risk to yourself, you give the order to the XO to

rise to just below the surface. You raise your periscope and the ESM antenna. Through the periscope you see nothing. Over the ESM you detect no radar — no enemy planes overhead looking for you. Next you raise two more antennas, your UHF receiving antenna and your laser transmitter.

"You tell the radioman on duty to send a laser burst transmission over the SSIX satellite to Atlantic Fleet Communications in Norfolk, requesting confirmation of your orders. Their response should be almost instantaneous. Instead you hear nothing. You wait. You are running out of time, you only have sixty-five minutes left. An hour and five minutes to launch. Still, no response from fleet communications.

"Against the dictates of everything you've been taught, you give the order to come up above the surface. Perhaps there is a shortwave receiver on board. It isn't likely, but it's possible. If there is such a radio, more than likely it will have a scanner, which will automatically seek out the strongest transmitting stations, like the BBC. No matter, several major broadcasters will be saying the same thing in several languages: Washington, D.C. has been the target of a nuclear attack. Incoming airliners over a hundred miles distant have reported seeing a mushroom cloud, until their communications suddenly went dead.

"Now you are filled with rage, the capital of your country has been obliterated. Your radioman hands you a FLASH-priority message from the TACAMO demanding to know why you're taking so long to launch; forty minutes have passed since he relayed the EAM to you. You send the order from the bridge to the missile control launch center to activate the fire control computers. Two minutes later the trigger is pulled."

For several seconds the stranger said nothing, the scenario the Third Reich scientist had just suggested having seized his entire imagination.

"The 707 doesn't have a rear stairwell like the 727. How do I exit the plane?"

A smile crossed Sabawi Hussein's face; he had anticipated the stranger's question. Unfolding a detailed drawing of an Iraqi Air Boeing 707 jetliner, he handed it to HYDRA, who studied the yellow-shaded space around the pilot's cockpit in silence.

"It has a hatch…"

"Exactly," Sabawi agreed. "The electrical and equipment access door. It's on the underneath of the fuselage so you won't get caught in the tailwing on your way out."

"Once I jump, who picks me up?"

"Submarine. We pick you up."

"Iraq doesn't have a submarine! Your whole Navy's nothing more than a handful of torpedo boats!"

"Not quite correct," interrupted Colonel Kamil. "At this moment an Iraqi crew is in Sevastopol, being trained to operate a rather old Foxtrot-class attack boat we have contracted to buy from the Ukrainians. They sold it to us for almost nothing."

"Remember," added Sabawi, "we have every desire to get you out of the TACAMO as fast as possible."

They both knew that if the American felt he had been abandoned in the TACAMO, the Iraqis ran the risk of his contacting Washington with information about his mission.

"Can you fly? Do you know how to fly jet airplanes?" Sabawi Hussein broke the silence.

"Yes."

"Boeings?"

"No."

"No matter. We have a 727, it's not that different from the E-6."

"Once TRAPDOOR is activated, you will only have six months, after that the one-time codes are obsolete," added Stemmler, guessing their guest already approved of their plan.

Sabawi Hussein looked sideways at his brother and raised an eyebrow. Colonel Kamil followed suit. The American stared off into space without a shred of interest.

"Will you accept the mission?" Sabawi asked at last. He had spoken softly but his question hung in the room, taking on a presence of its own. The American briefly returned his glance, then spoke without hesitation.

"Yes, but it's going to be very expensive."

"What do you want?" demanded Stemmler.

"I'm sure you understand, there's a real difference between performing the operation I just did for the Colombians and this. Whoever takes this on can never work in this business again. He will also be pursued with the full force of the combined American intelligence agencies — nothing will be left uninvestigated — I'll more than likely be caught. And if I'm not, I'll need enough liquid assets to survive and be able to move at a moment's notice."

"How much would that be?" asked Sabawi.

"Ten million dollars."

Sabawi Hussein cast a quick look at his brother, whose face, to his surprise, remained expressionless.

"Don't you think that's a bit much — "

"I'm neither a fanatic nor a true believer, but a professional who has no intention of being caught once it's over."

"There are other men, my friend, whom we could also contact," Stemmler added with a touch of insolence.

"I'm sure there are, *Doktor* Stemmler," replied the American, staring straight into the Nazi's eyes. "There are many others you could contact. I'm sure you sifted through their dossiers before you decided to call me here."

The American kept his gaze focused on the German, speaking without blinking, "and you decided you couldn't trust some of them not to run away with your money, turning you over to the Americans afterwards. You also decided that very few of them had the guts but not the expertise required for this project. And if I'm guessing correctly, you ruled out non-native English speakers …"

"Enough," replied Saddam Hussein. "We're convinced you're the one we want and we have the money. There's no need to haggle over this like a bunch of traders in a bazaar."

"Thank you, Mr. President," responded the American, "now I'd like to give a list of my conditions."

"Go ahead."

"First, I want every record of this meeting, every file, every dossier, destroyed. And I need to know who, if anyone, outside this room is aware of why I came here."

"No one," answered Sabawi Hussein.

"Good. Let's keep it that way."

"Secondly, after I leave here today I will never meet with anyone representing any of the Iraqi intelligence services again. If you have to contact me in case of an emergency, use this." The stranger slipped what looked like a regular cellular telephone from his pocket and tossed it to Colonel Kamil, who turned it over in his hand. Colonel Kamil had heard of such devices, but had never been able to obtain them, even after repeated requests during his equipment shopping sprees in Europe.

"What you're holding's a spread-spectrum, top-of-the-line CIA digital multiplexer that broadcasts over the KH-14A satellite on a bandwidth so wide it's almost impossible to detect. On top of that, it's equipped with a public key encryption algorithm developed by the NSA, so if it is detected, it's virtually impossible to decipher. As you can see it has a small receptacle on its side — " Colonel Kamil turned the device on its side, finding a female receptacle " — that's for the keyboard. All messages between ourselves from here on out will be in cipher text, not voice, for our mutual safety. By the way, if anyone were to find either one of our boxes, he wouldn't be able to retrieve anything from it without our keys.

"Third, I'll provide you with a list of twenty nominee accounts, located in a series of offshore banks. Each bank on the list has explicit instructions to forward any deposit received in these accounts to another account and another bank and has no idea who the real holder is. I also want the money broken down into irregular pieces before it's wired and sent from clean accounts which you have never used before and which have been opened by non-Iraqis and non-Arabs.

"I also want to be paid half up-front, and half after I finish the job."

"What else?" asked Sabawi Hussein, impressed by the stranger's thoroughness.

"If you need to send me a message, I want you to begin in clear text with the phrase, 'Who's speaking, please?' I'll respond in plain text with a simple code name. If you don't receive it, disconnect immediately."

"What name do you want to use?" asked Stemmler.

"I'm fond of the classics. Why not HYDRA?"

"HYDRA, what does it mean?" asked Saddam Hussein, leaning forward in his chair.

"He was a creature that was impossible to kill, if you cut off one of his heads, another simply grew back in its place."

"I like that," replied the dictator, standing up in his chair.

The meeting was over. The American shook hands with President Hussein, his brother, his brother-in-law, and Dr. Stemmler, then a sentry ushered him to the front door. A different plainclothesman was waiting by the same Volkswagen Passat, Baghdad's most common car, and returned him directly to the airport.

Chapter 8

In his apartment on 62nd Street in New York, HYDRA began a thorough examination of each step in his upcoming mission, desiring to leave no unnecessary portion of it to chance. Far from accepting Stemmler's analysis at face value, HYDRA sought out every publicly available piece of information he could find on America's strategic command and control system, WWMCCS. Sometimes he would grab a taxi and order it to drop him off at the New York Public Library, where he would sit for hours at a time, reading old federal government reports. For more recent works, he used a false name and credit card and had them delivered to a remote postal box, where he would pick them up.

Parcels poured in from the Brookings Institute, the Rand Corporation, the National Technical Information Service, the Naval War College, and the Government Accounting Office, which he would read until well past midnight. On a few of the documents, the titles alone were enough to increase his faith in Stemmler's story: *Worldwide Military Command and Control System — Major Changes Needed in its Automated Data Processing and Direction; Worldwide Military Command and Control System — Problems in Information Resources Management; Problems in the Acquisition of Standard Computers — Worldwide Military Command and Control System.*

The impetus for Wimex's structural design originated with computer entrepreneur David Packard, who, when he was Acting Secretary of Defense from 1969 to 1972, personally reviewed America's C3I capabilities and quickly came to the conclusion that the nation's strategic command system would more than likely collapse under a serious attack.

Antennas, radars, and command centers were all redesigned to make them more immune from the immediate aftereffects of a nuclear explosion, including massive doses of electromagnetic radiation, known in the jargon as EMP — electromagnetic pulse. Aging EC-135 aircraft, previously used as airborne command posts, were replaced with custom-built hardened Boeing 727s, known by strange names like Looking Glass and NEACP. But Melvin Laird, Packard's successor, later testified to Congress that additional protective shielding for the various nuclear command posts, power supply systems, computer rooms, and leased telephone networks would have prohibitively high costs, well beyond the resources of even the United States.

Meanwhile, early warning satellites to detect close-range submarine-launched ballistic missiles were installed, which would automatically alert ground-based bomber crews to take off at the first sign of an offshore launch. Unfortunately, all this effort failed to guarantee that a well-timed and well-planned launch of enemy SLBMs against U.S. strategic C3I targets and ground-alert forces still wouldn't totally succeed in neutralizing America's command authority, so the chain of command for the use of nuclear weapons in an emergency was drastically simplified. Now those authorities still remaining after a first strike were empowered to execute valid action orders in the absence of the original set of commanders. More than ever, America's submarine missile force was viewed as its last-ditch line of defense, linked to whoever remained in command by the single thread of the TACAMO. It was precisely these two countervailing forces which give GERALD's Trojan Horse its devastating power.

HYDRA lay on his back in bed for hours at a time, reviewing Stemmler's outline of the operation over and over in his mind, trying to find any flaw in it he could, before he actually decided to act. After several weeks spent viewing the operation through his own eyes, a sudden thought struck him like a thunderbolt: if they were to by chance become aware of the operation, the combined U.S. intelligence agencies would have no choice but to engage in a massive coverup, just like they had put into place after the Kennedy assassination. For if even a hint of his existence and his mission were to leak out, the world would be plunged into unimaginable chaos. On the other hand, he didn't underestimate the expertise of or the lengths to which the American security services would go to stop him if they were to get wind of his mission. Eliminating a handful of personnel in Operation BUNCIN was child's play compared to being pursued by the entire counterintelligence forces of the United States. This reality reinforced HYDRA's already firm belief that in order to succeed, each step of his operation would have to resemble an isolated act of criminal violence, giving the least hint of his existence.

The silence in his bedroom was suddenly broken by the soft ringing of his spread spectrum telephone. He hadn't been expecting any calls and watched its printer activate with veiled apprehension.

"Who's speaking, please?" Sabawi Hussein's question came across the line.

"HYDRA," HYDRA typed back.

"I'll be brief. You may want to cancel the mission. It's why we haven't sent the money yet."

"Why? What's happened?"

"GERALD's under surveillance."

"When did you find this out?"

"Earlier today."

"I'll call you back in ten minutes," HYDRA immediately typed back, then abruptly and hung up.

HYDRA sat up on his bed and faced the wall. He was furious, but at the same time, he told himself, the Mukhabarat was simply not a first-class intelligence operation, and he should have known that something like this would have happened. But there was nothing that he knew of that would tie him to GERALD, and with some luck, things would stay that way. Besides, even if the American secret services now suspected that a Trojan Horse had been inserted into their software, based on what HYDRA had read so far, if GERALD could be silenced, it would take them months, if not years, to locate it…

HYDRA flipped open the tiny laptop keyboard and punched in the Iraqis' number. Sabawi Hussein responded almost immediately.

"Who's speaking, please?" the text scrolled out.

"It's HYDRA. If you take care of GERALD, I'm still in."

There was a brief pause on the line.

"Done."

Chapter 9

The Assistant Director of Counterintelligence, David Woodring, walked into the FBI Director's outer office and smiled at the receptionist. The buzzer's sound always startled him, no matter how many times he'd heard it.

"He'll see you now, Mr. Woodring," the girl smiled.

Woodring got up and prepared to walk the full length of Hoover's fifty-foot-long corridor, when he saw Director Hubert Myers waiting for him outside the thick, oaken door to the large conference room with its impressive fireplace.

Woodring noticed Hoover's old oil painting of Harlan Fiske Stone had been removed from the mantlepiece. He waited for Director Myers to press the special button under his desk which told the receptionist he wasn't to be disturbed and also initiated a sophisticated series of electronic counter-measures designed to defeat any nearby bugs.

Myers, a recent Clinton appointee, was an unimposing lawyer who had previously worked in the Justice Department under Jimmy Carter, something, he knew, which did not endear him to his staff in an intelligence community which automatically feared Democratic liberals.

"What brings you back to Washington so fast?" Myers asked.

"I'm not sure," Woodring answered hesitantly. "I thought I was making a routine visit to CI-4 on the UNSCOM case, but when I get there they tell me that half the Mukhabarat goons just up and left the country. In and of itself that's bad enough, but combined with our problem in San Diego, it has the makings of a real disaster."

Director Myers was only too well aware of the facts; Woodring had briefed him about RABBIT before Woodring had made his presentation to the CI-5 Division in California. Myers had also just read the Senate Intelligence Committee's report taken in executive session about the I.A.E.A.'s failure to produce intelligence leads in its post-war inspections in Iraq. The chief inspector, Maurizio Zifferero, an Italian, had no concept of security and frequently discussed upcoming visits in bugged hotel rooms. Zifferero also had the cute habit of leaving his backpack filled with documentation of Iraqi nuclear sites behind in his hotel room. Meanwhile, on orders from Vienna, Zifferero would give the Iraqis up to twelve hours advance notice of each inspection, allowing them enough time to hustle pieces of strategic equipment out of one plant to another.

"You think I ought to bring this up with the NFIB?" Myers asked.

The National Foreign Intelligence Board was chaired by the Director of Central Intelligence (the DCI), and included the heads of the CIA, the FBI, the NSA, the DIA, the State Department's own intelligence branch, the Bureau of Intelligence and Research (INR), and representatives from other agencies and departments.

"Yes, sir," answered Woodring.

"Get your coat and let's go."

"Excuse me, sir?"

"The meeting's in ten minutes, you can ride with me in my car to F Street."

"But — "

"You're as ready as you'll ever be, Dave. Come on, we're already running late."

Even in morning traffic it only took Myers's limousine a few minutes to arrive in front of a separate gray building a block away from the Old Executive Office Building, next to the White House. The moment the Cadillac stopped, Director Myers was out of the door, almost jogging to the building's entrance, making it difficult for Woodring to keep up with him.

Once inside Myers and Woodring silently took their seats, since the meeting was already in progress and representatives from more than a dozen agencies were in the room.

"Well, Fred, I see you've brought a sidekick," uttered the DCI, Lincoln Daniels. Daniels had been Myers' predecessor at the FBI, before being appointed by Clinton as the new DCI. He had started as a fieldman under Hoover in the fifties and actually looked more like a patrolman than an agent — no neck, strong shoulders, and a large head framed with wavy silver hair.

All eyes were focused now on Woodring. Since Woodring had just been appointed Assistant Director after the election, he was an unknown quantity in the intelligence fraternity, a clannish group where reputations often hinged on the opinions of a relatively small group of people.

"Woody, why don't you just tell the group what you told me in my office?" prompted Myers.

"Ah, yes, sir."

Woodring cleared his throat, inventorying the various faces at the table: Frank Chalmers, Director of the National Security Agency, who had already been informed of RABBIT's existence; General Martin Praeger, Director of the Defense Intelligence Agency, the military's equivalent of the CIA; Daniels's Deputy Director of Counterintelligence (DDCI) at

CIA and Woodring's counterpart, Keith Axe; Air Force General Haywood Ford, Director of the National Reconnaissance Office (NRO), the "black" Air Force division charged with operating the community's fleet of surveillance satellites; plus representatives from the Drug Enforcement Agency and the Justice, Treasury, and Commerce Departments.

"As a matter of policy, we normally don't disclose ongoing CI investigations unless requested by Justice to do otherwise for national security purposes, and generally that only happens when there's a conflict with another agency.

"That said, I felt the board might be interested in the following two situations which I'll relate to you without any analysis on my part, so you can draw your own conclusions:

"First, about two weeks ago we received a set of photographs from INTERPOL taken at various European airports of a subject we'll call RABBIT." Woodring opened up his briefcase and handed a sheaf of surveillance photographs to Director Myers, who began to pass them around the table. "In the last thirty days, RABBIT's made three two-day-long trips to Europe. RABBIT's an analyst at FHI Systems in San Diego, and his real name is Victor Saleh. Saleh's a Lebanese-American, totally bilingual in English and Arabic, and is presently shopping for a new Mercedes on a G-10 salary. FHI systems is the chief contractor on the DCA's Wimex update.

"Second story: yesterday I got an urgent call from our CI-4 counterintelligence office in New York — they're covering the Mukhabarat agents assigned to the Iraqi Mission. When I arrived in Manhattan, I was informed the Iraqis had just cut the number of people in half they were devoting to reconnaissance of the Special Commission members — "

"They what?" demanded Keith Axe, the CIA Deputy Director Counterintelligence at CIA. Axe was Daniels' hatchet man, and his favorite pastime was crossexamining his associates at official meetings.

"Like I said, the Iraqis cut their New York force in half."

"How do you know that for sure?"

"Because my guys at CI-4 photographed them waiting for their planes at Kennedy." While Axe sat back in his chair with a grimace, the Director of NSA, Frank Chalmers, raised his eyebrows at his tablemate, General Martin Praeger, Director of the Defense Intelligence Agency (DIA). Praeger was more than happy to see "the Ax" put back in his place by the newcomer, Woodring. Unlike the directors of CIA and FBI, Praeger was not a new appointee as Director of DIA, and had managed to survive the transition from a Republican to a Democratic administration with his job intact. Utterly underwhelmed by Clinton's new team, and thinly masking his distaste for them, Praeger couldn't wait to see how they would all react to their first major crisis.

"Well now, I would say that's a very fascinating coincidence, wouldn't you, Keith?" Praeger grinned.

Woodring furrowed his brow and exchanged glances with Hubert Myers, his superior, who nodded for him to continue.

"Ah, there's one more thing."

The silence was deafening as all eyes returned to the new FBI ADCI.

"I had the boys at CI-4 in New York go through our old photo files, checking the stuff we took before we went to digital holography. RABBIT was a walk-in at the Iraqi Mission on January 18, 1991."

"Shit!" cursed General Praeger. "There's no telling what he's done! There's over 20,000,000 lines of programming in the whole system!"

"Frank? Anything to add to this?" asked Daniels, still trying to maintain his calm.

The Director of the National Security Administration, paused significantly before he replied: "If Dr. Saleh has indeed tampered with a part of Wimex, he may have just committed

the one act of sabotage to which we are the most vulnerable —
attacking our communications software."

"I thought our system was designed with safeguards to
prevent exactly this type of situation from occurring!" objected
Daniels.

"The system's safeguards were designed mainly to prevent
unauthorized use of the hardware," Chalmers rebutted.

"What are you telling me, Frank?"

"Just what I said. The Wimex system wasn't designed with
this type of thing in mind — it's over twenty years old, for
god's sakes."

"You mean a single disgruntled engineer can shoot off a full
complement of ICBMs just by altering the software? The
system's that weak?"

"Not exactly."

"Not exactly? What do you mean 'not exactly'?"

Chalmers was silent for a moment, then spoke, "The representatives from Treasury, Justice, Commerce, INR, and DEA
are going to have to leave the room."

"Gentlemen." Daniels motioned for the stunned members
of the aforementioned departments to wait outside the door.

A full three seconds after the last representative filed out
and the door was reclosed, Chalmers answered Daniels' question.

"The system is designed so that no nuclear missile will ever
be fired automatically, without a human interface between the
NCA and the device. That means any emergency action
message sent from the NCA has to be decoded and authenticated by a human being, not a computer, before any launch
order's going to be initiated. Since Dr. Saleh doesn't have access
to the one-time codes for the EAM's, there's no way he can
issue anyone a legitimate order to launch anything."

"So what else could this guy have done, Frank?"

"Something almost as bad," Chalmers replied. For the next fifteen minutes he gave the remaining members of the NFIB a crash course in trapdoors and Trojan Horses.

"Wait a minute!" Keith Axe protested. "That means a missile silo, or a strategic bomber, could suddenly become incommunicado!"

"Right," Chalmers agreed.

"Then how would we know what they were doing?"

"We wouldn't."

"What if Dr. Saleh had the codes, sent off an EAM, then activated one of these Trojan Horses — how would we be able to stop him?"

"You wouldn't, but Dr. Saleh doesn't have the authentication codes, so why worry about it?"

"Because someone else might try to get them. Someone a lot harder to catch than Victor Saleh," interrupted Woodring.

"Gentlemen?" Daniels spoke, trying to bring the discussion back to earth.

FBI Director Myers immediately responded:

"I say we burn Saleh as quickly as possible and find out if we've got a problem."

"Everybody agree on this?" Daniels surveyed the dozen faces at the table, and all were silent.

"Woody, he's yours."

A telephone next to Daniels unexpectedly rang and the DCI picked it up, furrowed his brow, then looked quizzically at Woodring.

"Woody, it's for you."

Woodring stood up, walked to the head of the table, and took the phone.

"Woodring."

Lincoln Daniels glanced worriedly at Hubert Myers as if to

say, "What have we gotten ourselves into?"

Woodring dropped the handset on the cradle, the color gone from his face.

"Dr. Saleh…he's dead."

"He's been hit?" Daniels demanded.

"They blew his whole house. Saleh was standing outside. They said it killed him."

"Surprise, surprise," muttered General Praeger.

"We've got to be careful, Lincoln. If people even start to think we might have lost control of just part of our nuclear arsenal, there could be a panic," Chalmers worried aloud.

"Woody, take my car and go back to your office and get in touch with CI-5 in LA and tell them to put a lid on this story. Keep our guys away from there for a couple of days and have the San Diego police say it's a gas explosion — anything but a terrorist bomb," Myers ordered.

"Yes, sir."

Once Woodring left the room, Daniels turned to his own Deputy Director, Keith Axe.

"By tomorrow morning I want a full-scale but quiet background check on Saleh's family in Lebanon. Use whoever you have to and give a copy of everything you find to Hubert."

Next, he turned to the Director of the National Security Administration. "Frank, I want you to review everything you've got from Iraq, the Mideast, UNSCOM and whatever else you feel is pertinent and see if your people can find any mention of something unusual."

"Yes, sir."

Next, Daniels looked at General Praeger. "Who's in charge of Wimex?"

"General Vaughn at DCA."

"Have him come to my office this time tomorrow. As far as

the Pentagon's concerned, he's got a sick relative somewhere. I want a full briefing on how the system works."

"Lincoln, what do you want to tell the Joint Chiefs about Saleh?" Praeger asked.

"For the moment, nothing, if that's OK with you, General."

"I can wait twenty-four hours, but, after that, we're going to have to talk."

"Fine. I expect to see you all in my office tomorrow at one o'clock," Daniels said, then immediately left the room, accompanied by Keith Axe.

Chapter 10

In December of 1978 a special investigator delivered a secret 280-page report to the House Select Committee on Assassinations regarding the activities of Lee Harvey Oswald in Mexico City from late September to early October 1963, directly prior to the assassination of President John F. Kennedy in November 1963. A copy of the document was also immediately made available to the then President, Jimmy Carter. Included in the report were several photographs of individuals whom both the CIA and FBI had represented as being Oswald visiting both the Cuban and Soviet embassies. Also included were eight written transcripts of telephone conversations between a man representing himself as Oswald and various Soviet officials which had been secretly taped during the same period. Finally, a lone tape-recording which had been retrieved by James Jesus Angleton from the home of the former station chief of Mexico City on the day of his funeral was also unearthed from the CIA's files and attached. It was immediately clear to any one who read the report and the transcripts, looked at the photographs, then listened to the tape that neither the faces in the photographs nor the voice on the tape recording belonged to Lee Harvey Oswald, but to someone else.

Upon receiving solid evidence that Oswald had been impersonated in Mexico City by others only a month and a half before the assassination, evidence which was deliberately withheld from the Warren Commission, a furious President Carter ordered his director of Central Intelligence, Admiral Stansfield Turner, to clean house. For, far from implicating either Russian or Cuban intelligence in Kennedy's death, the Lopez Report indicated that Oswald had been deliberately and unwittingly sent to Mexico City by the American intelligence services as part of a counterespionage mission, where he would claim to be a disenchanted leftist interested in assassinating John F. Kennedy, perfectly positioning him as a prime suspect if an actual assassination were to occur.

Many of those in the CIA's covert operations staff who were let go had trouble adjusting to civilian life and found it difficult to find employment; many more were rehired by the subsequent DCI, William Casey, after President Reagan was elected; and others, like David Blond, found being self-employed much more rewarding and learned to welcome their sudden change in status. Blond, himself, who had only been fifteen years old in 1963 and had had nothing to do whatsoever with Kennedy's demise, was later employed under contract by the CIA's Directorate of Operations as a tailor, a trade which he had learned from his father. During the Second World War, Blond's father, whose real surname was Stetzko, happened to have been a member of a Ukrainian nationalist group which called itself the "Nightingales" and whose members wore Wehrmacht uniforms and performed nasty tasks handed to them by the SS. Located in a displaced-persons camp by State Department intelligence agents, Stetzko was given new identification and recruited to fight communism in Eastern Europe, finally settling in New York.

At his shop on 53rd Street in Manhattan, Blond's father would receive envelopes filled with cash attached to pictures of foreign uniforms — Italian carabinieri, the Greek postal service, French delivery men, Guatemalan highway patrol, Iranian naval officers, and Cuban marines — accompanied by a list of required quantities and sizes. In September, 1963, he was surprised by a sudden request to make up two dozen various different uniforms based on pages torn from Texas law enforcement magazines. Two months later, Blond's father realized the implications.

In the meantime, the father-son team, with the help of their special friends, had built up a sizable portion of legitimate sales to local New York-area police agencies and private security forces, enough to easily allow them to do without the custom orders from Virginia. But David Blond, who finally took over the business entirely after his father retired at age sixty-five, would from time to time still fill certain orders whose origins were obviously illegitimate. Now, instead of limiting himself in this regard to Langley's true believers, he had decided that he would entertain clients of almost all persuasions, if, of course, their references checked out. In fact, at one point, Blond had provided over a score of different uniforms resembling those worn by various guard personnel at Kennedy Airport to certain gentlemen of Sicilian background, which had occasioned a subsequent visit by investigators from the New York Police Department. The NYPD had previously suspected Blond of similar endeavors, but had never been able to catch him at it.

So David Blond was hardly surprised to receive a call from a former client, a Colombian drug distributor who had found it was much easier to make his rounds disguised as a UPS deliveryman, who told Blond that a certain American was interested in his services and would arrive at noon, carrying a large package.

The moment HYDRA entered the waiting room, Blond guessed who he was and led him back to his private office.

"I assume you don't want to linger here any longer than's necessary," Blond suggested, taking a closer look at the man in front of him, "so let's get your measurements then." After setting the package on Blond's desk, HYDRA unfolded an advertisement he had torn out of *Skin Diver* magazine, handing it to Blond. It contained a lengthy list of measurements, allowing whoever filled it out to order a diving suit by mail from a firm based in Des Moines, Washington.

HYDRA removed his jacket while Blond pulled a tape measure from his pocket and waited for his guest to turn around before pressing against his shoulder with his finger.

"Left arm out, please."

HYDRA did as he was told and stretched out his left arm.

"Good. Stand still."

Blond held one end of the tape to HYDRA's belt and measured his pants length.

"Legs apart. Sorry, have to do the inseam."

HYDRA felt Blond pinch the tape to the bottom of his crotch.

"Arms up for a second." The tailor next stretched the tape tautly around HYDRA's chest.

"You don't know your neck size, by any chance, I suppose, do you?" Blond asked. Something about his new customer restrained him from asking to be allowed to put the measuring tape around HYDRA's neck.

"Sixteen."

"Good. We'll stick with that, then." Blond went over and wrote *16* on the advertisement from the diving magazine, then spent the next several minutes measuring HYDRA's wrist to elbow, wrist to armpit, ankle to crotch, ankle to waist, shoulder to waist and shoulder seam to crotch. Now standing in front of his guest, the tape dangling in his hand, Blond asked, "Now how can I help you?"

"Luiz told you I was coming?"

"Yes, certainly."

"And did he tell you what about?"

"No, he only said that I could rely on your discretion and that you were a friend of his father's in Bogota."

"Then you're aware of who Luiz's father is, I take it?" The American paused for a moment, catching the look in Blond's eyes.

"Yes, I know who he is."

"Good," replied HYDRA, pulling three patterns from his pocket. "I'd like you to take a look at these."

The first pattern was actually a series of drawings, containing two separate patterns of a winter flight parka and a diving suit plus mechanical drawings of an ICOM IC-MI5 handheld waterproof VHF marine transceiver and an ACR personal man-overboard strobe light.

Blond recognized the second pattern immediately as a uniform of the Naval Investigative Service, a counterintelligence unit of the U.S. Navy. Blond knew, of course, that counterfeiting such a uniform was a federal offense, which, if found out, could easily attract an investigation by the FBI, something he didn't want. On the other hand, whatever friendliness there had been in his new customer's manner had suddenly evaporated, having been replaced by an almost palpable chill which gave Blond butterflies in his stomach. The was tailor under no illusion as to what fate could easily befall him were he to refuse the implacable stranger, forcing him to go somewhere else to fill his order.

"Normally," Blond spoke slowly with great hesitation, "I don't do this type of work; there's just too much risk." His customer's eyes narrowed in response. "But if I do do this for you, I don't want to ever know your name or be given any information about where you live. You understand?"

The stranger nodded in response.

"The two naval uniforms will cost you twenty-five thousand dollars each. The parka I'll do for a thousand."

"That's extortionate!" HYDRA protested.

Blond's index finger lightly touched the part of the pattern which illustrated the uniform's lapels.

"These aren't just the insignia of an investigator. You're aware of that, of course?"

HYDRA paused a moment, while a cool grin formed itself on his face.

"Twenty thousand, then?"

"All right, twenty thousand, but nothing less."

"And I'd like it ready in thirty days."

"I can do that," Blond replied, folding up the pattern and slipping it into his jacket pocket.

"I'd like you to return once and only once for the fitting. You can wait here and I'll adjust them on the spot. Is that all right?"

HYDRA nodded affirmatively, then left the shop and hailed a taxi, disappearing into the noonday Manhattan traffic. After HYDRA left Blond carefully opened the box, extracting a regulation winter flight parka, ACR man-overboard strobe, ICOM handheld radio, and a pair of rubber fins which he spread out on his work table. Unconsciously rubbing his chin with his hand, Blond glanced at the first pattern, realizing all too well what it meant.

Chapter 11

The taxi soon dropped HYDRA off at an electronics discount house in midtown which regularly ran full-page ads in the Sunday issue of the New York Times. HYDRA asked a salesman to show him a Hewlett-Packard Model HP-100LX palm top computer, which, after examining carefully for several minutes, he told the salesman he wanted to buy. He paid for it in cash, then walked the few blocks to the post office branch he used for his mail drop and checked his box. A thick envelope from the Family Service Center Relocation Assistance Program Office at the Patuxent Naval Air Base was folded in half along with a brochure from Boeing on the specs of the E-6A, the modified 707 known as the TACAMO. He extracted them both and returned via taxi to his apartment on 62nd street, where he placed a discreet call to a local travel agent, asking her about flights to Baltimore, San Diego, and Seattle. After he hung up, he spent the rest of the afternoon reading. At 6:00 p.m. he walked to a neighborhood French restaurant and ordered a steak *au poivre* with a red Merlot, then caught a cab outside the Regency Hotel, telling the driver to take him to the United Airlines terminal at Kennedy Airport.

After successfully concluding the Operation BUNCIN affair for the Colombians, HYDRA had correctly guessed that someone outside the cartel was consulting it over its use of high-speed communications and cryptography, given the advanced level of the telecommunications equipment he had seen in Bogota. The Colombians' planes and helicopters were fitted with state-of-the-art over-the-horizon radars; their cellular telephone calls were digitally encrypted using unbreakable algorithms; and their bank-to-bank money transfers were wired through a maze of international accounts with the aid of sophisticated software programs, challenging even the relatively unlimited resources of the U.S. intelligence agencies to track them.

During an expensive dinner at an Italian restaurant Luiz had admitted to him that certain experts were, indeed, on his family's payroll. Some had formerly occupied cushy posts at companies a majority of whose revenues came from defense contracts, only to find themselves laid off as the military shrank in response to a lessening Russian threat. Others had previously been at firms which were unaffected by the federal government's shrinking military budget, but had succumbed to personal problems of their own, including, of course, drug abuse. There were so many candidates that the cartel had found it necessary to hire several talent scouts to work the

Silicon Valley, Boston, and Los Angeles areas to help it choose its new hirees.

A few days after his dinner with Luiz HYDRA received a plain-white envelope addressed to Russell Matthews which bore no return address and contained only a single sheet of paper: the resume of a certain Alex Castor. Castor's credentials fit HYDRA's needs to a tee: Stanford undergrad; grad work at MIT where Castor received dual masters of science in computer science and electronic engineering; five years at Bell Labs, followed by five more at GTE; then a stint at Mitre Corp in crypto, then nothing for two years. The next time HYDRA saw him Luiz explained the nothing part by tapping his nose with his index finger and laughing.

By evening, the mist had turned into light drizzle, making rings around the halogen lamps on the Van Wyck Expressway, and a faded orange glow hung in the sky like an electric cloud. Outside the terminal, swarms of taxis fought for precious road space, trying to unload their passengers in a small area crowded with waiting limousines, police patrol cars, and private automobiles. HYDRA allowed his driver to let him out on the sidewalk opposite the terminal, resulting in a brief series of angry honks and catcalls from passing cars who had been temporarily backed up behind him; he ignored them, paid the driver, then walked to the nearest crosswalk.

Giving his name as Russell Matthews at the United Airlines desk, HYDRA paid cash for a ticket on UAL Flight #5479 nonstop to San Francisco and boarded the plane thirty minutes later. Arriving a little after 10:00 p.m. local time, HYDRA took a taxi to the nearest airport motel, where he registered under his own name, prepaying for a one-night stay in cash.

☆ ☆ ☆

The next morning HYDRA had breakfast at the airport motel, checked out, got in his rental car and took the Junipero Serra

Freeway south, the state Highway 92 at the reservoir, and crossed 92 to reach Pacific Coast Highway 1. Castor lived south of Stanford in the Santa Cruz mountains in a town with the picturesque name of Bonny Dune. Bonny Dune was an isolated subdivision that ran all the way from the Pacific Ocean to two thousand feet in the nearby mountains and was crisscrossed by meandering roads interspersed with stands of tan oak and redwood.

After rechecking his map, HYDRA took the turn after Davenport, following Empire Grade Road along the northern boundary of U.C. Santa Cruz. Castor lived up in the mountains off an unmarked road just past the sign to Felton, the next town. HYDRA wound up a gravel road bordered by madrone trees, stopping at a battered gate made of old cyclone fence. He got out of his car and shoved it aside, driving another mile until he reached a clearing. An old stucco house with a shingled roof sat in the middle surrounded by six oak trees.

HYDRA pressed the doorbell twice and waited. It was about 10:00 a.m. in the morning and the suburban street was deserted, which made him feel better about renting the car in his own name. There was still no answer at the door, so he pressed the buzzer again, this time leaving his finger on the button, remembering how Luiz had tapped his nose when describing Castor. He heard a rumbling, then a voice.

"Yeah, just a minute!"

The door swung open, and a man with disheveled hair, rings under his eyes, and a stained shirt which had obviously been slept in stood before him.

"It's the man with no name," the man behind the door offered in greeting, chuckling nervously to himself. Alex Castor had no idea who HYDRA was, and had only been told a certain visitor would be arriving the next day around noon using the name Russell Matthews.

HYDRA said nothing.

"Come on in, Mr. No-name. Luiz told me you'd be coming."

HYDRA followed Castor through a living room littered with half-empty soda cans, old magazines, and dirty plates. A huge big-screen TV had been situated in the center, and CNN was playing with the sound off.

"You want a Pepsi or anything?"

"Sure."

Castor opened a filthy refrigerator and fished out two cold cans of Pepsi. HYDRA noticed Castor's hands slightly quivered as he handed him his, and that he sniffed involuntarily about every ten seconds.

Castor swept a heap of debris to one side of his kitchen table and pulled out two chairs, then sat down. HYDRA followed suit, setting the HP-100LX in front of him.

"That's a nice machine," Castor spoke, nodding toward the laptop. "Luiz says you want me to do something with it for you."

"Yeah."

HYDRA reached into his jacket pocket and extracted what at first resembled a .38-caliber pistol.

"Hey!" Castor involuntarily shoved his chair back, raising his hands in the air.

HYDRA slid the gun across on the table, slowly turning it so the barrel faced his own chest.

"Calm down. It's not a weapon."

Castor blinked in fright as the realization painted itself on his face. "*How'd you get this?* You know what this thing is?"

"Luiz told me you'd know how this thing works. Do you?" HYDRA pressed.

"Yeah. I know how it works. I also know you didn't get it from him. What exactly in hell do you want?" Castor was still standing behind his chair.

"I want you to make me an adapter for the computer that'll keep the gun from zeroizing after it's been downloaded."

Avoiding looking HYDRA in the eyes, Castor gingerly picked the gun up off the table and turned it over in his hands.

"Listen, No-name, I'm gonna be up front with you, since Luiz sent you here and I don't want any trouble with him or any of his kind. What I do for them is simply modify the boxes they give me to work a little better and a little faster, but I don't need a security clearance for any of the stuff they bring me." Castor held the gun so that its barrel pointed at the ceiling and shook it for emphasis. "If I touch this, if I'm even found with this thing in my house and the feds say that I stole it — I could get 10, 20 years no-parole. *Easy*," Castor sniffed and wiped his sleeve across his nose.

"I'll call Luiz then, and tell him you're not interested," replied HYDRA as if it wouldn't be a problem, pulled the special telephone out of his pocket, and flipped it open. Castor took a deep breath.

"Man, this is gonna cost you."

"How much?" HYDRA replied, still holding the open handset.

"Fifty thousand, and I want twenty-five of it right now. Up front."

HYDRA reached into his inside jacket pocket, slipping out a thick white envelope, tossed it on the table, stood up, and began to leave the room.

"You keep calling Luiz on that telephone of yours, No-name, and eventually they're gonna find you."

HYDRA stopped in the kitchen door, his head half-cocked in Castor's direction.

"The BUNCIN boys all had telephones just like that. I know 'cause I tracked them for Luiz. True, spread spectrum's pretty hard to find if you're not looking for it — but once someone knows you're using it, that thing'll act just like a beacon." HYDRA now faced Castor, the telephone still in his hand. "It's the codes. The codes inside that thing that'll give away your position.

"Look, even GPS — the Global Positioning System — the satellites for navigation — use spread spectrum. If they're looking for you and you're talking on that thing NSA'll pinpoint you within 10 meters."

HYDRA furrowed his brow; Castor's unsolicited speculations were getting on his nerves.

"You're the guy, aren't you?" Castor asked. "You're the guy they sent down there. Jesus, I should have known."

"If I were you, I'd keep speculations like that to myself," HYDRA replied, then walked out the door.

☆ ☆ ☆

On his return to New York he gave his cab driver the hacker's address on Wall Street, deciding not to stop first at his apartment.

The same guard on duty told the hacker that Fred Daniels was in the lobby, and HYDRA again took the elevator to the fifteenth floor, walking directly into the deserted office where the hacker worked.

"I've been working a lot of late nights for you," the hacker announced without preamble.

"Come on around, I want you to look at this — we don't have time to print it out."

HYDRA walked around the desk and peered over her shoulder as she grabbed a sack of McDonald's french fries off her desk.

"Want one?"

"No thanks."

Green letters all in capitals flickered on the monitor, NAV PAX RIV TDY ROSTER, ALL DIVISIONS.

"Which division do you want?"

"TACAMO Command."

"Hold on a second."

The hacker set the sack of french fries on the edge of the keyboard and typed in the password she'd stolen.

The screen blinked, then was filled with a list of acronyms, one of which was TACAMOCMD.

"That's it," she muttered to herself and entered the term with a second command.

"TDY ROSTER -TACAMOCMD -NAV PAX RIV," the screen answered back.

HYDRA carefully read each entry as the hacker scrolled through the list. Regular TACAMO crew members, none of whom HYDRA wanted, rotated out of Tinker Air Force Base, Oklahoma to either Pax River or Travis in California.

"Wait. Stop there," he ordered.

"Where? On Barton?"

"No, Gereke, right below."

"Just a minute." The hacker punched two keys, and Naval Air Force Reserve Lieutenant Junior Grade Jack Gereke's orders filled the screen.

"Can you print that?"

"Sure. Hold on." She punched a different key, then glanced back at HYDRA.

"How can we find out if he's ever gotten orders for Pax River before?"

"Easy. We just ask," replied the typist, and entered Gereke's name into a general search of the last twelve month's TDY.

Three full seconds later the words *File Not Found* blinked reassuringly on the screen. Gereke the weekend warrior. Meanwhile the hacker handed HYDRA a printout copy of Air Force Lieutenant Gereke's orders to report to Pax River on

March 15 from his residence in Kansas City.

"I need his personnel file," HYDRA spoke in a tone, indicating it was an order.

"No problem," chirped the hacker.

She typed in a command that automatically cleared the screen, then hit carriage return and typed in NAV PAX RIV MIL PERS.

"Welcome to Pax River Naval Base, login," the base's computer immediately responded.

The hacker just as quickly entered the password for the base's personnel files and in seconds retrieved a printout, listing a complete record of Lieutenant Gereke's military history, age, salient physical characteristics, base and home address and relevant telephone numbers.

"You want NIS next, right?"

HYDRA nodded affirmatively and in seconds the hacker logged onto the Naval Investigate Service computer system at its headquarters in Suitland, Maryland.

"Personnel again?"

"Right," HYDRA answered.

The words "Enter your password," appeared on the CRT screen, and the hacker accordingly typed in an eight-digit alphanumeric sequence. A menu containing an alphabet soup of acronyms popped up next.

"What department?"

"Courier transfer."

The screen blinked, and a second menu scrolled across it.

"Subdepartment?"

"Technical services."

"O.K.," replied the hacker, grabbing her Coke. "You wanna print this out?"

"If it's O.K."

"O.K? Like I told you they don't even know we're there, honey." She hit the carriage return, causing twenty-five resumes to slowly drop out of her HP laser printer into HYDRA's hands.

"What's next?" the hacker prompted, breaking HYDRA's concentration.

HYDRA looked up from the sheaf of papers, paused a moment, then spoke, "Let's run every one of these through Bangor's TDY, as far as you can so we can find who's already been there and who hasn't."

"Yes sir."

Just as the hacker logged off the NIS computer, HYDRA spoke up, holding one resume in his right hand. Technical Sergeant Peter Koester had just joined the NIS a month ago.

"Wait, try this name first," HYDRA said, giving her Koester's rank and serial number.

"No problem."

The computer operator cross-checked Koester's name with all previous visitors to Bangor Naval Submarine Base and came up dry.

"You wanna try anybody else?"

"No."

"What's next?"

"I need credit cards for those two identities, plus a third one," HYDRA spoke, looking up from the printout. "The third man's name is Russell D. Matthews."

Before the hacker could protest, he held up his hand to stop her.

"Not the actual cards themselves, just the numbers. Matthews probably doesn't have any, so go in and give him whatever you can. I'll leave it up to you. You can find Gereke's and Koester's in TRW credit reports — I'd like the files, too. But, whatever you do, don't get anything mailed out to any of them — I don't want to raise any unnecessary red flags."

"No problem. You want me to call you when I get them?"

"No," HYDRA firmly replied. "Just drop them in an envelope to this address." He handed her a plain white card, with his post office address written in pencil on it. "By the way, what's all this costing me?"

"Nothing. It's on the house. Courtesy of Luiz," the operator grinned.

HYDRA feigned mild surprise, but they both had known from the outset that the job was a courtesy of the boys from Bogota, and that there would be no haggling over the price or conditions.

HYDRA reached inside his jacket pocket, "I understand that you've been instructed to do me a favor and I want you to know how much I appreciate your cooperation ..." The hacker turned in her seat and watched him silently count out ten hundred dollar bills and lay them in her hand. "... on the other hand I want to be up front with you and tell you that if you ever repeat anything about what you saw or did here today to anyone — "

"Hey, don't worry — I — "

HYDRA held up his hand, again, interrupting her. " — I'll come back here and kill you myself. You understand me?"

"Yes."

"You sure?"

"I got the message, mister, believe me."

Chapter 12

General Curtis Vaughn, Director of the Defense Communications Agency, sat nervously beside General Praeger who was driving his wife's Toyota, as both men stopped at the security checkpoint outside CIA headquarters in Langley, Virginia.

All Vaughn had been told was that he was to prepare a rush briefing on the present status of the Worldwide Military Command and Control System for presentation to the Director of Central Intelligence at 1:00 p.m. that day; that General Praeger would pick him up; that the meeting was classified and that he was to wear civilian clothes. At first, Vaughn hadn't an inkling as to what the fuss was all about until he got a telephone call at his house that evening from one of his subordinates. Dr. Victor Saleh had died in an explosion at his home just as he was about to be arrested by the FBI. Even though local San Diego police were insisting there was no foul play, local newscasters had already found out that FHI Systems was involved in secret defense computer work.

The security guard made a brief telephone call to Daniels' security staff, then handed both men back their identification with two passes and waved them through. Praeger drove directly to the main entrance, parked, and motioned for Vaughn to follow him through the door. They entered a cavernous lobby with marble walls, the right chiseled with thirty-eight stars for agents who'd died in the line of duty, the left engraved with a quote from Saint John, "And ye shall know the truth, and the truth shall make you free." After showing their passes to a second guard, they were met by a receptionist who ushered them into a small private waiting room furnished with an Oriental carpet, chest and several matching vases. An elevator door opened slightly, and a young man in plainclothes said, "General Praeger, General Vaughn, please come with me." The two generals entered a small, private elevator, which Daniels's assistant took to the seventh floor, and ushered them into a second suite of similarly decorated waiting rooms. The security guard disappeared through a side door, leaving both generals momentarily alone.

For the next ten minutes neither general spoke to the other, since neither had the desire, under the circumstances, to engage in idle chitchat. Finally, a secretary with a pleasant smile on her face appeared and ushered them into a large and disconcertingly bright, spacious office framed by a forty-foot-long floor-to-ceiling window with a spectacular view of the forest below. The Oriental decor with its subdued rose and light mauve motifs gave the room a somewhat misleading air of comfort and tranquility.

But whatever pleasant feelings the room's interior might have normally instilled in Daniels's guests were not felt by General Vaughn the moment he caught sight of the meeting's other participants. Seated on two sofas were the Directors of the Federal Bureau of Investigation, National Security Administration, National Reconnaissance Office, and the State Department's Bureau of Intelligence and Research, plus a face Vaughn didn't recognize, which, Daniels informed, him, belonged to a certain David Woodring, who was the Assistant Director of Counterintelligence at the FBI. Vaughn knew that Woodring's presence could mean one thing only — spies.

Daniels showed Vaughn and Praeger to a pair of armchairs next to his, then began: "Curt, I know that General Praeger here has already told you that anything we discuss here today, must be kept absolutely secret from anyone. Repeat, anyone."

"Yes sir," Vaughn responded, partially clearing his throat.

"I'm sure you're by now aware of the recent killing of Dr. Saleh," Daniels continued. Vaughn blinked at the word "killing", no one had told him for sure that Saleh had been a murder victim. "Unfortunately, Director Myers has informed us that what took place might involve something much worse than a simple act of terrorism."

Now the muscles in Vaughn's back involuntarily tightened, creating a sharp pain between his shoulder blades. He fought to maintain his self control as the words seemed to march out of Myers' mouth.

"… after a thorough review of our old photographic files, we discovered that Dr. Saleh had visited the Iraqi Mission to the United Nations in Vienna more than two years ago."

The words Operation ARCHANGEL popped into his mind, and Vaughn felt almost physically ill. Saleh was the one who had run the battle systems of the F-15 four-ship that had disappeared. Now there would be no way to tell what damage he had done, until it was too late, and Vaughn didn't have to be told who would take the blame for it all. He guessed they would keep him on through the investigation, but, after it was over, his military career would be finished.

"Yes, sir. I see."

"Curt, what we'd like you to do right now is give us a quick briefing on the present status of the Wimex network, before we get into what Dr. Saleh may or may not have done while he was at FHI," Daniels ordered.

Vaughn fumbled with the legal-sized file folder he had brought with him, dropping a sheaf of papers to the floor. After he picked them up, he cleared his throat and began:

"The Worldwide Military Command and Control System is an integrated computerized communications and battle system designed to provide the President and the Joint Chiefs — or whoever's in control of the NCA at the time — control over our military forces. The Wimex data-processing system was designed for use under all conditions — peacetime to nuclear war — but, of course, has been augmented with many specialized capabilities designed specifically for use in a nuclear exchange.

"The system was designed both to provide downward communications connecting to the various forces, and also verified warning of attack to forces on alert in order to convince the enemy that our forces can and will be used against him if we are, in fact, attacked.

"Pre-attack operations are handled by Honeywell DPS 8 and 6000 computers, command center display systems are handled by Univac 1100s; war planning's on IBM 3080s and intelligence data handling's on VAX 11/780 front ends ..." General Vaughn paused a moment, surveying the faces before him, hoping someone would ask a question, but no one did. As far as everyone in the room was concerned, he had said nothing so far of any great importance. Vaughn resumed, "Wimex's two basic components are the National Military Command System, that is, the President and Joint Chiefs; the command centers of each of the services: Army, Navy, Air Force, and Marines; and other agencies, such as your own. The system's also designed to operate under a series of shifting commands, in case one or more is lost during an attack.

"The system's primary mission is to support the NCA during an attack, i.e., provide as much information as quickly as possible for a fast response. With this in mind an integrated set of programs called the Joint Operation Planning System — or JOPS — was developed to provide data support. Similarly, software was developed for a strategic nuclear war plan, the Single Integrated Operating Plans to be used by the Joint Strategic Target Planning Staff at SAC."

At this point several of the attendees had begun to shift in their seats; Vaughn still wasn't telling them anything that anyone couldn't have read in *The Joint Staff Officer's Guide.*

"Curt," General Praeger interrupted. "I think everybody here's pretty familiar with how our communications work, and, if it's alright with Director Daniels, I think our time would be better spent having you tell us more about the exact duties of the late Dr. Saleh."

Vaughn glanced at Director Daniels who nodded his approval.

"Yes, sir. FHI Systems was hired by us to review overall system architecture and response interfaces between communications and battle systems — "

"What's a response interface?" broke in Hubert Myers, tired of the endless jargon.

"A measure of how well and how fast the various individuals at the battle stations carry out the orders they're given by their commands."

"So what you're saying here — and correct me at anytime if I'm wrong — is that there's a Chinese wall between the people issuing the orders and the ones who carry them out, am I right?"

"Generally, yes."

"So Saleh's job was to review both the battle systems software and the communications software to see if one meshed with the other?"

"Yes, sir."

"What did you mean by 'generally'?" Woodring interrupted.

"Uh, that's what I wanted to bring up," Vaughn stammered, his face tensing up. "There was one instance after Desert Storm where we simulated a remote-directed nuclear strike — "

"What's 'remote-directed' mean?"

"Each plane's battle systems software was operable from a remote command via its communications hardware."

"Operation ARCHANGEL?" Woodring asked, raising some eyebrows in the room.

"Yes, sir."

"Weren't there some planes lost during ARCHANGEL?"

"Yes. But it wasn't any of the F-111Bs — the actual bombers, it was a — "

"Four-ship of F-15s?"

"Yes, sir."

"Was Saleh on the panel when the planes went down?"

"Yes."

"Exactly what other battle systems software did Dr. Saleh have access to, General?" asked Myers.

"Most of it."

"What's 'most of it'?"

"ICBM, Navy, sub fleet, SAC, Army artillery tactical nukes, you name it."

"To the best of your knowledge could Saleh have put a Trojan Horse or trapdoor in one or more of these programs?"

"Yes."

"How long do you estimate it would take your guys to find it, if one of these things had been put in there?"

"It could take months. Maybe years, depending how well it was done."

"And it wouldn't be necessary for Dr. Saleh, himself, to activate one of these programs, would it?"

"No. Not at all. Anyone with a little computer knowledge could do it, but what makes you so sure he did that, too?"

The fact that no one would respond to Vaughn's question made him all the more worried.

"Curt," Daniels prompted, "Frank assured us in executive session at yesterday's meeting of the NFIB that all nuclear battle systems have been designed to prevent a computer override. You go along with that?"

"Yes."

"Why?"

"The way each of them's set up, there's no way to load and launch without the aid of a human operator. In each case, it's a multi-step operation — it's not like a gun where you just pull the trigger."

"Thanks, Curt," Daniels spoke, cutting Vaughn off from further comment. "We may need you to talk to us again, so in the meantime, do me a favor and stay in the Washington area until further notice."

Vaughn's neck was flushed. He was about to protest, but thought better of it.

"No problem, sir."

After Vaughn left Daniels' office each of the attendees sat in momentary silence rolling the implications of what Vaughn had just told him over in his mind. Four F-15s were turned to butter, then disappeared off the radar, all because of an errant computer programmer in San Diego.

"My guess is the F-15s were just a demonstration," Praeger broke the silence. "Otherwise why should the Iraqis pull their men from the embassy three months later?"

"Why are we so sure there's a connection?" Myers asked.

"We're not," Praeger sighed.

"Keith," Daniels asked, turning to his deputy. "We have anybody inside Hussein's command?"

"No, sir. We don't. They're all Tikritis, relatives from his hometown — it's almost impossible to get anyone in there. Plus, Saddam's even killed some of them."

"How hard would it be to get someone in the country, then?"

"Into Iraq? It depends on what you want them to do," Axe replied.

"I'd want them to find somebody who'd know something more about Saleh and get them out."

"Snatch one of their top people? That could take months — if it's even possible. We'd probably have to bring in the Israelis. Besides, if the Mukhabarat's being pulled out, the operation, if there is one, might only be known to a handful of individuals — all very close to Saddam Hussein."

"Frank?" Daniels prompted, turning next to the NSA director.

"Most of our stuff's space-based — and Saddam got smart and converted all his command center communications with fiber optics, enclosed in gas-filled metal pipelines for security. Plus, if he's pulled his own men out, I doubt they're been told anything anyway, so we don't even know what we're looking for."

"I still think we have to look," Daniels spoke, almost as if to himself.

"Woody's welcome to come over to Ft. Meade any time it's convenient and we can show him what we've got."

"Hubert?"

"It's fine with me, if Woody wants to go." Myers glanced at his ADCI, who nodded his head affirmatively in Director Chalmers' direction.

"Gentlemen," Daniels spoke, "unless anyone's opposed I suggest we meet again on F street in one week to discuss any new developments. Agreed?" As the DCI surveyed the faces in the room, he received each man's murmured assent.

As Woodring walked out the door, Frank Chalmers strode alongside him and put a hand on his shoulder, "We have someone we use on special projects, that, if it's OK with you, I'd like you to liaise with him when you come over. You have any problem with that?"

"No. No, sir."

"Here's his name," Chalmers said, passing Woodring a blank white card with a name and number written on it. "I think it would be best for obvious reasons for me to skip the introductions — but I told him you'd be calling. He's expecting your visit about now, if that's alright?"

Woodring looked at the name and address on the card. Dr. Glen Hockaday, National Photographic Interpretation Center — Washington Navy Yard.

"He's not at Ft. Meade?"

"You meet him there and he'll give you a ride up, OK?"

"Sure. No problem. Let me clear it with Myers and I'll go right over."

Chapter 13

Woodring's feeling that Lincoln Daniels and the other members of the NFIB were already controlling the investigation of Saleh's death was confirmed the moment Chalmers handed him the card with the address of the National Photographic Interpretation Center (NPIC) on it. To outsiders, its headquarters was an old windowless yellow box in the Washington Navy Yard, but the highly secret National Photographic Interpretation Center was the child of the CIA and the equally nonexistent NRO, the National Reconnaissance Office, itself a joint-venture between the Air Force and CIA.

Satellite intelligence generally came in two forms, signals intelligence, called SIGINT, and photographic, called imagery. While the NSA at Ft. Meade concerned itself with the analysis of SIGINT, NPIC's major function was to process thousands of electronic photographs. And since the boys at Langley didn't like rubbing elbows with the DIA analysts at NPIC, the CIA had its own private imagery analysis section in Virginia with some long name like Imagery Analysis Service, so Woodring immediately realized that by sending him to NPIC Daniels was already going outside his own organization.

Woodring showed his pass, and the bluejacket at the door let him in, gave him a cup of coffee and escorted him right away into a darkened office. Its occupant, Dr. Glen Hockaday, was busy pinning what looked to Woodring like a dental x-ray onto an illuminated box.

Having done a quick background check on Hockaday before his trip to NPIC, Woodring found that Hockaday wasn't an imagery analyst at all, but a former Harvard classics professor and polyglot who knew ten languages. Before being posted to NSA, Hockaday had been at the Institute for Advanced Studies in Princeton, a prestigious think tank which was filled to the brim with former Ivy League professors. Which made Hockaday's presence at NPIC all the more suspicious, since NSA employees usually concerned themselves with signals intelligence at their own offices in Ft. George G. Meade. Hockaday also read Homer in the original Greek, Virgil in the original Latin, Proust in the original French, followed the libretto to *Tristan und Isolde* in the German, mused over the sexual habits of Bedouin potentates in classical Arabic, and followed the dialogue of undubbed Visconti films in the original Italian. Within a six-week period during a sabbatical to Istanbul, with the aid of a cab driver, he had constructed enough vocabulary from his knowledge of the probable Indo-European roots of Turkish to be fluent in that language, also.

"So you must be Woodring, am I right?" asked Professor Glen Hockaday of Harvard, Princeton, and MIT.

"Yes."

Such an intellectual type, Woodring thought, looking at the academic's tweeds and penny loafers. But Professor Hockaday, always in a rush, cut further musings short.

"Just got these," Hockaday said, pointing at a set of gray transparencies hanging in the air like mounted butterflies. "That's heat. That's not."

Hot spots were white. Cold was black. Sometimes it was the reverse.

"There's been a change, right," Woodring agreed, peering through the second set of transparencies mounted directly over the first. Still, it all looked like dots and splotches to Woodring, who wasn't used to seeing reports from the Directorate of Intelligence.

"Don't worry, we've already colorized them. Just for you."

The white dots had turned pink, surrounded mostly by green and gray. The pink blotches were more obvious.

"Weapons crates?" Woodring guessed, but he could tell by the shocked look on Dr. Hockaday's face that he had guessed wrong.

"Nooo," the professor paused, "weapons crates are orange.

These are pink."

"Came over this week?"

"Look at this." Hockaday handed a ship movement sheet to Woodring, who, at first, was confused by the lines of ETA's and ETD's and foreign names. Someone had taken it off Lloyd's computer — it wasn't from NROs.

"I still don't get it," admitted Woodring in defeat.

"No major flag freighters this time — just neutral and Japanese," hinted the roly-poly analyst, forcing Woodring to guess again as if he were a schoolboy.

"I don't get it." Woodring knew that several of the major arms-exporting nations often disguised their weapons shipments on neutral shipping, but that obviously wasn't the point. As Hockaday frowned, he refocused first on the ship movements chart and then on the infrared transparencies. "The volume is heavy…like if, if they're weapons crates," sputtered Woodring. He was at a total loss. *So many shipments on both Japanese and neutral shipping, so what was going on?*

Hockaday smiled annoyingly, giving nothing away, "It's not just the color," his didactic impulses overwhelmed him, "there are many more than that. More than even you could imagine."

"But you just told me they were pink."

"Anything with that density would be pink," Hockaday replied. His smile had a bit of a sneer to it this time.

"If this is a joke — "

"Joke? The joke is on the Germans, I assure you. These little crates are singing their heads off like a Southern gospel choir," Hockaday replied, peering down at Woodring's pass as if it were a dunce cap.

"I thought it was all based on light. I mean, on the heat. The relative heat waves — " Woodring stopped, when he saw a Cheshire cat's smile spread across the professor's face.

"You do want to know what it is, don't you?"

For a short man, Dr. Hockaday moved quickly, toodling through the huge corridor past the beige doors.

"Wait!" Woodring shouted after him and bolted out of the cubicle and startled a couple of passersby, whose eyes were immediately drawn to the color of his pass. He barely saw the door shut in time and grabbed the cheap metal knob.

"I'm not really NPIC, I guess Chalmers told you that already," uttered Hockaday, his voice lost in the cold wind racing across the yard.

"Why hasn't anyone given this stuff to NSC?"

"Oh, let's not discuss that here, too many little birdies in the air. Here it is!"

Hockaday was pointing at an Oldsmobile so old that Woodring winced before he could catch himself. The engine barely turned over and the White House messenger clapped his hands in the biting cold, while his breath began to fog the windshield.

"Where're we going?"

"To my real office, of course," laughed the Ph.D. It was Hockaday's idea of a joke.

Woodring raised his eyebrows and stared at the man who looked like a character from *Alice in Wonderland*. At first, the car lurched forward, struggling against the weather, but within a few minutes they had arrived at the entrance to the somnolent Baltimore-Washington Parkway. Each of them knew better than to make conversation on the way.

"No trucks," Woodring mused. A snow flurry began to reduce their visibility.

"No. None at all. Only bureaucrats and spies I'm afraid," Hockaday supplied, then they both lapsed back into silence.

☆ ☆ ☆

"The tower. The jewels are in the tower," spoke Hockaday,

nodding to their left.

Woodring almost missed it in the snow, the outline of a nine-story government building, stripped of personality and abandoned in the countryside. As they drew closer, he saw the Federal Protective Service guard teams wearing winter uniforms behind the cyclone fences.

"They've picked up our scent."

Woodring winced as a pack of attack dogs surrounded the black sedan and pressed their snouts against its windows. The car had just slammed to a stop outside a gatehouse with a single number on its front, 4.

"I don't have a — "

"Now you do.".

Hockaday slipped a pass out of his pocket, which had been properly labeled with Woodring's name and picture on it. The pass was attached to an elastic cord, so it could dangle under the wearer's neck, and Woodring put it on.

"Professor!" a guard saluted Dr. Hockaday, while a second bluejacket tapped the window for Dr. Hockaday to roll it down. A bayonet came into view as the beefy, FPS guard had a look at the doctor's special guest. The guard took the pass, checked Woodring's face again, then waved to the men inside the house.

"This is Mister Holland. He's quite all right," lied Hockaday in his patronizing way.

The bayonets dropped, and Woodring marveled how Hockaday acted as if he had handpicked the guards himself.

The moment both men crossed the threshold, a second group of bluejackets, who had been idly milling about several golf carts, snapped to attention and await the professor's order. Hockaday motioned to Woodring to join him in the golf cart wheeling up next to them and hopped on the vinyl seat. Startled passersby flattened themselves to the walls as the cart raced through the vanilla-colored corridors towards

DEFSMAC, the Defense Special Missile & Aeronautics Center, the NSA's electromagnetic nerve center. "Death-smack" is an electronic stethoscope whose input depends on the fleet of satellites directed by the Air Force's National Reconnaissance Office (NRO). Any sign or indication of a nuclear launch would be relayed immediately by DEFSMAC's analysts to the White House Situation Room, the National Military Command Center at the Pentagon, and finally, the underground headquarters of the North American Air Defense Command (NORAD).

A second squad of bluejackets stood outside DEFSMAC's unmarked doors, awaiting the arrival of the pair of visitors. Woodring couldn't help but be intimidated, since, until his arrival, no FBI personnel had ever been allowed to enter them.

Inside, a moving tableau of two-hundred-and-fifty technicians monitored an array of oscilloscopes, trajectory maps, country maps, ocean maps, space debris charts — all fed by a multibillion dollar system of satellites and listening stations which stretched across the world. In the center of the room a ray of light raced across the wall map, leaving hundreds of illuminated specks in its wake, which subsequently disappeared, until the light ray reswept the map and the pattern was repeated once again. Woodring noticed that country boundaries, indicating various states around the Persian Gulf, remained permanently lit in a soft, orange light.

Perhaps Hockaday was pulling it raw off the satellite, Woodring guessed, in direct contravention of the UKUSA treaty — the secret sharing agreement between the USA, the UK, Canada, Australia and New Zealand.

Hockaday ushered Woodring outside and jumped back on the waiting golf cart, whose driver rushed them down the corridor to an elevator. They exited on the fifth floor and walked one hundred feet to the right.

"This is my office," said Hockaday, pointing at the door.

Woodring nodded silently as Hockaday fiddled with the

keys and opened the door to his cubicle. He noticed a computer cursor blinking on and off like a lonely firefly at summer's end, before the professor flipped on the light. The corridors were deserted, except for the gray-uniformed Federal Protective Service guards at each end.

☆ ☆ ☆

"It's not a G-war, is it? So why all the equipment?" Hockaday, now the tutor, tested Woodring, his unwilling tutee.

"That was MILSTAR, wasn't it?" Woodring asked. The SIGINT satellite had told quite a story, but meanwhile Daniels hadn't told the White House or the JCS a thing.

"No. That was our own little star. In an orbit all its own."

"But the disposition, it was electronic, wasn't it?" Woodring didn't understand the discrepancy; the photographs at NPIC had told such a different story. Clearly, the deliveries of whatever it was had been disguised from infrared photography, but were somehow broadcasting a signal just the same. And the electronic map! The one at DEFSMAC had so many more dots than the one he had just seen at NPIC — they were all over Iraq! Woodring unconsciously rubbed the hair on the back of his neck, which felt as if it had stood up on end.

"It's sad, isn't it? None of the engineering students these days are ours — but at least the parts still are."

At first Woodring didn't know whether to take it as a joke, then quickly realized he had missed it. "Who?"

"No one knows about it yet…only Director Daniels and us," Hockaday replied, the friendly tone now gone. Saddam Hussein had just been sold a bill of goods, hardwired with special chips.

"It's nuclear, isn't it?" Woodring prompted.

"They're centrifuges for a nuclear separations plant — the parts are being warehoused all over the country."

"So why haven't the Iraqis ripped the bugs out?"

"Oh, they only sing upon command," Hockaday assured him. "They only oscillate when our bird comes over."

"But, the Germans — "

"Shouldn't reexport things they don't understand, should they?" Hockaday quipped, turning the lights back on. The professor's bonhomie vanished once again like a passing breeze. He leaned forward in his chair and stared straight into Woodring's eyes.

"Saleh's dead; the Mukhabarat's suddenly gone home; and Saddam's keeping a centrifuge plant in cold storage. That strikes me as a bit more than coincidental.

"If we're lucky — and I mean very lucky — someone else is going to have to be sent over to activate Saleh's second Trojan Horse, if there is one. Otherwise, we'll just have to wait it out."

Before Woodring could reply Hockaday turned in his swivel chair, quickly opened the Mosler wall safe, and pulled out a black notebook. Each page was identical in its pristine state, exhibiting the standard single-column of words in the original language for each topic.

"RAINBOW GOLD," Hockaday tapped into the computer terminal. He spent the next minute climbing the system's authorization ladder, then waited for it to double-check his clearance.

"You're cleared to the end of the RAINBOW," the message flashed across the screen for a split second and disappeared. Another security measure he had devised, just in case anyone were to leave an open terminal cleared to RAINBOW status, NSA's highest clearance.

"LIST ALL KEY SELECTION FILES," he requested next. His computer terminal asked Hockaday the proper medium for such a voluminous request.

"DISK, RAINBOW GOLD-GH," he told the system and logged off.

He had set it up, an electronic monster so powerful it could simultaneously monitor, analyze, and file into memory the thousands of telecommunications transmissions in over one hundred languages. The system's computers had been geared to detect keywords and their synonyms, automatically picking out the relevant conversations from thousands of transmissions for the auditors, who, if they heard anything interesting, would label it and send it to Transcription. But that was the problem — No one had been looking for a telltale message — until now.

"LIST ALL KEYS," Hockaday punched in the terminal, which immediately complied with his request. A list of various topics began to scroll across the screen from left to right.

"Here, take a look at this," urged Hockaday, handing the fresh printout over his desk to Woodring.

The titles of each Selection File struck Woodring with their brutal simplicity: PANIC, TERROR, ASSASSINATION, EXPLOSION, SURPRISE, CRASH…

Before Woodring could respond, someone knocked softly on the door.

"Come in!" ordered Hockaday.

A man larger than Woodring and almost twice the professor's size entered, stroking his mustache.

"Jackson, this is Assistant Director Woodring from the FBI. David Woodring, F. Jackson Tice."

Woodring got up from his chair with a worried look on his face.

"Don't worry, David, Lincoln and Hubert know all about this — it's their idea. You're just here to watch and learn."

Tice handed Hockaday a file which the professor unceremoniously folded open and read its contents.

"This is the complete list?"

"Why, yes, sir," Tice, his assistant, hesitated, knowing immediately Hockaday wasn't satisfied. "It was all that — "

" — I know, don't tell me: it was all that the Romance Languages Department could bring itself to produce."

"This is charming," the professor mused, scanning the single sheet of paper, "absolutely charming."

"So it's — "

"Worthless," Hockaday replied, neatly feeding the list of synonyms for the noun "hysteria" into what he called "his toaster."

"Now I'm going to lunch. Care to join us?" Dr. Hockaday commanded, in an accent, which if pressed, even he would have to admit was more than a bit affected for someone originally from Baltimore, Maryland.

Tice, not considering for a moment that refusal was an option, immediately agreed.

☆ ☆ ☆

Two hours later, after having listened to a luncheon discussion between Hockaday and his assistant about the existence of pagan shrines in late Byzantium, Woodring silently followed Hockaday, who was purposely ten minutes late, into the Transcription Department conference room. Each departmental head was seated before him, representing each language group in which the National Security Agency's monumental computerized eavesdropping project had an interest: Oriental, Slavic, Teutonic, Romance, Arabic, Scandinavian, Latin, Hebrew, Farsi, Urdu-Hindic, and Malay-Indonesian.

"When I taught Latin to Harvard undergraduates," Hockaday began without any introduction, "it was common to make a distinction between the basic literary idioms — classical Latin, for example, as represented by Virgil, varied considerably from silver Latin and also the idiom of the streets, *latina vulgaris*, exemplified by Petronius' *Satyricon*, which by the way was made into an excellent film by Fellini."

The head of Slavic languages department nodded slightly

towards his associate from the Teutonic department and allowed his eyes to dart back and forth in derision.

"So, I was somewhat shocked this morning, when my assistant gave me the key-list from a certain department for the noun 'hysteria.'"

Upon hearing Hockaday's last word, the head of Romance Languages felt an unwanted surge of adrenalin shoot through his body, making his head feel light.

"I'm afraid it's pretty third-rate stuff, which seems to have been culled from a college-level thesaurus," continued Hockaday, ignoring the looks of increasing shock on the face of each department head, but pausing a moment to focus on the chief of Romance Language's frozen grin. "Not only can one synonymously suffer from delirium, or agitation, or feverishness, or convulsions, in our language, but as you all don't need to be told — isn't it quite possible to go nuts, get crazy, or just to lose it, to boil over, if you will? Or, *panic* in low English, just as in high English one can be harrowed or psychoneurotic?"

"Excuse me, Dr. Hockaday, but by just whose authority have you been empowered to chair this meeting?" demanded the chief of Teutonic languages in an Austrian accent.

"My status is RAINBOW GOLD, which, if I have been informed correctly, gives me more than adequate authority to run this meeting as I see fit," Hockaday replied tersely, raising quite a few sets of eyebrows in the process. No one in Transcriptions had ever obtained RAINBOW status…and no one at the table needed to be told that RAINBOW GOLD was NSA-speak for "White House messenger."

"So vat do you vant?" the chief of the Hebrew Department kvetched. "I don't half all day."

"Don't worry, Hyman, this meeting is about over," Hockaday informed them. "By five o'clock I wish to see new key-lists with a minimum of fifty synonyms from each department."

"By five o'clock, this would be impossible!" the head of the Slavic Department protested. "I'm responsible for ten language groups, dialects — "

"Major languages only by today. Secondary in two days. Dialects within the week," Hockaday interrupted.

"Just what are we looking for, Dr. Hockaday?" the head of the Oriental Language Department questioned.

"*Une aiguille dans une botte de foin,*" Hockaday replied, repressing a grin of triumph as he saw the look of horror on Romance Language chief's face.

A needle in a haystack.

Chapter 14

The morning after his second visit to the hacker, HYDRA made himself breakfast in his flat, carefully reading the print-outs on each subject as he sipped his morning coffee. Koester, the NIS technician, was a few years younger than he was, but he thought it wouldn't make too much of a difference since Koester had never visited the Bangor Submarine base before. Gereke, the reservist, on the other hand, was in his middle thirties, and therefore a few years older than HYDRA, which, again, HYDRA thought shouldn't be a problem because no one had ever seen Gereke at Pax River before, either. But Russell Matthews, in his middle forties, was considerably older, and HYDRA had to weigh the not unimportant matter of how closely he wished to resemble Matthews versus how much disguise he, himself, could afford to wear. HYDRA also guessed that Matthews's hair, which was listed as "drk brn" in his file, had grayed somewhat after his stretch in Marion, and he should adjust his appearance accordingly.

After rereading each of the three files, HYDRA carried his dishes to the sink, walked down the four flights of stairs to the street and hailed a passing taxi on 62nd, giving the driver an address on the lower West Side, near the theater district. Carefully dividing his purchases amongst several different shops, HYDRA bought a salt-and-pepper colored wig at one, a matching mustache at a second, and a strawberry blond wig at yet another, then caught a taxi, having it drop him off at the post office branch near his apartment.

At the counter the clerk notified him that a package had just arrived from Washington State. HYDRA showed him Matthews' ID, waiting patiently while the clerk fetched it from storage. Holding the package under his arm, HYDRA walked the few blocks to his apartment, deciding he looked no different than any other pedestrian who had been out shopping.

After entering his room, he drew the curtains shut, tore the wrapping off the box, and unfolded a nylon-lined diving suit. Stripping off all his clothes, HYDRA donned the Farmer John-style pants and matching jacket, zipping up its banana collar. He took several paces back and forth, bent over and stretched, then paced around some more, checking the fit. Satisfied, he removed the diving suit and repacked it in its box, deciding he would send it later by messenger to David Blond.

Now wearing only his briefs, HYDRA went to his bedroom closet, shoved the suits aside, and extracted a Samsonite metal suitcase, a camera bag and a collapsible metal tripod. He dropped the camera case and the tripod on the sofa in his living room, and took the suitcase to the bathroom, setting it on the counter. He returned to the living room, counted out six paces, and set up the tripod in front of the sofa. Next, he opened the camera bag, removing a Polaroid Mini-Portrait Model passport camera. The Mini-Portrait model was constructed with four lenses instead of one, so that the user would receive a series of four identical photographs of the subject for each picture that was taken.

HYDRA returned to the bathroom, which he had redesigned with a large sink and matching mirror, and sat down on a padded vinyl stool of the variety found at makeup counters in department stores. He opened the metal case he'd left on the counter, unfolding it like a tackle box. A large, stamped manila envelope lay in the middle, which HYDRA extracted and slit open, taking out several color photographs. He propped the photographs in front of him against the mirror, and began to apply a dark makeup base on his face and neck and a layer of spirit gum on his neck.

One look at Matthews' face and he decided that the nose would be first. He scooped some putty out of the can and warmed it by kneading it in his fingers, giving it shape, until its surface was smooth, and positioned it upon his nose. He checked his handiwork from each angle, deciding to leave his face unshaven, since it would go better with the color. Now he feathered in the edges with the skin, alternately using a brush handle and an orange stick.

He blended some base color in his left hand, mixing it for a long time until he felt he had it right, then applied a dab of it to his nose with his fingertip. Now his hands moved quickly, spreading and applying it across his face before the colors changed. Shadow was next, which he applied to the nose by gently tapping it with his fingertips.

He opened the hatbox containing the salt and pepper wig and carefully positioned it over his head, glancing first at the row of Matthews' pictures, then at his own reflection in the mirror. He pressed his forefinger firmly against his forehead, then eased the wig gently down in back. Donning a blue denim workshirt he had purchased at Brooks Brothers, HYDRA returned to the living room, set the built-in delay timer on the Polaroid for ten seconds and pressed the shutter button. Returning to the stool, he sat down and faced the camera, which, after a short delay, automatically took his picture. Counting out the seconds to himself, HYDRA yanked out the film strip and peeled off the negatives. A quartet of Russell Matthews' stared impassively forward.

Satisfied with his work, HYDRA photographed himself as

Matthews three more times, just in case he needed any extra photographs. When he had finished, he went to his kitchenette, grabbed a dish, and picked up the vinyl chair on his way back to the bathroom.

He poured a moderate amount of acetone into a dish which he had set next to the sink and quickly screwed the cap back on the bottle. Dipping the cloth into the solvent, HYDRA dabbed it carefully on the edge of his scalp where the spirit gum had come loose. To free each adhesion point without harming his scalp was a laborious process, because the acetone was harsh on the skin and could cause burns, leaving dangerously visible marks on his head, and limiting his ability to adopt another disguise.

After gently removing Russell Matthews' wig, HYDRA dabbed more solvent across his scalp, forehead, and temples, until all traces of spirit gum were gone. In the medicine cabinet he found some cold cream and applied it to his scalp to reduce the risk of burning. He picked the blond wig out of the sink, and put it back in its hat box.

Now, because applying a second wig would irritate his scalp too much, he would be himself, and photograph himself without makeup as both Peter Koester and Jack Gereke. With the cold cream on his scalp, HYDRA returned to his bedroom closet, where he pulled out a shirt on a hanger plus a large, blue hatbox and laid them carefully on the bed. He opened the hatbox and extracted a surplus naval cap. Stripping off his shirt, he donned the white tunic and returned to the living room and sat on the padded stool, repeating the same process with the Polaroid passport camera he had performed disguised as Matthews. He shot several sets of pictures, both with and without the dress cap, since he didn't know which pose was required for proper identification purposes.

After he had finished shooting, HYDRA carefully packed up the equipment and accessories, redressed, and went to lunch at the French restaurant next door. Waiters were running back and forth carrying large plastic menus in their hands while the owner was busy taking reservations on the telephone. HYDRA, a regular, was quickly shown to an empty table and given his standard glass of wine, while he put in his order.

After lunch HYDRA walked to Madison Avenue and hailed a taxi, giving the driver an uptown address.

Chapter 15

Entering Manhattan's uptown traffic, his taxi exited East River Drive and in another minute came to a halt at the corner of 93rd Street and Third Avenue. HYDRA paid the Korean driver and walked the rest of the distance to a quiet bookshop in the middle of the block. A battered sign over the locked wire-mesh door read, *The Military Bookworm*. HYDRA pressed the service buzzer, then a loud solenoid switch was activated, and he let himself inside.

Rows of twelve-foot-high shelves were crammed with vertical and horizontal stacks of remaindered books, which dealt with a wide range of military matters as far back as the Roman legions to recent works on Operation Just Cause in Panama. A slim man with florid cheeks, sporting a blond mustache, stood behind the counter talking to a customer on the telephone, hanging up when he saw HYDRA.

"How can I help you?"

"I'm a friend of Luiz's. He told me he would give you a call about me," replied HYDRA.

At the mention of Luiz's name, the manner shifted and the eyes above the mustache narrowed. Recommendations from the Cali Cartel were taken very seriously for obvious reasons.

"Just a minute," the bookstore owner muttered, left the counter, and flipped over the Open-Closed sign hanging on the door.

"Come on back."

HYDRA followed him through a corridor of metal shelves into a tiny, cramped office.

"What do you need? A clean passport for Bogota? I can have it for you in a week — "

"It's a little more than that," HYDRA replied, flattening out a copy of the pattern he had just showed to Blond and slid it across the forger's desk. "You recognize this uniform, of course?"

Even though the Military Bookworm was filled with pamphlets and illustrated works devoted to various uniforms and insignia, the forger's knowledge of certain costumes came from a different source: a training course at Camp Peary in the early sixties.

"I recognize it," replied the forger, now training his eyes on HYDRA's. "It hasn't changed a bit." The forger smoothed out the pattern with the palm of his right hand, waiting for his customer to speak.

"I need a clean set of orders to visit Bangor on this date," HYDRA said, carefully handing the forger a slip of paper with Lieutenant Gereke's name and rank on it.

"Bangor?"

"Washington. Plus a full set of ID. Driver's license, credit cards, everything on the list."

The forger said nothing. Whoever had given his guest Gereke's legend obviously knew his way around the military.

"Next, I want a similar package on this man," HYDRA spoke, giving no hint to the forger that he was aware that this portion of his request was at all unusual. HYDRA handed him a second $8^1/_2$-by 11-inch sheet of paper, containing the relevant information on Sergeant Peter Koester, NIS's technical consultant.

The forger took the list and began to read it. Every piece of paper Koester could possibly possess was listed: MasterCard. Diner's Club. Amoco Motor Club. Even Blockbuster Video

Rental.

"Plus a visitor's pass for Gereke."

The forger carefully set down the sheet with Koester's specs on it.

"What for?"

"Trident tour at Bangor."

"Base passes are on regular paper, so printing them's no problem," replied the forger, eyeing the remaining printout in HYDRA's hand. "But if your guy's not expected, there's no way my codes are gonna match the Pentagon's."

HYDRA handed the proprietor a slip of paper from his shirt pocket. "These will be in each base's TDY."

The forger quickly examined the three sixteen-digit-long alphanumeric sequences which had been separately and simply entitled *Gereke-Bangor,* *Koester-Bangor,* and *Gereke-Pax River.*

"What's next?"

"Full ID package on this one too." HYDRA laid Matthews' file down like a hand of cards, spreading it on the table.

"All these people gonna look just like you, or what?" demanded the forger, shoving the printouts aside.

"Relatively, yes."

The forger reached into his shirt pocket for a cigarette and offered one to HYDRA. HYDRA held up his hand to decline, then reached into his jacket pocket and slipped out a letter-sized envelope, sealed with a piece of clear plastic tape. He handed the envelope to the forger, who carefully slit the envelope open with his index finger and spread the photographs across his desk, comparing them with the man in front of him. Except for the facial structure, HYDRA had managed through a change in hair color and other tricks to create a successfully misleading divergence from his normal appearance in each case.

"This is good work," the forger murmured, sifting through

the documents. "These will be fine."

"Luiz told me you could do it," HYDRA smiled. "Now why don't you tell me what your terms are."

"I'll be frank with you, just the way I am with anyone Luiz sends me. You and I both know the work itself will be no problem — it's the risk in this case that I'll want to be compensated for.

"I have no idea who these three men are, but it's obvious from their orders where Gereke and Koester are visiting — and whatever you're going to do there in their place may attract more than the normal amount of attention — to put it mildly."

"Meaning what?"

"Meaning that I want twenty-five thousand for the lot. In cash and up front."

HYDRA reached slowly into his opposite, inside jacket pocket, extracting a European-style wallet the size of a small checkbook and counted out twelve thousand five hundred dollars in fifty dollar bills.

"Compromise — I won't quibble over price and I'll pay you the rest upon delivery."

The forger stroked his mustache and sighed. The man in front of him scared him more than any other client he had ever had, and he thought better than to continue the discussion over terms with someone who had been referred to him by Luiz.

"Done."

Chapter 16

Once he left the Military Bookworm, HYDRA walked up 93rd Street to Madison and hailed a northbound taxi, telling the driver to take him to Kennedy Airport. For the second time HYDRA gave his name as Russell Matthews and paid in cash for a non-stop ticket to San Francisco on UAL Flight 4820, which departed in forty-five minutes. Arriving in San Francisco at approximately 3:00 p.m. local time, he rented a car in his own name for the drive to Bonny Dune. Less than an hour later, he pulled to a stop outside Castor's rundown redwood-shingled ranch house.

As he neared the door, HYDRA heard strains of rock music wafting across Castor's lawn. Pressing his finger on the doorbell, HYDRA hoped for his sake that Castor was relatively sober. Waiting a full thirty seconds, he pressed the bell a second time, doubtful that Castor could hear it amidst the din. Now worried that following Luiz's recommendation of one of the cartel's retreads had been a mistake, HYDRA tried the doorknob, finding to his surprise it was unlocked.

Inside, the music was even louder, and CNN was playing soundlessly on the big-screen TV in the debris-filled living room just as it had before. When the music stopped abruptly, filling the house with an eerie silence, HYDRA reached inside his jacket pocket and slipped out a Heckler & Koch P-9 9mm pistol, carefully checking his surroundings, before he called out Castor's name.

"I'm down here, down in the basement!"

HYDRA sighed to himself, shoved the pistol back inside his jacket, and found the open door leading to the shallow basement. At the bottom of the stairs he found Castor sitting on a high metal stool, hunched over an illuminated magnifying glass on a swivel arm made of stainless steel. Various pieces of electronic test equipment were stacked across a long C-shaped worktable, whose surface was littered with small plastic bins filled with electronic parts, tools, bits of circuit boards, and various handheld remote controls. Light green patterns danced up and down on a pair of spectrum analyzers.

"So, Mr. No-name, you finally decided to come back," Castor chuckled to himself as he peered through the glass without bothering to look up.

"Any problems?" HYDRA asked.

"I used to work on these babies, remember?" Castor sniffed, then wiped his nose with his shirt sleeve.

On the bench, the HP palmtop lay disassembled, its chassis covered with alligator clips, looking like an acupuncture patient. The laser gun he had given Castor was held vertically by a metal clamp, its point aimed directly at a tiny solar cell set in plastic. Behind the gun and computer were three television monitors whose screens glowed with a solid blue light.

"I wanted you to see this first," Castor spoke. "I managed to download the gun you gave me into my own computer without zeroizing it. Just a second — " Castor typed a brief command on the keyboard, and the screens of all three monitors were suddenly filled with text. Endless rows of 1's and 0's were each preceded by a date, expressed as MONTH: JANUARY; DAY: 05; YEAR: 1993.

"Those are the old keys for last semester's tour of duty. Each of 'em's 56 bits long, that's why there's so many 1's and 0's."

HYDRA nodded silently as Castor scrolled several pages of keys across the multiple monitors.

"Now, the day you want to transmit to whoever you're gonna transmit to, you're gonna have to use that day's key so you'll be sending an authenticated message, or else whoever you send it to's gonna decrypt a bunch of garbage.

"The second thing is this gun you gave me only's gonna work in one place — an SSBN — and somehow I don't think that's exactly where you plan on going — right?"

HYDRA paused a moment, then murmured without emotion, "Go on."

"So you're gonna have to know how to input that day's code into whatever box is in front of you — you may even have to print yourself out a physical key, depending where you're at — the technology's all different — or you may have to hand input it, and this adapter I just made you can't do all that for you.

You realize that, of course?"

HYDRA nodded affirmatively.

Castor displayed a grin filled with yellow teeth. "I see."

"Let's get on with it," HYDRA pressed, not wanting to give Castor's imagination any more time to dwell on the operation.

"There's not much more to it," Castor continued, with more than a hint of worry now in his voice. "To bring up the program, all you have to do once you've activated the machine is type in the password, T-E-S-T."

Castor entered the letters in himself and two seconds later the blank CRT in front of him came to life, filled with diagnostics.

"This is just boilerplate, in case anyone's looking over your shoulder — it doesn't mean squat.

"Next, you ask them for the gun and insert it into the adapter — " Castor disconnected the laser gun HYDRA had brought him and handed it to HYDRA. "Here, you do it."

After HYDRA took the gun from Castor's hand and gently shoved it into the female receptacle, the CRT screen went blank, then was filled with a different set of diagnostics.

"Same deal here — all this is just for show." Castor pointed at the keyboard, "here, you type it in."

HYDRA looked at him as Castor said the word "BULLS-EYE," then entered it into the laptop. Once again, the three large twenty-seven-inch monitors in front of them displayed a six-months supply of authenticated codekeys.

"One thing," Castor said, turning on his swivel chair so that he was face-to-face with HYDRA, "don't forget to tell them once you've downloaded their gun that it's been zeroized. If you forget, there's a small chance that one of them may wonder why, then mention it to someone else."

"Right," HYDRA murmured in assent.

"Now, when you want to pull up the codes again, I've wired

the HP so that they're stored inside a chip, not on its disk, in the small chance that someone decides to dump your disk to see what's on it. You'll need to protect it with your own seven-letter codeword which you can enter now." Castor hit the return key and all three screens went blank with a single question mark appearing on the furthest one to the left. "I don't want to know what it is for obvious reasons."

HYDRA thought to himself for a moment, then entered a seven-letter-long word which had special significance to only him.

"All right," Castor sighed, swiveling back around in his chair. "We're done and you owe me twenty-five thousand dollars."

"Right."

Without a hint of warning HYDRA slipped the P-9 out of his inside jacket pocket and shot Caster once in the sternum. The P-9's 9mm slug slapped into the technician like a hammer blow, toppling him off his chair into a cardboard box full of equipment. When HYDRA bent over the body, Castor's eyes were still open and his mouth was moving soundlessly and blood trickled across his chin. This time HYDRA aimed the P-9 squarely at Castor's forehead, uttering the word "BULLSEYE" as he fired his second shot. Still holding the P-9 in his right hand, HYDRA slipped a plastic baggie out of his side pocket with his left and jerked it open, showering the worktable with a half-ounce of pure, high-grade Colombian cocaine.

HYDRA stuffed the empty baggie back into his pockets, then extracted a clear pair of disposable surgical gloves, slipped them on and sat on the vinyl stool, its seat still warm from Castor's body. One by one HYDRA removed the alligator clips from the HP-100LX's chassis, then carefully reassembled the computer into one piece. He released the laser gun from its metal clamp and clipped the leads to the solar cell under it with a pair of wire clippers, stuffing the gun and the cell into his pocket. He next removed the two floppy disks stored on Castor's own computer and methodically searched the workroom for any others he could find, stuffing all of them into a discarded paper sack he found in Castor's wastebasket.

Now the screens of all three monitors were blank, save for a cursor and an automatic clock blinking at the bottom margin. Local time was 5:08 p.m. People were returning home from work, children were already home from school, and neighbors would be walking across their lawns. HYDRA decided to spend the remaining time until nightfall searching Castor's house for stray computer storage disks, in addition to the ones he had already located in the workroom.

A little after half past seven HYDRA walked out Castor's front door, wiping the doorbell clean with a tissue before he left. He drove past Felton, on local Highway 9, the cool mountain rushing through his open windows. In seconds, he reached the Pacific Coast Highway and retraced his path back to the San Francisco International Airport.

Chapter 17

The morning after his return from San Francisco, HYDRA took a taxicab to 53d Street in midtown Manhattan, giving the driver an address not far from the the tailor, David Blond. Before leaving his apartment, HYDRA had telephoned ahead, so the tailor was expecting him and immediately ushered HYDRA to his private office upon his arrival, after hanging a closed sign on his door.

When Blond turned around, HYDRA realized the tailor was wearing a pair of thin, transparent rubber gloves. He opened a large armoire, pulled out a long plastic bag, set it on a work table in front, and unceremoniously unzipped it, while HYDRA took off his sport coat.

"If you wish, we can try on the flight suit first," Blond suggested, awaiting HYDRA's approval.

"Fine."

Blond handed HYDRA a pilot's coverall, directed him to a changing booth and waited, hoping everything would meet his mysterious client's specifications. When HYDRA stepped out of the booth, Blond's only worry was that the normally loose-fitting flight suit would look too tailored on his physique, since HYDRA was in such good physical condition.

HYDRA stood before the mirror, admiring the tailor's work. Blond had cut everything exactly as the diagram indicated, including the pair of four-color unit patches on the right and left breasts and the tricolored American flag patch bordered in yellow on the left shoulder. HYDRA tried each of the diagonal zippered pockets which were placed asymmetrically below the breast patches, then the others on the midsection, thigh, and below the knee.

"It's not too tight in the shoulders?" Blond asked.

HYDRA stretched out both arms like a scarecrow.

"No."

"Good." Blond flipped the lid off a cardboard shirt box, extracting two folded canvas bags — one olive drab and the size of a briefcase with cloth handles, the other, a dark blue, the size of a camera bag with longer straps.

"These are regulation pilot's carryalls," Blond explained, snapping open first one bag then the other and handing them to HYDRA. "I thought you might like them."

"Excellent," HYDRA mused aloud. "I'd forgotten all about — "

"Now we should try on the shoes," the tailor interrupted, relieved now that his customer seemed satisfied with his initial work. Blond tore open a second box, pulling out a pair of all black, lace-up, rubber-soled regulation boots. "You want to try them on?"

HYDRA kicked off his calf-skin slipons. Blond held each boot as HYDRA stuck in his foot, then laced them up.

"Go ahead, walk around in them."

HYDRA did as he was told, amazed at how light each boot felt, even though it was a perfect replica of the Navy model.

"Special plastic," Blond smiled, "completely waterproof. It won't get heavier even if it's submerged for hours."

"Perfect."

Blond turned to the open plastic bag, carefully extracting a matching walking-out blue uniform and shirt on a hanger for a reserve naval officer travelling in the winter. HYDRA grabbed the hanger, returned with it to the changing booth, stripped off the pilot's coverall and slipped on the uniform and shirt. Looking at it first in the mirror in the booth, he had already decided it was a perfect fit, when he showed it to Blond.

"How is it?"

"Good, good," HYDRA murmured.

"Not too tight in the crotch?"

"No, not at all."

"How about the sleeve length?"

HYDRA shot his sleeves, then looked back at Blond and nodded.

"Cuff length?"

"Fine."

The plastic ID tag on his left breast read, *Lt. Jack Gereke*.

"Are you ready to try on Sergeant Koester's then?" Blond asked, pleased with himself.

"Yes."

Blond pulled a second long zippered plastic bag from his closet and set it, too, on the work table, slowly opening it, He handed it to HYDRA, who held it up in front of him, examining its detail. Then he produced a second coverall, similar in shape to the one he had designed for the pilot, Gereke.

This time there were no dramatic four-color unit patches over the breasts and American flag patch on the left shoulder, but only a plastic ID tag, which read *Sgt. Peter Koester.*

HYDRA took the garment and returned to the changing room, where he stripped off Gereke's coveralls, then donned Koester's, stepping outside for Blond to have a look.

"As you can see, it's the same size as Gereke's, just a different design, that's all."

HYDRA's eyes were immediately drawn to the pair of slim copper-colored felt bars sewn on the top of each collar — this was the NIS Technical Services classified ID patch for work in top-secret military installations.

He also noticed the zippers on the pockets ran horizontally instead of diagonally as before, and that the breast pockets themselves were symmetrical instead of asymmetrical. Also, the color of Koester's maintenance uniform was a dark navy, whereas Gereke's had been olive drab.

"Same fit in the shoulders?" Blond asked.

HYDRA stretched out his arms again. "Fine."

Blond knelt to the floor, looking at HYDRA's shoes.

"Cuff length looks the same," murmured the tailor to himself, then stood up. "You can use the shoes for both, if that's all right. There's no specific regulation requirement for NIS."

"Good," replied HYDRA, thinking it would be easier to wear in only a single pair of boots.

"Let's try the parka next."

Blond handed HYDRA the hooded parka he'd brought with him on his first visit, and HYDRA held it in his outstretched hand, checking the garment's increase in weight. Satisfied, he put it on over Koester's uniform and looked at himself in the mirror.

Perfect.

"Well, I think that's it, then."

HYDRA nodded, handed the parka back to Blond, and returned to the changing room, where he stripped off the custom boots and Koester's overalls, then redressed in the pants and sport coat he'd worn into the shop. He handed the pair of coveralls and boots to Blond, who, still wearing his rubber gloves, hung the uniforms back in the plastic bags and repackaged the boots in their box.

"I believe you owe me eleven thousand dollars," Blond stated flatly, stacking the bags and the parka on the table.

The hint of a smile passed across HYDRA's face. He reached inside his jacket pocket, fished out an envelope of moderate thickness, and set it on the table.

"One hundred and ten one hundred dollar bills. You can count them if you want."

"I don't think that will be necessary in this case," Blond replied, handing HYDRA the pair of plastic bags and then the shoe box.

HYDRA carried the packages through the stacks, flipped over the open-closed sign, unlatched the door and stepped out into the cool spring air. He walked several blocks before hailing a taxi, telling the driver to drop him off at 62nd Street and Madison.

Chapter 18

Satisfied with Blond's work, HYDRA hung the plastic bags in his closet, then walked to lunch at a neighborhood French bistro. After consuming a fresh lamb chop and washing it down with a glass of Vouvray, he took a taxi to 93rd Street and had the driver let him off at Third Avenue. Like the first time, he walked the rest of the distance, until he stopped under the Military Bookworm's battered sign. This time the proprietor saw him from behind his desk and immediately activated the solenoid switch which worked the lock. Before HYDRA could enter, a heavy-set Latino with a pockmarked face shoved past him, almost knocking him over, before disappearing into a waiting Lincoln Mark IV.

In his wake, the Colombian had dislodged volume six of *Die Heere und Flotten der Gegenwart*, part of a monumental series edited by Major General Graf von Zeppelin himself, which HYDRA picked up off the floor and handed to the thin proprietor with the large moustache.

"Sorry about him — but he had to catch the next plane to Cali — some problem, I guess. You want to come in back?"

HYDRA nodded affirmatively and the owner flipped the Open-Closed sign just as he had before, then ushered HYDRA through a row of shelves into an office filled with cardboard boxes in various stages of unpacking, stacked in no apparent order.

"Excuse the mess," sighed the proprietor. Then, pointing at an oblong wooden crate whose top lay on the floor next to a crowbar. "*Description de l'Egypte*, ever heard of it?"

HYDRA shook his head no.

"Just got it in from Amsterdam. Hard to get a complete set, because the previous owners stripped out the plates and sold them. Before his invasion Napoleon had it commissioned to impress the ancien regime, only a few hundred sets were ever made. Would you like to see a volume? The prints are beautiful."

"Sure."

The forger scooped out an oversized flat package, showering the floor with scores of plastic pebbles. He balanced it precariously on a small table laden with several uneven stacks of books and proceeded to unwrap it, revealing a large folio with a faded red leather cover. HYDRA watched silently as the forger deftly flipped through the first few pages, stopping at an engraving of an obelisk.

"Cleopatra's needle at Luxor: this one's usually torn out.

Nice, isn't it?"

HYDRA admired the engraving's detail, never realizing until then how much the First Consul thought of himself as another Alexander.

"Alright, enough of this," said the forger, slapping the book shut. "You've come here to admire my work, not Napoleon's." The forger turned to a small floor safe, spun the lock, and extracted a letter-sized file pocket. He pulled a thick wallet out first and spread its plastic pockets on the desk. Each pocket was filled with a different credit card.

"You can keep the wallet. It's for you. There're twenty-four cards inside it, based on the lists you gave me for Matthews, Gereke, and Koester." The forger slipped Gereke's Visa card from its pocket and handed it to HYDRA, who twisted it slowly in the light.

"Hologram's an exact copy — although I doubt anyone will ever check — it's the information embedded on the strip on the back that works the card."

HYDRA shot the forger a worried glance.

"Don't worry — strips on these babies are exact dupes of the ones on the list — if you're worried, try making a ten dollar purchase somewhere and let them run it through."

HYDRA felt the brown strip on the card's back with his forefinger, while the forger nervously twisted the top of his long moustache. HYDRA pulled each card, one after the other out of its plastic sheath, and checked it off a small list he had retrieved from his shirt pocket.

"These look good," he murmured. "I can't tell the difference."

"You can't tell the difference because they're real," the forger chided. "Blanks are from a friendly bank down in Colon."

HYDRA blinked in admiration. The cartel covered every detail of its operations, even down to smuggling blank credit cards from its banks in Panama to its forger in Manhattan. The forger slipped a second, thinner wallet from the file pocket and handed it to HYDRA.

"Driver's licenses for all three, plus some other miscellaneous picture ID you wanted."

HYDRA opened the wallet, examining each license under a nearby pharmacy lamp, then reinserted each piece and put the wallet in his pocket. Next, the forger handed him an 8 1/2-by 11-inch file folder, tab unmarked. Inside were two typewritten memoranda from Washington, D.C. with a series of code numbers in their upper right-hand corners, addressed separately to Gereke and Koester, instructing each to report to his respective base no later than a certain time and date. Maximum travel pay also given, with a note to inform base command whether recipient had decided to fly or drive.

"Now, I believe you owe me twelve thousand five hundred dollars," the forger uttered.

HYDRA grimaced, reached into his jacket pocket, and counted out the second payment in one hundred dollar bills, the forger twisting his moustache as he watched.

"Done."

HYDRA said nothing in response, watching the forger stuff everything back into the file pocket which he then took and let himself out the door.

Chapter 19

Instead of returning to his apartment after he left the Military Bookworm, HYDRA caught an uptown cab and told the driver to take him to La Guardia Airport, where he boarded USAir nonstop Flight 11 to Kansas City, the home of Naval Air Force Reserve Lieutenant Gereke. The flight was filled with a set of provincial-looking, middle managers in cheaply-tailored clothes mixed with a crowd of unattractive parents with even less attractive children. The only single women on the plane were the pair of overworked and slightly angry stewardesses who quickly informed HYDRA the only magazines on board were the airline's own publication inside his seat pocket.

HYDRA walked towards the rear of the plane, choosing a seat by himself. He listlessly flipped through the inflight magazine, avoiding a testimonial on chemical dependency by a famous country singer; skipping a piece by Shirley MacLaine on one of her previous lives; and ignoring an article on the town billed as the next Nashville: Branson, Missouri. Tossing the magazine in the empty seat next to him, HYDRA reconsidered the forger's advice regarding Gereke's orders to report to base. HYDRA realized, of course, that simply murdering Gereke would not be acceptable if the reserve pilot's corpse were somehow discovered and its existence reported to the Navy before the time of his arrival at Pax River. On the other hand, allowing Gereke to leave Kansas City for Washington would run the serious risk of losing control of the reservist once he boarded his flight, especially if Gereke left on a Sunday evening and decided to go straight from National Airport to base BOQ without even checking into a motel. A course of travel, HYDRA thought, that would be more than likely if Gereke were on a limited budget. A second risk was that Gereke would complicate his trip to Washington, leaving early and making a layover stop that HYDRA wouldn't know about until the last minute. The sound of the Boeing's landing gear being lowered into place was followed by a brief announcement that the plane was descending into Kansas City International Airport and would land in less than twenty minutes. From his window seat HYDRA examined the vast flat runway set alongside three donut shaped terminals surrounded by a sea of parked cars.

After the Boeing 737 landed and was taxiing towards the gate, HYDRA noted that no other planes took off or landed during the interim, while several of the gates at the terminal were empty. That the Kansas City airport would be operating far below capacity hadn't occurred to him and he filed the fact away in his mind for future reference.

"I hope you enjoyed your flight," the stewardess said automatically to each passenger as he filed out the aircraft, and as he passed, HYDRA nodded politely in return.

Upon entering the terminal HYDRA's suspicions of the airport's level of inactivity were confirmed — except for the passengers debarking from Flight 11, this part of the airport was almost deserted. HYDRA waited patiently by the luggage claim for fifteen minutes, picked up his single bag, found a taxi, and gave his destination as the Ritz Hotel located in the Country Club Plaza shopping center. Forty-five minutes later, after a drive through half-empty streets, he was deposited outside a curved and balconied hotel whose exterior with its Southwestern motif gave no hint of the faux-London-club design of its interior, complete with a large portrait in the style of Sargent hanging in the bar.

HYDRA presented Russell Matthews's American Express card at the desk, telling the receptionist he would be staying in Kansas City for the week to ten days on business. He was immediately led to his room by a friendly bellhop who explained the location of the hotel's various bars and restaurants during the elevator ride, while HYDRA listened in polite silence. For the next ten days HYDRA planned to make a meticulous examination of Gereke's existence, while at the same time maintaining as low a profile as possible at the hotel, so the less he said to anyone the better.

☆ ☆ ☆

When Jack Gereke signed up for the Naval Air Reserve, he had neither requested nor expected to receive orders to report to a squadron of the strategic significance of VQ-4 at Patuxent Naval Air Base. Before joining the reserves, Lieutenant Gereke had been a transport pilot flying 747s for the United Parcel Service. After he mustered out, he returned to college and studied accounting on the GI Bill, then became the CFO of a regional stock brokerage headquartered in Kansas City. Partly to relieve the tedium of the office routine, partly because he missed flying, and partly to supplement his income Gereke decided a year later to join the Naval Air Force Reserves. He made the usual commitment to report to camp a single weekend per month for the next eight years, in addition to agreeing to report for full-time duty for two weeks each year.

Otherwise Gereke's life was utterly predictable in almost every aspect. Every Monday through Friday Gereke would arise at 7:00 a.m., have breakfast, shower, then would walk from his one-bedroom bachelor apartment located in the Country Club Plaza across Brush Creek to the Board of Trade Building. Gereke would almost always leave the office between 5:30 p.m. and 6:00, sometimes stopping to have a drink in the first floor bar, but almost always returning directly home after that. Not being a salesman, he saw no need to attend the various openings and cocktails where the brokers often went, preferring to spend most of his spare time with his own set of friends outside work. Weekends were somewhat less predictable, with Gereke alternating between going out with one of his regular girlfriends on a date or attending various sports functions with his male friends.

☆ ☆ ☆

Thus, Gereke would have been quite shocked if someone had told him that, for more than a week, he had been the subject of surveillance by a professional whose last mission had entailed eliminating an entire crew of contract CIA agents. The Naval Reserve lieutenant would have been even more surprised to learn that not only had his movements been thoroughly watched, but, in addition, the locks to his apartment had been picked, his mail had been read, his personal effects had received a thorough search, and a permanent, encrypted FM digital transmitter which had a range of greater than one mile had been placed on his telephone line.

Chapter 20

The next morning HYDRA caught the first nonstop flight to Seattle. He arrived at 10:15 a.m. local time and immediately rented a Pontiac Grand Am at the airport's Avis counter, since Naval Air Reserve Lieutenant Jack Gereke's tour of the Naval Submarine Base at Bangor was scheduled to begin in an hour and fifteen minutes at 11:30 a.m. HYDRA followed Interstate 5 north where he took the exit for Edmond's Way which wound for 12 miles to the ferryport of Edwards. At Edwards HYDRA drove to the terminal area and purchased a ticket for passage to Kingston aboard the *Hyak*, one of the Washington State Ferry System's shapely triple-deckers. Since it was the middle of a weekday morning, traffic was light enough for HYDRA to board on the next departure.

Thirty minutes later the Grand Am drove off the *Hyak's* car deck into Kingston, a town which lay on the north of the Kitsap Peninsula on the opposite coast of the Puget Sound. HYDRA drove peacefully across the peninsula on a local road bordered on both sides by untouched forests. Turning off Highway 3, he took Trident Boulevard to the main gate, giving the security guard on duty Lieutenant Gereke's ID and telling him he had been scheduled to take the Trident tour.

After barely glancing at Gereke's driver's license, the guard rifled through a stack of papers, confirming Gereke was indeed on the Public Affairs Department's list, then issued the Pontiac a temporary pass and directed HYDRA to wait in the pass and ID office to the left of the gate. Ten minutes later HYDRA's group was met by Mary R. Lopez, Lieutenant Junior Grade, and also his tour guide for the day. Lopez, an attractive brunette in her early thirties, led her group outside to a navy-blue, 15-passenger Chevy van, and waited for them to take their seats before she picked up her microphone and began to speak.

"First of all, I want to welcome all of you to Naval Submarine Base, Bangor, where we're the home base for a squadron of 560-foot Ohio-class submarines. Today we're going to go on what's called the Trident Tour showing you one of three key elements of our strategic deterrent triad. The nuclear triad is composed of one, land-based missiles, two, manned bombers, and third, the Navy's fleet ballistic missile program, known as Trident. Trident, which takes its name from King Neptune's three-pronged spear, also can be broken down into three key components: the missile, the submarine and the base."

The van stopped for a moment in front of a second gate.

"Bangor is a closed base and the gate we are about to go through is our first level of security," Lopez informed them as she motioned the security guard to wave them through. The driver took the first left off Trident Road, passing the first building.

"On your left is the SUBASE Administration building. It provides offices for the base commanding officer, his staff, and Naval Communications Station, Puget Sound. The tower is used to transmit and receive messages for the commands on the base. Personnel Support Detachment is the next building on your left. This command is responsible for maintaining the records and pay for approximately 5,000 Navy personnel stationed here."

HYDRA checked his map, finding Hunley Road. The Public Affairs office had kindly highlighted the van's path with yellow magic marker indirectly that the tour would make a crude circle of the base. The van turned left again onto Tautog Circle which was filled with empty guard huts and abandoned security fences.

"This used to be the only entrance to the base and was guarded by Marines," Lopez explained. "Now, the Navy no longer uses Marines for gate guards. The base commanding officer is responsible for administering the Base Operating Services Contract which is currently held by Sharp Controls. The multimillion dollar contract supports the base mission by providing services through one multifunction contract. The contract employs civilians who perform jobs such as security guards, firemen, photographers, ground maintenance, and transportation drivers."

HYDRA was relieved to hear that a civilian security force had replaced the Marines. Presenting Gereke's papers to an outsider would be safer than having to show them to a guard from a rival service. They halted at a stop sign, went straight for a block, then turned left on Sculpin, passing a group of white buildings with weather-beaten facades.

"The buildings you see on both sides are from the 1940s. We are currently using them as offices. After the Navy purchased more than 7,000 acres in 1942, the base served as an ammunition transshipment point during World War Two, the Korean War and the Vietnam Conflict.

"Straight ahead is the public works area. Transportation and ground maintenance equipment and the offices for employees are here."

As Lopez droned on about the bachelor enlisted quarters to their right, HYDRA stared out the window of the van, realizing that no matter what direction he looked, his view was some part of the 7,000-acre facility. Its sheer size would help minimize the importance of the arrival of any single individual on the base, especially one who only intended to briefly visit the courier transfer shed, make a quick repair, then leave. The van turned and HYDRA noted the street sign indicated they were on Trigger Avenue. Two silver-colored pools of water reflected on his left.

"On your left are two man-made lakes. They are used for rainfall flood control and recreational fishing. Covered barbecue/picnic facilities, hiking trail (Boy Scout project), BMX trail and softball diamond are also in this area. As you can see it is an easy walk from family housing.

"Coming up on the left is outdoor gear issue. A service member can rent all kinds of equipment such as campers and camping gear, boats and fishing gear, and skiing equipment. Next door is an auto repair shop ..."

HYDRA ignored the descriptions of the auto parts store and gas station accompanying the repair shop and leafed briefly through the brochure that came with the map. Most of the brochure was filled with specs on the Trident submarine, which, HYDRA read, was quieter, faster, larger and more powerful than any submarine the US Navy had ever put afloat. Their 560-foot LOA made the Ohio-class two feet larger than the Russian Typhoon-class boats, but the Ohio-class still could boast a much narrower diameter at 42 feet. The Ohio boats also only displaced 18,750 tons when submerged, compared to the Typhoon's relatively bulky 30,000 tons. Ohio-class ballistic missile submarine's top speed of 30 knots was also three knots faster than the Typhoon's. And the Ohio-class $1.2 billion price tag per boat was a bargain compared with the potential destructive power of each sub's complement of twenty-four Trident ballistic missiles.

They passed the community service area on Pompano Street, where the credit union, library and more bachelor quarters were located, then turned right onto Thresher when Lopez resumed her narrative.

"On your right is the headquarters of Commander, Submarine Group Nine. He has administrative control of commands and units assigned in the Pacific Northwest and coordinates all submarine matters in the Pacific Northwest. Behind his headquarters are medical and dental clinics.

"Next is the Trident Training Facility. While one crew is at sea, the off-crew or crew on shore, spends a lot of time here. The training facility offers initial, advanced and refresher training. All systems aboard a Trident submarine are in this building, except for the nuclear reactor. This equipment is connected to computer systems to simulate at-sea operations and problems.

"Directly in front of us is the Off-Crew Administration

Building. Each submarine crew has a set of offices and class-rooms in this building. One crew has the submarine at sea and the other crew uses this area for their offices while ashore. When the submarine returns, both crews pack up and trade." Lopez clicked off her microphone and the van stopped abruptly in front of a security fence and guardpost which resembled the one at the main gate. HYDRA rechecked the map. The van had completed the first small loop and was returning to the intersection of Trident Road and Trigger Avenue. As the guards waved them through Lopez answered the question which had just formed itself in HYDRA's mind. "The base has several levels of security. The guards at the main gate and perimeter gates provide that first level of security. During heightened defense conditions, security guards are sta-tioned here as a second level. From here we proceed into the operational area, called the lower base. The number of people working in this is limited. There are no cameras allowed in the operational area," Lopez emphasized.

"On your right is Strategic Weapon Facility, Pacific. This command is responsible for the assembly, maintenance and storage of the Trident missiles. The buildings you see are for the assembly of the missile by Lockheed and other contractor personnel. This area is the third level of security, as you can see, this area has the highest security on the base. Additional security includes manned guard towers, double fences and numerous sensors. We have about 350 Marines stationed at Bangor. Their sole mission is to protect this area. The blue poles you see adjacent to the buildings are lightning rods."

So Lieutenant Gereke would have to pass through three security checkpoints and present his papers each time before he reached the communications shed, HYDRA thought to himself, taking a careful look at the third guardpost as they passed. At the second light, the van made a brief detour to the left off Trigger Avenue and entered a small circular drive, which surrounded an impressive set of missile replicas.

"Coming up on your right is a missile display. The Strategic Weapons Facility you just saw was used to produce the smaller Polaris missile in the 1960s, but the Polaris has since been replaced by the larger Trident. The Trident I is 34 feet high, 6 feet in diameter and weighs 71,000 pounds. Each missile costs about $13 million and has a range of 4,000 nautical miles, and each Trident submarine is capable of carrying 24 of these missiles. The Trident submarines are designed to upgrade to the much larger Trident II (D-5) missile…"

Powered by a solid-fuel rocket engine, possessing more sophisticated navigation equipment than the ICBM, each Trident C-4 carried eight MK 4 100-kiloton multiple independent reentry vehicle warheads (MIRVs) with a circular error of probability of less than 500 yards. Each MIRV warhead could either be aimed separately at eight different targets within the missile's footprint, or combined for a devastating single strike.

They exited the circle, returned to Trigger Avenue, then continued their gradual circle of the base, passing through a heavily wooded area, which Lopez informed them was maintained by a full-time forester. In addition a full-time game warden kept the lakes stocked with fish and watched over the base's population of deer, bear, wildcat, and geese. After that they passed a tall building where periscope maintenance was performed, when a muddy canal loomed in front of the van, slicing through the pines. "In front of the bus you can see Hood Canal," Lopez informed them as they turned a sharp right onto Sealion Road. "Hood Canal is deep enough that we could submerge a Trident as soon as it pulled away from the pier. In peacetime, however, the submarines make their transit to the ocean on the surface.

"The base owns 5 miles of waterfront. We are 155 miles from the Pacific Ocean. Through the trees on your left is our service pier. This is where the tugboats, security boats and other support watercraft are docked."

Passing the salmon ladder, they wound along the canal, then turned left, and went up a steep hill, where the driver pulled over to give the van's occupants a dramatic view of these giant docks, the middle of which was filled with the sleek black hull of the USS *Michigan* which was in for repairs.

"The Delta Refit Pier is controlled by Trident Refit Facility. It is the single largest piece of construction on the base. Each leg of the pier is 700 feet long, and from shore to apex is 1300 feet. Delta pier can accommodate three submarines — one on the north side, one on the south side, and one in the dry dock. The dry dock, which is parallel to the shoreline, is 700 feet long, 65 feet deep and 90 feet wide and holds about 21 million gallons of water. Each time before the dry dock is flooded with Hood Canal water, it and the submarine in the dock are washed down. The water then goes to a treatment plant above the Delta Pier before going into the county sewage system."

HYDRA checked his watch; the tour would be finished in fifteen minutes. Turning left on Seawolf Road, they entered in parking lot, stopping for a better view of a large wharf. Lieutenant Lopez spoke into her handheld microphone, "On your left is the Explosive Handling Wharf. It provides an enclosed, weather protected wharf for missile and torpedo loading and off-loading. The Trident I missile, enclosed in a protective canister, is transported from a bunker to the Explosive Handling Wharf on a flatbed truck. A crane hoists the container to a vertical position and swings it over to the appropriate missile tube on the submarine, then a winch lowers the missile into the hole. By the way, you may be interested to know that the Navy owns over 400 acres on the opposite side of Hood Canal as a buffer zone." Several of the passengers caught the joke, chuckling at the thought of an errant torpedo hissing across Hood Canal and exploding on impact on the opposite bank.

The next stop revealed a single pier, similar in construction to one of the Delta piers seen previously with one significant difference — the whole length of the pier was looped with a semicylinder of cable. Lopez explained its existence to those who didn't already know: "This 700 foot timber pier is built of nonmagnetic materials and looped power cables. Because a submarine is such a large metal object, it will acquire a magnetic charge, and since an electromagnetic charge is something that can be detected by aircraft and ships, giving away the submarine's location, its absence is important to the survival of the vessel. Everywhere else in the Navy, cables are manually wrapped around a submarine, as you can imagine, manual wrapping takes a lot of time. But at Bangor, a submarine can pull into the Magnetic Silencing Facility and in a few hours its degaussing is fully completed. Degaussing is similar to erasing an audio cassette tape. By the way, this procedure is not performed every time the submarine is in port, but periodically, each submarine drives over a range where the amount of magnetism is measured."

HYDRA rechecked his map. The tour was finished except for a last look at eastern side of the Strategic Weapons Facility. They were turning around, the driver was returning to the main gate via Flier Road. Halfway to the operational area gate, HYDRA caught a glimpse of an area guarded just as heavily as the Strategic Weapons Facilities, which Lieutenant Lopez pointedly ignored even though it could be seen right outside the window. Armed Marines stood in guard towers behind double cyclone fences, carefully eying them as they passed by. HYDRA guessed from the array of antennas and parabolic dishes that it was the home of the base's Naval Communications Station, Lieutenant Gereke's final scheduled destination.

Chapter 21

The next morning a spring rain loosened the hard earth, and the Dobermans which patrolled the grounds of the National Security Agency were unusually aware of any new odors or sounds in the air. At 6:59 a.m., the handlers felt their canine sentries struggle against their leashes, before they, the sentries on the grounds, saw the caravan of dark sedans snaking its way towards the guardhouse. The gatekeepers, too, had removed whatever remaining trace of humor they had been allowed to display, and greeted the first car with stiff salutes.

"Dr. Holland," the sentry barked, snapping to attention.

"Check each car; I know the rules," Woodring replied, rolling down his window.

Each automobile in the caravan was halted and thoroughly searched, its passengers and contents checked against a classified list which had just been hand-delivered by White House courier.

Instead of the usual single sentry posted at each end of the hallway, the floor housing the Transcription Department had been reinforced with an unnecessary additional platoon of FPS commandos armed with automatic weapons.

"This is Dr. Holland," Glen Hockaday announced to the platoon leader, whom the professor distinguished by the medallion on the peak of his SWAT-style cap.

"Yes, sir. Our orders are to check the ID of all personnel, Professor," the commando replied, placing Hockaday's plastic badge into what resembled a credit-card verification device.

"Alright, sergeant, but let's make it quick," Woodring snapped.

"Yes, sir! Hawkins, Montoya, get over here and verify these IDs!" the FPS sergeant barked at two of his men.

In a matter of minutes a heterogenous crew of twenty FBI and NSA personnel had been cleared through the temporary command post and gathered silently in a small cluster, facing Hockaday and Woodring. The ex-classics professor handed each man an identically sized computer printout and a threeby-five inch index card with a number on it. A small key had been scotch-taped to the backside of each man's card, giving him access to one of ten offices.

In each office two FBI counterintelligence agents met with the head of each language division in Transcriptions, in order to sift through the translations of the raw computer output. Hockaday's list of trigger words were cross-referenced with the word "Wimex" in all its possible variations, then fed into the largest bank of mainframe computers ever assembled in a single location inside the United States. In anticipation of the arrival of Woodring and his troops, a high capacity data link was also set up between Ft. George and the FBI's Counterterrorism Center to check for correlations between any of the speakers and a previous record of criminal and/or terrorist activity, with a particular emphasis put on Arab and Iranian residents of the United States and their associates abroad.

For the next twenty-four hours, the ten teams of specialists sifted through translations of thousands of telecommunications, finding many references to the various key words and their synonyms, but without ever finding a single cross-reference to the word "Wimex" or any of its synonyms.

Early the next morning, a young linguist from Harvard who had been assigned to work with F. Jackson Tice and was half-buried in the mass of paper spread across Tice's desk, spoke for the first time in hours.

"I think I found something."

F. Jackson Tice said nothing, got out of his chair and followed his assistant to the office directly adjacent.

"What is it?" asked Hockaday, looking first at Tice, then at the young linguist from Harvard.

"Sir, there's no Wimex matchup, but this ciphertext was recorded the day before Saleh was killed," the young Harvard student stuttered.

"Ciphertext?" Hockaday queried. "What group is it?"

"TCOM, Group 6-11."

Hockaday snatched the transcription from the student's hand, then turned to Tice. "Jackson, follow me back to my office." After Tice had shut the door, Dr. Hockaday allowed himself a smile. He immediately sat facing the computer terminal and typed in his password.

F. Jackson Tice read the corresponding index number on the computer index.

"TCOM Group L-11, 00605054," Tice responded, feeling something wasn't right.

Hockaday tapped in the transcription group code numbers and waited for his screen to respond. Seconds later a message in English scrolled from left to right across the screen. F. Jackson Tice winced as he heard Dr. Hockaday's sharp intake of breath.

"Bad news?"

"Tell Woodring I want to see him in here immediately," Hockaday spoke with a frightening gravity, handing him the transcript. "Then call Czarlinsky and tell him we're coming down."

Tice's eyes stopped dead on the neutral-sounding phrase: "Must consult TCOM for decrypt approval."

"My God! 'Consult TCOM for decrypt approval.' What's this supposed to mean, Glen?" demanded Tice, gripping the sheet so tightly his knuckles had turned white, but Hockaday was already at his door motioning for Woodring to come to his office.

"What's up?" Woodring asked once inside.

"We've got problems," muttered Hockaday under his breath. Hockaday handed Woodring the undeciphered transcript. Then, to Tice, "Jackson, call SWITCHBOARD and have them get a helicopter ready on standby."

"Yes, Glen."

"What's going on here?" Woodring asked himself aloud,

ignoring Hockaday's suggestion. "How come we have to get permission to decrypt?"

"Woody?"

Woodring looked up at Hockaday as if he were from another world.

"Let's go."

☆ ☆ ☆

On the way to the telecommuncations group Woodring and Hockaday passed row after row of various type of analysts seated in front of CRT screens connected to an array of sophisticated computing and signals analysis devices. Each man showed his pass to the guard at the desk, then once inside the door, they were immediately met by Ken Czarlinsky, TCOM's chief. After Dr. Hockaday made the introductions, he handed Czarlinsky a copy of the encrypted transcript.

"What's Group L? I don't remember ever hearing about it," Hockaday began pleasantly enough.

"It's a new spread spectrum group we just put together with the machine processing people, so we're not putting out much product yet."

"Then what prompted your group to issue this transcript to my department?" demanded Hockaday.

"We didn't issue it to your department; it probably just got sent up there in error. The sweep you ran was pretty broad, you realize."

"So what's spread spectrum?" asked David Woodring.

"Sorry for the jargon," Czarlinsky apologized. "OK, you understand how a cellular telephone works, right?"

"Kind of."

"OK, a cellular phone essentially takes an analog signal, the voice, and broadcasts it on a set frequency to a base station. If you happen to be listening to that frequency and you're in range of the device, you can listen in on the conversation unimpeded."

"Right."

"So, needless to say, there are many people who want the flexibility of cellular but don't like its vulnerability to eavesdropping."

"Right."

"So they generally do a couple of things to protect themselves — one, they can digitize the signal, so to an eavesdropper it'll sound like a fax line, second they can encrypt the digital signal, *plus* they can channel hop, making it harder for their transmission to be caught."

"Which type of challenge does all that present to TCOM?" interrupted Hockaday.

"Almost none. Remember, this is NSA. Almost every digital transmission generates its own signature, which we can locate and track; most of the encoding chips used in industry are only 16 bits, which we can break; and frequency hopping isn't much of a problem, because we can monitor them all at once and recapitulate the broadcast later."

"So why use spread spectrum?" Woodring asked.

"Instead of simple channel hopping, which, like I said, we can easily reassemble, a user sending a digital message over cellular spread spectrum just disappears into the ether. Poof!"

"Why?"

"Spread spectrum is very difficult to track, very tough."

"Why?" asked Hockaday.

"Well," Czarlinsky grinned, "it's simple, really. Instead of dividing the signal among a discrete number of channels, the users spread it like butter across the whole spectrum, so it more or less just disappears unless you're really looking for it."

"Why don't the stronger signals on all the other channels just wipe it out?" queried a perplexed Woodring.

"It's spread in the space between them. They don't even do a thing."

"Look, each channel's such a small part of the total signal, it only wipes out a millionth of the total bandwidth. That's just a minor bit of interference as far as the receiver is concerned. It'll just cancel it out, not affecting the final signal integrity at all."

Woodring blew air out his cheeks in confusion, feeling the beginnings of a slight headache around his temples.

"But TCOM *has* managed to intercept spread spectrum broadcasts, haven't they?" asked Hockaday.

"Of course, that's our business."

"So what is the intercept technology?" pressed Hockaday.

"Basically, high-order cyclostationary processing," replied Czarlinsky, unable to repress a grin.

"You mean higher mathematical analysis?" Hockaday shot back, putting Czarlinsky back in his place.

"Right. *Every* signal, no matter how weak, especially if it's encrypted, still has a signature — even one that's been spectrum spread."

"So you'd be able to locate the sender if he sent another message?" Woodring guessed aloud.

"Right."

"Based on what?" asked Hockaday.

"Periodicity, clock synchronization, system artifacts...preambles," Czarlinsky ticked off the list in his head, stopping when he saw the two blank faces in front of him.

"OK. Sorry. Look, if you have a computer and you encrypt a message into binary code and I have a computer and I have the key to decrypt that message — the ability to change a meaningless series of numbers back into a meaningful series of numbers — how does your computer know which number to start deciphering in the chain, so that its key will work?

Remember, if your computer starts in the wrong place, it'll just turn the encoded numbers my computer just sent you into a different set of gibberish."

"Both computers have a clock," Hockaday mused aloud.

"Bingo! That's what we call the synchronicity dichotomy, the key to cyclostationary processing."

"So why did you refuse to decrypt this?"

"Sorry, Glen, I'm afraid I can't answer that," replied Czarlinsky sotto voce.

Before Hockaday could press further, a voice at the door hollered out, "Dr. Hockaday! Doctor Hockaday! Are you in there?"

"Yes!" Hockaday testily replied.

"Call for you, sir," announced the Federal Protective Service guard, "On SWITCHBOARD!"

"I'll take it in here," Hockaday announced through the still closed door.

"But, sir — "

"I said, I'll take it in here!"

As soon as he saw the extension light flicker on Czarlinsky's telephone, Hockaday punched the button and raised the handset to his right ear.

"Yes, Lincoln…You what? It's outside now?…Yes, we can be on it." Hockaday hung up the phone and looked at it a moment.

"What was that?" Woodring asked.

"Lincoln's sent his helicopter. It's waiting outside. He knows about the transcript."

☆ ☆ ☆

An electric cart burst out the doors of Building No. 4, sped along Savage Road to the headquarters tower, circled around it, and slammed to a stop next to a Bell Huey HH-1H twelve-seater with civilian markings. The HH-1H was positioned into the wind with its rotors whining, ready for take off. Ducking to avoid the downwash, Woodring rushed after Hockaday into the open hatch, stumbling into the nearest seat just as the chopper rose off its skids. The pilot had inadvertently left on the intercom, and radio traffic from several nearby civilian and military bases was blaring throughout the cabin, making conversation impossible.

After the pilot had adjusted the throttle and collective to maintain altitude and heading, he performed a 360° spot turn to confirm his perimeter was clear, then moved forward, his nose pitched up in the air. At fifty feet of altitude, he crabbed into the wind to maintain a proper ground track, while Woodring stared out the window, watching the shrinking size of the traffic on the Baltimore Washington Parkway. The Huey raced along the northern suburbs from Maryland to Virginia, and in no time Woodring found himself looking at the Potomac, which wound beneath him like a silver snake in the cool noonday sun.

Across the Potomac and past the parkway, a single, seven-story, gray-white building rose before them, set like a toy on a lawn cut large square in the middle of a dense pine forest. The pilot banked steeply, giving Woodring a birdseye view of a cantilevered canopy, before they landed on the lawn twenty yards from the main door. A small crew in dark blue uniforms was running across the grass to meet them.

Ducking under the rotors, CIA security staff escorted Hockaday and Woodring into the lobby, waved them through the turnstiles at the entrance gate, and led them through the lobby up a short flight of stairs, leaving them in the same sitting room Generals Vaughn and Praeger had visited a week earlier.

The door to the DCI's private elevator opened, as if on cue, and the same assistant who had met the two generals before ushered them all inside. When they reached the seventh floor, Daniels' assistant took them directly to the director's office.

Chapter 22

Director Lincoln Daniels was sitting stonefaced at his desk, while in two chairs arrayed around him were Keith Axe, his deputy director, and Hubert Myers, Director, FBI. Axe rose from his chair, set a CD player on Daniels's desk, then turned it on. A pair of disembodied, computer-generated voices began to speak.

"*Who's speaking, please?*"

"*HYDRA.*"

"*I'll be brief. You may want to cancel the mission. It's why we haven't sent the money yet.*"

"*Why? What's happened?*"

"*GERALD's under surveillance.*"

"*When did you find this out?*"

"*Earlier today.*"

"*I'll call you back in ten minutes.*"

Woodring glanced at Hockaday in horror, the words "Consult T-COM for decrypt approval" mixed with the text of HYDRA's message swimming in his head. Axe hit the button a second time.

"*Who's speaking, please?*"

"*It's HYDRA. If you take care of GERALD, I'm still in.*"

"*Done.*"

A temporary silence gripped the room, the terrible reality of HYDRA's message holding them in its thrall.

Woodring looked from face to face, but no one returned his gaze.

Axe walked to the windows and started shutting all the

blinds, then the room went dark, and a silent film began to play on a small screen behind Daniels's head.

"I'd like each of you to watch this," Daniels spoke in the dark. "The film you're about to see was taken on the afternoon of Chauncey Laudon's death."

Laudon had been CIA Deputy Director of Operations under Kennedy, and later became DCI himself. He had perished in a mysterious fire at his home over a dozen years ago.

On the screen a grim-faced man in overalls suddenly appeared, jabbing a crowbar into the living room wall of Laudon's house, until he applied enough pressure to rip the panel from the wall. A second man immediately took the broken slab and passed an oval-shaped wand across it, repeating the process several times until he was satisfied it didn't contain any hidden bugs. Behind both men sat a six-foot-high metal rack of sensitive electronic equipment, blinking silently as they went about their work.

The scene abruptly switched to an oak-paneled study, where another pair of investigators was busying themselves by pulling every volume off the shelves of Laudon's extensive personal library and passing them through a small pair of stainless steel metal bars, similar to those found at airport security checkpoints. If nothing unusual was found, the book was unceremoniously tossed into a large black plastic lawn bag. Inside the upstairs bedroom, a third pair of technicians was sweeping every surface, while another tech monitored the results on a rack of equipment identical to the set being used downstairs.

The picture suddenly jerked, racing towards the equipment rack. A bright red light was flashing on and off on one of the many amplifiers, then several more lights began to flash, and the first technician furiously gestured to his partner with the wand in his hand. The expression on the face of the man holding the wand froze in terror—the neutron scanner to which the wand was connected was frantically indicating the presence of a large concentration of the almost undetectable plastic explosive, Semtex. Daniels' audience watched in horror as one of the techs next threw himself head-first through the second story window and disappeared from view. Then the film went blank.

"Jesus Christ," uttered Myers.

His face covered by the frozen image of the fallen house, Daniels spoke, "Several months after the film was taken, an anonymous package, containing a small address book was received at the Hoover Building. It was addressed to me, Lincoln Daniels, Director. After further investigation we guessed the address book had most probably been sent by one of Laudon's neighbors, who had found it in his yard and correctly guessed its owner.

"As I skimmed through its pages in my office, I immediately recognized several listings belonging to former agents of the Secret Service, CIA and the FBI...and listed right along with them were the names of several individuals who at one time or another had been logged into the FBI's national crime databank...Almost every one of the individuals in the databank had been prime suspects to one or more murder charges, most of which were never proven.

"When I met with the President that evening and explained the situation to him, he immediately ordered this entire group to be eliminated, using whatever means were necessary...Of the 15 individuals mentioned in the book, all of them were apprehended—except one."

"My God," whispered Myers.

"It took us some time to deduce how Laudon had managed to communicate with this group for such a long period and escape detection. We were a small team, but we checked hundreds of telephone logs, interviewed dozens of people, turned NSA upside down, until somebody came across an obscure memorandum from the Atlanta field office—" Suddenly Daniels's telephone rang, startling all of them.

"Send him in," Daniels spoke into the receiver and hung up.

A moment later, two security personnel escorted a tall black man with slightly gray hair in the door. For the next ten minutes a retired Atlanta police inspector told the astonished group how in 1980 he had interrupted an assassination in progress whose target had been Senator Edward Kennedy.

"They all insisted they were federal agents and flashed valid ID at us."

"Go on," Daniels urged.

"Well, we just didn't buy it—but, then, we didn't have much choice—"

"What do you mean 'much choice?'" Myers interrupted.

"We, ah, sir, were ordered by both the FBI and CIA, or what we thought was the CIA and FBI, to free the prisoners."

For the first time in his career the FBI Director felt goose bumps crawl across his skin.

"Free the prisoners?"

"Yes, sir, all three of them."

"Lincoln?"

"Neither our nor FBI's records have any mention of the event."

"Lieutenant?" prompted Axe.

"Yes, sir?"

"Why don't you tell these men what happened next."

"Well sir, to put it mildly, these boys were pretty well equipped. I mean they obviously came to do the a job—had everything—phony IDs, ski masks, ropes, government papers, pistols, thousands of dollars in hundred dollar bills, well, they even had commando daggers. Then I saw the box." Inspector Rainey abruptly ceased his dialogue and glanced at Daniels for permission to continue.

"Tell them."

"It was like a briefcase, and before I realized what I was doing, I had my men cover me while I opened it. I thought it was gonna be filled with drugs—it wasn't—it was a telephone."

"Tell them what happened next," Axe urged.

"Feds called Chief Clark and told him to give all the evidence back, even the diagram of Senator Kennedy's room—so we did. Except one thing, I kept the box. I'd left it at my home by mistake. Once I heard they told the chief to destroy all the evidence I just kept it. Put it in my attic and forgot about it.

"Months later I woke up in the middle of the night—thought my house was on fire or something, cause I heard a beeping sound and I thought it was the smoke alert. Then I realized it was the briefcase phone—someone was calling me on the box."

"Did you answer it?" Woodring asked.

"Yes sir. The caller said 'This is Laudon.' When I said 'Laudon who?', he hung up."

"The exact same box HYDRA's using," Axe stated with a grim finality. "9,600-bits-per-second, 30-kilohertz range, our software, our codes, the whole works."

Each attendee turned his head as Keith Axe passed him a manila envelope, sealed in wax. Hubert Myers wordlessly began to tear open the seal on his envelope, while the others followed, one by one.

No one in the room could believe the contents of the secret table enclosed inside the envelope. This one sheet of paper, seen on the front page of the *New York Times* would be enough to shake the government to its core, causing the collapse of the entire American intelligence community for decades.

On the left side of the list were a series of names and dates, while on the right was a corresponding set of summarized telephone conversations, listed by caller, date, and telephone number. No one in the room needed any further explanation as to the table's relevance, the names in the left-hand column were all too familiar: Martin Luther King, Robert Kennedy, Sam Giancana, Johnny Roselli, Federal Judge John Wood, Edward Kennedy. Edward Kennedy's name was listed with a corresponding set of HYDRA's telephone conversations to the right.

"As you can see from the record of the telephone transcripts before each of you, whoever was using this device was present before, during, and immediately after each of these...events."

"Hold on a second, Lincoln! You're saying this same type of device was used to make all these calls?" objected Myers.

"Not quite," Daniels replied. "After Lieutenant Rainey sent me his telephone, at the President's request we flew it to Cheltenham and had GCHQ find out what codes it used, then run a non-treaty search on all U.S. telecoms, radio, satellite, everything, looking for any transmissions using these same codes."

"You mean—" Myers began.

"That's right," replied Daniels, "Laudon changed the equipment but he kept the same codes as he upgraded. Otherwise we would have never found out."

For the second time the room fell into total silence.

"Gentlemen, Chauncey Laudon was insane," Daniels continued. "We'll never know what his true motivations were, but these tables make clear the extent of the damage he and his band of renegades caused this country. And I don't think I have to tell you that if even a hint that Chauncey Laudon was operating his own personal band of assassins were to get out, the whole national security apparatus of this country would risk being dismantled.

"Woody, starting now, you're in charge of tracking this man down and eliminating him," Daniels ordered, astonishing Woodring and the others by the ease with which he had just accepted the strong possibility that HYDRA was a former American intelligence officer. "I've already discussed this with the President and he's just signed an NSDD, which essentially strips any and all suspects in this case of their civil rights." At this point Axe handed each of Daniels's guests a copy of National Security Decision Directive No. 208, while Daniels continued speaking. "According to our in-house counsel, the Federal Emergency Management Act gives us the authority we need to support this, Woody. We've already gone to Judge Sachs and had him issue you enough blank warrants to tap any suspect's phones, read his mail, blackbag his house, hold him without a writ of habeas corpus or whatever else you feel you need to do."

"Yes, sir," Woodring replied automatically, then startled everyone by asking, "Sir?"

Daniels raised his eyebrows.

"I just have one last question for the Lieutenant," Woodring pressed, and Daniels allowed him to continue. "Do you have any idea at this time where any of the three men you arrested might be?"

"Yes, sir. I do."

"Wait a minute!" Axe protested. "You told us before you let them all go!"

"That's what I told you in 1980, Mr. Axe, but two years later I turned on my television set and saw Volz being taken into court by some Federal Marshalls—"

"Into court! Jesus! What was he charged with?"

"Murder. Harry Volz was charged with murdering a federal judge."

"Where is he now?" demanded Woodring.

"Volz's in Marion Penitentiary, sir," replied the police lieutenant.

"Thank you, Lieutenant," Daniels sighed, then picked up

his telephone.

A moment later the same two security personnel escorted him out of Daniels's office.

☆ ☆ ☆

The limousine ride back to Washington with his superior, FBI Director Hubert Myers, was possibly the most uncomfortable trips in David Woodring's life. For even though Myers's limousine was swept daily to check for bugs, Woodring didn't think it prudent to discuss the subject of their recent meeting at CIA headquarters in the car, and he was a bit surprised when Myers abruptly broke the silence as they rushed along Shirley Memorial Highway.

"Woody, I assume you're familiar with the Hostage Rescue Team?"

Woodring nodded affirmatively. He knew the bureau's fifty-man Hostage Rescue Team (HRT) was the chief civilian counterterrorist team available to the executive branch. Members of the HRT normally trained with military counterterrorist units, including the Navy SEALs, Marines, 82nd Airborne, and Delta Force, each of them often engaged in spirited rivalries with their competitors to see who could "neutralize" a terrorist attack first. Like its competitors, the HRT had copied many of the original training procedures and tactics of Britain's Special Air Service, including the SAS's all-black uniforms and balaclava hoods to hide its members' identities.

Myers informed Woodring that for the duration of the investigation he would be guarded day and night by a rotating force of twenty-four HRT agents in four six-hour-long shifts of six men each. On days when Woodring was inside the Hoover Building, his security force would be reduced to three men, with the remaining trio stationed at Woodring's house in Falls Church. Travel to cities outside Washington would be accomplished in a GSA-owned LearJet bearing civilian markings. It was understood that newly assigned security force would also accompany Woodring on any such trip.

Over the Potomac River Myers also ordered Woodring to immediately move his office from the eleventh floor of the Hoover Building to the FBI's Counterterrorism Center (CTC) on the seventh floor. Originally established by the CIA under William Casey in response to the hijacking of TWA Flight 847 in 1985, the CTC was the first time that CIA officers were ordered to cooperate with other government agencies in investigations of major terrorists. The CTC's formation almost caused a civil war between the analysts in the CIA's Directorate of Information and members of the clandestine service in the Directorate of Operations. Analysts in DI claimed their conclusions would be slanted or bypassed altogether if they proved to be unpopular, while covert operations staff in DO complained the formerly inviolate Chinese Wall between field operatives and headquarters was being torn asunder.

All of which paled in importance, when, in the early evening of December 21, 1988, a single jet airplane, Pan Am 103, flying to New York from London's Heathrow Airport, exploded in the sky 30,000 feet over Lockerbie, Scotland. Suddenly, the overall agent in charge of the CTC was given unlimited access not only to resources within the CIA, but also at the State Department, Federal Aviation Administration, FBI, Secret Service, and Pentagon. In addition, the CIA's multi-parameter extensive database on terrorism, a system known in intelligence circles as DESIST, was made available. DESIST tracks hundreds of different terrorists and their associates, their sources of funding, and any known contacts between them and the various secret services. After ending the Lockerbie investigation, control of the CTC was passed from the CIA to the FBI, which was a more natural choice, due to the bureau's role as America's major counterintelligence agency.

By placing Woodring temporarily in charge of CTC, Myers had cleverly positioned him to be able to request information from any of the CTC's member organizations without raising any eyebrows. Woodring's staff would be able to send cables to CIA offshore stations, liaise with friendly foreign intelligence agencies, demand access to desk officers and operatives at the FBI, FAA, State and the Pentagon, and instruct officers at the National Security Agency to perform communications intercepts. Some of which he might need to do, Woodring knew, if he were, in fact, trying to locate and neutralize a highly capable former American intelligence agent.

Director Myers's armored car bounced over the threshold of the Hoover Building's underground garage and sailed down the driveway, stopping suddenly next to a guardpost in front of an elevator bank. Three plainclothesmen with unfamiliar faces and muscular builds who were standing next to the regular sentry approached the car and opened its doors, then followed Myers and Woodring into the director's private elevator. When the elevator stopped at the seventh floor where the CTC's headquarters were located, the three plainclothesmen followed him out. Two of the trio took up preassigned posts at each end of the hallway, while the third accompanied Woodring as he strode past a row of apprehensive analysts seated at their desks. Woodring entered the empty corner office and locked the door behind him, leaving the third agent stationed outside his door, then picked up the telephone and ordered the the duty officer to ready his staff for an immediate flight to Marion, Illinois.

Chapter 23

Less than fifteen minutes after he had received Woodring's call, Joss Hall, Resident-Agent-in-Charge of the Carbondale, Illinois FBI regional office, leapt in his Oldsmobile 88 with three other FBI agents and raced sixteen miles across State Highway 13, veering off an access road near a tall water tower. Hall swerved left at the water tower, roaring past the parking lot and slamming to a stop, where he and his men were met by a pair of startled guards. Directly behind them was a wall of razor wire which fully encircled the U.S. penitentiary at Marion.

USP Marion is America's toughest lockup, the new Alcatraz for incorrigibles, prison gang leaders, escape artists and unmanageable felons so violent they must be separated from inmates in the nation's other prisons. Every one of its prisoners is in solitary confinement in an 8-by-8-by-6-foot cell restricted to only an hour a day, during which each inmate is allowed to walk along the corridor in his tier, before he is returned to his cell. Marion USP has no cafeteria, no prison industry, no group recreation, no visiting entertainment and no prison yard for inmates to mingle in. Prisoners amuse themselves by manufacturing alcohol from cornflakes dumped in toilets, carving miniature plastic knives out of toothbrushes, fashioning hacksaws from the metal frames of the air ducts, or by swallowing contraband and storing it inside their intestinal tracts.

"FBI, we're here to see Warden Joiner," Hall announced.

One of the corrections officers reached for a telephone, but Hall grabbed his wrist, holding it firmly.

"We're unexpected," Hall whispered, motioning to the guard to hang up.

After repeating the same performance at the security checkpoint in the lobby, the four FBI agents took the elevator to the warden's office on the sixth floor. A male secretary sitting next to a plate-glass window controlled the door with an automatic lock, separating the warden, Ed Joiner, from the outside.

"FBI, we're here to see Warden Joiner," Hall announced.

"Warden, there's a couple of men from the FBI out —"

"Send 'em in!" the intercom blared back.

Hall marched into a gold-carpeted room with a pair of green leather couches against the walls and an architectural model of the prison on a coffee table in its center.

"How can I help you?"

Joiner's expression hardened when he noticed all his visitors were wearing pins on their lapels.

"We have a National Security Intelligence Decision Directive regarding one of your prisoners," Hall responded immediately and pulled a piece of paper out of his pocket and set it on Joiner's desk.

"Volz's in Control Unit—we were told to keep him there by Washington— look this doesn't mean shit to me, we can't release people out of Marion without a judge's order...I've never seen one of these since—" the warden was interrupted by the telephone "—just a minute," At first all Joiner heard was static, then a special operator came back on the line and asked Joiner to hold a moment for Paul Henson, Director, U.S. Bureau of Prisons.

Warden Joiner involuntarily cleared his throat every few seconds, while Henson patiently enumerated the legal ramifications of a classified National Security Directive to him. "Yes, sir, uh hmm, uh hmm, yes, sir, I'll have him released from solitary myself—... no, no, no. No, sir, if you don't wish me to go personally, I understand of course...sure, sure, we've got a couple of extra unif—" Joiner stopped short. "Right," he answered, then hung up. Beads of sweat slipped down his forehead and stung his eyes and his palms felt like sponges. He avoided looking Hall in the eye as he spoke, "O.K., he's yours."

☆ ☆ ☆

Outside the Warden's office, Hall and his men were met by a squad of corrections officers handpicked from the regular staff, who were members of the Strategic Operations Response Team, better known to the inmates as the Goon Squad. Each officer carried a black Lifetime riot bludgeon, a three-foot-long hardwood club with a steel ball on its top, designed especially to tear the intercostal muscles between the ribs without breaking them.

Hall and his men followed directly behind, walking along the ranges filled with louvered concrete cells. Hall thought he noticed the smell of burning paint mixed in with general odor of human sweat.

"What's that smell?"

"Lock's being changed," snapped one of the guards. "Fuckers see the key more than once they go carve themselves a copy."

A red-headed guard wearing the uniform of the prison's Strategic Operations Response Team swung Volz's cell door open, stood away from him, so Volz couldn't slam the door on him. Two FBI agents stood behind the guard looking like twins with the same height, same build, and similar impassive expressions.

"Harold Volz?" Hall spoke.

"I'm Harry Volz, yes."

"O.K., let's move it."

"Who are you guys?"

"I'm Johnson and he's Johnson," Hall lied.

"Right. Mind telling me where I'm going, Johnson and Johnson?" asked Volz, getting up off the bunk.

"Yeah, Volz, we do mind." Hall motioned with his head towards the corridor then frowned at Volz as if he were wasting their time.

Volz made no response.

"You ready—or are we going to be here all night?"

Volz warily got off his bunk and let Hall lead him up a concrete stairwell to the sixth floor, where they stopped right before the metal door.

"Take off your shirt," ordered agent Hall.

Volz did as he was told and a second FBI agent handed Volz

some civilian clothes.

"What are these for? What's going on here?"

"Just put them on," snapped Hall, motioning Volz towards a small elevator. Volz entered the elevator to find a second pair of plainclothesmen inside, one holding the door-open button, while the other held a gun.

After the elevator doors shut, Volz examined his new clothes. The FBI agents had put him in expensive business suit with a tight-fitting custom-made cotton shirt underneath.

The moment the elevator door opened, the four FBI plainclothesmen duckwalked Volz across the asphalt- and gravel-covered roof, where the downwash of an incongruous Navy Sea King was blowing dirt in the air. When he leapt aboard, Volz caught a glimpse of Woodring's grim face through the open main rear door, realizing then what they must have come for.

Chapter 24

When Harry Volz awoke everything around him was pitch black, and when he raised up his head it bumped into something. It also felt as if he had the worst hangover of his life. The memory of Woodring's face inside the Learjet, the two black men who had opened his cell door at Marion, the helicopter on the penitentiary's roof, seemed to possess him in some way, repeating over and over in his mind. His hand touched a flat surface, then his other hand felt the same thing. For a moment he panicked—he was dead—it was over, the men who had picked him up had found out what they wanted and had disposed of him. Or else, he was about to die, but it was too hard to think about; memories flooded his mind without end.

His father's fist flew straight at his helpless face inside a gymnasium, missing him, smashing into a wall, and a bathroom was filled with a roaring agony. *Police! Police! Keep your hands up! Police!* He was a prisoner now, a prisoner of his mind.

The sluice gates opened and hundreds of visions rushed out. *Hey! You don't have a warrant for that!*

"Come on, Lieutenant, we're on your team."

Woodring watched the interrogator turn off the microphone and slump back in his swivel chair from exhaustion.

Volz's incoherent animal groans and screams played over a monitor in a glassed-in room where several grim-faced men sat, waiting for him to break.

"How much longer?" Woodring asked in disgust.

"He's ready now," the interrogator answered.

"Get him out. I want to get this over with."

Woodring watched through the one-way glass as Volz was carried into the room with his feet dragging and strapped into what resembled an electric chair, while a specialist attached electrodes to his body. His tongue was slack and hung out his mouth like a dog's.

Volz now faced a blank, mirrored wall, and the operator sat next to him at a wooden desk with a control board inserted in its top. A top-of-the-line, five-pen Lafayette polygraph would measure the response of Volz's respiration, blood pressure, heart rate, and electrodermal levels to the questions Woodring had instructed his team to ask.

"What is your name?"

"Volz...Harry Volz."

"That's good. Are you happy to be outside?"

"Yes, very hap-py."

"Where do you live?"

"I live in Marion...USP."

"Good, Harry. That's very good. Do you have dreams?"

Inside the hidden control room, a second pair of operators sat next to Woodring in swivel chairs, watching a duplicate set of pens march across the roll of polygraph paper.

"EDR's good," murmured one.

Two electrodes had been placed on the top of Volz's ring and index fingers to measure his skin's resistance to electricity by means of a galvanometer placed in the circuitry.

The second operator busied himself leafing through Volz's extensive medical prison record, reconfirming that no conditions existed which would adversely affect the test.

"Will you be telling me the truth today?"

"Yes."

"Good. Are you afraid I might ask you something you would prefer not to discuss?"

"Yes."

"That's alright. This won't take long."

"Look at his toes."

"What?" asked Woodring.

"Look at his toes, he's pressing them to the floor," repeated the operator in the control room, pointing at a television camera which had been focused on Volz's bare feet.

"Do you hear voices in your head?"

"No."

Woodring noticed the tip of Volz's big toe turn red as soon as the floor operator spoke.

"Check his tongue."

"You think he's biting it?"

"Have you ever had convulsions?"

"No."

"Blackouts?"

"No."

The operator next to Woodring flipped a switch on his console and whispered something into his hands-free headset.

The floor operator nodded slightly in response.

"Harry, are you squeezing your toes when I ask you questions?"

"No."

"You're sure of that?"

"Yes."

"Would you like to see a film of your toes?"

"No."

"When I just asked you about the film, did you bite your tongue?"

"No. Yes. No."

"Asshole," Woodring muttered to himself in the control room.

"Do you have dreams?"

"Yes...many."

"He's stopped using countermeasures."

The control room operator touched the responding chart with his finger, indicating to Woodring where a pattern of jagged sine waves had levelled out to form a regular pattern.

"Good. I have dreams, too. What did you dream about today, Harry?"

"Sheraton."

"The Sheraton Hotel?"

"Yeah, the hotel...airport."

Woodring slipped the small black address book Daniels had given him from his pocket and absentmindedly turned its pages, flattening it with his palm when he found Volz's name.

"Were you there in your dream?"

"Yeah, me and the others."

"Who were the others? Were they your friends?"

"Yeah, Colman and Bartel...old friends."

Woodring found the names of Bartel and Colman next to each other on the page opposite Volz's, while the agent next to him marked the number on the taped transcript which corresponded to Volz's mention of the two names.

"Harry, why did you and your friends go to the hotel?"

"To kill him…to kill the senator…"

The interrogator shot Woodring a glance, and he nodded for him to continue. Next to Woodring, sat Lieutenant Rainey, who looked on in horror.

"Who told you to kill the senator, Harry?"

"Bartel…Bartel got the job."

"Is Bartel your friend's first name, Harry?"

"No."

"Is Bartel his last name?"

"Yeah, Benn-ett. Bennett Bartel. Kinda rhymes."

"Yes, it does, doesn't it?"

During this exchange Woodring had picked up a headset to a secure telephone and began to issue a series of instructions in a soft voice.

"Harry, is Bennett Bartel your friend's real name?"

"No."

As he spoke Volz's eyes focused and refocused on the plate glass window behind which sat Woodring's interrogation team. Sweat poured off the killer's brow and soaked through his shirt.

Woodring noticed Volz was beginning to struggle with his bonds, hung up the telephone and whispered something in the ear of the tech next to him, who relayed the message to the operator on the floor.

"Harry, do you know if Bartel ever was in the service?"

"Who's back there?"

"Back where, Harry?"

"Who's behind that glass?"

"Harry, do you know if Bartel ever served in the armed forces?"

"I wanna know who's behind that window before I answer that." His eyes glistening like an animal's, Volz was now staring directly at the spot where Woodring was sitting.

Woodring picked up the microphone in front of him and pressed the transmit switch.

"Harry, this is Assistant Director Woodring. I'm sitting in the control room. What seems to be the problem?"

"Come on out where I can see you."

Woodring sighed and glanced at the operator next to him, then left his chair and made his way to the floor.

The interrogator sitting next to Volz noticed Volz's lip was trembling, while the polygraph's five pens began to jump erratically.

A door opened and Woodring stepped into the room without his jacket on, revealing a shoulder holster holding a .38.

"Give me a pen," Volz demanded.

Woodring nodded to the operator who in turn handed Volz a felt-tip pen and a single sheet of paper.

Volz wrote out two words, then folded the paper in half and held it in his right hand.

Woodring strode forward in three quick steps but Volz was too fast for him and yanked the paper back, holding it near his mouth, causing Woodring to stop short.

"What do I get?"

Woodring said nothing, but kept his gaze fixed squarely on Volz's hands.

"Come on, what do I get?"

Woodring remained frozen in place, shifting his glance

almost imperceptibly towards the operator.

Volz saw the motion out of the corner of his eye, but the electronic charge racing up his spine into his brain arrived at the speed of light. His right hand froze where it was, then shook violently as the slip of paper wafted to the floor. None of those present would ever forget the animal savagery of Volz's cry.

"Get him out of here!" Woodring snarled, unfolding the paper in his hand.

China Lake.

Chapter 25

Lincoln Daniels suddenly glanced at his watch and set down the book he was reading, then picked up the telephone to talk with the sentry who was posted outside his house.

"Yes, sir."

"David Woodring is coming by with another man, and as far as you're concerned this visit is off the books. You know what Woody looks like, and as long as his guest isn't holding a gun to his back, let 'em pass," Daniels ordered.

Inside the sentry's car the words, "*WOODRING, DAVID, FBI, ADCI, CHEROKEE BLAZER, VA #555-573*", flashed across a small CRT mounted in the dash. A moment later, the sentry saw a pair of headlights belonging to Woodring's Cherokee Blazer rounding the island to the north of Daniels' home. The sentry unsnapped the leather strap which held a mini-Uzi under his armpit, but stayed inside his car as he had just been ordered. He watched Woodring's Cherokee speed down the sidestreet and lurch to an abrupt halt in front of Daniels' white colonial. The ADCI sure seemed seemed to be in a hurry, the sentry thought. Woodring had just left his Blazer parked halfway up the curb and was jogging up the path to the DCI's front door. The second man was unable to maintain Woodring's pace and lagged behind the FBI Assistant

Director. The sentry took careful note that both Woodring's and his companion's hands were outside their coats and empty.

Lincoln Daniels opened the steel-reinforced front door without a word, let both men inside, and immediately slammed it shut behind them. Daniels had every motivation to keep the identity of Woodring's companion a secret, even from his own security staff, since the very existence of the third man was one of the administration's greatest secrets. The DCI's other visitor was a special White House courier, whose sole function was to relay urgent messages from the Commander in Chief to a restricted circle of individuals in the various intelligence services, usually regarding certain executive directives which specified an existing threat to the national security. In the trade he was known as the Messenger of Death.

"Our stress analysis guys just finished looking at Volz's test," Woodring half-gasped, worried by the look on Daniels's face. "They say it's real."

Daniels held a thick, spiral-bound notebook in his hand, whose cover read in red and black block letters: RAINBOW CLEARANCE, CHINA LAKE SPECIAL OPERATIONS WEAPONS FACILITY.

"You'd better go to China Lake tonight, and take one of our planes. I've already called Andrews and made the arrangements."

"Yes, sir."

Outside Daniels' home a small, red warning light appear on the sentry's dashboard, followed by an earsplitting tone which jolted him in his seat. Next, the words *HOMESDALE ETA 1:00 MINUTE* flashed across his CRT and the sentry felt his armpits grow moist. Translated into English, the message had just informed him that a helicopter would be landing in Lincoln Daniels's back yard in less than sixty seconds.

The agent burst out his car door and shoved his suit coat aside as he ran around Daniels's house. He was just in time to catch Woodring and his two bodyguards jogging towards a HH-1H, which was hovering above the lawn.

Chapter 26

Not many aircraft in the government's fleet of civilian transport were capable of making the 2,600-mile-long journey from Andrews Air Force Base in Maryland to the China Lake Naval Weapons Center in California nonstop. In fact, there were only two, the Gulfstream C-20A and the Boeing C-137. They were modified versions of the Gulfstream III executive jet and the Boeing 707-120 airliner, and had a range of 4,718 and 5,150 miles respectively. Upon boarding Daniels's helicopter, Woodring was informed that a Gulfstream C-20A had already been preflighted by the 89th Military Airlift Wing Command and was waiting for him and his men on the tarmac. When the HH-1H Huey arrived at Andrews' Heliport fifteen minutes later it was met by two vans filled with HRT agents who escorted Woodring to the end of runway 7 whereupon Woodring and his platoon of bodyguards boarded the C-20A.

According to a hastily filed and false flight plan, United Airlines Flight No. 5575 from Washington D.C. to Los Angeles had just departed.

The first five hours of the flight passed without incident; the Gulfstream passed from one Air Route Traffic Control Center to another, appearing all the while to be strictly maintaining the parameters of its flight plan. Woodring had ordered the HRT pilot to broadcast all radio contacts over the public address system in the cabin, so he would be immediately apprised of any change in the airplane's status, and right before Flight 5575 crossed the Nevada-California border, Los Angeles Center recontacted the plane.

"Cherokee Six One Tango, squawk one two zero six and ident."

"Cherokee Six One Tango, squawking one two zero six," repeated the Gulfstream's pilot.

The controller inside the Los Angeles Air Route Traffic Control Center rechecked the position of the plus sign which represented Flight 5575 on his monitor. Below the plus sign, in addition to the jet's four-digit transponder code were two more numbers which indicated its altitude in feet and its speed in knots. Both readouts indicated that Flight 5575 was far north of Las Vegas, way out of its flight path for landing at LAX. The controller had just asked the pilot to push the IDENT button on his transponder to give the controller's radar beacon system more data.

He did a double take when the standard 1200 transponder code was replaced with ID number 0101. ID 0101 was an unusual Federal Emergency Management Act code which meant: the flight you have just contacted doesn't exist.

Meanwhile, an increasingly nervous controller at China Lake Naval Weapons Center was watching FEMA ID 0101 cross the Panamint Mountains at 500 miles per hour, heading directly into China Lake's 1,800-square mile restricted military operations area. He pressed the toggle switch on his console, then began to speak into his headset.

"Aircraft on China Lake, descending to flight level two zero zero, squawk zero three one two."

The familiar pattern of a short-range civilian radar transmitter suddenly expanded, indicating whoever was flying ID 0101 possessed unusually powerful transmitting equipment, but the analyst ignored it, he was busy rifling his desk for a special one-time code pad. He nervously flattened the code book in front of him, double checking the three-letter message he had just received. After deciphering Woodring's message, he punched a certain number into his telephone.

"Base security," the operator responded.

"Give me Sergeant Roberts."

"Just a minute."

"Roberts," the sergeant said, picking up his telephone.

"We've got a zero-one flight ETA here in fifteen minutes and they want you on the tarmac with a ladder and three jeeps the moment they arrive."

The sergeant slammed down the phone, jabbed three sentries who were asleep in the guard hut and ordered them to follow him out onto the runway each in a separate jeep. The C-20A roared past, its tires searing the runway as the tiny four-vehicle convoy raced after it. The pilot threw the pair of Rolls-Royce Fll1-RR-100 turbofans in reverse, drastically slowing his runway speed.

The plane stopped and as Roberts neared the aircraft in his vehicle, its hatch flew open, framing a pair of plainclothesmen holding Heckler & Koch MP5-5D2 submachine guns.

"Jesus," he muttered under his breath, hoping the base controller hadn't misinformed him about their new arrivals. The moment he lined up the ladder to the hatch, two plainclothesmen leapt down it two steps at a time and flashed their IDs in his face.

"FBI. Stay where you are. You pull out a weapon and we'll shoot a hole through you."

Roberts and his astonished ground crew watched as ten more plainclothesmen filed down the ladder, followed by Woodring, who ordered Robert's men out of the jeeps, leaving them under guard by a pair of agents, before Woodring raced across the runway into the gloom.

The first security checkpoint Woodring encountered lay directly outside the airstrip. He raised his hand and the two jeeps behind him screeched to a halt.

"My name is Dr. Holland," Woodring told the Marine in the guardhouse without emotion.

The sentry jerked alert at the special name, instantly noticing the two plainclothesmen in Woodring's jeep had their hands on their holsters. The fourth passenger, sitting in the front seat next to Holland and dressed as a civilian, said nothing.

"Yes, sir."

Woodring's jeep sped through the gate, the two sentries watching the dust rise off the road in its wake.

Woodring repeated the same procedure at the next four guardposts, until, finally, at the fifth, he handed a wary female sentry a copy of NSDD 208, waited for her to read it, then demanded she escort him to Dr. Brimbecombe's private residence. Dr. Ernest Brimbecombe was the civilian commander of the Special Operations Weapons Facility and also possessed a combined Ph.D. in nuclear physics and engineering. Caught totally unawares by Woodring's arrival, Brimbecombe came to the door of his ranch house in his robe and slippers, since no one in Washington had even called him about an unannounced visit.

"Dr. Brimbecombe—" the sentry began to explain.

"I know this man, thank you, corporal," muttered Brimbecombe, frightened by the name Holland on Woodring's plastic name tag.

"I want my people around the house," Woodring spoke in no uncertain terms, startling Brimbecombe even more.

"All right," answered Brimbecombe, surprising the sentry with his immediate acquiescence.

No one said anything until she left, leaving Brimbecombe alone with David Woodring and Detective Rainey.

"Dr. Brimbecombe, I have come here under the authority of National Security Decision Directive No. 208, a copy of which I am allowed to show you before we begin our search," Woodring announced, then slipped the sheet of paper into Brimbecombe's hands.

Brimbecombe read the document in shock, immediately recognizing the National Security Council crest and the texture of the special paper.

"*What is this? What do you want?*"

"We're looking for the man who used this box." Woodring handed the startled base commander a copy of HYDRA's transcript and a matching spec sheet for the spread spectrum multiplexer.

"Who's GERALD?"

"We're pretty sure it's a reference to Dr. Victor Saleh—"

"Saleh? The one in La Jolla at FHI?"

"Right."

"You're saying one of our people's tied up in his—"

"We think he might have worked here."

"*An employee of ours?*"

"Probably an ex-employee," Woodring relented a bit. "But since we don't know how far back we're going to have to look, I want to access to the records of everyone who's come through here for the last fifteen years."

"*The last fifteen years? You mean you don't know his name?*"

"No. We only have two individuals who may have seen his face. One is in detention, the other is standing right in front of you," responded Woodring, nodding towards Detective Rainey.

"We'll have to go to the command center to get the files," sighed Brimbecombe. "Wait here a second while I put on my clothes."

Woodring snapped his fingers and the FBI HRT plain-clothesman stationed outside came to attention.

"Yes, sir?"

"I want an escort to the command center—ten men."

"Yes, sir."

Two jeeps, each packed with four heavily armed HRT agents, sandwiched Woodring and Brimbecombe as they sped to the command center in a third. Brimbecombe began to believe his life might really be at risk, but the short ride through the cold mountain air was uneventful. The column came to a halt outside a manned guard post protected by a twelve-foot-high chain link fence with floodlights on each corner. Woodring leapt out, shoving his ID in the sentry's face.

"Bring those with us," Woodring commanded, and two FBI agents hefted two legal-sized record storage boxes from the back of their jeep, following Woodring inside past the startled guard. A second pair of agents motioned for Dr. Brimbecombe to follow them inside.

"You've brought a duplicate set of records? Why was that necessary?" Brimbecombe gasped, watching Woodring's agents arrange stacks of yellowed files on the desks.

"Doctor Brimbecombe, I'd like you to pull the names of everyone who had any type of disciplinary problem here whatsoever, can you do that on your computer?"

"Yes."

Ten minutes later the somewhat nonplussed base commander handed Woodring a short, one-page-long printout with ten names on it.

"Great. Pull each of their files and give them to him, picture ID showing."

Brimbecombe glanced at Rainey, then punched in a series of numbers on an electronic lock which opened the door of an inner room, and disappeared inside.

"I want you to pull the same files he pulls and turn them so the picture IDs are showing and hand them to him with the one matching it from the safe," Woodring instructed the two agents.

Brimbecombe handed Lieutenant Rainey the file folders he had pulled from his safe, as did Woodring's man, and the police detective carefully examined the ID photographs of each pair, before setting them aside.

"Nope. Not here," Rainey said, both his hands pressed against the desk.

"Figures," muttered Woodring. "All right, hook that thing up and let's see what's next."

One of the HRT agents slapped a small laptop computer on a desk, plugged a CD ROM unit into it attached to two small speakers, then inserted a floppy disk which contained the name of everyone who had ever been stationed at China Lake, and typed in a series of commands. The CD ROM contained a master list of death certificates which had been recently created by the Social Security Administration to guard against computer fraud, of which it had been a serious victim.

Seconds later, the HRT agent handed Woodring a printout of over a score of names. Edwin D. Bailey had died on May 26, 1951, more than two decades before the Weapons Center had even been in existence.

Inside the vault, Brimbecombe quickly found Bailey's file and opened it, folding it back so that the ID photograph was revealed, then handed it to Woodring, who in turn handed it immediately to Detective Rainey.

"That's him. But—"

"But what?" demanded Woodring.

"When I saw him in Atlanta he had red hair and a beard, like I told you."

Woodring grabbed the file out of Rainey's hands. "Fax this to Daniels over CRITIC,"

Woodring ordered one of his men, "Then call and have the jet preflighted, we're going back." A quick look at the contents of Bailey's file had been enough.

Chapter 27

Generally unknown to the American public is the fact that the White House office complex contains two Situation rooms instead of just one, the endless repetition by the media of the phrase "White House Situation Room" notwithstanding. The original, or older, Situation Room does, in fact, lie in the basement of the west wing of the White House. It is a traditional dark, wood-paneled conference room with a large oval table in the middle which seats twelve and is small enough so that all the participants can hear and speak to one another. Along the room's perimeter another fourteen chairs are arranged so each member of the President's National Security Council can bring along one of his staff for backup. Traditional access to the old Situation Room is through an entrance visible to the omnipresent White House press corps—and anyone else who might choose to make a study of the Executive branch's comings and goings.

The second, more recently constructed Situation Room, or "Room 208" as it is known to the White House staff, is found in the Old Executive Office Building, which itself lies directly next to the White House. The Old Executive Office Building traditionally houses the President's National Security Council staff, the group responsible for keeping the chief executive informed on foreign policy (and not to be confused with the National Security Agency at Fort George G. Meade, an intelligence organization). After a raft of terrorist incidents in the 1980s, a certain aggressive former NSC staffer in the Reagan Administration named Oliver North lobbied for and succeeded in having Room 208 outfitted with the latest electronic gadgetry, computers, visual display equipment, and a combination lock on the door. The "crisis center", as Room 208 is sometimes also called, also possesses a long wooden conference table situated in the middle of the room. Meetings of the President's national security advisers which, sometimes by their very nature sometimes demand a clandestine setting, are often held in the Situation Room in the Old Executive Office Building instead of in the White House basement in order both to avoid the prying eyes of the White House press corps and also to allow the participants to arrive at as many different entrances to the complex as possible. And, in fact, before dawn that morning several key members of the Executive branch had received an abrupt summons to do just that—each invitee was told to report to Room 208 at 7:00 a.m. sharp and given a specific entrance to use with no further explanation.

And after each participant arrived inside the Old Executive Office Building, exited the elevator on the second floor and walked into the corridor, he found himself immediately surrounded by a full platoon of heavily armed Secret Service agents who, in a highly irregular fashion, were holding unsheathed automatic weapons at port arms.

After passing through the throng of Secret Service and entering Room 208 each invitee immediately realized what he had already begun to suspect—that he had been called to an assembly of the President's national security high command: seeing each other in attendance were Al Gore, Vice President; Lawrence Maddox, the President's chief of staff; J. Mark McDowell, National Security Advisor; Lincoln Daniels, Director, Central Intelligence; Hubert Myers, Director, Federal Bureau of Investigation; Frank Chalmers, Director, National Security Agency; Air Force General Haywood Ford, Commander, National Reconnaissance Office, Sunnyvale, California; Air Force General Olsen, Commander, Defense Special Missile and Astronautics Center (DEFSMAC), NSA; General Praeger, Director, Defense Intelligence Agency; and finally, Wesley Reynolds, the FBI official in charge of Command Black, a secret division of the bureau's Hostage Response Team which acts as the federal government's secret nuclear operations commando group.

Each attendee was also immediately aware that the combined presence of such an unusual group could mean only one of a few things: either America was about to go to war, a remote possibility given the present geopolitical situation and the noticeable absence of the Joint Chiefs of Staff; or, secondly, a declaration of Condition STARE DECISIS under the Federal Emergency Management Act was about to be made due to an event which each invitee would have preferred to never have to contemplate, e.g., nationwide rioting; or, finally, some other emergency that directly affected the security of the nation.

A small spotlight now illuminated the humorless face of Lincoln Daniels, and behind him a large area map of the world slowly revealed itself on a built-in movie screen. Major cities were noted by small red lights which blinked on and off.

No one spoke a single word.

There was a knock on the door, and Daniels checked his watch, then motioned to the Secret Service agent standing beside him to allow a second set of guests to enter. Each attendee at the table nervously shifted in his seat as a mixed crew of technicians, drawn from several different intelligence agencies, wheeled in several tall metal racks, each packed with obscure electronic instruments, and immediately went to work.

"This will only take a moment," Daniels apologized to the group.

Every square inch of every surface in Room 208 was subsequently swept and reswept by a range of devices, each one specifically designed to home in on different emanations across the entire electromagnetic spectrum.

"Excuse me, General Ford, would you mind standing up?" one of the sweepers asked the Commander of the National Reconnaissance Office.

The general grimaced, said nothing in response, and got out of his chair and faced the specialist.

"Would you hand me your pen, please, sir?"

"Here," Ford replied in open disgust.

The specialist gingerly inserted the pen inside a hollow metal cylinder built into one of the devices on the rack.

On the other side of the room one of the technicians winced as he passed his bizarrely shaped wand past the door of an innocent-looking console, stationed next to the south wall.

"What is it?" muttered his superior, now hovering over his shoulder.

"I'm getting something—several milliwatts—can't tell if it's the lamp or the table…" the specialist confessed.

"Anybody know anything about this table?" the senior specialist suddenly asked the assembly in a loud voice.

"This is ridiculous," groaned General Olsen.

"I've never seen it in here before," answered McDowell, the National Security Advisor.

"Get it out of here, pronto," ordered FBI Director Myers, motioning to two of his own people.

The sudden sound of a powerful electric drill only served to heighten the unbearable level of tension in Room 208. Lincoln Daniels held his left index-finger to his lips to indicate that everyone should remain silent. The President's chief of staff bit his lower lip and stared straight into space. *It was like a cancer, growing and gnawing at his insides.* Specks of plaster flew into the air amidst the unholy racket—now several technicians had gathered about the gaping hole in the wall of the New Situation Room, one drilling, another pointing a long vacuum rod in the same direction, which resembled the shotgun microphone often used by the networks at football games, while a third man now scooped up the debris and fed it into a machine.

A single light began to flash on the console of the amplifier which was analyzing the debris.

"Bingo!" whispered the senior man.

"Shit," Frank Chalmers, Director NSA.

"Gentlemen."

Lincoln Daniels had just called the meeting to order. The attendees who were sitting nearby noticed that as he broke the seal on the binder in front of him, the DCI's hands were shaking.

"As Director of Central Intelligence of the United States, I feel compelled to inform you that a conspiracy involving one or more components of our strategic nuclear forces is believed to exist—" Daniels paused to clear his throat, it was already dry as a bone. Meanwhile each man looked at his neighbor with apprehension. *Had the DCI just gone mad?* "—each of you will find a summation of what we have found so far spelled out in his binder—"

"Director Daniels!"

"We believe that one or more Americans have been contracted," Daniels continued, ignoring the objection, "who has had previous involvement with one or more of our intelligence agencies."

"Jesus!"

"Director Dan—!"

"I knew he should have never left that maniac in power," muttered Praeger, openly embarrassing Vice President Gore.

"Silence! Gentlemen! Silence! There's no time for interruptions!" McDowell, the National Security Advisor, shouted.

Lincoln Daniels took a deep breath, glanced at the Vice President, then sighed. "None of our intelligence regarding this, this—" Daniels stuttered, not wanting to give the incident a name "—all the evidence we have found supports the conclusion that this is much more than just a terrorist operation—"

☆ ☆ ☆

Outside Room 208 a pair of Secret Service agents holding Uzi submachine guns stopped David Woodring at the door. Woodring was holding a small CD player in his hand.

"Just a minute, sir."

"Excuse me?" Woodring asked.

"What's that?"

"Classified."

"Sorry, sir. We're gonna have to have a look."

"No way, pal. Call Daniels and tell him David Woodring's outside. Now!"

"Just a minute."

One of the Secret Service agents picked up a handset and murmured something into it.

"O.K. Sorry, sir." The agent stepped aside and let Woodring enter the Situation Room.

The Deputy Director blinked twice when he saw all the faces gathered around the table.

"Thanks, Dave," his superior, FBI Director Myers told him and motioned for Woodring to hand the disk player to Lincoln Daniels.

The telephone in front of Daniels rang, and he picked it up and grunted a response. A second later, two technicians the group hadn't seen before wheeled in a four-foot high metal rack. Without saying anything Daniels set the tape recorder on the table, then left his chair, so that one of the technicians could take his place.

"Who are these guys, if you don't mind my asking, Lincoln?" asked the President's chief of staff.

"They're ours," muttered General Praeger, Director DIA.

"And ours," sighed Frank Chalmers, Director NSA.

The tech in Daniels' chair ignored their conversation and

busied himself typing in several commands on a keyboard. A screenful of diagnostics suddenly illuminated a large 27-inch monitor positioned on the metal rack.

Next, his partner pulled a small gray box from the tray and set it next to the tape recorder and plugged it in its side.

The diagnostics suddenly disappeared and were replaced by the single word, *Ready.* Woodring stood behind the tech in Daniels' seat and addressed the group.

"The telephone conversation you're about to hear was deciphered last week at NSA. The two speakers were detected using a 9,600-bits-per-second, 30-kilohertz-range, spread-spectrum multiplexer telephone which broadcasts direct to satellite. The date of the transmission is January 15, 1993, the day before Dr. Victor Saleh was murdered at his home in California."

Each attendee then turned his head as Woodring passed him a manila envelope, sealed in wax, then pressed the play button on the CD players, activating an artificial simulation of HYDRA's conversation with Sabawi Hussein.

Listening in stunned silence, General Praeger wordlessly tore open the seal on his envelope, while the others followed suit, one by one.

All eyes were riveted on the FBI Assistant Director, who was still speaking. "As you can see from the record of the telephone transcripts before you, neither speaker could be identified since actual voice transmission never occurred. The individual referred to as HYDRA in the text is believed to have obtained his transmitter from the Special Operations Weapons Facility in China Lake. The encryption method used matches that given to an Edwin D. Bailey in the base's files.

"Edwin D. Bailey is a dangerous man—quite capable of carrying out any number of missions Iraqi intelligence may have hired him for. If you haven't done so already, I think if you take a quick look at his resume, you'll agree with me that this individual's received more than enough training to pose a significant threat, if, in fact, he's become involved in a conspiracy related to the death of the late Dr. Saleh."

The room was totally silent except for the occasional rustling of paper; Anyone reading Bailey's resume could see how expert his qualifications were: June, 1972, Bailey enrolls in 4th Airborne Training Battalion, United States Army Infantry Center, Fort Benning, Georgia, then is posted to 3rd Brigade, 82nd Airborne Division. A year later Bailey receives additional training Special Warfare Center, Fort Bragg, then sees duty in Guantanamo Bay, Panama and Honduras, after which he joins 5th Special Forces Group. Returns to Fort Bragg where he specializes in weaponry, operations and intelligence, in addition to taking 25-week-long signals course, after which Bailey becomes a member of the Blue Light Operations Group. Reader should note that Blue Light Operations Group is predecessor organization to Special Forces Group Delta, i.e., Delta Force. Reader is advised to refer to Central Intelligence, Langley, Virginia for list of any further activities.

"Where's Bailey's DO file?" demanded Praeger, holding his copy of Bailey's resume in the air.

Woodring nodded at the tech in Daniels chair, who replaced the disk in the CD player Woodring handed him from his briefcase, turned on the machine and the television monitor suddenly came to life, its screen filled with the same pattern of jagged lines. No transcripts were passed out for the conversations the group was about to hear.

"*FBI! Open up!*"

"*Don't shoot. We're cops!*"

"*Jesus.*"

"*Thank God, you guys ar—*"

"*Shut the fuck up!*"

"He's got the book!"

"Shutup, Bartel!"

"What book?"

"Inspector Rainey, I'm afraid you're going to have to hand over any evidence you may have gathered here today, including this man's appointment book."

"Are you crazy? These men are about to kill Senator Edward Kennedy! This here is the floor plan of his hotel!"

"Inspector, need I remind you that the Senator is in Washington, D.C., at this moment?"

"Bullshit! Mr. FBI, or whoever you really are! We're booking these three right here and right now! And if you have a problem with that, I've got a problem with you, Mister!"

"You can't let these cops—"

"Shut the fuck up!"

Daniels's sonorous voice now filled the darkened room. "The conversation you just heard was recorded by GCHQ in Cheltenham—we just got a copy of it yesterday. It apparently was transmitted accidentally and we wouldn't have even known to look for it, except that we have an eyewitness—"

"Eyewitness to what, Lincoln?" demanded National Security Advisor McDowell.

"What are you saying here?"

"Edwin D. Bailey was attempting to assassinate Senator Edward Kennedy while in the employ of the United States government."

"He what?" cried Vice President Gore.

"Lincoln, what's going on here?" interrupted McDowell.

"So whose side is he working for now?" shouted the chief of staff.

Woodring nodded at the tech at Daniels' side, who doused the lights, which had the immediate effect of quieting the room.

"The film you're about to see was taken when I was Director of the FBI…" Daniels began to explain as the screen was filled with the picture of Chauncey Laudon's house. While the silent movie played, Daniels reiterated the story he'd told Woodring and Hockaday in his office about Laudon's secret band of assassins.

Again the room fell into a stunned silence as each intelligence chief struggled with the implications of Bailey's role as a paid government assassin. If Bailey was indeed HYDRA, any investigation of his whereabouts would have to be managed with kid gloves, given the risk to the government of his involvement in an illegal assassination team run by the CIA.

"This is blackmail! Sheer unadulterated blackmail!" spat out General Praeger after the film had ended.

"That's right, gentlemen," agreed Hubert Myers. "That's exactly what this is. The message here is simple. We go public—he goes public."

"And ruins all of us," grumbled Chalmers.

"Not just us," muttered the chief of staff.

Daniels took back control of the meeting with his next comment. "Before we met, I showed the film you just saw to the President at Camp David. His instructions were explicit: we are expressly forbidden from launching any raids into Iraq—since we have no way of knowing how much the Iraqis actually know about Bailey's past, we also obviously have no way to predict what Saddam's reactions would be after an attack. Obviously the President doesn't want to risk the almost certain chaos that would result if Hussein chose to make this thing public.

"I also believe everyone in the room has seen a copy of NSDD 208 and is familiar with its contents, and after speaking with the President, he and I and Hubert all agreed that

Assistant Director Woodring continue to run the investigation until Bailey is located and apprehended. NSDD 208 grants Mr. David Woodring full power to use whatever resources of the United States government to track Bailey down," here Daniels paused, "and let me emphasize to you, gentlemen, that, in this case, the rules of engagement are unlimited."

All eyes returned to the Assistant Director, their new temporary superior. Woodring was the youngest man amongst them, but there was no doubt in anyone's mind what his fate would be if he failed to find HYDRA. Also, the last thing any of them wanted was to be charged with the task of investigating the remnants of Laudon's band of assassins, an investigation which had previously proven to be a fatal endeavor for those who had had the misfortune to be assigned it.

Sitting next to Daniels with his hands flat on top of his attache case, Woodring stared straight ahead, avoiding looking at the others. Two HRT watchdogs stood against the wall behind him, increasing his isolation. Nothing in his career could have prepared Woodring for the position he found himself in now—busting up Mafia families and chasing spies could hardly approach being given absolute police power over the whole United States.

Daniels paused a moment and took a drink of water, giving anyone who had a question time to ask it. No one did.

The next meeting was scheduled at the NFIB offices on F Street two nights hence; all were expected to attend except General Ford who had to return to Sunnyvale. Woodring left the room first, followed by his pair of bodyguards. The platoon of Secret Service agents outside the door immediately parted way for them immediately in a mute demonstration of Woodring's new position.

Chapter 28

Fishing boats rocked in the water next to busy crab stalls as Woodring's car limped along the Southwest Freeway in Washington's evening rush hour. Finally, after half an hour of waiting, he took the South Capitol Street exit past the empty Skyline Inn, then turned right, whizzing past the weed-filled junkyards of Anacostia. He skidded to a stop outside the Potomac Electric Power Company plant next to an area criss-crossed by abandoned railroad tracks, shoved open his door and disappeared into the ramshackle building opposite. Inside, he was met by a pair of plainclothesmen, and Woodring barely nodded as all three took the elevator to the eleventh floor.

Thirty special agents, the entire membership of the CI-3 Division, breathlessly awaited Woodring's arrival. They were seated amongst ten rows of metal desks in a room whose only feature was an ancient wall map of the United States showing areas once off-limits to Soviet diplomats. Woodring swept into the room accompanied by several HRT agents who took up positions on its perimeter. He slapped Daniels's compact disk recorder on the nearest table, then spoke without introduction: "The pair of telephone conversations you're about to hear were deciphered two days ago at NSA. Transmission was made on a 9,600-bits-per-second, 30-kilohertz-range, spread-spectrum multiplexer telephone which broadcasts direct to satellite. We know a lot about it, because it was made by us. Only one thousand of them were ever produced, and they were then issued to Special Ops Command at China Lake, and whoever was assigned a box was also assigned his own personal code key. Records at China Lake indicate the key used to encrypt this transmission belonged to a certain Mr. Edwin D. Bailey.

"This intercept was decoded strictly by accident—the only reason the techs at Ft. Meade did it was because whoever was using the box didn't know his broadcast was being

encrypted by an old algorithm, called DES, which dates back
to the seventies. DES's key length is only 56 bits, so it didn't
take Allo Group that long to run all the possibilities.

"One last item—the date of the transmission is January
15, the day before Dr. Victor Saleh was murdered at his home
in California."

Woodring snapped open a battered briefcase, extracting a
set of copies of Bailey's resume, each with an 8½-by 11-inch
enlargement of his original ID photograph attached. After
passing a set to each attendee, he pressed the play button on
the CD recorder.

"*Who's speaking, please?*"

"*HYDRA.*"

"*I'll be brief. You may want to cancel the mission. It's why we
haven't sent the money yet.*"

"*Why? What's happened?*"

"*GERALD's under surveillance.*"

"*When did you find this out?*"

"*Earlier today.*"

"*I'll call you back in ten minutes.*"

Woodring snapped off the CD player, pausing to inform
his audience that the second conversation was recorded ten
minutes after the first on the same night.

"*Who's speaking, please?*"

"*It's HYDRA. If you take care of GERALD, I'm still in.*"

"*Done.*"

The room was totally silent: each special agent was rereading Bailey's resume, already making the connection to Saleh's
death.

"If Dr. Saleh has, in fact, inserted a Trojan Horse into our
command and control system," Woodring spoke, reading his
agents' thoughts, "we believe Bailey's the one who's been

recruited to activate it. Unfortunately, we also found a little problem with Bailey's records. When I cross-checked Edwin D. Bailey's ID number with the Social Security's master disk at China Lake, the Social Security disk said that Edwin D. Bailey of the same number had died at two months old on May 26, 1951. Then, when I checked with Daniels before I got here, I found out CIA had no Edwin D. Bailey in any of its files."

Before anyone could ask a question, Woodring gave them their orders. "Until he is found, I want everyone in this room to drop whatever you're doing and think about nothing else than arresting the man known as Mr. Edwin D. Bailey.

"You can go anywhere you want, interview anyone you want, stay at any hotel you want, detain anyone you want, tap any phone, black bag any house, follow any car, go to any military base—you name it, it's covered in this NSDD." Woodring slapped the directive on the table. "And if you find him, don't, I repeat, don't kill him."

"Why not?" someone asked.

"Because he may not be acting alone," Woodring snapped.

☆ ☆ ☆

After the meeting at CI-3, that morning Woodring returned to the Counterterrorism Center in the Hoover Building and made a routine request to the Pentagon for the records of the 4th Airborne Training Battalion U.S. Army Infantry Center, Fort Benning, Georgia and the records of 3rd Brigade, 82nd Airborne at Fort Bragg. Woodring also made a direct call to the commander of the U.S. Army Special Operations Command at Fort Bragg, requesting records of the 5th Special Forces Group. His third call was to the Commander, Joint Special Operations Command (JSOC) at Pope Air Force Base in Fayetteville, North Carolina. JSOC is a combined services operation whose real purpose is the responsibility for Navy SEAL Team 6 and Special Forces

Detachment Delta (better known as Delta Force), whose predecessor unit was Blue Light, of which Bailey had been a member.

Within twenty-four hours over 2,000 computerized files were transferred by the respondents to the CTC over high-speed satellite data link which Woodring, in turn, parcelled out to the staff of CI-3 on Half Street. For the next ten days a team of twenty special agents worked the phones, setting up appointments for their associates, who, in turn, dispersed throughout the United States and its possessions to interview former members of Bailey's various military units.

Meanwhile, Woodring decided to review the CTC's extensive files on America's Special Operations Forces, rereading a secret briefing paper on them which had been prepared for the FBI's elite Hostage Rescue Team (HRT). The Delta Force, the successor unit to Bailey's Blue Light Group, was itself only a small part of the U.S. military's special operations structure which encompassed four separate commands, totaling over 45,000 men. As a result of the lack of inter-service cooperation in Operation URGENT FURY, the codename for the invasion of Grenada, the Joint Chiefs decided to unify all Army, Navy, and Air Force Special Operation forces seven years later in 1987 under a single entity, the United States Special Operations Command (USSOCOM), headquartering it at Fort McDill, Florida. Under USSOCOM's umbrella are the Army's Special Operations Command, Air Force's Special Operations Command, the Navy's Special Operations Command, and a separate Joint Special Operations Command (JSOC).

USSOCOM's largest force is the Army's Special Operations Command (USA- SOC) based at Fort Bragg, North Carolina. USA-SOC contains a diverse set of units, including the 74th Ranger Regiment, various Special Forces groups (better known as the Green Berets), 160th Army Aviation Regiment, and 96th Civil Affairs Battalion and 4th

Psychological Operations Group. The 75th Ranger Regiment is essentially an elite infantry unit specializing in ambushes, urban warfare and lightning attacks, while the Green Berets and the 160th Aviation Regiment emphasize insertion, extraction, and infiltration behind enemy lines.

The 75th Ranger Regiment is divided into three battalions, the 1st, 2nd, and 3rd, each of which has 606 personnel and is based at a separate location: 1/75 at Hunter Army Airfield, Georgia; 2/75 at Fort Lewis, Washington; and 3/75 at Fort Benning, Georgia. Training begins with a ten-week-long course conducted at the Ranger School, also located at Fort Benning, Georgia, and students are usually U.S. Army officers and NCOs who have already undergone both Army and Air Force training. The Ranger course emphasizes mountaineering, patrolling, navigation, survival, weapons handling, ambushing, recon, and hand-to-hand combat. Before being allowed to join a Ranger unit, graduates from the school must pass an additional three-week Ranger Indoctrination Program, whose initials, RIP, Woodring suspected, were not entirely a coincidence. Emphasis of the Ranger Indoctrination Program is physical stamina and performance with constant monitoring and supervision. Only between fifty and seventy percent of the applicants survive the program. Graduates then spend 52 months with a Ranger Battalion in the field before returning to the Ranger School for final training.

U.S. Army Special Forces, better known as the Green Berets, are essentially the Army's primary counter-insurgency, guerrilla-warfare force. Candidates must possess "secret"-level security clearance to receive training, and volunteers are often typically former Rangers or members of 82nd Airborne. Emphasis of SF training is on the individual, with six basic qualification courses available for each man's occupation specialty. Each Green Beret must choose at least one of the qualification courses in order to graduate. The six specialties include: signals, a 25-week course in radiotele-communications and encryption; medicine, a 39-week course in preventative medicine and minor surgery; engineering, a 25-week course in demolition and construction; weapons, a 25-week course in all types of armaments; operations and intelligence, a 16-week course in intelligence techniques; and detachment officer, a required 19-week course for all future SF officers.

USA-SOC trains its special forces with every imaginable type of weapon, sight, optics, communications gear, and vehicle which the Army has in its arsenal, essentially sparing nothing in the education of its troops. Special Forces' weapons training also includes the use of other nations' armaments, in case American weapons aren't available in a battle situation. Thus, SF commandos become expert with not only the standard-issue M6A2 assault rifle, but also the Russian AK-47, German G3 assault rifle, Israeli Uzi and the German Heckler & Koch MP5-SD2 submachine gun. Night operations are enhanced by the use of AN/PVS-7A night-vision goggles, AN/PAQ-4 laser aiming lights and AN-TAS-6 thermal acquisition sights.

Navy Special Operations Command operates the Navy SEALs (Sea-Air-Land units) which were established in 1962 from a predecessor unit, the Underwater Demolition Teams (UDTs). Trained like the Green Berets to operate in groups of approximately a dozen men, the SEALs' primary mission is also infiltration behind enemy lines. Required courses, lasting up to two years, include a twenty-five-week-long marathon course, blandly entitled the Basic Underwater Demolition/SEAL, whose rigor is unmatched in the American military. Basic UDT training begins at Coronado Naval Amphibious Base, California. Emphasis is put on physical conditioning, field exercises, boat handling, land-warfare tactics, hydrographic reconnaissance, weapons handling, demolitions and communications. Trainees are driven to learn to operate for days on end with a minimum of sleep, while performing exercises like carrying 300-pound boats on long beach runs.

The fifty percent of the class who normally graduate go on to Fort Benning, Georgia, for a three-week course in basic static-line parachuting. After that, students return to Naval Amphibious School at Coronado where they are instructed in how to operate small, battery-powered, open submersible swimmer delivery vehicles (SDVs), an underwater version of a motorcycle. After ten weeks of SDV training, students are taught explosives handling and neutralization, and use of biological and chemical munitions in a thirty-three-week-long explosive ordnance disposal (EOD) course which takes place at either Huntsville, Alabama or Indian Head, Maryland.

Like the Army, the Navy showers its special forces units with a wide variety of specialized equipment. Weapons used include the CAR-15 assault rifle, the Stoner M63A1 light machine gun, in addition to the more traditional Heckler & Koch MP5, McMillan 7.62mm M86 sniper rifle, and the older but highly accurate M-14. Besides the SDVs, SEALs are also trained to operate seven-man inflatable boats, open-and closed-scuba systems, hand-held sonar and other underwater communications devices.

Air Force Special Operations Command's mission is to transport the men and equipment of the first two groups to their battle sites. Long-range transport is provided by the fixed-wing propeller-driven MC-130H Combat Talon II. On short-range hauls or where vertical landing's required, the 42,000-pound MH-53J Pave Low IIIE helicopter is used. Combat support is provided by the AC-130U Spectre gunship, equipped with computerized fire controls to allow its 150mm howitzer and its 25mm and 40mm cannons to saturate specified areas with projectiles.

But what interested Woodring most was the highly secretive Joint Special Operations Command (JSOC) headquartered at Pope Air Force Base which had the responsibility for Special Forces Group Delta, Navy SEAL Team 6, and the "Nightstalkers", a special operations helicopter unit that is part of 106th Aviation. The three units under JSOC's command constitute the U.S. military's prime counterterrorist force. Men chosen to serve in any of the three are culled from the best of the other special forces units, and recruits for each are required to endure additional rigorous retraining to qualify. JSOC, itself, was a bureaucratic stepchild of the Joint Task Force (JTF) organized by Secretary of Defense Harold Brown two days after the spectacular failure in April, 1980 of Operation EAGLE CLAW, the mission to rescue the hostages at the U.S. embassy in Tehran. Now, for the first time, elements of the three services were told to report outside their normal chain of command to a single Army general at Ft. Bragg. JTF's original command structure was drawn up by Colonel Charlie Beckwith and Commander Richard Marcinko, founders and commanders of Delta Force and Navy SEAL Team 6, respectively.

Slow to respond to the terrorist threat and fearful of creating military units with police powers, America's military leadership changed its opinion on the need for counterterrorist units after witnessing events in Europe in the 1970s. In 1977 Colonel Charles "Black Beret" Morrell, Commander 5th Special Forces Group, was instructed by Major General Jack Mackmull, Commander of the John F. Kennedy Special Warfare Center, to create a stopgap unit until Delta Force could be certified for operations. Morrell selected forty men, including Edwin D. Bailey, from the 5th Special Forces Group and codenamed his temporary unit Blue Light. At the same time, Colonel "Chargin' Charlie" Beckwith, a gruff Vietnam SF veteran and commandant of the Special Forces School at Fort Bragg was charged by Army Chief of Staff General Bernard Rogers with the creation of a permanent counterterrorist unit, Special Forces Detachment Delta. Fearful that Morrell's temporary unit would derail Delta's formation, Rogers lent his full weight to the project and backed Beckwith to the hilt. As a result Delta was certified for operations on November 4, 1979.

Delta Force recruits are usually senior non-commissioned officers (NCOs) drawn from Active Army, Army Reserve, or Army National Guard units. Training sessions are held only twice a year and are for 100 candidates each, each of whom must have passed stringent background security investigation, been screened for psychological abnormalities, and taken thorough physical and eye examinations. After passing the next stage of intensive physical testing, which includes an 18-mile-long speed march and a 40-mile land navigation exercise complete with 55-pound rucksack, the few remaining volunteers are sent to Fort Bragg to the high-security Special Operations Training Facility. A 19-week course reviews skills learned in former special forces units, plus teaches evasive and aggressive driving, how to manage hostage situations, lock picking, car theft, and weapons improvisation.

Realizing that for it to be effective, the Joint Task Force would have to possess the capability to target maritime objectives, Navy action officer and former SEAL Richard Marcinko recommended to William Crowe, who was then deputy chief of naval operations, the formation of a separate SEAL Command, which Marcinko thereinafter referred to as Navy SEAL Team 6. (Confusingly at that time there were only two other SEAL teams in existence, Team 1 and Team 2, six of whose platoons had already received CT training; ergo, the number 6). Marcinko was given his command and went to work designing a special training cycle for volunteers to his unit, almost all of whom were picked from SEAL Teams 1 and 2 and therefore were already graduates of the BUD/S course at Coronado, the airborne course at Fort Benning, and the EOD course taught at Huntsville and Indian Head. Marcinko's recruits were divided into two teams of three platoons each, then ordered to undergo a nonstop schedule of shooting, jumping, diving and CT hostage-rescue exercises. The Navy's budget for SEAL Team

6 was even more liberal than for the other two teams combined, with Marcinko's men receiving more ammunition than that issued by the Navy for the entire Marine Corps. Equipment included rustproof stainless steel Smith & Wesson .357 revolvers, all-weather camouflage suits, Gore-Tex camouflage parkas, British-made reverse-weave nylon lines for fast roping, plus a pair of customized armored Mercedes 500-series sedans and four Mercedes jeeps for use in European operations.

The Navy's Office of Security and Coordination had also instructed SEAL Team 6 to create "black hat" units to perform terrorism awareness exercises at U.S. Navy bases both in the U.S. and abroad. One such unit, known as the "Red Cell" according to an unattached report, tested how base personnel would respond to a terrorist threat by "penetrating base outer perimeters by climbing fencelines at day or night, using false ID at gates, commandeering gates, or running them. Terrorist tactics enacted on bases included the bombing of personnel, support assets, and critical strategic assets, and the taking of hostages and barricading within facilities on base." The report concluded: "Navy antiterrorism specialists demonstrated the vulnerability of installations to terrorist tactics at fourteen U.S. Navy bases." A dense footnote at the end of the briefing paper mentioned an Army Intelligence division called Intelligence Support Activity, or ISA. Woodring was astonished to find that ISA had 283 agents in over a score of offices and was designed to support both Delta Force and SEAL Team 6 in their intelligence gathering needs, filling in the gaps for CIA.

He skimmed over the history of JSOC's third component, the 160th Special Operations Aviation Regiment (SOAR), also called the Night Stalkers. Headquartered at Fort Campbell, Kentucky, the regiment was equipped with the latest in special ops aviation equipment, including the AH & MH-6 Little Bird helicopters. SOAR had recently distinguished itself in operations against Iran in 1987-88,

Operation Just Cause in Panama, and, finally in Desert Storm.

The final section, which was also separately classified as "compartmentalized top secret", wasn't devoted to a military unit at all, but was a short exegesis on the Department of Energy's little known Nuclear Emergency Search Team (NEST). NEST is headquartered in Germantown, Maryland, but most of its equipment is based at offsite locations, including Nellis AFB, Nevada. NEST's task is to protect America's nuclear facilities and storage areas and to recover any nuclear material stolen by criminals or terrorists, or to otherwise counter any threat of nuclear terrorism. Created by President Ford during his administration, the unit was so secret Congress didn't learn of its existence until three years later. In case of a nuclear emergency the Nuclear Emergency Search Team has its own fleet of special aircraft, ground vehicles, and radiation detection equipment at its disposal. The unit's rules of engagement are essentially totally unlimited. *But HYDRA isn't going to steal a bomb,* Woodring *thought, he doesn't have to.*

Now exhausted, Woodring absentmindedly leafed through the briefing paper's extensive bibliography. Endless government documents were cited: congressional reports, training manuals, mission statements, personnel evaluations, CTC profiles of foreign terrorists, basing requirements, and finally reports by various military investigative units, like the Army's CID and the Navy's NIS. He blinked; he didn't remember reading anything in the report which covered illegal improprieties. Flipping backwards in the text, he found mention of a separate document in an obscure footnote, entitled the Criminal Investigations Annex. Apparently, USSOCOM hadn't bothered to include it in its report to the HRT. Woodring grabbed his telephone, placed a direct call to the Special Classified Intelligence Group on the second floor of the Pentagon, and asked to speak to General Ronald Finley.

☆ ☆ ☆

Thirty minutes later the CTC computer operator notified Woodring he had received a transmission from the Pentagon which was over 2,500 pages long and would take twenty minutes to print out. Woodring redialed General Finley, asking him if he'd sent the correct file. Finley told him to read the summary introduction, pages one to seventy-five, then he'd understand. Woodring sighed, picked up his telephone again and instructed the computer operator to temporarily halt the mammoth printout and bring him the first seventy-five pages. Two minutes later the summary introduction to the Criminal Investigations Annex lay on Woodring's desk.

After taking a quick glance at its contents, Woodring was surprised to find that all three of the elite CT units, the Delta Force, SEAL Team 6 and ISA, had each been the subject of a corruption probe. Department of Defense investigators had uncovered various instances in each unit of financial irregularities, lax discipline, and failed operations that sometimes even resulted in litigation: ISA Lieutenant Colonel Dryden, convicted in 1985 for fraud involving $90,000 in missing funds...security director of Naval Weapons Station, Seal Beach, California, kidnapped, beaten, stripped of his clothes by seven members of SEAL Team 6's Red Cell unit, sustains serious injuries, then sues...eighty-five members of Delta Force convicted filing false travel vouchers in Beirut...finally the founder of SEAL Team 6, Commander Richard Marcinko himself, was convicted for conspiracy and sentenced to twenty-one months at Petersburg. On the other hand there was never any mention of Bailey's old unit, Blue Light.

While Woodring was rechecking the annex's table of contents, the computer room called again. The full 2,500-page-long printout was ready. After the six-inch-thick document was dropped on his desk, Woodring carefully lifted it up by the bottom, extracting the last twenty pages. Quickly checking the index he found no reference to the name Edwin D. Bailey.

Woodring leaned back in his chair as far as possible, clasping his hands behind his head and yawned, then flipped forward and grabbed the telephone, dialing the extension of Charlie Thompson, CTC's computer programmer.

"Chuck, can you come in here a second?"

There was a brief knock on the door and Woodring told Thompson to come in and sit down. The analyst was in his late twenties, had big eyes and a friendly disposition.

Woodring spoke slowly and calmly, "I want you to take this file and extract every name in it—" Woodring caught the look of concern on the programmer's face, and immediately qualified his request. "—I want only the file names, you understand, there's only about two hundred." Thompson grinned a bit. "Cross-file each subject with his social security number, then check the operational file and look for any cover names and ID and cross-file those. We may not have the ops files on a lot of these, so you'll have to make me a list of what you need and I'll wire Finley to get them."

"Yes, sir."

After Thompson left, Woodring returned to the next section of the executive summary of the investigations annex which was was entitled *Psychological Profile—CT Operations Forces.* "Army and Navy staff psychiatrists have found most CT operations forces to possess the following common characteristics: nonconformist, physically aggressive, outwardly tranquil, risk-prone. It should be noted by the reader that these same characteristics also fit the profile of the average criminal. Therefore, it should not have come as a great surprise to either JSOC or USSOCOM that a certain minority of applicants were discovered to have indulged in criminal acts."

ASSESSMENT OF COMPUTER ATTACK
ON WWMCCS INFORMATION SYSTEM

PARTS I & II

Chapter 29

That same morning HYDRA arose early in his apartment on East 62nd Street; he needed as much time as possible to prepare for his departure. After taking a shower and rinsing himself off with cold water, and still only wearing a towel, HYDRA pulled the vinyl clothing bags and the hatbox from his closet and laid them on his bed. He put on his clothes, dressing in a casual sports jacket and slacks, then slipped the large wallet from the bottom drawer of the nightstand in his bedroom. He took it to the kitchen, setting it on the table and unfolded it with the palm of his hand. He methodically extracted every piece of ID, arranging them in three separate rows, representing Matthews, Gereke, and Koester. Taking his own wallet out of his back pocket, HYDRA replaced his own ID with that of Matthews's, then put his regular wallet back in his pants pocket and the large one in his inside jacket pocket.

He found the croissant he had purchased the day before at the next-door bistro and ate it with a simple glass of orange juice. Checking inside his refrigerator, HYDRA took out a carton of eggs, a jug of milk, three oranges, and several bananas, pouring the milk down the sink and putting the fruit and eggs in a trash sack which he left by the door. The last thing he needed during his absence was to upset the landlord with the smell of rotting food.

Returning to the bedroom, HYDRA pulled a large suitcase from under the bed and opened it next to the pair of vinyl fabric sacks. He first unzipped the bag containing Gereke's uniform and coveralls and took them out, then neatly folded them in two, setting them each on top of the bag. Pulling up the cloth along the perimeter of the right side of the suitcase, HYDRA found the zipper underneath and pulled it 360°, releasing the suitcase's false bottom. He stuffed Gereke's outfits in the space, then pressed the bottom firmly into place and zipped it shut. Koester's uniform was next, which he simply packed in the regular part of the suitcase on top of Gereke's.

Finally, he opened the hatbox, lifting out the hat which was still lodged inside its cardboard protector and set it inside the left half of his suitcase, surrounding it with socks and underwear. In his bathroom he turned off the water to his sink and toilet, then grabbed the suitcase, pausing a moment as he passed the kitchen to reexamine the refrigerator and the freezer. With his other hand he scooped up the sack of fruit before he left, then double-locked the door behind him.

Outside he walked to Park Avenue where he caught a taxi in front of the Regency Hotel.

"La Guardia Airport," he told the driver.

Upon his arrival at National Airport in Washington, D.C. a little over an hour later, HYDRA fetched his bag and entered a stall in the nearest men's room, replacing Russell Matthews's ID with that of Peter Koester's. At the United Airlines ticket counter he picked up Koester's prepaid ticket for Flight No. 95 which was scheduled to arrive at SeaTac International Airport in Seattle at 7:25 p.m. local time.

Chapter 30

The McDonnell Douglas DC-10 carrying the passengers on United Airlines Flight 95 arrived at Sea-Tac twenty minutes late due to a rainstorm which had blown in from the southwest, the direction of the area's prevailing storm winds. Occasionally, as it had happened on the evening of HYDRA's arrival, low level winds coming off the ocean split in two at the tip of the Olympic Peninsula; one portion rushing south around the Olympic Mountains, and the other blowing north through the Juan de Fuca Straight. Both fronts had converged in the Puget Sound, causing a violent thunderstorm to ensue. As he waited for his luggage on the airport's ground floor, HYDRA watched the sheets of rain pound against the floor-to-ceiling glass panels, illuminated by occasional lightning flashes. He cursed his luck; he hadn't planned on bad weather, but he feared that arriving a day late at Bangor SUBASE would risk raising some eyebrows. He had booked himself a room at the Nendels Suites hotel in Bremerton and planned to catch the ferry, but due to the weather HYDRA decided to change his plans to drive the whole distance, circling Puget Sound via Interstate 5.

Using Sergeant Peter Koester's ID, HYDRA presented himself at the Thrifty Car Rental counter, a different rental agency than he'd used on his previous visit, and rented a Chevy Lumina , telling the agent he'd only need it for one night. Thrifty's lot was outside the airport off the South Pacific Highway so HYDRA waited for the shuttle on the curb, which, even though it was covered, was being swept by rain-soaked gales. When the shuttle arrived, HYDRA threw his luggage in the trunk, then clambered aboard, the only passenger. The van's wipers vainly fought against the wind as the driver maneuvered it through a sea dotted by the airport's lights, blinking on and off in the storm.

Once they arrived inside the rental building, HYDRA handed Koester's papers to the agent on duty, who told him that a Thrifty employee could go out into the lot and fetch his car for him. While he was waiting in the office, HYDRA took a local map and reviewed the route to Bremerton. Essentially, he would be circling south and westwards around Puget Sound, crossing the Narrows Bridge at Tacoma to reach the Kitsap Peninsula where the base was located. A flash of lightning lit up the room, immediately followed by a thunderclap as the Chevy Lumina materialized through the glass. A carhop in a yellow slicker and matching hat popped out the door and ran around it, opening the trunk.

HYDRA threw his luggage in the trunk and took the wheel. Visibility was at most thirty feet, but since the highway was deserted HYDRA quickly found his way to the interstate without any problems. On I-5 cars headlights came in and out of focus as they rushed past, leaving a spray in their wake. As he neared Tacoma the storm's intensity increased and several drivers had already pulled over to the curb and stopped. Rain pounded on his windshield, and the only thing HYDRA could see in the rearview mirror were his own eyes staring back at him.

He sucked in his breath and rechecked the speedometer. His speed had dropped to twenty-five miles per hour. The Lumina was one of the last vehicles still traveling on the interstate. HYDRA could barely read the exit sign at Fife and reminded himself there were only three more between him and 132. Downtown Tacoma was deserted, with traffic lights blinking on and off on empty streets. A mile later HYDRA found Exit 132, Bantz Boulevard-Highway 16, and followed Highway 16 north up the Peninsula. At Port Orchard, where Highways 16 and 3 converged, lightning flashed across the sound, illuminating the turbulence of the waves. He passed through Navy Yard City on 3, carefully watching for the turnoff to Kitsap Way.

The town of Bremerton, where he'd booked a room under the name of Sergeant Peter Koester, lay halfway between Tacoma and Bangor SUBASE on the Kitsap Peninsula directly west of Seattle across the sound. Bremerton was also the site of the Puget Sound Naval Shipyard, a 680-acre Navy overhaul and repair base. In the downpour HYDRA barely found the sign; taking the exit at the last moment, he looped around it, proceeding east parallel to Oyster Bay.

Squinting in the gloom, HYDRA saw the red-and-white sign for his motel, Nendels Suites, and pulled into the lot under a covered awning. The rain was still so intense it was almost impossible to make out the other three buildings where the rest of the rooms were. Hanging plants flew violently back and forth, while the drive was littered with overturned potted trees. A lone girl was behind the desk, lit only by a fluorescent light.

HYDRA shoved open the car door, and trying to avoid being doused by a gust of wind, he ran around the Lumina and yanked open the lobby door.

"How ya' doin'?"

"I'm wet," HYDRA told the desk clerk, smiling involuntarily at the combination of red lipstick, nail polish and excessive hair.

"Me, too."

HYDRA stared at her blouse, made transparent by the rain, revealing a pair of full breasts trapped inside a lace brassiere.

"Let me guess?" the clerk teased him, looking at his coveralls, "you're in the Navy."

HYDRA said nothing, only grinning in response. The girl's hardened nipples showed clearly behind her blouse and she had a full mouth and a look she learned from fashion photographs.

"Sergeant Koester?" she asked, mispronouncing the name, so that it rhymed with "firster." "Sergeant Peter Koester from Washington, D.C.?"

"Kester," HYDRA corrected her.

"Oh, sorry. We've got your room ready if you can get to it. It's in Building Two."

Chapter 31

By early Monday morning virtually every agent in the Washington, D.C. CI-3 field office had already departed for one of the capital's civilian or military airports to begin the search for Edwin D. Bailey. Pairs of agents simultaneously boarded civilian flights at Washington National, Dulles, Berwyn Heights and Baltimore-Washington International airports, while their associates boarded chartered MATS transports at Andrews AFB, Fort Belvoir Military Reservation, Bolling AFB, and Fort George G. Meade. In addition, two teams were given specific orders to fly directly to New York and Los Angeles to parcel out to the counterintelligence units their files relevant to their respective geographical areas. At the same time, Woodring dispatched seven separate teams of Justice Department lawyers, giving each team orders to visit the headquarters of each of the regional Bell telephone companies and inform its top executive of the existence of a FEMA warrant granting the FBI unlimited powers to tap any line it so chose.

Leaving nothing to chance, Woodring had instructed his men to install a wiretap on the home and office telephones of every interviewee prior to his interview. Due to the expected volume of intercepted material, all lines scheduled to be wiretapped were doubled up and rerouted to Fort George G. Meade, where employees of the National Security Agency would immediately begin to sort and transcribe every conversation until Bailey was found. Meanwhile, Harry Volz and Police Inspector Lindsay were moved to an undisclosed FBI safe house located in the suburbs of the capital which was guarded day and night by a select team of HRT agents.

Woodring had quickly decided that the first interviews would be Bailey's former commanders at Fort Benning and Fort Bragg. On the other hand, he doubted that the instructor in charge of Bailey's company in the 4th Airborne Training Battalion at Fort Benning would remember much, since each of the "Black Hats" in charge of 4th Battalion's four separate companies was responsible for training over 5,000 men per year. Likewise, Woodring didn't expect to hear anything significant from the commander of the 3rd Brigade, 82nd Airborne Division whose normal strength was approximately 3,000 men, or from his instructors at the Special Warfare Center, who were responsible for training not only potential candidates for the Special Forces, but members of all the U.S. armed forces in addition to selected civilians from other government departments. But quite a different situation would apply to Colonel Chuck Morrell, Commander, 5th Special Forces Group. Even though the 5th Special Forces Group included three battalions, a headquarters element and support organizations amounting to over a thousand people, Morrell had handpicked the members of Bailey's Blue Light unit himself, originally limiting strength to only forty men.

Woodring had scheduled initial interviews with the commanders of the 4th Airborne Training Battalion, instructors of the Special Warfare Center, the colonel in charge of the 3rd Brigade, 82nd Airborne, and Colonel Morrell at 5th Special Forces Group at approximately the same time to prevent one from tipping off any of the others, in case one or more of them might have any knowledge of Bailey's unusual affliction.

Chapter 32

Even though he had been alerted that Woodring had located Bailey's file at China Lake, Ken Czarlinsky, chief of the TCOM Group at Ft. Meade, continued to analyze the HYDRA tape, desperately looking for some anomaly which would tell him more about its origins. On the same Monday morning Woodring's agents were flying out of Washington on both civilian and MATS jets, Czarlinsky told his wife, who hadn't seen him all weekend, that he was still at the office. Czarlinsky then called F. Jackson Tice, who also had been working late that weekend, and invited Tice to share a cup of coffee.

"Square root of seven," sighed Czarlinsky, leaning back in his chair.

"I dare say," F. Jackson Tice replied, not knowing at all what the department chief had meant. Tice's forte was languages, not random number generation.

"It's good equipment, I can say that much."

"That's good to know since it's ours."

"DOE designed its boxes to key off an irrational number — insured that they'd have steady supply of truly random digits."

"I see."

"The ones with the new codes are impossible to crack — we

don't waste much time on actual decryption, but we got lucky on this one."

"Thank God," Tice agreed and stroked his moustache thoughtfully, hoping Czarlinsky wouldn't ask him a technical question.

"Usually we look for just signatures — RF, digital, anything we can find."

Tice nodded slightly to indicate his continued attentions, even though he had no idea what Czarlinsky meant.

"With the quality of reception we've got here, we can amplify any signal, literally pull it apart, then find the anomalies in it, you know, the glitches even a manufacturer doesn't know are there."

"Glitches. Right, Ken."

"Once we find an anomaly, then the sender has a signature. That's what we look for, the glitch, the bad part that produces its own special static."

Tice suddenly understood — once TCOM had found an anomaly in the sender's transmission, it could identify that sender over and over again, making it easier to locate him.

"Also, since HYDRA's not operating over an ILC, he didn't have to slow his message down to 9,600 bps and cram it into a 3,000-kilocycle range for voice like a telephone."

"Oh, indeed."

"I wish we had more on disk, though."

"Too short?"

"Too short? It's like a hiccup," Czarlinsky muttered, absent-mindedly staring at the knobs and disks on his console.

Chapter 33

Early the next morning HYDRA awoke at 6:30 a.m., showered and shaved, then opened his suitcase, pulling out Sergeant

Koester's coveralls and regular boots. He slipped on the boots and coveralls, checking his appearance in the bathroom mirror one last time before he left his room to have an early breakfast. Several other visitors dressed in Navy uniforms were already seated in the dining room, having begun their day early in order to be able to report to base by 7:30 a.m., the usual time. No one paid much attention when a blond-headed man wearing coveralls entered the room and found himself an empty table near the front.

The waitress who came to HYDRA's table was the same girl who had been at the reception desk the previous night. She grinned at the handsome stranger, knowing he hadn't expected to see her again so soon.

"Good morning, Lieutenant. Did you sleep alright?"

"No problem, and you?"

"I slept all right."

Her uniform was stretched tightly across her chest, revealing her ample figure. Like the night before she was wearing red lipstick and nail polish, but this morning, HYDRA noticed, her hair seemed to have more body, falling across her shoulders and down her back.

"Is this your first visit? I haven't seen you here before."

"No. I've never been to Washington."

"Where'd you come from?"

"From D.C."

"I went there once — with my parents. I had a good time."

HYDRA said nothing.

"Oh, I guess you want to order. You know what you want?"

"Two eggs sunny side up and bacon with some coffee and orange juice. Make the coffee black."

The waitress took his order, turning a few heads as she returned to the kitchen. HYDRA resumed reading the Seattle *Times*, when a small headline at the bottom of the first page caught his attention. *Protestors expected at Bangor SUBASE for arrival of* USS Eisenhower. While base security would understandably be heightened, HYDRA guessed the presence of the protestors would have the unintended effect of creating a greater feeling of sympathy on the part of base security for arriving visitors dressed in uniform. If he were lucky an "us against them" mentality would prevail, making his task all the easier. If he were lucky.

"Breakfast's here."

HYDRA folded up his newspaper as the waitress served him his food. As she set down his plate her hair brushed his face and her breast was only a few inches from his mouth.

"Are you coming back tonight?" the waitress asked.

HYDRA looked up from his plate into her eyes. Sergeant Koester was going to have a little fun while he was in Bremerton.

"Yeah, I'll be back. Why?"

"Well, I thought you being new to the area and all you might want someone to show you around."

"You're not working tonight?"

"No. Tonight's my night off. But I can meet you here if you want."

"Meet me at my room at seven."

The waitress would have preferred the lobby, but something in Koester's manner made her suddenly go along with him. She smiled slightly, then left his table.

After the waitress left, HYDRA quickly finished his breakfast and returned to his room, where he unpacked the HP-100LX palmtop and the spectrum analyzer from his suitcase, carried them to the car and put them in the trunk. Pulling out of the hotel drive, HYDRA followed Kitsap Way along the bay, taking State Highway 3 north to the town of Silverdale on the opposite end of Dyes Inlet. Five miles north of Silverdale HYDRA found the Bangor Exit on the right and followed it across the highway. On Trident Boulevard a few protestors had already arrived, scattered in several small clumps each dedicated to a different sign. HYDRA saw one placard decorated with the outline of a mushroom cloud behind a large "X" and smiled to himself. In just a few more days the anti-nuclear lobby would achieve quite a different status in the public's mind. Just outside the main gate HYDRA turned right and pulled to a stop in front of the Pass and ID Building, where he presented Sergeant Koester's papers to the civilian security guard on duty.

"Many protestors out there yet?"

"A few," HYDRA replied.

"They come here every year about this time. Must be the weather — there's nothing else for them to do."

The guard brought up the TDY roster on his computer, then checked Koester's order number against the base's, and, finding a match, issued HYDRA a temporary pass. Noticing Koester was crypto-cleared, the guard decided to let HYDRA choose how he wanted to check in. "You want to talk to the duty officer or call communications commander yourself?"

"It's my first visit. I'd better call my command."

"Suit yourself. Strategic Weapons is 4525. Phone's over there. Just dial the extension number to get through."

"Thanks." HYDRA walked to the telephone, picked up the handset and dialed the four-number extension.

"Strategic Weapons, Sergeant Robinson."

Chapter 34

The next morning at Ft. Meade, F. Jackson Tice received a second call from the chief of TCOM Group, Ken Czarlinsky. Czarlinsky refused to divulge his purpose over the telephone for requesting that Tice come down to his office immediately.

"Watch this, Mr. Tice."

Tice watched the CRT screen of a nearby spectrum analyzer as Ken Czarlinsky replayed the HYDRA fragment.

A jumble of luminescent spaghetti performed a meaningless dance before his eyes.

"Fascinating, Ken, umm."

"Exactly, Jackson. It's so obvious I can't believe I missed it"

"It is?"

"Look at that screen and tell me what you see!"

Czarlinsky pressed the button and the dancing lines on the spectrum analyzer suddenly froze in position.

F. Jackson Tice tugged thoughtfully at his moustache, issuing only a knowing murmur.

"Look at that! Clear as a bell! They're not a fast Fourier transform at all — he's got himself a new set of chips!"

"Not Fourier?" asked Tice, now totally perplexed. "Why not?"

"He almost outwitted us,"

"How?" Tice asked, capitulating.

"Oh. Sorry, Jackson," Czarlinsky apologized, turning away from the screen. "Look, everything these days that involves conversion of analog to digital and back again uses the same technology in its chips called the fast Fourier transform, taken from the nineteenth century mathematician — " Czarlinsky tapped on the CRT screen with his finger. "Fourier realized that complex waves, no matter how messy, are actually combinations of hundreds of perfect waves — these regular waves are like the building blocks, and the Fourier transform puts them all together!"

"So it's nothing more than a formula?" ventured Tice.

"Exactly. But, as my screen shows here, HYDRA's not using FFT at all."

"But how does he go from analog to digital then?" asked Tice, feeling like a genius for getting this far.

"I would have never seen it, if it hadn't been for Dr. Roy."

"The Indian from Bell Labs?"

"You know him?"

"Well, I've met him a couple of times with Glen, he's really not in my field — "

"I would have never realized."

"Thank God."

"Wavelets. Just like those chips that Dr. Roy showed to us."

"Wavelets?"

"From that company in Cambridge. Roy's always into the soft aspects of the problem — it's unbelievable what he did with that call-routing formula."

Tice vaguely remembered that the famed Dr. Roy of Bell Labs had singlehandedly rewritten the 125-page-long formula which governed how all AT&T's long distance telephone calls were switched, cutting the cost to Ma Bell of switching every call in the United States 15 per cent without so much as adding a bolt in additional hardware.

"The Fourier transform is the exact same thing — twentieth-century hardware and nineteenth-century software!"

F. Jackson Tice took a second look at the frozen image on the CRT screen, trying to divine the meaning of the waves.

"So Dr. Roy's developed a new formula for digital conversion, too?" asked Tice.

"It's always the Indians. Why is that?"

"What, you mean in mathematics?"

"Inside the old conversion chips everything but the math was up to date! Every CD player, modem, telcom, its most important chip was working on an ancient formula from the 1800s — no one gave it a second thought."

"Amazing."

"It's right on the screen!" Czarlinsky emphasized tapping the glass screen. "Instead of recording every change, each variation like FFT, wavelets just look at enough changes to recreate the image. Don't you see? It's an entirely more efficient formula!"

"So how old are they?"

"HYDRA's chips?"

"Yes, when were they made?"

"They're experimental, they're not even being manufactured yet."

"But — "

"But don't you get it? HYDRA isn't Bailey — Bailey would have never retrofitted his box with these chips and not changed his codes."

The two sentries stationed in the glass booth outside the Defense and Missile Special Aeronautics building raised their eyebrows as Professor Glen Hockaday raced down the steps two at a time, then suddenly stopped, and desperately fumbled in his coat pocket for his car keys. A second later his old Buick roared down Savage Road, quickly disappearing over the first hill.

When he reached the gatehouse at Building No. 4, Hockaday tossed his holographic pass at the startled bluejackets inside, rushing into the reception room. There he was met by Tice who led him directly to Czarlinsky's office.

Hockaday summoned up enough energy to shake Czarlinsky's hand, then found the nearest chair.

"Jackson just told me you've found something."

Chapter 35

HYDRA only had to wait ten minutes at the Pass and ID

Building before Sergeant Pat Holt, the officer on duty at the Strategic Weapons Facility, came to pick him up. Holt, a Marine in his early twenties, knew enough to handle any visitor from the Naval Investigative Service with kid gloves, since the NIS had authority to investigate anything it wanted to on the base.

"Sergeant Koester? Sergeant Pat Holt at your service."

HYDRA returned Holt's firm grip and smiled politely, saying nothing.

"Your first time here?"

"That's right."

"If you give me your papers, I'll take care of security, if that's OK?"

"Great," HYDRA said and handed the Marine his papers. Holt nodded at his shoulder bags and the two suitcases on the floor.

"You want me to take your equipment and put it in the car?"

"Thanks."

Holt grabbed all the bags under one arm in bellhop fashion, lugging them outside to a faded olive-drab Chevy station wagon, and shoved them in the rear. HYDRA let himself in the passenger door and waited.

"See any protestors?" Holt asked, after he got in the car.

"Just a few scattered around."

"Colonel says more of them'll show up by this afternoon. With the Cold War over you'd think they'd find something else to bitch about."

"Some people never give up."

"I guess so."

Holt stopped at the second security gate and handed his and HYDRA's passes to the civilian security guard, who looked

HYDRA up on his computer, then waved them through. Instead of circling the base as the van had done on the tour, Holt turned off Trident Road onto Trigger Avenue, stopping at the operational area gate, handing their passes for the second time to another civilian guard. Directly ahead were two manned guard towers connected by a double fence topped with barbed wire, which protected the Main Operational Area where the Strategic Weapons Facility was located.

The pair of Marines inside the third guardpost took their time looking over the passes Holt just handed them, then one of them left his hut and peered in the passenger window of the station wagon to double-check the picture on Sergeant Koester's ID with HYDRA's face in the car. Satisfied, he waved them through.

☆ ☆ ☆

At Nendels Suites, Pamela Michaud served her last breakfast customer and was walking out the lobby when the daytime manager, Mr. Howard, shouted her name from behind the front desk.

"Yes?"

"Marcie didn't show up today. I need you here."

Marcie was the alcoholic maid from Silverdale who was always late. Pam was furious. She cleaned rooms all day-she'd be exhausted by the time she was supposed to meet Peter.

"Mr. Howard, please. I can't."

"Pam, I don't really have any choice."

Giving him a look of uncontrolled fury, Pamela stormed off to the tiny employee locker room where she stripped off her waitress outfit, tossed it on the floor, threw open Marcie's locker and yanked out a pair of dark blue slacks and matching blouse. She put them on, grabbing a mop and bucket, then cursed at herself for forgetting the vacuum cleaner and went back and got it. When she returned to the lobby, Pamela slammed the bucket on the floor, spilling some water and startling a customer at the desk.

"What rooms am I supposed to clean?"

Mr. Howard pretended to ignore her. He was still busy with the customer.

"What rooms?" she repeated menacingly.

"Second floor — all of them — can't you see I'm busy?" Howard snapped, throwing a ring of keys in her face.

She was tempted to tell him off and quit right there on the spot, then immediately thought better of it. More than anything, Pamela Michaud wanted out of Bremerton and at the moment was willing to do anything that would speed her departure. It was only when she exited the service elevator that she remembered that Peter was staying in Room 204 down the hall. A smile crossed her face. Sergeant Peter Koester was about to get the cleanest room on the second floor.

Now she looked around — the corridor was deserted, which was good, since she didn't want Peter to discover her wearing Marcie's awful uniform. She stopped at the door to Room 204 and had to insert several keys in the lock before she found the one that fit. After that she dragged the bucket, mop, and vacuum cleaner inside and was already in Peter's room. She felt a curious feeling of relief. Peter was from a big city; from the other side of the country; she would make sure he would fall in love with her and take her away with him. She knew she could compete with any woman on the peninsula, but worried what the girls in Washington were like. Maybe they were all young and just as attractive as she was. Pamela let the mop fall to the floor as she stood in front of the full-length mirror on the closet door. Her reflection looked ridiculous — a girl in thick-soled sneakers and blue pajamas. Impulsively she unbuttoned her blouse, revealing a pair of full breasts straining against a wired-lace bra. She unhooked her brassiere and cupped her breasts in her hand, turning from side to side, admiring their fullness.

Bending over, she slipped off her shoes and pants — she would clean Peter's room wearing only her panties, then tell him about it if things worked out. Pulling the mop and bucket into the bathroom she decided to do the hard part first and clean the bath and tile. Thinking how good it would look that evening, she poured Lysol into the bowl, sprayed and scrubbed it. A toothbrush in a cup and battery-powered Braun shaver on the sink were the only souvenirs Peter had left behind to remind her of his existence. She dropped the scrub brush back in the bucket, telling herself he'd never know if she took a look around, but then she couldn't tell him about cleaning his room with no clothes on. The whole floor was quiet, the guests had departed to the nearby bases, including Sergeant Koester, who most probably wouldn't be back for hours.

Pam walked into the suite and turned on the television to mask the sound of drawers being opened and closed just in case anyone was listening outside the room. A couple of pairs of socks. Underwear. Regulation tee shirts and an airline ticket folder. Pam gingerly picked up the folder and opened it, sucking in her breath when a pair of receipts fell upon the desk. A stub remained in one for Peter Koester's return flight, Sea-Tac to National Airport. The second ticket contained only a receipt made out to R. Matthews for a different flight on USAir from La Guardia to Washington. Pam felt a sinking feeling in her stomach. Who was R. Matthews? A girlfriend of his from New York? She was probably staying in his apartment in Washington, D.C., while he was in Bremerton, waiting for him to come back.

Angrily, Pam methodically opened and shut all the remaining drawers, looking for anything she could find which would further inform her about the identity of R. Matthews. Finding them either empty or containing only hotel property, she slid back the closet door, found HYDRA's suitcase and threw it on the bed. It was an old Hartmann with combination locks. Locks which most people left at their factory setting of 1-1-1. She turned both dials to triple one, then tried the latch. It popped open automatically. If Peter Koester was fucking Roberta Matthews she wanted to know about it before their date that night.

She rifled through the clothing, all folded and neatly arranged in stacks, finding no evidence of letters, pictures or other items lovers normally exchange. While she felt under a pile of shorts, her right hand caught on something sharp which gave her a small cut. Pushing the shirts aside, at first she couldn't find what could have nicked her — the whole interior of the case was lined with light fabric. Curious now, she slowly ran her hand along the inside perimeter when she felt it again. Raising the lining up from the bottom, she found the zipper head and pulled it around all four sides of the suitcase, releasing the double bottom.

☆ ☆ ☆

"TDY said you're headed for the tin can, that true?" Holt asked HYDRA after they'd passed the guardpost.

"That's it."

Marine Sergeant Holt, deciding to avoid further conversation with the crypto-cleared tech from NIS, drove the rest of the way along Tecumseh Street in silence. He stopped in front of a concrete-block code shack surrounded by its own cyclone fence and guarded by two solemn-faced Marines in front. Holt handed HYDRA back his ID and opened up the trunk for him so he could remove his computer and spectrum analyzer. HYDRA grabbed his equipment, then presented his base pass to the Marine on duty.

"Your name, sir?"

"Sergeant Koester."

"Where'd you TDY out of, Sergeant Koester?"

"Washington, NIS."

"Why're you here?"

"TOD, software change, the rest is classified."

"Just a minute." The Marine took HYDRA's papers and entered the code shack, returning a couple of minutes later.

"All right, Sergeant, you can go inside."

☆ ☆ ☆

Sitting half-naked on the hotel bed, Pam held the oversized wallet in her hands and slowly pulled out one piece of ID after another, before returning each to its proper slot. Russell Matthews, New York Driver's License. American Express Card, Lieutenant Jack Gereke. Blockbuster Video, Russell Matthews. Missouri Driver's License, Lieutenant Jack Gereke.

So who was Sergeant Peter Koester?

Her heart racing, she dropped the wallet back into the suitcase's false bottom, and picked up the neatly folded leather holster, discovering it held an almost weightless plastic gun. She unsnapped the leather safety guard, carefully pulling the gun from the holster, turning it over in her hands, then pressed a button and a clip fell out, fully loaded with almost weightless bullets.

☆ ☆ ☆

HYDRA walked inside the communications shed where he was met by a pair of NSA-cleared Navy technicians wearing plain uniforms and holstered sidearms. While he handed one of them his base pass, the other unsnapped the leather safety strap on his holster, leaving his hand on his gun as per regulation.

"Who are you?"

"Sergeant Peter Koester."

"Where'd you TDY from, Koester?"

"Washington, NIS Headquarters."

"What for?"

"Technical Operations Directive — software mod followed

by a TEMPEST check on the laser gun."

"Why weren't we notified about this before?" Both men's unblinking eyes were fixed on HYDRA, impatient for his reply.

"Motorola delivered the chips late. McPhee just got 'em last week, even though he was supposed to have gotten them two months ago. So he wanted me to haul my ass out here asap before he got a call from Ft. Meade."

"Great," sighed the one holding HYDRA's ID and TOD order. "How're Mark's kids doing, anyway? Last time I saw 'em was three years ago."

"Sheila's still at Country Day and Bill's on varsity — Mark says he's a natural athlete."

"He still play golf?" asked the one with his hand on the gun.

"Oh, yeah, he's got the same old four-handicap he's always had — "

"I thought it was five," the other interrupted. HYDRA's face froze. His eyes involuntarily darted to the unholstered gun.

"Jerry, stop fuckin' this guy around, it's his first visit for godsakes."

"Sorry," grinned the second tech. "We get pretty bored in here. Come on back and let's get this over with."

☆ ☆ ☆

Pam put the Glock back in its holster, snapped it shut, wrapping the strap around it as she'd found it and set it next to the large leather wallet and the maps, then zipped the false bottom shut. After that she refolded and repacked the clothes on top of it, closed the suitcase, and turned the combination locks to a random setting hoping Peter hadn't memorized where he'd left them. Next she checked all the dresser drawers, making sure all their contents were in reasonable order and that they were all firmly closed.

She quickly put on her bra and the rest of her uniform and left, then cleaned the remaining rooms on the second floor in record time, before leaving the hotel without saying a word to anyone.

☆ ☆ ☆

While HYDRA was being watched by the man with his hand on the gun, the second Navy cipher clerk had his back to them. Kneeling in front of a floor safe, he was fiddling with the lock. Scattered around them were teletype machines and CRT monitors, whose blank screens were only occasionally disturbed by random blips.

"Here it is."

He handed it to HYDRA with a smile who took the laser gun and set it on the nearest desk. HYDRA unpacked the HP-100LX computer and the DKD-1810 spectrum analyzer from their vinyl cases and plugged the analyzer into the palmtop. Next he plugged the DKD-1810's wand into the analyzer, waved it in the air, and hit a key on his computer.

"Got to see if the sniffer's working."

The Navy code clerk nodded in understanding. He'd been through several TEMPEST checks before. HYDRA silently took the adapter cord Castor had made for him and plugged it first into the HP-100LX, then into the laser gun, an operation the code clerk hadn't seen before, but which didn't surprise him.

"Here goes nothing," HYDRA murmured as he pressed the trigger. The palmtop's LED screen momentarily displayed a pattern filled with dancing waves, then went blank.

HYDRA opened the gun and deftly removed its original chips, then slipped a UV-resistant plastic case from a pocket in his coverall, set it next to the gun and opened it, revealing an identical pair of chips.

"OK, after I put these in, I've got to check them against the first set, but, they're set so I'm not going to zeroize them when I do it, all right?"

The clerk nodded appreciatively, watching HYDRA press the trigger a second time to recording stray emissions with the DKD-1810.

"That's it, we're done."

Chapter 36

The arrival of a Gates Learjet C-21A belonging to the 89th Military Airlift Wing caused barely a stir at Fort Bragg, the base known as the "Home of the Airborne." Its passengers, the four teams of two FBI agents, deplaned without incident, were met by four separate jeeps driven by Army CID officers as requested and driven to their separate destinations. Overhead a squadron of UH-60A Black Hawk helicopters roared past at low altitude, disappearing over the banks of Smith Lake.

At 148,000 acres in size, Fort Bragg is one of the largest military bases in the world and is the home of XVIII Airborne Corps, the 82nd Airborne Division, the "Golden Knights" Army Parachute Team, in addition to the 1st Special Operations Command (SOCOM). Assigned to SOCOM's command were several Special Forces Groups, including the 5th commanded by Colonel Chuck "Black Beret" Morrell.

Neither of the two agents who had been assigned to interview Colonel Morrell had ever been in the military in his life. Joe Kelly was a former street cop from D.C. and his partner, John Barrone, had joined the FBI directly after college. Even though both agents were in their late thirties and highly experienced in the field, they both felt ill at ease in the foreign environment of the Special Forces Camp. They were used to controlling the field, knowing they always had the option of calling for whatever additional support they needed if a situation required it. But today's visit was different. Chuck "Black

Beret" Morrell commanded a force of over one thousand highly-trained men, all of whom were in the immediate vicinity and had been trained to follow the colonel's orders without question.

They came to a halt in front of a nondescript two-story barracks building guarded by two MPs who immediately stepped aside once the two CID agents escorting Kelly and Barrone showed them their ID. The MPs told them Colonel Morrell's office was only twenty feet down the corridor to the right, where a corporal, acting as Morrell's secretary, sat outside behind a metal desk. The corporal had a quizzical look on his face as he was saluted by his unexpected visitors.

"How can I help you, gentlemen?"

"We're here from the FBI. We'd like to speak with the colonel for a moment," replied Agent Kelly calmly.

"Just a minute." Before the corporal could pick up his telephone, one of the Army agents leaned forward and grabbed the handset out of his hands. Colonel Morrell walked through his office door, about to give an order to his aide, when he stopped dead in his tracks. Wearing olive drab jungle fatigues and spit-shined jungle boots, Morrell looked every bit the hard-eyed soldier in his green beret.

"Can I help you, gentlemen?"

"Colonel, we're from the FBI. We'd like to speak to you a second," Kelly repeated. The CID agent released his grip on the corporal's telephone, letting him hang it up.

"What about?"

"Sorry, sir, but it's classified. We'll have to tell you in private."

Morrell looked at his aide, then the pair of CID agents, then Kelly and Barrone.

"All right, come on in. Don, hold all my calls."

Morrell's office was comfortable enough with its carpeting

and wood-paneled walls. The blinds were shuttered, muting the noonday light.

"Make yourselves comfortable," Morrell said, pointing to a couple of armchairs.

Before Kelly sat down he slipped an envelope out of his jacket pocket and handed it to Morrell across his desk.

"Colonel, my instructions are to ask you to read this document before we go any further — " Whatever friendliness remained in Morrell's demeanor vanished as he ripped open the envelope and read the words National Security Decision Directive No. 208 at its top. "... authorizes us to ask you any question concerning any personnel present or former and any of their activities and operations no matter what security classification they may carry. Also, — "

"Enough," the colonel snapped. "Why did you come here?"

Kelly blinked, then opened an attache case, pulling out a legal-length file with Bailey's photo stapled to its cover and set it on the colonel's desk. Morrell took one look at it, refusing to pick it up.

"Where'd you get this?"

"I'm sorry, colonel, but our orders — "

In a violent motion Morrell scooped up Bailey's file, then pulled a pair of reading glasses out of his tunic pocket and put them on. "I haven't seen this man in over a dozen years since he was in Blue Light."

"So you remember him," prompted Kelly.

"Yes, Mr. FBI, I remember Captain Bailey."

"Why?" asked Barrone.

"Why? Because during the whole time I've been in the Army I've only met a handful of men like him, that's why."

"Bailey was exceptional?"

"Exceptional? Captain Bailey was the best we ever had. He practically sailed through the Q Course — and let me tell you, it's a lot tougher than Basic Airborne — His GT scores were top one percent. You read the file, didn't you?"

"Did CIA contact you about him?"

Morrell paused a moment, glaring back at the pair of CI-3 agents across his desk. "You don't know where he is, do you? That's why you're here, isn't it?"

Kelly and Barrone glanced at each other, before Kelly answered. "No. We don't know where he is. We were hoping you could help locate him for us. We want to talk to him."

"One day a man showed up at the Warfare Center. He'd been talking with General Jack, then they sent him over to see me."

"Did he give you his name?"

"He didn't have to, one look at him and I knew where he was from."

"Do you remember his name?" asked Barrone.

"Yeah. I remember it. It was a bad joke. Axe. Keith Axe. Chauncey Laudon's hatchet man."

"Axe?" Kelly gasped. "Are you sure? At the time he was stationed in Mexico City — "

"Where he ran Operation BUNCIN."

"What do you know about that?"

General Morrell picked up the copy of the NSDD, slowly crumpling it into a wad of paper. "Nobody's bothered to tell you, have they? How many men'd the FBI put on this, anyway, fifty, a hundred, more? Pretty funny, coming here in a Learjet to locate a dead man.

"Here, you can take this and stuff it up the ass of whoever wrote it," Morrell snarled, tossing the wad at Kelly, who caught it just before it hit him in the face. "Edwin D. Bailey is dead. You got that. Dead. D-E-A-D. Dead."

"He — "

"He was a good officer. The best. He put it all together and they killed him."

"Good to see you back," the familiar FPS sentry told Woodring at the gatehouse, taking Woodring's ID and sticking it into the confirmation slot.

☆ ☆ ☆

Woodring merely nodded in reply. He hadn't slept for over seventy-two hours. The guard handed him his card, then he sped along Savage Road to Building No. 4, where he slammed to a stop, leapt out of his car, and rushed up the concrete steps to the glass booth at the door, tossing his pass at the sentry inside before jumping into a waiting golf cart. Woodring ordered the driver to take him to the elevator immediately then grabbed the vehicle's built-in telephone and dialed Czarlinsky's office to warn him of his arrival. Exiting the elevator, Woodring grabbed the clipboard offered to him by the second sentry at the hallway's end, barely scrawling his signature on it before he tossed it back at him.

Chapter 37

HYDRA returned to Nendels Suites a little before noon, his trip to Bangor having taken much less time than he expected. He parked outside his room and brought the HP-100LX with him in the off-chance the rental car were stolen and shoved it in his closet next to his suitcase. Even though it was cool outside, his coveralls were soaked with sweat, so he stripped them off and took a hot shower to cleanse the memory of Sergeant Koester's visit to the code shack.

So far he had been lucky. No one appeared to be looking for him, following him, or asking anyone he knew about his whereabouts. If the authorities were seeking anyone at all, it was probably Edwin D. Bailey, a name, HYDRA had been assured by the Colombians, guaranteed to throw his pursuers into confusion. Stepping out of the shower, he toweled himself off, glad to no longer be wearing Koester's coveralls. He absentmindedly opened the dresser drawer, grabbed a fresh pair of socks and underwear and put them on without noticing anything amiss. The clock on the nightstand said exactly twelve noon, giving him more than enough time to check out of the hotel and to leave Sea-Tac that afternoon or evening on the next available flight to Kansas City. He would leave a message at the front desk, telling the waitress that he was called back to Washington on important business, so she wouldn't start calling around to look for him.

He slid open the closet door, lugging out the men's suiter and threw it on the bed. His trip to the code shack had been such a breeze for a moment he entertained the horrible thought that the authorities were already onto him, letting him steal the codes only to arrest him later. He turned the suitcase upright and placed his thumb on the dial, then sucked in his breath when he saw the combination above the right lock, 9-4-8. After closing the suitcase, he normally always reset the right dial to 7-2-7 as a simple security precaution, in addition to turning the left dial 6-5-6, which wasn't anywhere near its present setting.

Now his mind was racing. Where had they picked up his trail? New York? Washington, D.C.? Seattle? The hotel? The base? His memory was a frantic blur of indifferent ticket clerks and smiling airline stewardesses, anonymous cab drivers and employees at car rental booths. Perhaps it was the hacker's fault. Had she botched the entry into the TDY? Letting the suitcase fall back on the bed, he sat down beside it, rolling over all the possibilities in his mind. Castor was dead — it couldn't have been him. Or had he been picked up in Iraq? Maybe even betrayed by one of Saddam's inner circle. In that case, he asked himself, why hadn't he noticed any surveillance until now? But there hadn't been the least hint of anyone since he left New York. He checked the locks again, letting the air out of his lungs, then on impulse turned both of them to 1-1-1. If his trail was red hot, then it was already too late to escape. The hotel would already be infested with FBI. But when he'd just pulled into the hotel parking lot it was empty. The latches clicked and he spread the suitcase open, immediately seeing that someone had clumsily rearranged his clothes. Running to the window, he parted the curtains from the side, quickly glancing outside. No one.

In one swift motion he unzipped the false bottom, grabbed the Glock, unleashed it from its holster and threw himself along the wall beside the door to his room, holding the gun at ready. He heard nothing. Grabbing the doorknob, he kicked the door open, letting it crash against the closet, fully expecting to be bum-rushed by an angry pair of SWAT commandos. His heart was beating in his chest like a jackhammer; he had to think, think about who could have rifled through his suitcase since he'd left that morning.

He quickly closed the door, then began pacing back and forth in his room. Biting his lower lip, he forced himself to slow his mind down, to rerun every event of the day through his head from after the moment he woke up until he returned to his room. Showered, shaved, breakfast, chat with the waitress, return to the room to grab the equipment, throw it in the car and go. Told the waitress to meet him at 7:00 that evening in his room. Stupid. Never involve a third party unnecessarily. Showered, shaved, threw the dirty towels in the tub — he raced to the bathroom door — Of course, he told himself, it had to have been the maid. Professionals would have reset the dials to their original settings. Still holding the Glock in his right hand, HYDRA sat on the bed, furious with himself. Deciding he had nothing to lose, he picked up the telephone with his left hand and dialed zero for the front desk.

"Nendels Suites," the operator chirped.

"Hi. This is Sergeant Koester in 204. Is there any way of finding out who cleaned my room today?"

"Why sir? Is anything wrong?"

"No. No. No. I'm checking out and I just wanted to leave

her a tip. It's a habit I picked up on duty in the Orient."

"Just a minute," the operator sighed.

HYDRA cradled the telephone against his shoulder, while he faced the door with the Glock in his hand.

"Sir?"

"Yes."

"Pamela Michaud cleaned your room. The regular maid on duty called in sick, if that's any help."

"Great. No, that's wonderful, thanks a lot," HYDRA effused and hung up.

The little bitch had tossed his room! But why? She couldn't possibly be FBI — she was an idiot! A waitress, for godsakes. What in the hell could she have possibly been looking for? He found himself standing up, pinching the bridge of his nose with his eyes closed. Maid duty. What does she do? The bathroom, change towels, make the bed, change the sheets. But she's not the regular maid, so she quickly gets bored. Maybe she's resentful at being called on duty at the last minute on the day of her big night out? It hadn't occurred to him until now, that if Pam saw Sergeant Koester as a potential meal ticket out of Bremerton, she might only want to sleep with him if she were sure he was unattached.

Bored. First she'd try the drawers, not the suitcase. Open it. Socks, underwear, a shirt — for a split second his eyes froze on the ticket folder, before he scraped it up and unfolded it in his hands. Sgt. B. Koester — National-Sea-Tac, Sea-Tac-National. Right next to a mystery receipt for R. Matthews, his secret girlfriend. HYDRA unconsciously dropped the receipts on the desk and stared at his reflection in the mirror above. So far he'd only asked to leave her a tip, but in a homicide investigation, that would be enough. The telephone rang, jarring his thoughts, forcing him to make up his mind.

HYDRA scooped up the ticket, pulled a shirt and a pair of slacks out of the suitcase and hurriedly slipped them on, trying to ignore the insistent ring of the telephone. He slammed the suitcase shut, carrying it with him out of the room as he raced down the short stairway to the parking lot.

☆ ☆ ☆

Now seated around a bank of CRT screens in Ken Czarlinsky's office at TCOM in Ft. Meade were David Woodring, Dr. Hockaday, F. Jackson Tice, and Czarlinsky himself, the department chief.

"This is a fast Fourier transform," Czarlinsky spoke, tapping his CRT screen. Woodring stared intently, to him it looked like a plate of electronic spaghetti. "The point is, FFT's relatively old software hidden inside new hardware — it's not the best way to solve the problem." Czarlinsky tapped a key on his console, and an entirely different image displayed itself on the monitor. "Now here's the same message sent in the same code using wavelets which are much more efficient."

"O.K. Let's review," Woodring sighed. "You're telling me even though HYDRA was using Bailey's code key, he isn't Bailey because Bailey's chips were the old ones, whereas HYDRA's are newer ones that use — "

"Wavelets," added Hockaday.

"Wavelets, thanks. And as far as you know, none of these new chips using wavelets have ever been issued by the manufacturer to any government agency, right?"

"Right," Czarlinsky agreed.

"HYDRA knew we'd find the message? HYDRA knew about Bailey trying to kill Kennedy? He knew about Chauncey Laudon?"

Czarlinsky's phone rang, interrupting everyone's thoughts.

"TCOM. Just a minute."

Czarlinsky handed the handset to Woodring. Agent Kelly was calling him over a secure line from the FBI field office in Fayetteville, North Carolina. The CI-3 agent immediately informed Woodring that it was Keith Axe who'd recruited Edwin D. Bailey for Operation BUNCIN, but that Bailey had been killed in Central America before he could have ever tried to kill Senator Edward Kennedy in Atlanta.

"Shit!" Woodring cursed, slamming down the phone. "Shit! Shit! Shit!" Then, just as quickly, Woodring picked the handset back up to call a chopper.

Chapter 38

HYDRA was headed west on Kitsap Way, unconsciously circling Oyster Bay and driving in his car away from the hotel. Once he was in the car he found it was easier for him to compose his thoughts. In a more relaxed fashion he reviewed the situation in his head. Having found the ticket stub for R. Matthews, Pam had most likely jumped to conclusions and gone through his luggage, finding the full set of IDs for Lieutenant Gereke and Russell Matthews in addition to the plastic gun.

He turned left at the first light, keeping close to the water, following Rocky Point Road along the peninsula, until he saw the sign for the yacht club. He pulled into the half-empty parking lot next to a pay telephone and picked up the directory he'd taken from the hotel, checking the listings for Michaud. Spreading the city map over the steering wheel, HYDRA quickly located her address. She lived near the shipyard on Chester Avenue which HYDRA guessed was a cheaper part of town.

He pulled out of the lot, retracing his route, until he returned to Kitsap Way which he took east towards the bridge. At the end of the avenue a tall cyclone fence masked the outlines of mothballed ships lying in the harbor. In five minutes, he reached Chester and turned right, passing a life-sized sign of a ballerina in a tutu, advertising the local dance school. Stopping outside Pam's building, HYDRA put on Koester's dress hat, pulling it down over his forehead.

The apartment house was a nondescript two-story brick building with an unkempt lawn, surrounded by a low wooden fence. HYDRA left his car, walked along the footpath, and entered the unlocked foyer, where he checked the mail boxes. Michaud was No. 2C upstairs. The musty smell of uncleaned carpet hung in the air and the sound of a television droned in the background. HYDRA took the stairs two at a time, careful not to make too much noise. He stopped outside Pam's door, standing motionlessly in the corridor, waiting several seconds before he knocked.

"Who is it?" asked a muffled voice.

"Pam?"

"Who is it?"

"It's me, Peter, I've come to talk to you."

"What about?"

"I think we both know why I'm here, Pam."

The door opened an inch, and HYDRA was careful to insert his foot in the crack just in case.

"Pam?" He gently shoved it open. She was sitting on an old daybed, the makeup on her sullen face clearly streaked by tears.

"What?"

"You shouldn't have gone through my luggage, it wasn't right."

Pam wiped the tears from her eyes, then she saw the gun in his palm and the look of betrayal on his face.

"No!"

☆ ☆ ☆

HYDRA leaned over Pam's corpse, checking her neck with his right hand for a pulse. Her expression was frozen in place, and a small red hole glistened in the middle of her forehead, while a large blood stain bloomed across her blouse. HYDRA noticed her hair reeked of the odor of cigarettes, which he detested, and that there was an ashtray filled with butts on the nightstand. Satisfied she was dead, he stood where he was, his eyes scanning the perimeter of the small apartment, before he went to work. It wouldn't do, he thought, to risk Sergeant Koester becoming a suspect in a homicide; in a worst case, Navy command, finding out about his double's visit to Bangor SUBASE, could order the fleet to switch its nuclear operations to the alternate set of authentication codes, nullifying the ones in his palmtop computer.

He found the lighter fluid in the kitchen cabinet above the sink, returned to the living room and liberally doused both the corpse and the daybed, emptying the can, then tossing it aside. Next he lit a match and flicked it on Pam's body, creating an instant funeral pyre. Sprinting to the kitchen, he knelt over the pilot lights, blew them out, then turned the gas burners on full bore. Without looking back, he dashed to the door, shut it rapidly behind him, and clambered down the stairwell to the outside.

Chapter 39

David Woodring jumped out of the helicopter before it had even landed, almost twisting his ankle as he hit the ground. Axe's lawn was covered with an amalgam of commandos in combat gear, regular FBI agents, and guards from the CIA's own internal security staff. Woodring ignored them all as he ran across the lawn towards the open door, a crowd of HRT commandos following in his wake.

Pressing his face against the small window of the front door, he frantically rang the doorbell, while holding a mini Uzi in his other hand. Then he saw it. The shadow of a man, hanging upside-down, cast by the setting sun on the foyer wall. Woodring checked the clip on his automatic, then shot out the lock, pushed the door open and rushed inside, while six HRT agents stormed in behind him. Keith Axe's body was twisting around and around anchored to the living room ceiling fan. His corpse had been disemboweled and parts of its intestines had spilled out over the large sofa onto the rug in the sunken living room.

Grasping an outsized pair of plant trimmers he had fetched in the garage, one of the HRT agents immediately unfolded a stepladder and clambered up it. After he cut the hangman's rope, Axe's corpse fell into a large black plastic lawn bag, held by his partner. He cut the corpse's intestines with the sang-froid of an obstetrician clipping a baby's navel cord, handing the remnants to his partner to drop into the bag. Woodring issued orders for the others to clean up the rest of the mess, and his men dashed about the scene, removing the sofa cushions, rolling them up in an Indian-patterned rug from under the coffee table and shoving them into another lawn-size black bag.

"The sofa! Take it to the van! Now!" Woodring yelled, and a second pair of agents instantly materialized and carted the offending piece of furniture outside, tossing it into the open rear doors of the waiting van.

Chapter 40

Back in his room at Nendels Suites, HYDRA heard the unmistakable sounds of fire engines, then saw them outside his window racing along Kitsap Way. He picked up the telephone, waiting for the receptionist to come on the line.

"Front desk," she replied, the siren echoing in the receiver.

"This is Sergeant Koester in Room 204, can you have my bill ready in fifteen minutes?"

"Yes, sir."

"Thanks."

Rechecking all the drawers and then the closet to be certain he'd left nothing behind, HYDRA left the room with his suitcase on one arm and the HP-100LX on the other. He put them in the trunk of his car, then drove to the front entrance to settle his bill.

"Did you have a good stay?" The desk clerk, another young woman about Pam's age, asked.

"Excellent."

"Any problems?"

"None that I couldn't handle."

"Good. Here, Mister Koester," she smiled, sliding the bill across the counter. "If you just sign this, you can be on your way, we've already confirmed your credit."

"Great."

Walking back to his car, HYDRA performed several quick mental calculations in his head, comparing one scenario to another in regards to his relative risks and merits. While it would clearly be advantageous for him to ditch Koester's identity as soon as possible, such an action entailed the risk of having it appear that the sergeant, who had asked about the girl at the hotel, was purposely fleeing the scene of a homicide. Clearly, either turning his rental car back in Bremerton or even abandoning it there ran the risk of doing exactly that. For a while, at least, HYDRA decided, it would seem much more normal to the local investigating authorities to learn that Koester, acting as if he had no idea of the fire, simply returned his car to its point of origin, i.e., Sea-Tac Airport, then disappeared.

As he neared Chester Avenue on 6th Street HYDRA saw a thick column of smoke in the air, rising above the two-and three-story buildings against the pale outline of the Olympic Mountains in the distance. Traffic was already blocked off by local police, stationed at the interaction in several separate cars. The Washington State Ferry was only a few blocks away adjacent to the shipyard, and, since the weather had cleared, would be a more convenient way to return to the airport.

☆ ☆ ☆

One hour after HYDRA had boarded it in Bremerton, the ferry docked at Pier 52 in the Colman Terminal on the Seattle waterfront. Cars of passengers discharged simultaneously at separate decks, and HYDRA only had to wait a minute before he drove the Lumina down the ramp. I-5 was directly opposite the terminal, and he took it south in order to return to the airport. Since it was a clear day, HYDRA decided Sergeant Koester would first return the Chevy to the Thrifty Car lot, and then change his identity back to Russell Matthews, who had never been to Bremerton or Bangor and had never met Pamela Michaud.

At the rental lot, HYDRA left his keys at the desk, telling the agent behind the desk he was in a hurry, then caught the shuttle, getting off at the nearby Holiday Inn in Renton which was only minutes from the airport.

A bellhop carried his suitcase to the front desk and he had to stand in line behind two businessmen, waiting for them to check in before the reception clerk could get to him.

"How long will you be staying with us, Sergeant Koester?" asked the desk clerk.

"Just tonight, my flight leaves early tomorrow," HYDRA lied. "If I'm running behind, you have automatic check out, right?"

"Yes we do. Just drop your key in the box there and we'll mail you your copy of the bill."

"Great."

"You're in Room 312. Take the elevator to three, get out and turn right. It's halfway down the hall."

"Thanks."

Once he was inside his room, HYDRA stripped off his clothes and took a shower, cleansing his skin so that it would be prepared for what was next. After he had dried off, HYDRA wrapped a towel around his waist and opened the door a crack, slipping the Do Not Disturb sign on the outside doorknob. He opened his suitcase on the bed and rifled through the contents until he found a sealed plastic pouch which he tore open, extracting a salt-and-pepper wig. He set the wig and his makeup kit on top of the desk of drawers in front of the mirror and went to work making himself up as he'd done in his apartment on 62nd Street. His flight for Kansas City wasn't scheduled for departure until 8:00 p.m., so HYDRA would rely upon the cover of darkness to disguise the obvious use of cosmetics.

Chapter 41

Upon Woodring's entrance into the offices of the Counterterrorism Center at 7:00 p.m., typists remained still at their keyboards, investigators held their hands over telephone mouthpieces, analysts looked up from their desks—all eyes glued to the assistant director as he passed by their desks.

"Thompson, Lanier, Drexler, Mendoza, in my office."

The four individuals just summoned hastily left what they were doing and sprinted after their superior into his office. Again, Woodring spoke without preamble, this was no time for idle talk. "Charlie, I want you to get on-line with all the major credit card processors tonight. Visa, MasterCard, Banc One, Citibank, State Street, American Express — whoever's clearing the transactions and run a check on every name in the Criminal Annex. Look for any sign of significant activity — gun shops, airline tickets, car rental, hotels — you name it.

"Jim, I want you to take the INTEL personnel file in DESIST and locate every officer who's presently not in his assigned office and profile where he went, where he's going. Times, dates, hotels, everything. You work around the clock. Personnel's unlimited. You run out of people here, tell me, I'll get you DP people somewhere else.

"Steve, same goes for you, call the Pentagon and hook into the locator databases for the Army, Navy, Air Force and Marines, and cross-check every base's TDY roster with Jim. You find a match, give it to Asher at CI-3 and he'll run it down.

"George, you're the facilitator. Anybody the other three can't get on the phone, you find for them. I don't care who you have to call, where you call them, or at what time, get it done. Someone doesn't want to help, immediately threaten him with arrest. He gets nasty, detain him incommunicado at the nearest field office."

That evening bank officials in New York, Boston and Ohio were commuting home in their limousines, eating dinner at their homes or in restaurants, or working at the office were contacted by local FBI agents and told to gather up key members of their credit card data processing staff and have them return to work. Officials at data processing departments located in Phoenix, Los Angeles, Rapid City, and San Francisco were, for the most part, still at work and simply told to select employees to remain at their posts for further orders. Pentagon computer operators living in the capital environs were quickly located and told to report back to work immediately. Night communications crews at CIA, DIA, INR, NSA, NIS, CID, and all other intelligence agencies immediately went to work supplying the CTC with travel data on all employees who weren't at their desks.

In his office, exhausted, Woodring loosened his tie and lay down upon his sofa and attempted to take a catnap amidst the endless phone calls from FBI field officers, demanding confirmation of their orders.

☆ ☆ ☆

At 10:18 p.m. Pacific Time HYDRA arrived in Las Vegas on America West Flight 1748. He exited the plane, double-checked the monitor to confirm Flight 359 to Kansas City was still scheduled for its 12:33 a.m. departure, and proceeded to the America West ticket counter in the airport's main lobby, his mind still occupied by events in Bremerton. Even though the girl was dead, there was still the risk she had mentioned either Matthews's or Koester's name to someone before she died, endangering HYDRA's use of both IDs. Koester's trail had ended in Bremerton; now he'd let Matthews's stop in Vegas.

"Can I help you?" asked the ticket clerk.

"I'd like to go to Kansas City on your next flight."

The clerk brought up Flight 359 on his monitor; it was almost empty.

"First class or coach?"

"First class."

"Aisle or window seat?"

"Aisle."

"Your name?"

"MacDonald. Earl MacDonald."

"That'll be $469.00, Mr. MacDonald."

HYDRA handed the clerk five one hundred dollar bills from his wallet, and since first-class customers dressed in jackets and ties hardly fit the airline's profile of suspicious passengers, the clerk asked for no corroborating ID when he handed Mr. MacDonald his ticket.

"Have a good flight."

Chapter 42

By 2:00 a.m. Eastern Standard Time preliminary reports from the Armed Forces' locator computers, the major airlines reservations systems, the various intelligence agencies' operations department and the major credit card processors had already begun to pour into the FBI Counterterrorism Center's computers over high-speed satellite and fiber-optic data link. Since Woodring had already ordered Charlie Thompson to input the names of the individuals listed in the Criminal Annex to the briefing paper on the Special Operations Forces, this was the first batch of names to be cross-checked against the mass of incoming files.

Included in the mass of data were fifty different passenger name records (PNRs) from five separate airline reservation systems for the name Russell Matthews. The Russell Matthews who was listed in the Criminal Annex and who was being cross-checked by Woodring's staff had formerly belonged to a "black hat" unit of SEAL Team 6 called "Red Cell" whose mission had been to clandestinely penetrate U.S. Navy bases. Unfortunately for Matthews, he had shown a little too much enthusiasm during an exercise which occurred at Naval Weapons Station, Seal Beach, California, a result of which was that the base's security director sustained serious injuries and sued the Navy for damages. Matthews was immediately discharged, tossed out of a unit he'd been in for more than a decade, after which the Navy lost track of him. But the Social Security Administration and the IRS had not. His last known address was in Greenwich Village, New York, where he had become a dee-jay at a local bar, playing records five nights a week until well after dawn. A cross-check with the NCIC indicated Matthews had also subsequently been picked up by New York Police in 1988 on a weapons charge, then later released without trial.

Taking the credit card numbers from the passenger name records sent by the reservations systems and matching them against the customer files given by the credit card processors, one of Thompson's analysts quickly eliminated all those whose social security numbers failed to match the ex-Navy SEAL's, leaving him at first count with no remaining PNRs. That notwithstanding, a moment later both the analyst and Thompson were knocking on the door to Woodring's office, jolting him awake.

"I think we've got something," Thompson spoke.

Sitting upright on his cot, Woodring rubbed his eyes.

"Tell him," Thompson ordered.

The analyst glanced first at Thompson, then at Woodring, then cleared his throat. "Uh, we got five PNRs on a guy named Matthews — and an ex-SEAL with the same name got into trouble in an incident at Seal Beach — Anyway, the credit card on one of the Matthews' PNRs isn't on any of the TRW reports."

"What bank?" asked Woodring.

"Excuse me?"

"What bank issued the card?"

"Oh, sorry. Uh, it's Banco Interoceanico Unitado. Some bank down in Panama — " The analyst stopped when he caught the look of concern flash across the other two men's faces. "Anything wrong?"

"No. Go ahead," Woodring prompted.

"Last month Matthews with the funny card made two trips to San Francisco from New York, stopping in Kansas City on the last one. Also, two days ago an R. Matthews boarded the New York-Washington shuttle, using a ticket he'd purchased for cash at a USAir ticket office in Manhattan earlier this week. The guy with the same card just departed Sea-Tac Airport in Seattle on America West Flight 1748 at 8:00 p.m. bound for Las Vegas, ETA 10:15 p.m. local time."

Woodring looked at his watch, which said almost 6:00 a.m., long past the arrival of the American West flight into Las Vegas.

"We checked the airline," Thompson added. "Flight arrived on time. No problem on board. Las Vegas office's looking for the stewardesses now to see if anyone remembers Matthews. His PNR doesn't list a hotel."

Woodring pinched the bridge of his nose with his fingers,

his eyes closed. First it was Bailey, the assassin, now Matthews, the dishonorably discharged Navy SEAL. The search for Bailey had not only been a monumental waste of time and resources, it had unearthed a major scandal tearing at the fabric of America's ability to conduct intelligence operations. HYDRA was leading them by the nose, sending them down one blind alley after another, whose only commonality were scandals committed by various government personnel.

"Isn't there a Navy base in Seattle?" Woodring asked.

"There're two," replied Thompson, who'd just been calling the Pentagon for TDYs. "Bangor SUBASE and the shipyard in Bremerton."

"Check their rosters ahead of the others, see if Matthews has been there. Check with local police in Seattle to see if anything else unusual has happened, same with San Francisco, and put the DESIST team on those areas and check out anything that doesn't match up. I'll call McDonald at CI-4 and have them pick Matthews up if he's in New York."

"But I thought he was in Las Vegas!" protested the analyst.

"What do we do about Banco Interoceanico?" Thompson interrupted, not waiting for an answer. "Without their help VISA can't flag Matthews' purchases."

"Call the commander of Howard Air Force Base and find out what special forces they've got down there, and have them get a team ready to move in with some DP people, if we decide to use them."

"If?" repeated Thompson.

But his question was interrupted by Mendoza knocking at the door. Woodring quickly waved him in.

"George, call the Las Vegas field office and fax them this picture," Woodring unceremoniously ripped the photograph out of Russell Matthews' service file and held it in his outstretched hand for Mendoza to take. "Have them liaise with local police there and check everyone departing any airport within a hundred mile radius starting now. If Matthews is found, I want him taken immediately to the air force base at Nellis and put under heavy guard. Under no circumstances is he to be taken to a local jail."

"Yes, sir."

Chapter 43

At 6:45 a.m. an FBI SWAT team hit Matthews's apartment in the Lower East Side, bursting through the door in classic fashion and catching Matthews in bed with a female patron of the bar where he worked. Seeing his bedroom full of heavily armed men, Matthews put up no resistance and shouted at the hysterical girl next to him to shut up. Meanwhile, a score of CI-4 agents methodically tore the hapless ex-SEAL's apartment apart, slitting open all the furniture, ripping up the floor, tearing out the walls, and mangling every appliance, while several others conducted aggressive interrogations of Matthews and his girlfriend in separate rooms.

☆ ☆ ☆

"Woodring," the assistant director answered, picking up his telephone. As McDonald made his report, Woodring looked at his watch, then looked at the airline guide he'd folded in half on his desk. The next connecting flight from Las Vegas to New York wasn't until 6:56 a.m., meaning the Russell Matthews in Las Vegas couldn't have possibly taken a civilian flight in time to return to his apartment earlier that morning.

Charlie Thompson swept into Woodring's office, the worried look on his face introduction enough.

"We just cross-checked Bangor SUBASE's TDY roster with the Navy locator and found that yesterday a Sergeant Peter Koester visited Bangor's Strategic Weapons Facility. CI-3 just checked with NIS and they say Koester's in DC — he never went to Bangor."

"That's him."

"Bangor's TDY says the reason for Koester's trip was classified. Clearance is Operation TEMPEST. You want us to call the base?"

"No!" Woodring stated firmly. "I'll send a team up from CI-5. What time is it now?"

"Almost seven."

"Call Half Street and have them put enough men on the street to surround Building 200 in the Washington Navy Yard. Starting the moment they get there anyone that leaves they detain on the spot. Oh, one more thing. After I leave, turn off their telephone system."

Thompson blinked. "How do I do that?"

Woodring was already out the door, when he stopped for a moment: "Call the phone company."

☆ ☆ ☆

After receiving Woodring's call, CI-5 agents who had been standing by at the Los Angeles field office on Wilshire Boulevard rushed to the eleventh floor elevator, taking it nonstop to the basement parking lot. At 3:10 a.m. in the morning the deserted interstates allowed the men from CI-5 to reach Los Angeles International Airport in only fifteen minutes. Their two dark sedans skidded to a stop outside a private hangar off Vista Del Mar, where a MAC Gates Learjet C-21A was already preflighted for the emergency trip to Sea-Tac International Airport.

☆ ☆ ☆

Morning traffic in the capital was heavy, but the Washington Navy Yard was only minutes away from FBI Headquarters. Upon his arrival, Woodring was met discreetly at the door by a pair of special agents from CI-3 who had already taken over the front desk. One of them escorted Woodring directly to the

Office of Commander Mark McPhee, who himself was being babysat by a second pair of CI-3 special agents. McPhee could barely restrain his fury at the audacity of the FBI agents, and it was all he could do to prevent himself from pulling his service pistol out of his top desk drawer and shooting them both on the spot. Woodring's sudden arrival in his office only further infuriated him.

"Who are you?"

"David   Woodring,   Assistant   Director   of Counterintelligence."

McPhee blinked, then got right to the point. "The FBI's Assistant Director of FBI Counterintelligence didn't drive all the way out here just for fun, Mr. Woodring."

Woodring reached into his jacket pocket, then handed the envelope across the desk.

National Security Decision Directive were the first words that caught McPhee's eye.

"We have a spy in here, Mr. Woodring?"

"No."

"Then — "

"Next shift change is at seven-thirty, right?"

"Yeh, but — "

"I want to talk to Sergeant Koester. The SCI computer room'll be fine, if you don't mind."

"By my watch Koester should be here in ten minutes, and I suppose that piece of paper you just handed me is good enough for SCI clearance. You want to go on down?"

Woodring stood up and grabbed his coat, following McPhee to the nearest elevator.

A moment later, Woodring sat alone at a small table on the raised floor inside a large clean room, whose walls were lined with mainframe computers. A brief knock at the door and a young sergeant entered, already a bit intimidated by the no-

nonsense look on Woodring's face.

"Sergeant Koester. I'm David Woodring, Assistant Director of Counterintelligence with the FBI. Before we begin this discussion, let me just say one thing. If you tell unauthorized individuals about this conversation, you will be subject to prosecution under Title VIII, United States Code, Section 794(c) — the maximum penalty for which is death. You understand that?"

"Ah, yes...sir." Koester, who was all of twenty-five, grew tense, then blew air out of his cheeks in relief.

"You haven't recently visited Bangor SUBASE, have you?"

"No. No way, sir. I wouldn't have forgotten something like that, Jesus."

"You're TEMPEST cleared, aren't you?"

"Yes, sir."

"Can you give me a brief summary of your TEMPEST duties?"

"Brief, sir?" repeated Koester.

"Relatively, yes."

"Ah, sir? Is it alright to show you the files? I think that may help explain." Koester looked hesitatingly at the two plain-clothesmen on either side of Woodring.

"Go ahead, but make it quick." Woodring motioned for the two CI-3 agents to accompany Koester to his office.

Woodring's jaw went slack when he saw Koester reenter the conference room with his arms filled with two large storage boxes. "What in the hell is that?"

"You said you wanted — you want TEMPEST, right?"

"Shit," Woodring muttered under his breath. "Set it on the table and sit down and shut up."

Woodring yanked the cardboard lid off the first box and grabbed a one-inch thick sheaf of computer paper. Each sheet had dual vertical borders which were formed by repetition of the four-letter acronym, SIOP. The text, itself, was liberally sprinkled with a host of abbreviations, including TACAMO, ULF, EAM, NAVSTAR, TDOA, AUTOVON, WWMCCS, NCA, and USCINCEUR. The color drained from Woodring's face as he mechanically flipped from page to page, going faster and faster as he went. Suddenly he slammed the stack of papers on the table.

"What's SIOP?"

"What, sir?"

"*SIOP*, Koester. What's it stand for?"

"Single Integrated Operational Plan, ah — "

"Plan for *what*, Sergeant?"

"Ah, well, Director Woodring, you have to understand that, that these printouts — "

"*What's it the plan for, Peter?*"

"For war, sir."

"*What war? What?*"

"Ah, sir, I think I'd like to see Commander McPhee before I — "

Woodring flew across the table and in the blink of an eye had Koester hammerlocked facedown upon the floor with his FBI service pistol jammed into the Sergeant's left ear. "I thought I told you this conversation was just between us — you tell McPhee anything and I'll blow your head off myself!" Woodring snarled, pressing his gun further against Koester's temple.

"All right! It's OK! I made a mistake! Jesus!"

Koester turned his head towards the ceiling, Woodring had gotten off him and was bent over the second box, rifling through its contents. There they were by the hundreds for every level of command and alert: the Emergency Action Messages which allowed the President to access the Worldwide

Military Command and Control System (WWMCCS), the Joint Chiefs of Staff, and the Commander in Chief of U.S. Forces Europe (USCINCEUR), the high command during Situation HAMMERCUT, nuclear Armageddon…

Koester slid back into his chair and his hands shook as he fumbled with a cigarette.

Woodring was still reading as he spoke, "Anyone at Bangor ask you about this stuff, Pete? Anything about a printout?"

"No, sir. I never heard a word from them - like I told you."

"Just a minute." Woodring flew out of the door to the computer room, issuing orders to a pair of agents as he went. "Hold him here until you hear from me." Racing along the corridors out the front door of the building, Woodring was immediately met by several more men from CI-3 who followed him to his car.

"Put on the siren!" he shouted to the driver. "Take me back to the Hoover Building," he added out of breath, then uncradled the handset to the cellular telephone and punched in the number for the Counterterrorism Center. "Pick up Curtis Vaughn and bring him to my office."

☆ ☆ ☆

Almost exactly two hours after it had left Los Angeles International, the Gates Learjet carrying the crew of CI-5 agents touched down at Sea-Tac International Airport, where it was met by a caravan of unmarked sedans which had been hastily assembled by the agent in charge of the local FBI field office. During the emergency telephone call to his home from David Woodring, the agent-in-charge was also notified that, until further notice, the ten men he was supplying from the local office were to take their orders from CI-5, Los Angeles.

Racing southwards on Interstate 5 with sirens blaring and lights flashing in the predawn gloom, the four-car caravan reached Tacoma in record time. It swerved onto exit 132 following State Highway 16 around the sound, heading north to Silverdale. Forty minutes later the four sedans skidded to a stop on Trident Boulevard outside the main gate, and Special Agent Johnson demanded to speak with the duty officer, since the Pass and I.D. Building would be open for fifteen more minutes. After receiving a frantic call from the civilian sentry, the night duty officer ran out of the administration building on Hunley Road, jumped in his car, and drove the short distance to the main gate, where he encountered a group of plainclothesmen milling about a line of unmarked cars.

"Lieutenant Brookfield?"

"Yes?"

"FBI Counterintelligence," replied Special Agent Johnson, flashing his ID in Brookfield's face. "We have orders to seal off this base."

Chapter 44

At 6:00 a.m. Central Standard Time a Yellow cab dropped HYDRA off at the front door of the Ritz Hotel where he had stayed on his previous visit to Kansas City. He took the escalator to the lower level and exited out the parking lot, walking the short two blocks to Lieutenant Gereke's apartment on foot. It was still dark, and a light snowfall began to fall like dust on commuters' windshields, making them wonder if their return treks home would be delayed by inclement weather.

Holding his suitcase in his hands, HYDRA walked up Wornall past a row of shops, taking the stairs through the parking lot which led to Gereke's apartment building. He checked his watch. It was only 6:15 and Gereke didn't usually awake until 7:00, so, in theory, the Naval Air Reserve Lieutenant was still in his bed asleep. HYDRA inserted the key the lock service had made for him into the lock, slowly turning the handle. Gereke's room was pitch black, except for the soft green blinking light of the an electronic clock of a VCR. While waiting for his eyes to adjust to the dark, HYDRA carefully set the suitcase on the floor, then moved slowly towards the single bedroom, holding the Glock in his hand.

In a single motion he strode to within two paces of the bed, grabbed an extra pillow, wrapping it around the Glock, and fired and two quick rounds into the lieutenant's sleeping form. Gereke's body jerked spasmodically, then went limp, his now open eyes staring in shock at the ceiling. HYDRA reached over the corpse, checking for a pulse with his left hand, while still holding the Glock in his right. Satisfied, he sprinted to the front door, latched the nightlock, and threw on the lights, then ran back to the bedroom where he stripped the covers off the bed.

Slipping a heavy lawn bag out of his jacket pocket, HYDRA snapped it open and put it around the corpse's feet, pulling it all the way up past Gereke's head. After tying it closed, HYDRA dragged the corpse to the bathroom where he dumped it into the bathtub, then went to Gereke's kitchen to search for a small bowl and a chair.

HYDRA brought the bowl and the chair back to the bathroom, then extracted the makeup kit from his suitcase, emptying the contents into the bowl. He found a handcloth nearby, dipped it into the acetone solution, and began the laborious process of removing Matthews's salt-and-pepper wig. As he had done previously, HYDRA soaked the towel in solvent and wiped it across his scalp and forehead to remove any remaining traces of makeup and spirit gum which he had used to hold the wig in place, then applied cold cream to the sorest points to prevent inflammation.

Returning to his suitcase, he unfolded the white shirt and matching winter blue dress uniform Blond had tailored for him and donned them in front of Gereke's mirror. All he was missing was the naval cap, which was in a hatbox he had unpacked and lain upon the bed. Retrieving it, he fitted the navy hat over his head, packed up his things, then turned out the lights and left the room. Walking back to the Ritz on foot, he reentered the hotel through a service entrance, taking the elevator to the main lobby, where he caught a taxi for the airport.

☆ ☆ ☆

At the Pentagon two CI-3 plainclothesmen entered the outer office of General Curtis Vaughn, Commander of the Defense Communications Agency, calmly presented their credentials to his secretary, then walked past her directly into the general's private office.

Chapter 45

As Woodring was driving back to the Hoover Building a tall, blond-headed man wearing a dress naval cap presented himself at USAir ticket counter in the Kansas City International Airport.

"Where to today?"

"Washington, D.C."

"Do you already have your ticket?"

"Yes," HYDRA replied, handing it across the counter.

The clerk confirmed Lieutenant Gereke's reservation on Flight 674 in his computer. "Any baggage?"

"Just this one," HYDRA hefted the Hartmann through the slot, and the clerk handed him back his ticket claim with the check stapled inside.

"Flight 674 departs in fifteen minutes from Gate 5. That's two gates to the left. Have a good flight, Lieutenant."

"Thanks."

☆ ☆ ☆

On the seventh floor of the Hoover Building inside the Counterterrorism Center a very nervous General Curtis

Vaughn sat inside David Woodring's office, listening to the ADCI field telephone calls from New York, Los Angeles, Las Vegas, Seattle, and finally Silverdale, Washington, the location of Bangor SUBASE.

"Woodring." Woodring paused, glancing neutrally at Vaughn. "Hold on a second, I'm going to put you on the speakerphone." Fearing the call was from Bangor, Vaughn felt a line of perspiration form across his brow.

"Woody, I'm sitting with the pair of crypto-clerks here who met with Sergeant Koester." Agent Johnson's mock joviality resonated in the room, putting Vaughn more on edge. "Their names are Gene Braden and Terry Hammer."

"Right," Woodring replied. "Gentlemen, I am David Woodring, Director of Counterintelligence, FBI, and I'm sitting next to General Vaughn whom you've already heard of. Before we go any further I want to confirm that Agent Johnson has read you your rights under Title VIII."

"Yes, sir," replied each man, knowing Section 794(c) essentially granted him no rights at all.

"Did Agent Johnson show you Matthews's picture?"

"Yes, sir," both men answered.

"It wasn't him," added Braden.

"You're taking into account, different hair color, maybe even a wig, shaved head — "

"Yes, sir. There's no way Koester would have been Matthews, sir. Absolutely no way," Sergeant Hammer emphasized.

"Sergeant Braden? What do you think?"

"I agree with Terry, sir. Koester didn't look like that fax picture at all. No way."

"Thanks," sighed Woodring.

"Why don't you begin by telling me and General Vaughn exactly what you did during the time Sergeant Koester was in the communications shed."

☆ ☆ ☆

USAir Flight 674 arrived at National Airport in Washington, D.C. precisely on schedule at 11:05 Eastern Standard Time, allowing HYDRA the whole afternoon to claim his baggage, rent a car, and make the sixty-five mile journey to the Patuxent River Naval Air Station. The package of information HYDRA had received from the Morale, Welfare, and Recreation Office made a point of informing all visitors that there was no public transportation to the Patuxent River area from any of the three major airports in the Baltimore-Washington, D.C. metropolitan area, so before his arrival at Washington National, HYDRA, using Lieutenant Gereke's ID and credit cards, had booked a car which he picked up after a thirty minute wait for luggage. At 11:40 he set out upon Maryland Highway 5, following a course through the freshwater wetlands which were roughly parallel to Patuxent River on his left. Carefully maintaining the speed limit, he passed endless stands of leafless trees rooted in the local creeks and streams.

☆ ☆ ☆

"He knew McPhee's kids' names, their schools, everything," Hammer's voice wailed over Woodring's speakerphone.

"What did he want?" demanded Woodring, shooting a look at Vaughn.

Neither of the two cryptographers immediately replied.

"What did he want?" repeated Woodring.

"Uh, he wanted to do a TEMPEST check ..."

"A TEMPEST check on what?"

"On the gun — "

"Shit!" muttered Vaughn under his breath.

"Excuse me?"

"What gun?"

"On the laser gun — "

"He's got the codes!" Vaughn interrupted a second time, but Woodring, by violently waving his hands, shut him up.

"He told us he was coming to change the chips and had to check the gun."

"He brought his own chips?" Woodring pressed, now staring at Vaughn for some help.

"Yes, sir."

"Sergeant," Vaughn spoke. "What did he do with the set of chips that were inside the gun before he came?"

"Well, General, he took them with him."

"He *what?*"

"He took them with him."

Vaughn motioned to Woodring to turn off the box. "He's got the codes. They're on the chips. In theory, if he takes them out of the gun it'll zeroize, but I doubt he went to all that trouble for nothing."

"What do you mean?" Woodring asked.

"Can you turn them back on?"

Woodring pressed the button.

"Terry, this is General Vaughn, again."

"Yes, sir."

"What equipment did Koester use to conduct the check?"

"A DKD-1810."

"A what?"

"It's a spectrum analyzer, sir — Portable, with a wand."

"He bring anything else?"

"Uh, I don't remember."

"He brought a computer," added Braden, the other clerk.

"A nice one, an HP-100LX palmtop."

"*A computer? What for?*" demanded Vaughn.

"I don't know. Said he had a program in it for the DKD — how was I supposed to know — he — "

Vaughn motioned violently for Woodring to shut off the speakerphone cutting Braden off in mid-sentence. "He's downloaded the codes into the computer. We're fucked."

"What are they good for? A submarine, or what?" Woodring asked.

"They're good for everything. The whole fucking ball of wax — "

"What — "

"That's right. Not just the sub fleet — "

"Fleet?"

"ICBMs, bombers, tacticals, all of it."

"For how long?"

"For how long? For the next six months, that's how long! Because the subs are gone on patrol that long."

Their conversation was interrupted by the ringing of one of Woodring's other lines.

"Woodring." For the next two minutes the agent-in-charge of the Seattle field office described the fire at Pamela Michaud's apartment building in Bremerton. "They think it was arson? …She worked at the motel…she cleaned his room…alright, thanks."

A third line began blinking on and off before Woodring had time to hang up.

"Woodring."

The special agent-in-charge of the Las Vegas field office was calling to give his preliminary report on the city-wide search for Russell Matthews. No one by that time could be found anywhere in the city and no one at America West airlines recognized the fax ID photo of Matthews sent by CI-4 in New York. The second Matthews was gone. Vanished into thin air. Woodring hung up and punched three digits into his keypad.

"Charlie, I want you to check all the flights departing Las Vegas Airport after 10:00 p.m. last night, print out every PNR, match it up with its owner, and find out where they are." Woodring hung up, not waiting for the inevitable protest. The task he had just requested couldn't be realistically accomplished in less than a week, but he had no other choice.

"Woody?"

Woodring blinked. He'd almost totally forgotten General Vaughn was sitting in his office across his desk.

"I'm going to have to call General Shelton on this, unless —"

"No. Go ahead. We have no choice. Tell him the meeting's at seven sharp at the NFIB."

"You realize, of course, Shelton'll probably want to bring the Joint Chiefs."

"I realize, and there's nothing I can do about it."

"I should get going."

"Right," Woodring answered, staring into space. "Right."

☆ ☆ ☆

Deciding that Lieutenant Gereke, like himself, would have favored civilian over military food, HYDRA decided to stop for a leisurely lunch at the Comfort Inn Beacon Marina in Solomons, Maryland, eight miles from Pax River's main gate. As he turned off Highway 235 and passed over the bridge on Route 2-4 HYDRA knew he had arrived when a pair of FA-18 jet fighters roared overhead at less than 1,000 feet.

Hovering over the docks filled with sailboats was a four-story white colonial beacon station with a bright red roof. HYDRA passed the inn's namesake and parked his car outside a restaurant called The Captain's Table. He entered the bar which was dark and had pictures of old boats and marinas on the wall.

"Can I help you?" asked the hostess.

"You want a booth in the bar or a table in the restaurant?"

"I'll take a booth."

"No smoking?"

"Fine."

"Right this way, then," replied the hostess, showing HYDRA to an empty booth.

☆ ☆ ☆

Grille lights blinking in unison, four unmarked cars plowed through the morning fog along Flier Road inside Bangor SUBASE. Turning sharply onto Tang Road, they exited a dense stretch of pine forest and raced across an expanse of concrete towards the docks of the Explosive Handling Wharf. Crew members wearing orange vests on the USS *Eisenhower* and a pair of nearby tugs stood frozen in their respective decks, having just received a call from the commander about a boarding party. Sixteen Counterintelligence agents piled out the car doors, lining the right dock, while linehandlers reattached ropes to large iron eyelets on both docks. One of the tugs which had been positioned astern the USS *Eisenhower* cut the ones holding it to the sub, letting them drop into the water, and steamed forwards towards the space between the docks.

The tug's crew gathered up the rope from the linehandlers on both docks, then, after the tug had come alongside the *Eisenhower*, tossed the lines to the hands on deck, waiting for them to reattach them to the opposite end of the craft. Since the *Eisenhower* was 560 feet long and weighed over 50,000 tons, Special Agent Johnson decided on the spot he and his men wouldn't wait for the lengthy docking process and would board the sub immediately. A personnel transfer boat pulled alongside the dock, taking a dozen of the FBI agents aboard, then steamed slowly towards the *Eisenhower*.

The sub's commander stood in the open hatch on the bridge with a grimace on his face as he watched his craft being pulled slowly back to shore. A thousand questions were racing through his mind; on the radio the base commander had been circumspect, not only refusing to give any reason for recalling the *Eisenhower*, but also ordering him point blank to fully submit to the authority of Special Agent Johnson of the FBI. FBI? What in the hell had happened?

While the personnel transfer boat pulled alongside the dull gray hull of the *Eisenhower*, a certified diver stood watch on the sub's deck just in case one of the boarding party slipped and fell into the cold water of the Sound.

Chapter 46

Patuxent River Naval Air Station is located at the southern-most tip of the state of Maryland on the west bank of the Chesapeake Bay, and is surrounded by water on three sides — the Patuxent River on the north, the Bay on the east, and the Potomac River on the south. The base's major activity is the Naval Air Test Center, where many of the Navy's most advanced aircraft weapons systems are tested and evaluated. The Naval Air Test Center had its origins in the air war of World War II during which hundreds of combat-experienced pilots arrived to test new airplanes.

By Navy standards Patuxent River Naval Air Station is a large base with a population of 3,400 active duty personnel and an additional 6,000 dependents. Expanding under the Korean and Vietnamese Wars, squadrons such as Airborne Early Warning, Antisubmarine Warfare, Oceanographic Development, and Naval Air Transport were later added, although the ASW squadrons were transferred in the 1970s to Brunswick, Maine and Jacksonville, Florida, as the helpful four-color booklet from MWR informed HYDRA. Also, in

1975 the Test Center itself underwent a sweeping reorganization, establishing it as the Navy's principal center for development testing. Strike Aircraft, Antisubmarine Aircraft, Rotary Wing Aircraft and Systems Engineering Test Directorates were set up to evaluate aircraft by type and mission.

After he had finished lunch at the Captain's Table, HYDRA checked his watch, paid his bill, then got in his car and followed Route 2-4 back across the bridge to Highway 235 which led directly to Pax River's main gate. It was about 2:00 p.m., giving him more than enough time to report for duty at Fleet Air Reconnaissance Squadron Four by three o'clock, when Gereke was due. As he passed a Foodland Store off Three-Notch Road on the base's perimeter, HYDRA found himself waiting in a line of cars two lanes wide. At the head of the line, two officers wearing white sailors' caps and matching leggings with orange safety vests were checking each driver's ID and issuing them instructions.

HYDRA drummed his fingers impatiently on the steering wheel; waiting for his turn, he flipped on the car radio and scanned the FM dial for something to listen to. Blaring rock music was followed in turn by crooning country singers; the Berlin Philharmonic Orchestra playing Mahler's Third Symphony, more rock, oldies, jazz, and finally, an announcer's voice: "… Jackson at WPGC Radio FM ninety-five live in the capital. In official Washington rumors are flying over the sudden death of Keith Axe, the Deputy Director of Central Intelligence. CIA Public Affairs issued a statement claiming Axe was the victim of a sudden and massive heart attack, but residents who live nearby house reported seeing an unusual amount of unmarked vehicles on the scene in addition to the arrival of a helicopter — " HYDRA punched the power button off, his hand shaking slightly. Axe's death couldn't have been an accident, it had to be connected to Edwin Bailey, which meant a search of some kind had already begun.

All at once the car window was filled with a security officer's face who was rapping on the glass.

"Hey! Roll down your window!"

HYDRA glanced in his rearview mirror — he was boxed in from behind. There was no way to escape except on foot; then, remembering he was Gereke, he jerked open the window, an apologetic smile on his face.

"You OK in there?" asked the security guard.

"Fine, fine, thanks. Just had my radio on too loud."

"I need to see some ID."

"Just a minute." HYDRA fumbled with his wallet, and pulled Gereke's papers from the glove compartment, handing them to the guard.

"Lieutenant Gereke, you need to go to Building 409 Command Duty Office and check in. Just take this road about a half-mile and it's on the right before the intersection."

The guard motioned to a one-story red-brick building a few feet away. HYDRA thanked him, rolled up his window, and put the car in gear, trying to concentrate while the potential ramifications of Axe's death flooded into his mind. Obviously, the search for Bailey had gone some distance to cause the death of someone as important as the former deputy director, which worried him, because it would only be a matter of time until Bailey was located and whoever was looking for him realized he wasn't the one with the telephone. Then what? What about Matthews and Koester? How long would they last if Bailey had already been blown? He barely noticed the intersection ahead in time and jerked his steering wheel, swerving off the road into the parking lot of Building 409. He was careful not to rush around the car, but walked to the trunk, pulling the vinyl bag containing his flight suit and the HP-100LX in its leather case.

Inside there were two short lines a couple of men deep, and HYDRA took his place behind a P-3 pilot assigned to Air Test and Evaluation Squadron One, dressed in a uniform similar to his own. He fingered the strap of the HP-100LX, checking to be sure it was there.

"Your orders, please, Lieutenant," asked the crewcut security officer behind the counter. After HYDRA handed his papers across, the clerk entered the sixteen-digit alphanumeric sequence into his computer, searching for Lieutenant Gereke in the base's TDY roster. During the short delay the clerk compared HYDRA's face with the picture on his ID and back again without comment. Once he brought up the record, he gave Gereke his orders.

"You're to report to VQ-4 no later than 15:00 hours. That's the hangar up the street on Cedar Point, you can't miss it. Next."

☆ ☆ ☆

"Commander, I am Special Agent Forest Johnson of FBI Counterintelligence Division 5 in Los Angeles. My men and I have been authorized to board this sub by National Security Decision Directive No. 208 which was issued two weeks ago by the President, a copy of which you can read now, if you wish. If you do wish to read the document, after doing so you must return it back to me."

Commander Bart Thomason, dressed in a full-length bright orange coverall and a navy blue cap stood stonefaced on the bridge. Directly beneath his special observation platform the XO and the Chief Officer of the Watch listened to Johnson in stunned silence, while another two crew members occupying the two fins attached to the conning tower were observing the FBI agents on the docks with their binoculars. The black man in the short raincoat who had just given the speech had been set aboard the deck by a personnel transfer boat along with more than a dozen plainclothesmen just after the sub's communications officer had received a classified cable to return to port. The chill March wind was blowing in the agent's face, making his eyes water.

"I got the cable. What the hell is all this about?"

"Sir, we have reason to suspect that someone may be impersonating one of your crew members."

"That's ridiculous! I'm personally familiar with every man aboard this vessel!" retorted Thomason, refusing to budge an inch.

"Sorry, Commander, but our orders are clear — we'll have to interview them all."

"Jesus Christ."

☆ ☆ ☆

After HYDRA left the Command Duty Office, he got back into his rental car and drove the short distance along Cedar Point Road to the hangar housing VQ-4. Separated from the road by a double cyclone fence, VQ-4's hangar resembled the Strategic Weapons Facility at Bangor. And, in a similar fashion to the Strategic Weapons Facility at Bangor, the entrance to VQ-4 was guarded by a pair of Marines stationed in a guard hut, one of whom motioned for HYDRA to stop his car. Walking around to the driver's window, the sentry demanded to see HYDRA's ID and orders. After double-checking them in the base's TDY roster, he lifted the barrier, letting HYDRA pass through. Standing before him was rather battered looking building with rows of paint-stained translucent windows and bright red metal doors with a three-story high four-color circular emblem painted on the wall above. The VQ-4 squadron's emblem showed the profile of a black figure in a spy's cap, holding three bolts of lightning above a white cloud. Behind the circle, a banner read "FAIRECONRON FOUR."

HYDRA parked his car and walked through the red door, finding himself in a dingy office filled with cheap metal desks and fading, slightly bent partitions, occupied by the other thirteen members of the crew for his flight.

"Lieutenant Gereke?"

"Yes," HYDRA replied.

"I'm Lieutenant Bob Higgins. We'll be on the flight together." Higgins was a short man with etched features and slicked-down hair. "Let me introduce you to the rest of the crew."

☆ ☆ ☆

"Your name, please?" repeated Special Agent Johnson.

"Lieutenant Randy Power," replied the watch officer, squinting under the halogen light. A second FBI agent, standing next to Forest Johnson in the crew's mess, was holding a portable camcorder, focusing it on the subject of the interrogation. A cable had been strung from the mess to the wardroom on the deck above out the bridge access truck to a building opposite the deck, where the code clerks Hammer and Braden were being held.

"Your Social Security Number?"

"555-54-0265," intoned Lieutenant Power on the television monitor.

A plainclothesman sitting next to Hammer raised his eyebrows as if to ask the question, is this the one, but Hammer nodded his head back and forth, followed by Braden in quick succession. The agent whispered something unintelligible into the hands free headset.

"Where were you born?"

"Eugene, Oregon."

As the watch officer gave his response, Johnson received the news over his headset. "Thank you, Lieutenant, that will be all. Get the next man," Johnson told the agent next to him.

A tall, blond man was led into the room by a pair of agents and shown a chair.

"I'm   Forest   Johnson,   an   agent   with   FBI

Counterintelligence. Before I begin asking you any questions I want to inform you that if you mention this conversation to any unauthorized individuals, which, for the moment, as far as you're concerned is anyone but me, you will be subject to prosecution under Title VIII, United States Code, Section 794(c) — the maximum penalty for which is death. Do you understand what I just said?"

"Yes sir."

"Fine. What's your name?"

"Clark Titus."

"What's your rank and position?"

"Lieutenant, Engineering Officer, sir."

"What's your mother's maiden name, Titus?"

"Beatrice."

"That him?" asked the agents next to Hammer and Braden.

"No. No way."

"What's your father's first name, Lieutenant?"

"Patrick."

"Negative. Repeat, negative," intoned Hammer's captor.

☆ ☆ ☆

"This is Lieutenant Anderson, my copilot," Lieutenant Higgins spoke, motioning to a tall man with dark hair, who shook HYDRA's hand.

In turn Higgins introduced HYDRA to half a dozen other crew members, saving the men who were on HYDRA's shift until last.

"Lieutenant, this is Lieutenant Bacon. He's on VLF."

A short man with thinning hair smiled at HYDRA and offered his hand.

"Lieutenant Sheldon on HF and UHF."

A medium-built man with blondish hair nodded in

HYDRA's direction.

"Our two authenticators," Higgins said with a hint of sarcasm, introducing HYDRA to a pair of slightly overweight technicians named Drew and Bruning. Besides authenticating Emergency Action Messages, Bruning and Drew also had the more mundane tasks of operating the TACAMO's interior communication system, plus a host of ancillary control and monitoring equipment.

"And not to forget Lieutenant Jameson, who operates our high frequency," Higgins added, turning to a taciturn-looking scientific type.

"You been on one of these before?" Bacon asked.

"No, can't say that I have," HYDRA replied.

"What'd you do your hours on, then?"

"Mostly E-3s," HYDRA replied, remembering Gereke's resume.

"Hey! I haven't seen it, but they say you won't have any problem — the message board on the TACAMO's an exact duplicate of the AWACS, so you should feel right at home!"

"That's what I've been told," offered HYDRA.

☆ ☆ ☆

In the darkened room on the seventh floor of the Hoover Building, David Woodring and several of the staff members of the Counterterrorism Center watched Special Agent Johnson conduct his ninety-second interview with a crew member of the USS *Eisenhower.* On a second screen appeared the faces of the two code clerks and the pair of agents holding them.

"What's your position on this submarine?"

"Battlestations OOD," replied a short, intense-looking Hispanic.

"No way," Hammer's voice filled the room. "He's way too short."

"I agree," added Braden.

"Negative on this one. Subject's too short."

"How many more to go?" Woodring asked aloud.

"At least sixty, sir," replied Lanier.

"Shit!" Woodring cursed. "This'll take forever!"

"... and before I begin asking you any questions, I want to inform you that if you mention that you had this conversation — " the sound of Johnson's voice was interrupted by the insistent ringing of a nearby telephone.

"Woodring...right...a fire...arson...she was shot ..." Woodring slammed down the telephone, then picked it up again and sent a direct order to Agent Johnson to expedite the Bangor interrogations.

Due to Pax River's role as the Naval Air Command's principal site for in-flight meeting, in any given year its busy air traffic control officers handle over a quarter of a million movements (takeoffs and landings) from the base's runways. For that reason, the appearance at 2:50 p.m. of Navy Airliner 63918, a large Boeing E-6A, on Taxiway A, behind a de Havilland U-6A Beaver, an old single-engine, orange and black demonstrator, was little cause for concern. Besides concerning themselves with the two planes about to take off, the base controllers already had to contend with a pair of McDonnell Douglas/British Aerospace T-45A Goshawk development and three T-38 Talon supersonic advanced trainer aircraft which were already aloft and maneuvering inside the base's 7,000 square miles of airspace.

Inside the cockpit of his E-6A TACAMO, Lieutenant Higgins listened to the controller give his final instruction to the demonstrator before takeoff.

"Pax Tower, de Havilland Four Five Two Five Intersection Ten ready for takeoff."

"De Havilland Four Five Two Five, Runway Six Two, cleared for takeoff."

The little orange de Havilland took off down the runway, leaving the ground right before Johnson Road.

"Boeing Six Three Nine One Eight, remain this frequency, taxi to ramp."

While the air controller was directing Captain Higgins to move onto the runway, in the rear of the E-6A its eight communications officers were busy bringing their own onboard radios and command links online. Based on the design of the AWACS E-3, the TACAMO is a nuclear hardened derivative of the Boeing 707-320B commercial aircraft, which was ordered to replace the previous fleet of propeller-driven Lockheed EC-130s. Equipped with custom-designed, fuel-efficient GE-SNECMA CFM-56 engines instead of the usual Pratt and Whitneys, the TACAMO could stay aloft for over sixteen hours and a total of seventy-two hours with additional in-flight refueling, more than enough time to conduct operations in a nuclear exchange.

Its complex communications system, originally developed by Rockwell International and later augmented by equipment from other manufacturers, was designed to function as a manned relay link between the National Command Authority and the SSBN fleets in both the Pacific and Atlantic. In place of the usual passenger seating compartments found in a Boeing 707 commercial airliner, the E-6A's cabin was partitioned into separate compartments housing its communication staff, sleeping quarters, no-break power supply for its electronics, computing and radio receiving and transmitting equipment.

Communications Central was where HYDRA, along with five other officers, was seated in a comfortable high-backed cushioned chair attached to separate metal tracks located in the middle of the cabin. Of the six men in the communications crew, Lieutenant Jack Gereke had the most important post, that of Communications Officer, allowing HYDRA to control the routing and transmission of every incoming message.

"Pax Tower, Boeing Six Three Nine One Eight at intersection Ten ready for takeoff," Captain Higgins's voice echoed over HYDRA's headset.

"Boeing Six Three Nine One Eight, Runway Six Two cleared for takeoff."

HYDRA felt the four turbojets rock to life, moving the 340,000-pound armored aircraft.

☆ ☆ ☆

"Come on! Let's hurry this up! Get me the next guy in here!" shouted Special Agent Johnson. "You, Goodman, get another chair over here, we'll do two at a time! Come on! Move it! Move it!"

Inside the crew's mess FBI agents dashed about, trying to fill all of Johnson's commands at once. A second special agent from CI-5 sat in a chair next to his superior waiting to interrogate his own subject, while Johnson conducted his.

"Where are they? Get them the fuck in here!" Johnson ordered. Two fresh faces winced under the camcorder's bright light, as they were hustled past the metal door and slammed into a pair of empty chairs.

"Hi. I'm Forest Johnson, special agent with FBI Counterintelligence." The agent next to Johnson was muttering the same phrase. "... before I ask you any questions I want to inform you that if you mention this conversation to any unauthorized individual ..."

"What's your name?" Johnson asked.

"Loputo, Phil."

"Rank and position, Loputo?" asked the second agent

"Electrical Operator, Lieutenant."

"Rank and position?"

"Chief Petty Officer, sir. Lieutenant."

"What do you think?" asked the special agent sitting next to Braden.

"No."

"No what? Which one is no? The tall one or the skinny one or both? Come on, we don't have all day here."

"Neither."

"What about you?" he pressed Hammer.

"It's neither. No way they're him."

"Great."

Hearing the negative report over his headset Johnson suddenly terminated both investigations. "Bring the next two in now! Come on people! Hurry! Hurry! Hurry!"

Lieutenants Gilham and Loputo were unceremoniously dragged from their chairs, both more relieved than shocked at how quickly their interviews had ended.

Chapter 47

As the interrogations at Bangor SUBASE continued, the Boeing E-6A which HYDRA was on cruised in an easterly direction over the Atlantic at an altitude of almost 40,000 feet, leaving whatever weather disturbances there were below. Seated in front of a computer-aided display/keyboard terminal and wearing a handsfree headset, HYDRA was already busy entering messages from Fleet Communications in Norfolk into the TACAMO's Message Processing system for routing and transmission by one of the five other operators. They had just been ordered to participate in an upcoming drill involving the entire Atlantic SSBN fleet.

A fact little publicized by the military authorities in the United States is that the nuclear strategic forces are constantly and continuously running drills which simulate their reactions and responses under an actual nuclear attack. The underlying reason for constant drilling is quite simple: in a system as critical as America's strategic nuclear forces, nothing can be left to chance. Constant drilling causes the participants to memorize each step, increasing efficiency and reducing their response times to a minimum; reveals flaws in communications, computer and weapons systems; and shows, most importantly, which individuals are not capable of handling the stress of nuclear-weapons related duties.

The operator sitting next to HYDRA, Lieutenant Andy Bacon, ignored his teleprinter as it spat out a series of last-minute instructions from Fleet Communications.

"You sleep OK last night?" Bacon asked, noticing HYDRA looked a little bleary-eyed.

"Sure. Fine."

Bacon hit the return key on his console, and a moment later his CRT screen revealed the latest version of the E-6A's entire schedule, beginning with its departure at Patuxent Naval Air Station that afternoon at approximately 3:00 p.m. local time.

"Remember, we're not on-line yet. This isn't a hot box unless it's activated, like I told you at the base."

"Right."

Bacon checked his watch, then spoke as he typed, "OK, now we'd better review the alert ladder — we have to do this thing in the slim chance I've been disabled. You ready? This could take a while."

After HYDRA nodded affirmatively, Bacon punched the return key, bringing up a short list in green block letters which now glared on the screen. The file name, HYDRA noticed, was a single word, LADDER. An alert ladder organized in brutally simple fashion to allow a harried President to make a quick retaliatory response to a nuclear attack. The words "DEFCON-5, DEFCON-4, DEFCON-3, DEFCON-2, DEFCON-1," flashed upon the screen.

"OK, there're five rungs total, but all we care about here are the last three, the ones you see on the screen. For us,

DEFCON 3 means simple alert, DEFCON 2, reinforced alert, and DEFCON 1 is general alert, got it?"

HYDRA nodded affirmatively in response.

"NCA, CINCLANT, COMSUBLANT, SSBN, UNIT, SYSTEM," appeared next.

HYDRA watched the analyst hit a second key and almost instantaneously the screen was filled with a single question, "NCA, AUTHORIZATION APPROVED?"

"OK, that's the National Command Authority. You have to wait here until someone enters the command code for the President."

Bacon hit the TEST button on his keyboard and, in fascination HYDRA watched the screen reply:

"COMMAND STATUS CONFIRMED, SECDEF AUTHORIZATION APPROVED?"

"OK, here you wait for the Secretary of Defense to input his." Bacon hit the button YES on his keyboard, and the appropriate response appeared next.

"CINCLANT AUTHORIZATION APPROVED?"

Bacon hit the YES button again, and waited. "Now SecDef's telling the CIC Atlantic Fleet to get his act together and tell COMSUBLANT who and when to nuke."

"CINCLANT TARGETS APPROVED?"

"YES."

"Here the CIC approves the targeting list."

"TRANSMIT TO COMSUBLANT?"

"YES."

"Then he sends the message to sub command."

"COMSUBLANT TARGETS APPROVED?"

"YES."

"Then they confirm."

"REPEAT CONFIRMATION, COMSUBLANT TARGETS APPROVED?"

"YES."

"They reconfirm."

"FINAL CONFIRMATION, COMSUBLANT TARGETS APPROVED?"

"YES."

"FINAL CONFIRMATION RECEIVED, STANDBY FOR TARGET LIST."

"Then we recap."

The screen blinked twice, and HYDRA watched in astonishment as it began to rapidly scroll through an endless series of Russian-sounding names and acronyms. Finally, the two sentences,

"LAUNCH AUTHENTICATED — OPERATOR A?"

"LAUNCH AUTHENTICATED — OPERATOR B?"

appeared on the screen in tandem, one directly below the other. Bacon turned to HYDRA, a weird grin on his face.

"This is for us. This is where Tony and Pete on either side of us have to turn their keys before we can relay the targets to the fleet. They've both got to type in their personal codes and do it within twenty seconds of each other or the whole thing's history, right?"

"Right."

"Now, in a drill, the orders coming out of Norfolk are unauthenticated, so nothing's going to happen."

"OK, so let's get started," Bacon muttered to himself. Bacon added and as an afterthought punched his return key, clearing HYDRA's screen.

"We just did the big one."

"Russia?"

Bacon winked in response.

"Now let's keep in mind that that whole process might take up to twenty-five hours from a warning issued out of NORAD to the CIC to going through the whole command sequence for battlefield use."

"Twenty-five hours?"

Bacon swiveled in his chair and grinned conspiratorially at HYDRA. He had guessed immediately what the other man was thinking.

"Watch this," whispered the analyst as he typed the word NUCFLASH on the keyboard, then the number 1.

"WARPLANS, COUNTRIES, CITIES, OTHER."

"Okay, let's say the CIC wants to make a surprise attack on France. First we select the countries list," Bacon spoke and hit a single key, "then we locate the target city on that list — " the screen was instantaneously filled with a short list of strategic French cities and French military bases, " and presto."

"Now let's say the naval base at Toulouse has gotta go...all you do is find its number on the screen and type it in like this and wait."

"TARGET: COUNTRY: FRANCE, BASE: TOULOUSE, CONFIRM?" queried the CRT.

Bacon hit the YES button and HYDRA watched the screen blink back, "ATTACK ON TOULOUSE CONFIRMED, NEXT TARGET?"

"Pretty quick response, huh?" Bacon grinned.

"How does it work?"

"Simple. CIC punches in his NUCFLASH code and he achieves total system override over both NMCC at the Pentagon and CINCLANT in Norfolk. Target selection is actually made by a computer deep underground in Fort Ritchie, Maryland, and if that's blown away, by Looking Glass or Kneecap, whichever's left. That way, the CIC, who's a civilian, doesn't have to get bogged down in weapons systems decisions, like whether to use SSBNs, SSNs, B-52s or other aircraft, on ground and naval tactical nukes, etc., etc., etc."

"Situation HAMMERCUT," HYDRA muttered.

"Exactly," Bacon agreed. He surreptitiously glanced at the other operators, and covering the microphone on his headset, leaned closer to HYDRA's face. "Rumor is, that's today's drill — but you didn't hear it from me."

Chapter 48

From his seat in the darkened command room inside the SIOC Woodring and several of his staff members watched the last two interrogation candidates being led into the mess of the USS Eisenhower.

"Your name please?" sighed Special Agent Johnson, visibly exhausted from the endless questioning.

"Thomas Layton."

"That's not him!" Woodring exploded. "He's not on the boat! He's not on the goddamned boat!"

"... Buckner, Chip," answered the second crew member in the background.

"Then where is he?" asked Lanier.

"Somewhere he can use the codes," Woodring spoke, then turned to Thompson, his computer specialist. "Charlie, I want you to call the Pentagon and get their locator records on anybody, repeat anybody, who's scheduled to visit any base having anything to do with with nuclear operations for yesterday and today —" Woodring was interrupted by his telephone. "Woodring...right...yes, sir...right away." From the look on Woodring's face, Thompson guessed Hubert Myers was calling from his office. "I've got to go," Woodring announced, disappearing out of OPS1 into the corridor.

Accompanied by two HRT commandos, David Woodring dashed into FBI Director Myers's outer office, running past the receptionist down the full length of Hoover's fifty-foot-long corridor, where another pair of HRT agents stood guard outside the thick oaken door to Myers's office. The sentries immediately waved Woodring through, pushing open the bulletproof door to the large conference room with its impressive fireplace.

Sitting in his chair in an office, lit only by the lamp on his desk, Director Myers barely stirred as Woodring entered. "The President just called," he gloomily announced. "If I'm approved, I'll be the new DCI." Woodring didn't know whether to congratulate his superior or not due to the circumstances surrounding his promotion.

"In any event, we're already late to the NFIB. You're ready to go, I hope?"

"Yes, sir," Woodring answered, out of breath.

"The car's waiting downstairs."

Woodring followed Director Myers and his pair of bodyguards to Myers's private elevator, his shirt soaked with sweat. In seconds they reached the basement garage where the Director's car was waiting for them along with four HRT agents, each perched on a separate motorcycle. The small motorcade roared out of the Hoover Building's Pennsylvania Avenue exit on its short trip to the National Foreign Intelligence Board Headquarters eight blocks away.

From the car window, Woodring spotted several plainclothes teams dressed in anoraks, walking German shepherds along the street, watching for any unusual signs of activity. They had just been informed to take unusual precautions and detain any suspicious persons in a specially designated facility not connected to the capital's corrections system. Woodring had also ordered an FBI SWAT team to be choppered in from Quantico, Virginia to man twenty different rooftop locations.

In fact, by 5:00 p.m. that evening the building having the NFIB had had a complete change of staff, picked from the various armed services' commando groups, most of whom were expert shots with small arms, although other skills were represented in abundance. For these men alone, the mask had harshly been removed, while they were making the last leg of their trip to Washington aboard a Chinook transport helicopter. A man they had never seen before, after introducing himself as the Assistant Director of the FBI, issued them the most bizarre set of orders they had ever heard in their careers. *If any member of either Director Daniels's or Director Myers's staff or any other official from the FBI, CIA, or any other agency should make any untoward motion towards anyone, this individual should be immediately restrained by whatever force is necessary. Failure to apply such force will subject all affected personnel to immediate courts martial.*

When they arrived, plainclothesmen surrounded Myers's car, forming a human shield around the FBI director and his assistant as they entered the NFIB. The corridor was lined with a mixture of HRT plainclothesmen and SWAT personnel all holding unsheathed automatic weapons.

Once assembled, each attendee to the second meeting wore a more somber mien than before, since each felt he was now a victim of a scheme whose sophistication had been greatly underestimated. News of Keith Axe's murder mixed with rumors of terrorism and assassination squads were already racing like wildfire around official Washington. Equally disturbing to all those who had participated in the first emergency session was the unexpected presence of Secretary of Defense Rutger Chase along with the Joint Chiefs of Staff, who, obviously for security purposes, had been told to attend without wearing their usual uniforms.

Once again Woodring and Myers were late; all the other participants had already arrived and were in their seats. But unlike the previous NFIB meeting Woodring had attended with Director Myers, this time the attendees were awaiting the arrival of the two FBI men before convening the proceedings.

All eyes followed Woodring as he made his way to the empty chair next to the right of Hubert Myers. Behind Director Myers a pair of technicians followed, wheeling in a rack of equipment identical to that used previously in Room 208 next door. Wordlessly and quickly they swept every inch of every wall, then, when Lincoln Daniels motioned to the participants, each man stood up in turn and was subjected to an electromagnetic search. Nothing unusual was found, and Daniels reluctantly called the meeting to order.

"Gentlemen."

All heads automatically turned and faced Lincoln Daniels at the head of the table.

"At the specific request of the President the originally scheduled topic of tonight's meeting, the case of Captain Edwin D. Bailey, has been tabled until a later date. I believe Assistant Director Woodring has recently demonstrated beyond a reasonable doubt that Captain Bailey is not HYDRA and that further discussion of Bailey's whereabouts will only delay HYDRA's capture." Before anyone could protest the sudden removal of Axe's death and Bailey's disappearance from the agenda, someone knocked on the door causing Daniels to pick up his telephone. "Send him in," grunted the DCI.

A pair of Secret Service agents stepped through the door, escorting a solemn and haggard Bill Clinton. Each participant rose from his chair, tonelessly uttering the words, "Mr. President" under his breath. The President shook no hands, and proceeded swiftly to the opposite end of the room, where he set an empty chair at the head of the conference table. A pair of bodyguards remained standing next to the wall on either side of him.

"Lincoln," the President spoke in a harsher voice than normal, "let's get on with it."

"Thank you, Mr. President," the DCI paused and noisily cleared his throat. "I believe Director Woodring has some news for us."

Woodring performed a last minute arrangement of the four stacks of papers in front of him, then spoke in the detached, matter-of-fact tone of a medical doctor delivering a piece of bad news, "I'm afraid that yesterday HYDRA managed to breach the security of Bangor SUBASE.

"He was traveling under the guise of Mr. Russell Matthews, a Navy SEAL, dishonorably discharged due to an incident which occurred at Seal Beach, California, in an obvious attempt to mislead in the same manner he's used with Bailey.

"For his arrival at the base, he used the identification of a certain Sergeant Peter Koester. The real Sergeant Koester is employed as a technical services courier at the Naval Investigative Service. In an interview conducted by myself and General Curtis Vaughn with two clerks of the Strategic Weapons Facility coderoom while two of my agents were present, the two clerks testified that they allowed the person they believed was Koester to open up the laser encryption gun, remove its chips and insert two replacements, then to administer an Operation TEMPEST evaluation to that same gun.

"Employees Hammer and Braden also stated that Koester, in addition to carrying a regulation device known as a spectrum analyzer, also had in his possession what appeared to be a miniature personal computer — "

"Director Woodring!"

"Director Woodring!"

"Silence! Gentlemen! Enough! One question at a time!" shouted National Security Advisor, J. Mark McDowell.

"Shit!" cursed Frank Chalmers, Director, NSA, "those bastards let him download the codes!"

"Exactly," Woodring agreed in resignation.

Several of the participants looked at each other in disgust, while General Robert Shelton, Chairman of the Joint Chiefs, left his chair and stood in front of the World Situation Chart. He flipped a switch, and scores of glowing dotted arcs traced their paths across the Atlantic.

"A text of the Single Integrated Operation Plan has been provided and is in your binders," Shelton informed his stunned audience in a neutral tone.

Each attendee felt his skin crawl as he read the transcript with its twin vertical borders formed by the four-letter sequence, SIOP. No one in the room had to be told that SIOP stood for Single Integrated Operational Plan, the nation's complete operations plan for full-scale nuclear war. Thousands of Emergency Action Messages (EAMs) for ordering execution of every possible option of the SIOP were also listed in their entirety, along with the particular mode of communications to be used for each.

"What does this mean? That whoever has the codes can launch an attack?" demanded Al Gore, the Vice-President, looking up from a page entitled, EAM NO. 1247 TO SSBN EISENHOWER VIA TACAMO.

"That's right," answered General Olsen, Director of the Defense Special Missile and Aeronautics Command.

"So how long would it take to reprogram all the Emergency Action Messages?" demanded Larry Maddox, the President's chief of staff.

"I can answer that," General Vaughn replied, and all eyes focused on the director of the Defense Communications Agency. "At any one time the National Military Command Center has about 5,000 total shelters, strategic bombers, SSBNs, and tacticals to alert. Many of the platforms that have EAMs built into their hardware which would have to be ripped out, reprogrammed and replaced. In other words, if the order was given to rewrite, it could take months to execute."

"Let's assume, General," Larry Maddox continued, "that this HYDRA has gotten hold of the launch codes — could he go ahead and execute some part of this plan?"

"Only if he convinces whoever's he's talking to that he's the

Commander in Chief and that he's got a damn good reason."

The President blinked, then pulled a plastic card the size of a credit card from his shirt pocket and tossed it on the table. No one picked it up. "Then what good are they to him then? Whether he's impersonating my voice or not, we just tell him there's no deal, we're not gonna launch!"

"That's right, Mr. President."

"What about the second case?"

"Well, you've got it in your folder there, right in front of you."

"General, this document's over a thousand pages long!" protested Maddox.

General Vaughn cleared his throat and looked straight at Maddox. "The final section of the plan, labelled Situation HAMMERCUT, includes a provision for the CIC to override the National Military Command Center and take over the command center's processing and display system and issue orders directly over the MEECN network himself, after having picked his targets."

"But I thought you just told us, that any launch order's going to run into human interference as soon as it reaches WWMCCS!" Maddox objected a second time.

Vaughn said nothing, looking first at the President, then to General Shelton, Chairman of the Joint Chiefs, with a pained look on his face.

"Excuse me, gentlemen," Mark McDowell interrupted. "I can understand the military's reticence to delve into this area — but, at the moment, I really don't think we've got much choice."

The President gave a slight nod of his head for Shelton to respond to Maddox's question. "I think we must all realize that once Situation HAMMERCUT has been declared, the capability of the National Command Authority to respond to an ICBM attack is quite different than the speed at which we could respond to a rogue cruise missile attack, if it happened to be launched just off our coastline.

"As we all know in the case of an intercontinental ballistic missile attack, NORAD would have about five minutes to initiate a conference of all the appropriate watch officers of each command center and another two minutes to receive authorization to use the joint operating planning system's computers to retaliate in time to avoid an X-ray pin-down — "

"What's that?" asked Al Gore.

"The Sovs, sorry, the Russians could explode four or five SLBM warheads exoatmospherically," Gore furrowed his brow in noncomprehension "that is, predetonate a few nukes about three hundred miles up to neutralize our existing communications — "

"But Bob, I thought we installed a fiber optics communications system for just that very reason," inserted Clinton.

"We did, Mr. President, but I think we all have to realize here there's really no way to measure what effect that a sudden pulse equal to literally tens of thousands of accelerated lightning bolts would have on our command structure — "

"So what happens in HAMMERCUT?" Clinton interrupted.

"If the NCA decides we're the subject of a cruise missile attack launched by SLBMs off our coasts there is essentially almost no time to do anything else but release retaliatory authorization as soon as possible — "

"Who can issue it?"

"The NCA."

"You mean the President, of course?"

"Not exactly, Mr. President. Under HAMMERCUT any strategic commander can execute the order — "

"Like who?"

"Ourselves, NORAD, SAC, EUCOM in Brussels, CIN-CLANT, CINCPAC, or the Military Airlift Command at Scott Air Force Base in Illinois and about twenty other commands —"

"*Twenty others?*"

"Mr. President, it's important to note that the operators on duty will have to confirm first that the MEECN network has, in fact, been knocked out, before they would be liable to carry out any kind of preemptive order — no matter who issued it to them."

Chief of staff Maddox summarized, "So, General, even in this case, it would be highly unlikely that anyone in the field would launch, if, after they check in with the command center over the MEECN network and they find everything's OK."

"That's right."

"But what if their communications net's been jammed by a Trojan Horse?"

General Shelton sighed, then leaned forward in his chair with an irritated look upon his face. "I think, Mr. Maddox, that it would be highly unlikely that anything, except a direct nuclear explosion, could succeed in crippling every method of communication to our strategic forces all at once."

"Curtis, do you agree with that?" asked the President.

"No," replied General Vaughn. "Not in this case."

Vaughn knew he had nothing to lose, his career at the Pentagon was finished, so he decided to go down fighting.

"That's right, I don't agree. Ever since the thing began, we've always been one, two steps behind this HYDRA. Everything he's done so far is the hallmark of a first-class professional who knows exactly where he's going. He's got the codes and he's going to take it all way."

"So what can we do to stop him?" asked Bill Clinton sotto voce, his voice starting to crack.

Vaughn looked the Commander in Chief straight in the eye as he spoke, "Mr. President, I say we order every strategic nuclear asset to stand down, starting now."

General Robert Shelton traded looks of consternation with

his five subordinates, then nodded at Admiral Alexander who already had his hand half-raised in the air, demanding to be allowed to speak.

"Admiral," muttered President Clinton.

"Mr. President, with all due respect to General Vaughn, who, I understand, is quite upset about this attack upon his command, I think it's important to realize here that with the SSBN fleet, at least, the Navy can't just flip a switch and have each sub stand down its missile tubes. We'll have to notify the fleet at sea over the ELF to ascend to laser depth en masse — something I'm sure that won't go unnoticed by our Russian friends. Besides, as I understand it, Mr. Woodring's already detained the crew of the *Eisenhower* at port in Bangor so there's no way this HYDRA's going to be able to do anything there — "

"With all due respect to your position, Admiral Alexander," Clinton interrupted, "I don't think we have any choice. Bob, how do I give the order to stand down?"

"We'd send out a FLASH-level PINNACLE Report from the National Military Command Center, Mr. President."

"Can we do it from here?"

"Yes, sir, if you authorize it."

"Mr. President, what do you want to tell the Russians?" pleaded Admiral Alexander.

"I'll get to that in a minute!" Clinton snapped. "Curtis, if I authorize a general stand down, are we in the clear?"

"No."

Clinton's face clouded over. "You just told me — "

"Excuse me, Mr. President," Frank Chalmers, Director of NSA, intervened, "I'm afraid that General Vaughn hasn't fully explained the implications of what Dr. Saleh has done — "

"Godamnit! I want to know right now! Can I put an end to this or not?"

"No, sir."

"*Why not?*"

"It's very likely that the compromised platform will never receive the PINNACLE report, if Dr. Saleh's tampered with the communications software — "

"That's bullshit!" Clinton erupted. "What do we have a million men in uniform for? Shut all of it down NOW! I want you to check every silo, every airplane, every control center and every ship this man could have boarded or anyone else — I don't give a shit what it takes — get it done!"

No one in the room dared to break the silence. None of them were sure if President Clinton were still in control of his faculties, and, if he weren't, what exactly they were supposed to do about it. The President had just proposed a temporary unilateral disarmament of America's entire strategic nuclear forces, something that in their worst nightmares none of the participants had ever imagined.

"Mr. President," General Shelton ventured, and President Clinton nodded to the Chairman of the Joint Chiefs to continue.

"Do you want to hand me your code card?"

President Clinton mechanically scraped the laminated card off the table and handed it to Lincoln Daniels next to him.

Shelton picked up the telephone next to him and dialed the telephone number of the Crisis Management Room at the National Military Command Center at the Pentagon where a duty officer immediately responded.

☆ ☆ ☆

"Crisis Management Room, Captain Bryant speaking." Bryant was seated at a twenty-foot-long console with two other officers, above which was an equally long panel of plastic buttons similar to those found on office telephones which represented direct lines to hundreds of different bases and command centers. Bryant's eyes widened and his body tensed up the moment Shelton gave his name and rank, then issued him a properly authenticated command to execute Operation BROKEN ARROW, a massive computer exercise where each of 5,000 nuclear platforms would receive simultaneous orders to reject all Emergency Action Messages for the next twenty-four hours, whether authenticated or not.

"Shit," Bryant uttered, hanging up the handset with a shaking hand. Lieutenant Colonel Jacobs who was sitting next to him, saw Bryant's face had turned ashen.

"What?"

"That was Shelton. He just gave the order to stand down. He was with the President."

☆ ☆ ☆

"CINC-SAC," General Dick Turner announced.

Air Force General Turner was the Commander in Chief of the Strategic Air Command (SAC), based at Offutt Air Force Base just outside Omaha, Nebraska. The Strategic Air Command is in charge of land-based strategic bombers and underground missile sites throughout the United States. In 1990 its air order of battle included 178 B-52G Stratofortresses, 96 B-52H Stratofortresses, 61 FB-111A, and 97 B1-B bombers, plus 450 Minuteman II, 500 Minuteman III, and 50 MX Peacekeeper Intercontinental Ballistic Missiles, in addition to over 3,000 air-launched cruise missiles available to the B-52, FB-111, and B-1 bomber fleets. In an emergency situation, the Commander in Chief could also order up one or more of the SAC's fleet of thirteen EC-135 airborne command posts, known by the more familiar name "Looking Glass", which General Turner would do immediately after making his next phone call.

"Get me Admiral Scott," Turner said flatly, then depressed the switchhook and dialed his Deputy Chief of Operations on duty inside the base's new underground command post.

☆ ☆ ☆

"Major General — " the chief of staff stopped short, interrupted by the Commander in Chief. "Yes, sir…right away, sir…you are now authenticating," General McCord brought up a screenful of codes on the CRT in front of him "… yes, sir, BROKEN ARROW confirmed." McCord severed the connection, blew the air out of his cheeks, stared straight ahead of the eight quiet display screens through the window in his office, then punched a second line, connecting him to a third general in in one of the glassed-in offices next to his.

"You've got it on your screen? …Right, I'm authenticating," McCord spoke nervously, entering the code numbers on his terminal. "Execute…BROKEN ARROW now."

BROKEN ARROW was just one of many scenarios developed by a little-known division of the Strategic Air Command called the Joint Strategic Target Planning Staff (JSTPS). Consisting of some 300 ex-SAC-bomber-missile-crew members and Navy submariners, JSTPS more than any other group is responsible for developing the Single Integrated Operational Plan (SIOP) of the United States. In reality, SIOP is a misnomer, because it really involves a full range of responses developed with every conceivable circumstance in mind. A system of IBM 3080 mainframe computers with VAX 11/780 front ends was designed to produce detailed plans for execution for the JSTPS staff, based on almost any conceivable enemy strategy, including theft of the nation's authentication codes.

The moment Generals Turner and McCord put BROKEN ARROW into action, 5,000 Emergency Action messages simultaneously poured out of SAC's computers, warning every command center possessing nuclear weapons to stand down for the next twenty-four hours and to refuse to accept any further EAMs, whether authenticated or not. At the same time, military intelligence agents from Army CID, Navy NIS and the Air Force Intelligence Agency were ordered by the

NMCC to report immediately to every one of the 5,000 platforms, save for the eighteen SSBNs already at sea and the TACAMO already aloft over the Atlantic Ocean.

The set of Emergency Action Messages intended for the SSBN fleet at sea and emanating from SAC Headquarters at Offutt Air Force Base wasn't, of course, able to reach its intended recipients instantaneously. Since the major strategic value of the SSBN fleet is the enemy's inability to locate it before or after an initial surprise attack, nuclear submarines on patrol tend to cruise at depths too deep to be reached by most radio frequencies. Ultra-high frequency (UHF) broadcasts via satellite can, at best, penetrate only a few feet of water before being dispersed. Very-low frequency (VLF) signals, transmitted either from Fleet Communications in Norfolk, Virginia or by the TACAMO overhead can penetrate only fifty feet at best, while the recently developed SSIX satellite blue-green laser communications system can penetrate as low as 225 feet.

Thus, at normal cruising depths only one method exists to contact a SSBN at sea, the Navy's Extremely Low Frequency (ELF) radio transmitter located in the Upper Peninsula region of Michigan, possessing an antenna over twenty miles long. Because the available bandwidth of ELF is so small, the data rate possible from this system is only one bit per minute, meaning the three-letter Emergency Action Message for Operation BROKEN ARROW required a full twenty-four minutes to transmit.

Inside the TACAMO the three radio operators who were wearing handsfree headsets suddenly heard a loud, insistent tone which repeated six times, paused a full second, then repeated a second six times. At first, all of them, including HYDRA, assumed that Fleet Communications was signalling them that day's drill had begun. Instead, HYDRA, sitting in Gereke's position as communications officer, watched the following short cable automatically appear on the screen of his Message Processing System:

Z151504ZMAR

COMPARTMENTALIZED TOP SECRET

FM: CINCLANTFLT

TO: TACAMO

INFO: CINCSAC

1. ASSUME SITUATION BROKEN ARROW IN EFFECT IMMEDIATELY.

2. BE READY IN TEN MINUTES TO CONFIRM ABOVE TO USS OHIO, USS GEORGIA, USS GEO W CARVER, USS NEVADA, USS JOHN C CALHOUN, USS MICHIGAN, USS WILL ROGERS, USS ANDREW JACKSON, USS ALABAMA.

Before HYDRA even finished reading the FLASH cable he felt a hollow feeling in his stomach. Events were racing ahead of schedule — this wasn't a drill — the authorities had somehow happened onto Sergeant Koester's visit to Bangor and had gone into a panic.

"Jesus, someone's got the codes," Bacon spoke aloud, standing over HYDRA's shoulder, giving him a start.

HYDRA summoned all his forces, trying to regain his composure as he wondered to himself how nervous Gereke would be if he were in the same situation, "You mean this isn't a drill?"

"No, this isn't a drill. This is the real thing."

"What do we do now?"

"What do we do? We watch the screen — look, they're already taking over."

HYDRA watched in horror as BROKEN ARROW's logic chain rapidly unfolded before his eyes.

*** BROKEN ARROW DEFCON-2 REINFORCED ALERT. STANDBY. ***

*** BROKEN ARROW *** BROKEN ARROW *** BROKEN ARROW ***

NCA AUTHORIZATION APPROVED?

YES.

COMMAND STATUS CONFIRMED, CINCLANT AUTHORIZATION APPROVED?

YES.

REPEAT CONFIRMATION, CINCLANT AUTHORIZATION APPROVED?

YES.

FINAL CONFIRMATION, CINCLANT AUTHORIZATION APPROVED?

YES.

FINAL CONFIRMATION RECEIVED, STANDING BY FOR TACAMO CONFIRMATION...

FINAL CONFIRMATION RECEIVED, STANDING BY FOR TACAMO CONFIRMATION...

FINAL CONFIRMATION RECEIVED, STANDING BY FOR TACAMO CONFIRMATION...

The last phrase, STANDING BY FOR TACAMO CONFIRMATION now scrolled endlessly down the monitor while an incessant high-pitched alarm tone rang in the operator's headsets.

"What are you waiting for? Route it to me!" Bacon shouted over the intercom, snapping HYDRA awake. HYDRA punched a key on his console, then turned in his chair to watch Bacon confirm receipt of the FLASH-level alert over the VLF. Meanwhile, a second operator was busy sending a backup confirmation via UHF over the Fleet Schedule Communications System.

Now both messages popped up on HYDRA's CRT; it was the communications officer's duty to first encrypt them, then release them into the message processing center for transmission. He automatically entered the command to first send Bacon's message to the VERDIN transmit terminal for anti-jam MSK coding and modulation and security encryption, then released it to the TACAMO's powerful 200-kilowatt VLF transmitter for transmission over the airplane's 25,000 foot-long dual trailing wire antenna. Seconds later he performed a similar procedure for the UHF transmission, uplinking it to an FLTSATCOM satellite 23,000 miles overhead.

Chapter 49

Thirty minutes after Woodring's request for the records of nuclear operations personnel was relayed to the Pentagon, high-speed printers in the Counterterrorism Center inside the Hoover Building came to life, spewing out the records of 753 individuals who had been scheduled to arrive in the last forty-eight hours at the 50 U.S., and 160 foreign bases possessing nuclear weapons. Sent along with the 753 files was a large chart listing all 210 bases and names of each squadron assigned to each base. A brief synopsis describing the duties of each and every squadron was also set out in 200-page-long Appendix, which was labelled *U.S. Nuclear Forces.*

The moment the printers went silent, computer operators in the CTC gathered up the entire printout and rushed it to Charlie Thompson in the Strategic Information Operations Center on the fifth floor. He immediately began to parcel out the various personnel files to his staff, who, in turn, telefaxed them to the relevant FBI field office for immediate action. Since up until now only the counterintelligence staffs in Washington, New York, and Los Angeles had been involved in the investigation, Special-Agents-in-Charge of the remaining fifty-four field offices were somewhat shocked by the proviso in these orders specifically requiring them to travel to the bases listed by the fastest possible means of transportation, regardless of cost or ownership. In other words, each SAC was suddenly empowered to commandeer any transport vehicle, whether publicly or privately owned, in or out of use, to accomplish his mission. None of the SACs had to be told what was happening: the text of the order regarding vehicular seizure had been lifted verbatim out of a secret set of regulations regarding a nuclear terrorist attack developed by the Federal Emergency Management Agency.

Four and a half minutes after the message was received aboard the TACAMO, an alarm bell went off inside the radio room of the USS *Alabama*, signifying an Emergency Action Message had just been sent over the ELF. The communications officer, Sean Kiefer, naturally assumed the message would inform them to ascend to antenna depth to receive additional orders for that tour's scheduled drill and had grown used to waiting patiently while the radio duty man transcribed the message on high speed tape. The communications officer set the code book in front of him and opened it. The book was a one-time-pad cipher which descrambled the three-letter groups broadcast over the ELF.

Rumor had passed amongst the tight-knit submarine fraternity at Kings Bay of a Situation HAMMERCUT drill, so the communications officer wasn't surprised by the arrival of so short a message, but his complacency was dashed by an incessant and loud buzzing tone.

"ELF's gone off!" shouted the duty radioman.

"*It's what?*" gasped the communications officer. Looking at the flashing lights over the ELF radio, he turned to the captain. "What do we do now?"

Captain Frank Parker took one look at the lights flashing over the ELF, then gave the order, "Battle stations. Alert-one."

Meanwhile the duty radioman handed the transcription of the ELF to the communications officer who flattened his codebook on the console.

"This is garbage," he uttered to himself.

"All hands, man your battle stations!" blared over the intercom.

"This is garbage!" Kiefer repeated, this time more loudly.

Captain Parker, about to order his XO to ascend to antenna depth, turned abruptly towards Kiefer. "It's what?"

"It's garbage, sir. There aren't even any letter groups, just numbers — "

Parker tore the message out of Kiefer's hand, examining the transcription himself. Never in his entire career as a submariner had he ever heard of the ELF ceasing transmission, much less transmitting unintelligible messages.

"Must be the radio, check it out," he muttered, then turning to the XO, "let's take her to laser depth."

The XO blinked; in a normal exercise Captain Parker would have ordered him to ascend to sixty feet below the surface, high enough for them to send up the UHF antenna to receive direct radio transmission from the COMMSAT satellite overhead. But laser depth at 225 feet was much lower, allowing the *Alabama* to remain more deeply submerged as it awaited further transmissions from Atlantic Fleet Communications from Atlantic SSIX, the communications satellite developed exclusively for the SSBN fleet.

"Diving officer, make your depth two-two-five feet. Repeat, two-two-five."

Chapter 50

After a considerable amount of study both by in-house analysts from the Department of Defense and outside consultants retained from various private contractors and think tanks, the entire strategic command apparatus of the United States was rearranged in order to be able to respond as quickly as possible to a surprise nuclear attack from any remaining command post. Open telephone lines were established between the National Military Command Center (NMCC) at the Pentagon, the North American Aerospace Defense Command (NORAD) at Cheyenne Mountain, Colorado, the Strategic Air Command at Offutt Air Force Base, Nebraska, the

Alternate National Military Command Center at Ft. Ritchie, Maryland, "Looking Glass", SAC's airborne communications center, and "Kneecap", the National Emergency Airborne Command Post for the President. The various command centers were, in turn, all independently linked with the commanders-in-chief of the various nuclear forces throughout the United States, Europe, Korea and the rest of the world to enable any surviving command center to direct whatever nuclear forces were remaining.

A second set of analysts, similar to the ones who had formulated procedures and responses for a surprise nuclear attack, also redesigned the system used by the military to respond to crises, and formulated a complex series of Crisis Action Procedures to be followed by the Joint Planning and Execution Committee at the Pentagon under the Joint Chiefs of Staff. Phases One through Six were, in fact, outlined in some detail in *The Joint Staff Officers Guide*, a document whose contents General Robert Shelton had either memorized or studied at some length. But the system's emphasis was in executing plans, not in ordering itself to shut down, and whatever mission Victor Saleh had designed for HYDRA to carry out depended on exactly that, Shelton thought on his way back to the Pentagon.

Upon his arrival at the River Entrance to the Pentagon, General Shelton and his entourage immediately took a private elevator to the second floor and proceeded directly to the National Military Command Center, where they arrived in less than ten minutes due to the building's unique design. A crisis action team had already arrived, immediately augmenting the NMCC's normal staff by some one hundred individuals. A thousand separate telephone lights were blinking on and off, while scores of operators, each holding a partial computer printout in his hand, spoke at once over a variety of telephones. Literally the entire force of the various military intelligence services was being summoned into the field at once, being issued thousands of simultaneous instruction sets by the NMCC's powerful computers.

Advance units from the Air Force Intelligence Agency had already arrived and were already reporting in from several of the Strategic Air Command's twenty-five bases, since many of the intelligence officers who had been notified were located at the same base that they were assigned under BROKEN ARROW. Meanwhile, all twenty-six of the major command posts that were tied into the Wimex network were now occupied by an outside monitoring staff composed of intelligence officers from the service relevant to each command.

Shelton was sitting at a table in the Crisis Center Room, surrounded by members of his Joint Planning and Execution Committee who were advising him and the other Joint Chiefs of their options under BROKEN ARROW. A young lieutenant-colonel wearing glasses with tortoise shell frames had the floor.

"He's already had the codes for over twenty-four hours — we've got to go to POLE VAULT."

"Harry?" Shelton turned to the Vice Chairman.

"Agreed."

"Admiral?"

"He's right, we've got no choice," agreed Admiral Alexander.

Alexander's vote was quickly seconded by Chiefs of Staff for the Army and Air Force and the Commandant of the Marine Corps. Their solemn faces were being simultaneously teleconferenced to the other twenty-six command centers where they were being viewed on large-screen television monitors by each command staff.

"Mr. President?" Shelton spoke into his microphone.

"Agreed," Clinton's raspy voice broke the silence, his face automatically occupying everyone's screen. The President and the rest of the National Security Council were seated in the Situation Room in the White House basement.

"Mr. President, are you authenticating?" Shelton asked automatically.

"Yes."

Each participant watched an aide then hand the President a portable keyboard, pointing to a card Clinton had in his hand and gesturing, showing Clinton how to type in that day's codes. Clinton looked at the aide, then entered the codes into his machine. Upon receipt of the authenticated message, a computer clerk downloaded a large CD-ROM disk into the NMCC's computers, instantly instituting Situation POLE VAULT across the entire World Wide Military Command and Control Network. Once Situation POLE VAULT was declared, the communication paths of all 5,000 nuclear platforms were doubled up and copied back to SAC where they would be continuously monitored in order to locate and isolate anyone attempting to input an Emergency Action Message, whether authenticated or not.

☆ ☆ ☆

At the NMCC banks of blinking red lights which represented each separate nuclear platform turned from red to green. In seconds every light had changed color except for twenty-three which were still blinking red. Of the twenty-two red lights still blinking, eighteen represented the nine SSBNs afloat in the Pacific and another nine in the Atlantic; the remaining three represented SSBNs at port, and finally, the remaining light represented the single TACAMO plane presently aloft over the Atlantic. Due to the time lapse involved in relaying the order to surface over the ELF to the subs submerged the various sub commanders were only now receiving the previous set of authenticated orders regarding Operation BROKEN ARROW.

☆ ☆ ☆

Inside the TACAMO, HYDRA watched the digital readout of his CRT, knowing that in just seconds he had no choice but to release the orders for BROKEN ARROW to Andy Bacon, the VLF radio operator sitting on his left. Now the clock read 00:00:00, time to send. The final commands appeared on HYDRA's CRT, requesting the operator on either side of him to enter his own separate authentication code. While each was typing in his code, two rows of three asterisks each appeared on HYDRA's screen, giving him the cue to type the pound sign symbol on his keyboard twice. While each operator was turning his key, releasing the encrypted message from SAC back to the Message Center, HYDRA had just captured his fellow operators' separate pair of authentication codes and committed them to storage in his terminal. Next, HYDRA hit the return key on his console, releasing the EAM sent by the Strategic Air Command over the TACAMO's 200-kilowatt VLF transmitter to the sub fleet below.

Chapter 51

FBI Director Myers and David Woodring ran into the underground lobby of the Hoover Building, flipping their badges at the guard, then grabbed Myers's private elevator and took it express to the fifth floor. When it arrived they rushed down the corridor past the office of the assistant director of Command Investigation Division, towards the pair of HRT commandos who were stationed next to the red Restricted Access sign outside the SIOC, one of whom was already entering the special code. After the sentry punched in the combination, he turned the special lock, opening the door just in time for both men to dash through.

"Commander Reynolds is in the conference room," the duty officer informed them.

"Yes, sir — " the duty officer stopped speaking, Director Myers and Woodring had already run down the corridor past the control room, where Woodring entered OPS1, stopping at Charlie Thompson's work station.

"Did we get it?"

Thompson gestured towards the other nearby cubicles, each filled with a busy analyst talking rapidly into the telephone, his desk stacked with computer paper. Thompson picked up the 200-page-long annex and handed it to his boss.

· "This came for you."

Woodring read the title, *U.S. Nuclear Forces*, then snatched the document out of Thompson's hands, returning with it to his office.

The moment he sat down at his desk, Woodring now immersed himself in the reports, refreshing his memory on America's nuclear arsenal. At first, he was overwhelmed by the immensity of forces required to operate and maintain the United States' strategic forces — every day over 115,000 personnel were performing operations, maintenance, security, custody, and C3I duties at total of 210 military bases in the U.S. and Europe in addition to related facilities belonging to the Department of Energy and the Defense Nuclear Agency.

He dropped the Appendix on his desk, leaned back in his chair and stretched, sighing deeply. What had HYDRA done so far? he asked himself. He'd downloaded the codes, codes good for the next six months. Woodring somehow doubted HYDRA was going to wait to use them — he was smart enough to know he couldn't afford to. So where did he go?

A bomber base? Woodring closed his eyes, reviewing the text of the appendix in his head. Only a portion of the aircraft belonging to the Strategic Air Command were preflighted and ready to take off at a moment's notice. This month, as was noted in *U.S. Nuclear Forces*, they were the 319th Bomb Wing at Grand Forks Air Force Base in North Dakota and the 7th at Carswell Air Force Base in Texas. Carswell had B-52s, but the 319th at Grand Forks, had B-1Bs, a much harder plane to fly than a B-52.

A missile base? These were more problematical because there were several of them, their operations were spread out over thousands of square miles, and HYDRA wouldn't need to know how to fly a strategic bomber. The 150 Minuteman II ICBM silos and related control centers operated out of Whiteman Air Base, for example, were spread over a 10,000-square-mile area throughout the state of Missouri. Woodring noted wearily that a whole host of redundant control centers had been installed at each missile base upon recommendation of the Joint Strategic Target Planning Staff to prevent nuclear decapitation in the event of a Soviet surprise attack, further complicating the search for HYDRA.

For the moment Woodring ruled out the SSBN fleet, since the only sub scheduled to leave in the last forty-eight hours was the *Eisenhower*, which CI-5 had already examined with a fine-tooth comb. He also thought it was unlikely HYDRA was planning an attack on either the manufacturing facilities belonging to the Department of Energy or on the storage facilities under the Defense Nuclear Agency — both HYDRA's stealing the launch codes and the fact that the actual bombs themselves were specifically designed to decouple physical possession from acting control mitigated against physical theft.

Whoever had the codes, had control, Woodring thought to himself. And whoever had the codes could give commands — in a worse case, making people obey his commands if they were convinced they were legitimate.

So was HYDRA at a command center? Woodring snapped forward in his chair and flipped through the appendix to the chapter entitled, "Worldwide Military Command and Control System — WWMCCS." The first page was a diagram composed of small black triangles and circles linked to larger hollow circles representing host computer systems and labeled with acronyms like NMCC, ANMCC, USEUCOM, PACWRAC, LANTCOM, MAC, CCSA, MASTERIMP, NEACP (ANDREWS), etc. Over thirty-two different locations possessed either host computers, terminals, or the intermessage processors linked into Wimex, not including any of the airborne command centers, like the Looking Glass, one of which had just been launched in the last hour. The telephone rang, interrupting Woodring's thoughts.

"OPS1...yes sir...right."

Hubert Myers was calling in from the conference room. Woodring ran out of OPS1 into the conference room, finding Director Myers engaged in a teleconference with J. Mark McDowell in the White House Situation Room. Next to Myers with a grim look on his face was seated Wesley Reynolds, head of Command Black, the top secret counterterrorism group, which in case of a nuclear emergency would provide the necessary ground forces to the Nuclear Emergency Search Team headquartered in Germantown, Maryland, with branch locations in Nevada, California, Colorado, and Washington, D.C.

Created by executive order of President Ford in 1974 after an extortionist threatened to detonate a nuclear bomb in Boston, Command Black had the widest purview of all the federal counterterrorist units, whether military or civilian. Unlike the rest of the military, Command Black didn't share its channels of communication, but received its orders in person by presidential courier. Electronic communications, instead of being conducted over WWMCCS or CRITIC were sent over the President's FEMA network — a separate communications net authorized by the Federal Emergency Management Act to be used after a nuclear attack.

To further prevent the press from discovering the unit's existence, FBI authorities never missed a chance to emphasize that membership in neither its elite Hostage Rescue Team nor its various SWAT teams was composed of permanent employees — that both were largely "paper units", only to be activated during emergencies, which, in fact, was true. The staffing of Command Black, however, was anything but temporary; most of its members had never even seen the inside of an FBI field office and wouldn't know what to do if they were in one. Picked from an eclectic mixture of military CT units and various intelligence agencies, Black Commandos were given an intensive one-year-long training course in nuclear operations in a separate wing of the FBI training facility at Quantico, Virginia, then shipped to another secret facility at the Federal Law Enforcement Training Center in Georgia for a second year-long field course whose focus was identifying, locating, dismantling, and defusing live nuclear weapons of all types. Another unpublicized facet of the course at Glynco were drills whose major purpose was acclimating Black Commandos to firing upon "friendly" troops, in case a renegade unit of the U.S. Armed Forces were to attempt to steal or detonate one of their own nuclear weapons. Methodology of both U.S. and foreign CT forces was also scrutinized in order to help neutralize an attack by a determined professional, or group of professionals, who possessed capabilities equivalent to the group's.

A courier who had just arrived from the White House Situation Room, carrying a copy of President Clinton's freshly signed National Security Intelligence Decision Directive activating Reynolds's unit, handed the NSIDD to Director Myers while the others looked on.

"The President wants to know how soon you can be at Andrews," McDowell pointedly asked Commander Reynolds.

"Can I take a helicopter?"

"Commander Reynolds, you can have your pick of any aircraft military or civilian in the D.C. area. We just want you at that base."

"We'll take care of it," Myers said with finality.

"Thanks Hubert," replied McDowell, then the large screen went blank.

Turning to Woodring, Myers asked him to fill him in on the arrival of the locator files from the Pentagon.

Chapter 52

It only took two minutes for the USS *Alabama* to ascend less than two hundred feet to laser-depth, but once it reached 225 feet, the submarine started taking rolls, suddenly listing five degrees. Inside the control room, already rigged for red, Captain Parker told himself the failure of the ELF was simply an unannounced twist in an otherwise routine missile drill, a fact which would hopefully soon be confirmed by Fleet Command. The rest of the crew, who had no knowledge that the ELF had ceased transmitting, were busy performing routine checks of their sequence lists, quietly talking to themselves as they ticked off item after item.

Inside the missile control center, technicians, their faces illuminated by racks of equipment lined with small white lights, monitored their systems, while the two launch team members stood before identical control pads, each containing twenty-four columns, one for each missile tube. Sonar operators sat in the reduced light, monitoring their consoles, not expecting to detect any activity.

"Level at two-two-five feet," reported the XO.

"OK, let's talk to OSCAR," Captain Parker ordered his communications officer.

OSCAR, or the Optical Submarine Communications by Aerospace Relay, is a blue-green laser installed on the geostationary SSIX satellite which transmits messages by pulsing laser light over the 450-550 nanometer frequency bandwidth. A petty officer pulled a control lever, raising a special antenna mast tipped with photovoltaic cells.

"Laser mast up."

Sean Kiefer eyed his radio console in anticipation, waiting for some kind of message from Fleet Communications, telling him the ELF had gone out. Silence took hold of the control room, the crewmen sitting silently at the wheels, while Captain Parker and the XO stood behind Kiefer, who nervously flipped a couple of toggle switches on his console, rechecked the frequency, tapped his headphones, then let out his breath.

"Nothing."

Chapter 53

"SSBN 733 CONFIRMS RECEIPT BROKEN ARROW." The *Nevada*.

"SSBN 726 CONFIRMS RECEIPT BROKEN ARROW." The *Ohio*.

"SSBN 630 — INTERRUPT — TX INTERRUPT — TX INTERRUPT —"

While HYDRA was watching the confirmations just sent by the sub fleet to Fleet Communications being rebroadcast on the TACAMO's Message Processing System, another second loud tone interrupted the confirmation list, signaling transmission of a second EAM from Norfolk, which automatically appeared on HYDRA's CRT.

Z151532ZMAR

COMPARTMENTALIZED TOP SECRET

FM: CINCLANTFLT

TO: TACAMO

1. ASSUME SITUATION POLE VAULT IN EFFECT IMMEDIATELY.

2. WILL NOW RETURN TO CONFIRMATIONS.

A thin line of sweat formed itself across HYDRA's brow, he remembered from his readings that Situation POLE VAULT was a companion to Operation BROKEN ARROW, whereby any EAM received by any of the nuclear assets would be relayed back to SAC for immediate analysis in order to trace its sender.

"REPEAT TX: SSBN 630 CONFIRMS RECEIPT

BROKEN ARROW." The *John C. Calhoun.*

"SSBN 727 CONFIRMS RECEIPT BROKEN ARROW."
The Michigan.

Four subs, HYDRA thought, with only five to go. The first
major test of the Trojan Horse, a false confirmation by the
ninth submarine that it had received the BROKEN ARROW
EAM, was about to take place.

"SSBN 729 CONFIRMS RECEIPT BROKEN ARROW."
The *Georgia.*

"SSBN 619 CONFIRMS RECEIPT BROKEN ARROW."
The *Andrew Jackson.*

HYDRA turned in his seat to find Bacon biting his lower
lip and looking over his shoulder at the screen.

"SSBN 659 CONFIRMS RECEIPT BROKEN ARROW."
The *Will Rogers.*

"SSBN 656 CONFIRMS RECEIPT BROKEN ARROW."
The *George Washington Carver.*

"Come on, *Alabama,*" Bacon urged.

"SSBN 731 CONFIRMS RECEIPT BROKEN ARROW."

"Whew!" Bacon sighed. "We're in the clear."

Next the Message Processing System's CRT blinked twice,
then both men watched as POLE VAULT's logic chain scrolled
out next.

POLE VAULT DEFCON-1 ALERT. STANDBY

*** POLE VAULT *** POLE VAULT *** POLE VAULT
***

NCA AUTHORIZATION APPROVED?

YES.

COMMAND STATUS CONFIRMED, CINCLANT
AUTHORIZATION APPROVED?

YES.

REPEAT CONFIRMATION, CINCLANT AUTHO-

RIZATION APPROVED?

YES.

FINAL CONFIRMATION, CINCLANT AUTHORIZA-
TION APPROVED?

YES.

FINAL CONFIRMATION RECEIVED, STANDING
BY FOR TACAMO CONFIRMATION...

FINAL CONFIRMATION RECEIVED, STANDING
BY FOR TACAMO CONFIRMATION...

FINAL CONFIRMATION RECEIVED, STANDING
BY FOR TACAMO CONFIRMATION...

The phrase STANDING BY FOR TACAMO CONFIR-
MATION was accompanied by an incessant high-pitched
tone over each operator's headset, signaling them to relay the
EAM for POLE VAULT. HYDRA immediately routed the
FLASH-level alert to both the VLF and UHF operators, signaling them to prepare confirm receipt messages for release to
Fleet Communications. While the replies appeared almost
instantaneously on his monitor, his hand trembled as he
entered the commands first to encrypt them, then to release
them to the processing center for transmission.

☆ ☆ ☆

As the individual commanders of each sub in the Atlantic and
Pacific fleets radioed confirmation of his receipt of the
Emergency Action Message for Situation POLE VAULT to
Fleet Communications, General Shelton and his crisis management staff kept their eyes peeled on the two banks of
blinking lights labeled COMSUBLANT and COMSUBPAC,
which represented the Atlantic and Pacific submarine forces
respectively. Under each column was listed the nine SSBNs
and their respective numbers presently at sea under each
command, including SSBN 732, the USS *Alaska*. One by one
the lights switched from red to green as a disembodied com-

puter voice repeated the SSBN's name and number over the intercom. Now, only one light remained red, SSBN 732 the USS *Alaska* in the Pacific Fleet, and a hush came over the entire room.

"SSBN 732 CONFIRMS RECEIPT POLE VAULT," echoed the computer's voice as the last light blinked to green.

Shelton heaved a sigh and glanced at Admiral Alexander, who was staring at the display while scattered applause broke out amongst the staff. Now anyone who entered an Emergency Action Message would automatically be prevented from initiating an actual load and launch sequence, while, at the same time, SAC's computers would identify the sender's location allowing him to be apprehended by the nearest counterintelligence forces.

☆ ☆ ☆

In the E-Ring of the Pentagon, inside a room whose door was innocuously labeled U.S. Navy Flag Plot, several admirals had gathered to monitor the electronic wall charts showing the position of the U.S. Navy's nuclear submarine fleet. Normally, the only other people in the room were an NSA-cleared cryptologist and a senior chief radioman, but after General Shelton had arrived at the NMCC that had changed.

Vice Admiral Harold Fremont, Commander Submarines Atlantic Fleet, stood next to his aide, Captain Fred Hulen, silently reading a copy of the receipt confirmations from the Atlantic sub fleet the cryptologist had just handed him. In front of them all nine status indicators for the Atlantic Fleet now read SURFACE TRANSIT, whereas minutes ago each had said SUBMERGED OPERATIONS. The usual blue dot representing each SSBN was now flashing red as a result of General Shelton's implementation of Operation BROKEN ARROW.

The moment it appeared over a blacked-out runway at Andrews Air Force Base, ground crewmen waving flashlights directed the Bell Huey HH-1H carrying Wes Reynolds where to land. The HH-1H bearing Reynolds had left the courtyard of the Hoover Building immediately after the termination of the meeting in Strategic Information Operations Center. Ten minutes before the helicopter's arrival the Emergency Action and Coordination Team at the Department of Energy had sent an encrypted message to Andrews tower, telling them to clear all runways until further notified for several unscheduled landings of Command Black personnel.

Obeying the flashlights' firefly trails the pilot landed directly outside an empty hangar, extinguishing his engines. Two dozen men in civilian clothes, sitting along the hangar's perimeter, watched the hatch jerk open and Wesley Reynolds clamber down the ladder with two adjutants in his wake. Inside the hangar one of the NEST commandos stood up, snapped his fingers, and pointed at four of his men. Each of them went to a separate corner of the hangar towards a rack of amplifiers similar in scale to those which had been used to clear Room 208 and switched them on. But unlike the spectrum analyzers which had been used to analyze the Situation Room for bugs, each rack was filled with a series of signal generators to perform exactly the reverse function: each signal generator would broadcast white noise over a range of frequencies to defeat any eavesdropping device still undetected after the thorough search made earlier in the day.

While Commander Reynolds and his pair of adjutants were waiting to be given the all clear, they examined the stacks of equipment littering the hangar's floor. Fast attack vehicles, crates containing inflatable boats, SDVs, stacks of overwhites, MI6A2s, M203 40mm grenade launchers, ten-power Leopold scopes, M24 sniper systems, Barrett 82A1 .50-caliber semiautomatic rifles, LST-5C satellite radios, HALO and HAHO jumpsuits, AN/PVS-7A night-vision goggles with AN/PAQ-4 infrared lights attached, and a crate of new Heckler & Koch

MP5K-PDWs lay strewn about the hangar. Only after a single white light flashed atop each of the four metal racks could Reynolds address his men.

Two dozen men now stood in formation directly facing their commander, awaiting orders. Reynolds glanced at his electronic watch and realized it had just ceased to function.

"At ease, gentlemen. Make yourselves comfortable, there's no need to stand. In fact, after you hear what I'm about to tell you, you may be glad you're already sitting on the ground."

As the unit broke formation and took their places on the floor, Reynolds surveyed the faces of each team member, reviewing each man's file in his mind. Many had been drawn from the Armed Forces, various special forces units, while others had been recruited from various intelligence agencies. Every major ethnic group America had to offer was represented, and the unit as a whole possessed the ability to communicate in over thirty languages.

"Men," began Reynolds, "your mission today is to capture and eliminate a man who we believe has as his mission to illegally initiate the launch of a nuclear ballistic missile from one of our own military bases."

A swift exchange of silent glances took place in Reynolds's audience.

"For reasons that I am not at liberty to discuss, we believe at this time that the individual we are seeking is an American citizen with previous counterterrorist or intelligence experience. Unfortunately, as they say, that's the good news I have to tell you. I'm afraid have to admit as of this moment that we are not even certain of that."

Dead silence reigned throughout the hangar. A feeling of uncertainty took hold of each man as he realized that he would have to wait for his prey to take the next step.

A hand shot up.

"Commander Reynolds, what're our orders?"

"Simple. Sit here and wait."

☆ ☆ ☆

The brief euphoria which General Shelton and his crisis management team had enjoyed only a few seconds earlier at the National Military Command Center was rudely shattered by a sharp buzzing tone, similar to the one HYDRA had just heard inside the TACAMO, followed instantly by a computer-generated announcement, "EMERGENCY ACTION MESSAGE NO. 3256 TO GRAND FORKS AIR FORCE BASE 319th BOMB WING FROM MILITARY AIRLIFT COMMAND."

"He's at Shiloh!" shouted the lieutenant-colonel. Shiloh, Illinois was the location of Scott Air Force Base, home of the Military Airlift Command.

"Call that Control Center now!" Shelton ordered, and an operator with shaking hands punched the telephone extension, immediately connecting the commander of the strategic bomber wing to the NMCC.

"It's dead!" gasped the operator, turning in his seat.

"Seal off the base! Seal off the fucking base!" roared General Jacobs, Air Force Chief of Staff.

☆ ☆ ☆

"CINC-SAC," answered a visibly shaken General Dick Turner who had also just heard the Emergency Action Message blaring over his intercom. "Yes sir." Turner told General Shelton, then ordered the aide next to him to patch him through to General Mike Shelby, who was both Commander of the 319th Bomb Wing and also superior in rank to the actual base commander at Grand Forks Air Force Base.

Turner's aide turned towards him, the horror showing on his face. "No one answers, sir."

"Goddamnit, send him a teletype then! Tell Shelby the EAM's not from us!"

"Sir, the teletype's ready, if you'll authenticate—"

"Shit!" Turner cursed, punching in his codes into his console as fast as he could, then reaching for the key, he immediately turned it without even looking.

☆ ☆ ☆

Buried beneath 1450 feet of granite inside Colorado's Cheyenne Mountain, a roomful of space-track and early-warning analysts sat at their desks in total silence at the North American Air Defense Command (NORAD), watching the activity of the NMCC, SAC, and White House Situation Rooms on three separate display screens. A fourth screen, which had been tuned to the real-time transmissions from a quartet of third-generation Defense Support Program (DSP) early-warning satellites, and until that moment had been flashing alternately from one to the other, now showed only the transmission from that DSP hovering over the North American Continent.

Although somewhat confused in the general public's mind with the Strategic Air Command (SAC), NORAD's function is a primarily defensive one of providing the National Command Authority with an early warning and trajectories of every missile and/or bomber attack. As such, NORAD employs a wide range of missile warning systems in addition to the geostationary DSP satellites, including a second nuclear detection satellite system installed in the Global Positioning System satellites, in addition to older and separate ground-based phased array, dish, scanner, tracker and backscatter radars.

In theory the moment an ICBM was launched, even if it was from a base inside the United States, NORAD's analysts would be able to provide instant warning to the NCA and also be able to plot its flight profile, determining the missile's eventual target. But this time, as General Ernest Hueter, NORAD's Commander-in-Chief, knew, there would be no need to plot the azimuth of Emergency Action Message No. 3256, all he had to do was look it up in his copy of the *Single Integrated Operational Plan.*

☆ ☆ ☆

"*What's the target?*" demanded President Clinton, the color drained from his face.

Secretary of Defense Chase grabbed the telephone in front of him, automatically connecting himself with General Turner at SAC Headquarters in Omaha. "Dick, the President wants us to display the targets for EAM 3256...thanks..." Chase hung up the telephone and one of his aides turned the volume down on the other screens, reducing the combined audio outputs from NMCC, SAC, and NORAD to almost a whisper, while a second aide checked a code number in a manual, deleting the DSP satellite display of North America on Screen Four, which blinked twice, turned solid blue, then revealed the following:

EAM 3256

FM: MAC SCOTT AFB
T0: 319TH BOMB WING GRAND FORKS AFB

*** HAMMERCUT DECLARED *** HAMMERCUT DECLARED ***
HAMMERCUT DECLARED ***

AIRCRAFT NO. 32
TARGET: DESNOGORS
COORDINATES: 54 06N 033 20E

AIRCRAFT NO. 33
TARGET: BALAKOVO
COORDINATES: 52 02N 047 47E

AIRCRAFT NO. 34
TARGET: ZLATOUST
COORDINATES: 55 10N 059 40E

AIRCRAFT NO. 35
TARGET: POLYARNYY, MURMANSK

COORDINATES: 69 14N 033 30E

AIRCRAFT NO. 36
TARGET: OMSK
COORDINATES: 55 00N 073 24E

AIRCRAFT NO. 37
TARGET: BYKHOV AF
COORDINATES: 53 31N 030 13E

AIRCRAFT NO. 38
TARGET: BELAYA AF
COORDINATES: 52 56N 103 34E

AIRCRAFT NO. 39
TARGET: PETROPAVLOVSK-KAMCHATSKIY
COORDINATES: 53 01N 158 39E

AIRCRAFT NO. 40
TARGET: SVOBODNYY
COORDINATES: 51 24N 128 08E

AIRCRAFT NO. 41
TARGET: SARATOV
COORDINATES: 51 34N 046 01E

AIRCRAFT NO. 42
TARGET: VOLGOGRAD
COORDINATES: 48 45N 044 25E

AIRCRAFT NO. 43
TARGET: IVANOVO
COORDINATES: 57 00N 040 59E

"Jesus Christ! That's most of Russia! This is insane! He's going to start World War III!" Clinton shouted, apoplectic.

"Countermand, goddamnit! Countermand!" yelled secretary of Defense Chase into a telephone.

Exactly sixty seconds after it was announced over the Worldwide Military Control and Command System, Emergency Action Message 3256 was repeated by the same computer voice over the public address system of all thirty-eight nodes of the WWMCCS Information Network, alerting each that the retaliatory strike of twelve B-1B bombers which had just been released under Situation HAMMERCUT was still in force and had yet to be countermanded. The NEST team both nearest to Scott Air Force Base, the source of the false EAM, and also nearest to Grand Forks Air Force Base, the location of the 319th Bomb Wing, was stationed at Nellis Air Force Base in Las Vegas, too far to be of any use in the next four to six minutes as the pilots raced to their planes.

Chapter 54

Lieutenant Bacon swung around in his chair, leaning towards HYDRA's screen just as the alarm buzzer went off again.

The monitor blinked once, and the Message Processing Center automatically began relaying Emergency Action Message 3256:

Z031545ZMAR
COMPARTMENTALIZED TOP SECRET
FM: MAC SCOTT AFB
TO: 319TH BOMB WING GRAND FORKS AFB
INFO: MAC
//T000000//

*** HAMMERCUT DECLARED *** HAMMERCUT DECLARED *** HAMMERCUT DECLARED ***

1. EMERGENCY ACTION MESSAGE 3256.
2. AWAIT FURTHER TX.

"Holy Christ!" Bacon muttered, "they're at Scott Air Force Base!"

"What do we do now?" HYDRA asked, acting panicked.

"Nothing. We just hope to hell they stop whoever it is who just sent that EAM or we're gonna be fried."

The rest of the communications crew turned in their seats,

their faces etched with fear. The whole SSBN fleet had just ascended to the VLF depth, been ordered to accept no further EAMs, only to be followed immediately by a rogue transmission from the command center at the Military Airlift Command, confirming that the sudden institution of Operation BROKEN ARROW and Situation POLE VAULT had been anything but a test.

Of all the hundreds of participants in the various command centers, only HYDRA felt relief. So far, Victor Saleh's plan was working like a well constructed mechanical clock, whose every movement forced his enemies, no longer knowing if the information they were receiving was valid or not, to respond with increasing desperation.

Chapter 55

Inside the OPS1 command room David Woodring and Director Hubert Myers sat transfixed in front of five giant television monitors, watching chaos simultaneously break out at NORAD, SAC, the White House Situation Room, and the NMCC. Every form of secure communications between Scott Air Force Base in Illinois where the EAM had originated and at Grand Forks Air Force Base in North Dakota, its destination, had suddenly collapsed. Meanwhile none of the authorities in command had any way of knowing whether EAM No. 3256 was real, i.e., authenticated or not, and would have to wait to watch the radar to see if the 319th had scrambled its bombers, or, on the other hand, if the announcement was a fraud.

"How long till they get in the air?" demanded Director Myers.

"They can be out of the ready rooms and taxiing down the runway in two minutes," Woodring answered, reciting what he'd just read in *U.S. Nuclear Forces.*

A red telephone next to Myers rang, indicating an incoming call over the CRITIC network, the direct line to the White House Situation Room. "Myers, yes sir ..." While Myers spoke, the oversized monitor, which until recently had been displaying a view of North America transmitted by DSP satellite, blinked once, switching to an overview of Grand Forks Air Force Base. The obvious outlines of a dozen immobile B-1B bombers glimmering on the screen were for the moment the only activity registering on the base.

Myers grabbed a second telephone, speaking hurriedly, "Wes, it's a go. They want your team at Shiloh as soon as possible." Slamming down the telephone, Myers turned to Woodring, "Call SAC St. Louis and tell him to use every available man to seal off Scott Air Force Base, and after you do that send a FEMA teletype to Missouri and Illinois Highway Patrols and put them under the SAC's control along with whatever local police you feel you need."

"Yes, sir."

Members of Woodring's staff who had heard Myers's orders were already at work on the telephones or typing on the telex, preparing to relay the calls to Woodring and get his approval to send the encoded alerts. In his right hand Woodring absent-mindedly clasped the copy of *U.S. Nuclear Forces*, still opened to the page containing the block diagram of the WWMCCS network. On the next page, which he hadn't yet had time to read, was a footnote, indicating that the thirty-third and thirty-fourth nodes of the Wimex Information System were on standby, since its users, the VQ-4 TACAMO Squadron at Pax River and VQ-3 at Travis Air Force Base in California had been grounded by President Bush in early 1991, reduced for budgetary reasons to conducting occasional random flights to keep the crews alert.

"Your call to SAC St. Louis on two!" yelled an analyst from a nearby desk. Meanwhile another assistant shoved a sheaf of telexes in front of Woodring, whose vertical borders were labeled with the ominous four-letter acronym FEMA, standing for the Federal Emergency Management Agency. As Woodring blindly initialed a telex copy, the Special-Agent-in-Charge St. Louis came on the line, and Woodring confirmed his orders,

"Henry, we've got a FEMA-1 Level alert—someone just released an Emergency Action Message at Scott Air Force Base — take the fastest possible transportation and shut down its command center, using whatever force is necessary. Understood? …Good. In about two seconds you're gonna get a telex appointing you district commander; stay there with your men and wait for the NEST team to arrive. Understand?"

"Your call to Grand Forks SAC on one!" shouted Lanier in the background.

"Henry, got another call, 'bye," Woodring informed the SAC St. Louis, pressing down his switchhook to switch him to the next call, where a voice was already speaking on the line.

"… reached the Grand Forks office of the Federal Bureau of Investigation. Agents are unable to come to the phone right now. At the sound of the tone please leave your name, date, and the time you called. If this is an emergency, please call the Bismarck office at area code 701-465—"

"This is a tape! No one's there!" Woodring protested. "Get the SAC's home number, call Bismarck, find out where he is!"

The FBI resident agency in downtown Grand Forks was only fifteen miles from the air base adjacent to Kelly's Slough National Wildlife refuge, which would have allowed the resident-agent-in-charge to arrive on base in under ten minutes and report back to Washington via his car radio, but the five agents in the Grand Forks office just happened to be out.

"Where's the nearest highway patrol?" Woodring shouted, wondering to himself if he would be able to convince a branch office of the North Dakota State Highway Patrol to intercede with a bomber wing of the Strategic Air Command.

"Resident agent Fairview Heights on two," announced

Lanier.

"In person or on tape?"

"It's him."

Woodring punched the extension, cursing under his breath. Fairview Heights was only ten miles from Shiloh and Interstate 64. The resident agent could be at the base in minutes. "Steve? David Woodring, Deputy Dir—you got the telex? Right, we think he's in the command center…No, communications down, we can't contact them…right…right…right." Woodring agreed and hung up. Resident Agent Steven McKay and five fellow agents ran to their cars and left for Scott Air Force Base immediately.

Chapter 56

Two minutes after it had first been announced, Emergency Action Message 3256 blared for the third time over public address systems at SAC, NORAD, the NMCC, the White House Situation Room, the CIA's Operations Center and DEFSMAC at NSA. Inside his command post under Cheyenne Mountain, General Ernest Hueter, CINC-NORAD, was watching the picture transmitted by DSP Satellite West when the picture went suddenly blank.

"DSPS WEST's off the air," a technician's voice announced over the p.a. system.

Hueter grabbed his telephone, instantly connecting him with his second- in-command, Major General Martin Shafer. "Marty, what the hell's going on? …You're sure? …How can you tell? …Just a minute…CINC-NORAD…no, General, it's out, all transponders are down…no, we don't know why…just a minute—"

Now all Hueter's telephone lines were blinking, he was being flooded with calls about the loss of transmission from the other command centers, but ignoring them, he gave precedence to an incoming call from Clinton's National Security

Advisor, J. Mark McDowell, inside the White House Situation Room.

"CINC-NORAD…no, like I just told the JCS, it's dead…we don't know why, Mr. McDowell. Hold on a second—" A bright halogen light went on inside Hueter's office, illuminating his face as a television camera broadcast his picture to the other command centers. The acronym CINC-NORAD flashed on and off at the bottom of the screen.

"This is General Ernest Hueter, Commander-in-Chief NORAD. The President has requested me to inform you that DSPS WEST, whose display you were just watching, has stopped broadcasting. Repeat, DSPS WEST is off the air."

"General Hueter, we have to confirm that those planes have taken off," McDowell interrupted.

"I'll check the other warning systems now," Hueter replied, then punched the extension button for his second-in-command, instantly reconnecting him. Hueter began speaking before Shafer even had a chance to announce his name and rank.

"Marty, call DESFMAC and tell them we want to check for tower chatter coming out of there—then call NPIC and find out if they have a KH-11 anywhere near Grand Forks."

"Yes, sir."

Hueter punched a second extension, connecting him to the operator who monitored the eight large display screens above the operations pit. "Hank, I want a full sensor display on Grand Forks Air Force Base; I'll monitor the command centers up here. As soon as you get anything from NPIC put it on display."

"Yes, sir."

Hueter's telephones now began to ring incessantly, but he again punched the incoming line from his second-in-command.

"Sir, NPIC says the nearest KH-11's fifteen minutes from

target; DEFSMAC's got nothing over North Dakota either. A LACROSSE is thirty minutes out, MAGNUM's ten and VORTEX's twenty."

"Great," Hueter cursed.

The KH-11, a 30,000-pound, 64-foot-long, 10-foot-diameter monster with two huge mirrors had the highest photographic resolution of any surveillance satellite in orbit. The LACROSSE, VORTEX, and MAGNUM satellites were designed to pick up radio signals and analyze their origins, thus being able to provide verification that the B-1B squadron was communicating with Grand Forks tower.

"Then call the Minneapolis Traffic Control Center and patch them in."

"Yes, sir."

While General Hueter was speaking on the telephone the pictures of the various command centers dropped off NORAD's display screens and were to be replaced by real-time maps of NORAD's various atmospheric warning systems. Each display screen was labeled in the upper righthand corner with designations like DSPS WEST; PAVE PAWS, Sector 7; PARCS; BMEWS: Thule, Greenland; OTH-B: Sectors 1, 2 and 3; OTH-B: Sectors 4, 5, and 6; and OTH-B: Sector Center.

"PAVE PAWS just went out," announced a second technician. PAVE PAWS was a phased array radar located at Robins Air Force Base whose coverage area included eastern New York State.

"It what?" demanded Hueter.

"It's dead. No signals from anywhere. Goodfellow, Beale, Cape Cod, Robins—they're all off the air."

On Display Screen Two sectors 2, 5, 6, 7, and 8 began flashing on and off, confirming what the technician had just reported.

"OTH-B Sector 2 is down," a third operator announced. A

second display screen, illustrating the atmospheric warning coverage of North America of NORAD's over-the-horizon backscatter (OTH-3) radars by sector, started blinking on and off.

"OTH-B Sector 4 just went off. OTH-B Sector 6 is down. Now Sectors 3 and 5. All sectors OTH-B now off the air." Every pie-shaped sector was blinking on the screen, including the piece covering Grand Forks, North Dakota.

Hueter grabbed his ringing telephone, fighting off a feeling of sinking despair.

"CINC-NORAD." It was Shafer, his number two in command.

"Robinson just called me from NPIC, KH-11's gone off the air."

"Have they talked to Sunnyvale?" Hueter asked automatically. Sunnyvale, California was the home of NRO's, "Big Blue Cube", the operations headquarters for all America's surveillance satellites. Several of Hueter's other lines started ringing in unison. "Just a minute," he said, putting Shafer on hold.

"Hueter."

The caller was Carter Marshall, Director of NSA's Defense Special Missile and Aeronautics Center (DEFSMAC), where the data from NRO's SIGINT satellites was processed.

"It what?" Hueter gasped. Marshall just informed him DEFSMAC had lost all contact with the MAGNUM satellite nearest Grand Forks.

"BMEWS Thule has just ceased transmission," an operator's voice blared over the intercom, interrupting the conversation.

"DSPS EAST has just ceased transmission. Repeat, DSPS EAST has just ceased transmission," another voice announced.

Dropping his telephone, Hueter stared at the bank of display screens in horror: NORAD had just lost contact with every one of its sensors—now save for a visual sighting of a report from Minneapolis ARTCC, there was now no way to tell if the B1-B bombers were in the air or not.

Chapter 57

"Bismarck SAC on line one!"

"Grand Forks RAC on two!"

Woodring punched the extension for line two, connecting himself with the agent-in-charge of the Grand Forks office.

"Dan, David Woodring. Where are you? ...You're in the office? ...Good. You saw the teletypes? ...Look, I've got no time to explain, just get in your car and drive like hell to the air base; we need to get visual confirmation on a squadron of B-1B bombers! ...Right! Thanks!"

"Everado Police line three!"

Woodring punched line three, leaving the Bismarck special-agent-in-charge on hold. His headset was instantly filled with static, Officer James Cullen, a member of Everado, North Dakota's three-man police force, had been reached on the portable telephone in his car.

"Hello! ...Hello! ...Can you— this is David Woodring, Assistant Director—Assistant Director with the FBI! . .. The FBI! Can you see the air force base from there? ...the base, the air force base...can you see it? ..." Woodring covered the boom microphone with his index finger, stage whispering to Mendoza, "he's across the highway! Set us up!"

One of the operations specialists rushed to the conference room to fetch the television camera which Director Myers had just used in his teleconference with the White House, while a second desperately adjusted the controls on his console, patching Woodring's call through to the other command centers and speaking sotto voce into his headset, "FBI SIOC and Everado Police, Channel 7...FBI SIOC and Everado Police, Channel 7."

"This is an emergency. FEMA Level-1 Alert. You know...excuse me...you know what that means?" Woodring's voice echoed throughout the SIOC, and a bright floodlamp illuminated his face which appeared instantly on one of the five giant monitors.

"...Federal Emergency Act?" Cullen repeated amidst the static.

"Right! Look, Jim, we need you to tell us—" more static disrupted Woodring's urgent plea. "Jim, are you still there?"

"Yes."

"We need you to tell us if you see a squadron of B1 bombers taking off!"

Static prevented Cullen from answering; the noise amplified over the public address systems in the various command centers was unbearable, having the unintended effect of suddenly focusing the attention of every participant inside the NMCC, NORAD, SAC, and Room 208 on Woodring's picture.

"Sorry, you're gonna have to repeat that!"

"Can you tell us if any bombers are taking off?" Woodring repeated.

"Yeah, sure. How many?"

"Twelve!"

"Are there any taking off now?"

"No."

"O.K.! Stay on the line! Don't hang up! We need you to stay there—" a blast of interference cut Woodring off "—we need you to stay there and watch!"

"No problem."

☆ ☆ ☆

Dead silence reigned in every major command center as the Joint Chiefs, President Clinton, his National Security Council, operators at both NORAD and SAC, all waited for Officer Cullen's report. Woodring's tense face glowed on each of their display screens, beads of sweat glistening on his brow.

"RAC on two," Lanier whispered in the background.

"Patch him on," Woodring ordered.

"David?"

"Yes, Dan."

"I'm on Highway 2, and I don't see anything."

"OK, keep on the line."

☆ ☆ ☆

"That bastard! It's a fucking false alarm!" General Shelton muttered under his breath at the Pentagon.

Members of his staff avoided each other's gazes as they looked contrite, victims of a giant computer hoax.

☆ ☆ ☆

At NORAD every operator remained frozen at his console, helpless to analyze events without any warning sensors to give them data input. General Hueter sat at his desk with his eyes glued to the display from the SIOC, almost missing his own operator's announcement.

"Minneapolis ARTCC on Screen Three."

Hueter blinked, he had almost forgotten having told Shafer to call the FAA's Minneapolis Air Traffic Control Center. Now display screen three glowed with the familiar image of a high altitude civilian radar, its green sweep rotating every few seconds a full 360°. The screen was blank, not a single plane was in the air. Within the terminal's control area, all civilian pilots had been automatically grounded after the release of the first EAM.

"Nothing," Hueter muttered to himself.

☆ ☆ ☆

"Grand Forks SAC on Screen Three! Grand Forks SAC on Screen Three!"

Woodring picked up the teleconference line, waving to his staff to put himself back on camera.

"Woody? Hello, Woody?"

"Dan, where are you?"

"I'm at the base. I'm with General Poston now. Everything's OK."

"Put the General on."

"Hold on."

"Hello?"

"General Poston?"

"Yes?"

"This is David Woodring, Assistant Director, FBI. All I need you to do is confirm that no B1-B bombers have taken off from your base."

"Does this have something to do with why our communications—"

"General, there's no time for questions now. Let me remind you that this conversation is being teleconferenced to the entire NCA. I repeat, have you or have you not issued an order to any of the 319th Bomb Wing to take off?"

"Hell no!"

☆ ☆ ☆

At SAC General Dick Turner's attention was broken by an aide, tapping him on the shoulder.

"What is it?" Turner asked.

"Sir, communications with Whiteman are down. What—" The aide's message was interrupted by a blast from the warning buzzer, which was automatically followed by the announce-

ment of a second Emergency Action Message. "EMER-
GENCY ACTION MESSAGE NO. 2714 TO WHITEMAN
AIR FORCE BASE FROM CINCEUR."

Chapter 58

"That's in Frankfurt!" Maddox blurted out in the White
House Situation Room.

"Jesus Christ!" cursed McDowell. "How do we know if it's
another false alarm?"

"We don't," replied Secretary of Defense Chase with finality.

The SAC display screen blinked, then was filled with the
following target data regarding Emergency Action Message
No. 2714, flickering against a solid blue background.

EAM 2714

FM: CINCEUR
TO: 351ST STRATEGIC MISSILE WING CONTROL CENTER 17
WHITEMAN AFB

*** HAMMERCUT DECLARED *** HAMMERCUT DECLARED ***
HAMMERCUT DECLARED ***

MISSILE NO. 19
TARGET: VLADIMIROVKA AF
COORDINATES: 48 19N 046 13E

MISSILE NO. 20
TARGET: PLESETSK MISSILE TEST BASE
COORDINATES: 62 72 N 040 28E

MISSILE NO. 21
TARGET: ACHINSK
COORDINATES: 56 15N 090 30E

MISSILE NO. 22
TARGET: SEMIPALATINSK
COORDINATES: 50 23N 080 10E

MISSILE NO. 23
TARGET: DOMBAROVSKIY
COORDINATES: 50 46N 059 32E

MISSILE NO. 24
TARGET: KAMENKA
COORDINATES: 53 11N 044 04E

MISSILE NO. 25
TARGET: BOBRUYSK AF
COORDINATES: 53 08N 029 12E

MISSILE NO. 26
TARGET: GREMIKHA
COORDINATES: 68 03N 039 38E

MISSILE NO. 27
TARGET: TROITSK
COORDINATES: 54 05N 060 40E

MISSILE NO. 28
TARGET: CHERNYAKHOVSK AF
COORDINATES: 54 36N 021 48E

MISSILE NO. 29
TARGET: ROSTOV-NA-DONU
COORDINATES: 47 14N 039 42E

"How many minutes before launch on this?"

"Under HAMMERCUT, they can't wait any longer than ten minutes in order to avoid X-ray pin-down," answered Secretary of Defense Chase.

☆ ☆ ☆

"Kansas City SAC on five!"

Woodring punched the extension on his console, picking up, "Max, Woody in D.C. You'll get a confirming telex on this in about ten seconds—look, someone, or something, just sent a false Emergency Action Message to Whiteman Air Force Base...right, as in launch ICBMs—how far's your office from—…OK, take a helicopter, just shut it down…"

"Commander Reynolds on two! Commander Reynolds on two!"

Director Myers, sitting in the cubicle adjacent to Woodring, immediately launched into conversation, "Wes, how far are you from Whiteman? … *Two hours!* Jesus, that's not enough time!"

☆ ☆ ☆

"Kansas City ARTCC on Display Screen Seven."

At NORAD General Ernest Hueter watched in increasing horror as the Kansas City Air Traffic Control Center's radar was patched into Cheyenne Mountain. Every warning sensor NORAD possessed was still off the air, forcing him and his roomful of operators to monitor the two bases which had just received the Emergency Action Messages over civilian radar.

☆ ☆ ☆

Special Agent Stephen McKay of the FBI Resident Agency based in Fairview Heights, Illinois raced along Interstate 64 at over one hundred miles per hour, braking as he skidded onto the exit ramp for Scott Air Force Base. He had been reached in his car as he was leaving the local grocery store and given a rush order by Woodring to contact General Charlie Hackett, the base commander to confirm the validity of EAM 3256, from Scott AFB to Grand Forks.

When the sentry on duty at the main gate caught sight of a Ford LTD bearing down Scott Drive with its red grill lights blinking, he picked up his telephone only to find the line was dead. The LTD swerved to a halt behind two others on line and McKay burst out the door, running towards the guard hut waving his badge in his left hand, screaming "FBI! FBI!"

Airman Joe Schirmer automatically unsnapped the holster holding his nine millimeter and stepped out of his hut with his right hand resting on his gun.

"Stephen McKay, FBI. You're gonna take me to General Hackett."

"By whose authority?" Schirmer snapped.

"The President's."

☆ ☆ ☆

Now every telephone line in the SIOC was ringing. Special agents who were checking out the identities of the 753 locator records received from the Pentagon were beginning to call in from different bases, while police, highway patrol, and FBI units who had been alerted to investigate Scott, Grand Forks, and Whiteman Air Force Bases were relaying their various reports. In the midst of the chaos one of Charlie Thompson's analysts handed him a fresh printout from the computing center in the Counterterrorism Center. As an afterthought Thompson had decided to cross-check the names on the 753 locator records for any possible previous visits to two bases: Bangor SUBASE and China Lake.

Naval Air Reserve Lieutenant Jack Gereke, who had just reported for duty at Pax River that afternoon, had also apparently taken the Trident Tour at Bangor SUBASE almost two months earlier.

"The Trident Tour?" Thompson asked, furrowing his brow. "You mean he was a tourist?"

"Right."

"You checked this with the base?"

"Yes, sir. Gereke just took the tour—and they're sure he left afterwards—they keep track."

"Just a minute."

Thompson leapt out of his chair and dashed over to Woodring, slapping the single sheet of paper on Woodring's desk.

"What's this?"

"I cross-checked the latest batch of the locator records with TDYs at China Lake and Bangor—this guy took a tour of Bangor two months ago."

"St. Louis SAC on two!" yelled an operator.

"Tell him to wait!" Woodring shouted, then turning back to Thompson, "What's 'VQ-4 Squadron TACAMO' mean?"

"It's right here, in your book." Thompson pointed at the opened page of *U.S. Nuclear Forces*. "Take-charge-and-move-out. The aircraft linked to the NCA—"

"Like the Looking Glass?"

"Fairview Heights RAC on one!"

"Tell him to hold!" Woodring snapped.

"Right. It's linked to the Looking Glass and Kneecap; there's one over the Atlantic and one over the Pacific twenty-four—"

"Where're they based?"

"Tinker Air Force Base in Oklahoma—"

"Not on the coasts?"

"Well, the squads are at Pax River and Travis in California—"

"Sacramento SAC on three!"

"St. Louis SAC on one!"

Woodring turned in his seat, issuing a sharp order, "Lanier! Drexler! Take all my calls—I don't want to talk to anyone, unless they've found HYDRA or they've seen a missile launched. Understand?"

The two analysts nodded their heads, then immediately returned to their telephones, fielding call after call.

"Who flies them?" Woodring resumed.

"What?"

"Who flies them? Air Force? Navy? SAC? Who?"

"Naval Air Force, of course. Usually Naval Air Reserve—"

"*Reserve?*"

"With rotating crews."

"With rotating crews? Would the crew members always know who each other were?"

"Some of the reservists are filling out their hours, so they wouldn't necessarily know everybody in the squad—"

"Hold on a second." Woodring punched a button on his console, immediately linking him to the NMCC. "David Woodring, get me General Vaughn!"

"Impossible," Captain Bryant replied, "he's not here."

"Where is he then?"

"Computer room."

"Switch me there!"

"I can't, lines are jammed!"

"What—"

"Just a minute! One opened up! I'll put you through!"

Woodring bit his lower lip as another operator came on the line.

"Computer Room, Captain—"

"This is David Woodring FBI, I want to speak to General Vaughn."

"Hold on."

A second later, as if in a miracle, Vaughn came on the line, "What do you want?"

"What that admiral said about every sub having several modes of communication—"

"Look, Woody, do you have any idea what's going on here? I've gotta go—"

"Wait! The TACAMO! What if HYDRA's on the

TACAMO!"

"He can't be on the TACAMO! It's been grounded for god-sakes!"

"We show a flight took off this afternoon!" Woodring protested.

"Look, Woody—ELF, VLF, blue-green laser, satellite UHF, it's all sorted by computer. Turn that off and the master's running blind."

"You mean—"

"I mean each sub only knows what it hears and if your guy's on the TACAMO then one of the subs has gotta be cut off!"

"But—"

Vaughn hung up. He was under too much pressure as it was, trying to restore communications to Whiteman and Grand Forks. Suddenly, the enormity of it struck Woodring like a hammer blow.

"Call Pax River and get the name of anyone who could have possibly reported for duty today and yesterday and give them to Lanier. When you get the files I want every one of them checked out a.s.a.p.—use whatever personnel's available—counterintelligence, criminal investigations, local police—confirm these guys really reported to base, get on the phone, whatever, you know the drill." Before Thompson could nod his assent, Woodring punched another button, and was back on the line with the duty officer in OPS2. "I need the helicopter." Then, "patch the commander of Andrews Air Force Base onto the pilot's intercom...right." Woodring ripped off his headset and ran towards the vaulted door, screaming "Get it open!" to the pair of HRT agents, standing by the lock.

"Take charge and move out," Woodring muttered under his breath in the corridor, running to the bank of elevators, hoping he'd get there in time.

The moment the elevator first arrived, Woodring shoved

his hand in the crack, rammed the door open, slapped his ID card into a slot above the OPEN DOOR button and punched EXPRESS to the lobby. Every second lasted an eternity— passing each floor took longer than forever.

Woodring burst out the half-open elevator , scattering a waiting crowd, then, seeing the rotors of the Bell Huey HH-1H stirring up the leaves through the glass, barreled out the nearest door, running with his head ducked towards the open hatch just as the chopper was rising off its skids.

"Where to?" yelled the pilot, turning in his seat.

"Andrews!"

Chapter 59

After he had failed to receive a transmission over blue-green laser from COMMSAT, Captain Parker became increasingly worried and ordered the USS *Alabama* rigged for ultraquiet operations. All non-essential lights were turned off with only the soft green glow of the CRTs and colored gauge-faces remaining. Idle crew members were confined to their bunks, while turbine generators and circulation pumps were either shut down or put on slow speed. The public address system which was used during normal operations was turned off, while Captain Parker and the remaining crew in the control room had all donned handsfree headsets to minimize any remaining noise.

Men sat silently in front of weapons consoles, missile controls, sonars and reactor gauges, the majority of which were still convinced they were in a drill.

"Six zero feet," the diving officer spoke sotto voce.

"Raise VLF antenna," added Captain Parker.

"Five five feet," announced the diving officer.

The second time the loud buzzer shattered the silence of the Communications Center of the E-6A each operator turned in his swivel chair towards HYDRA, who was now holding a Glock Model 18 fully automatic pistol in his right hand.

"Hey!" Bruning protested, his eyes darting from the gun to HYDRA's face.

Open-mouthed, Bruning now had a hole in his chest and was falling forward when HYDRA fired consecutively at Drew, Bacon, Jameson and Sheldon, each of whom died still strapped to his swivel chair. The Glock's trigger mechanism allowed its user to fire multiple shots faster than any other handgun available, and HYDRA killed all five in less than two seconds.

Still holding the Glock in his hand, HYDRA unhooked his seat belt and left his chair, dashing behind the communications consoles to retrieve the knapsack containing his HP-100LX. Once he returned to his seat, he ripped the cover off the knapsack, flipped on the small computer's power switch, bringing the HP-100LX's blank CRT screen to life. After entering the first password into the palmtop, he swiveled in his chair, hitting first the return key, then the dollar sign on the console of the Message Processing Center, causing two blinking question marks to appear on Message Center's CRT. Turning back to the palmtop, HYDRA entered the second seven-letter codeword, known only to himself, in order to retrieve authenticated codekeys he had stolen from Bangor SUBASE. Holding his index finger down on the spacing bar, HYDRA quickly scrolled through thirty days of codes, stopping at **MONTH: MARCH; DAY: 15; YEAR: 1993**, that day's date. Below the data entry were two letters, A and B, each followed by a 64-bit-long binary number which was divided into sixteen 4-bit-long blocks, which HYDRA carefully began to enter into the console of the Message Center.

After he entered the NCA's authentication codes into the Message Center of the TACAMO, its display blinked off and on three times then went blank. Letting out his breath in relief,

HYDRA tugged at one of the zippered pockets of his flight suit, extracting a cylindrical device which he fitted over the authentication key at Bruning's post. Returning to his seat, HYDRA tapped the return key on the console of the Message Center, then entered the word NUCFLASH, followed by the number 1, then hit the return key again.

"WARPLANS?"

"COUNTRIES?"

"CITIES?"

"OTHER?"

After WARPLANS, HYDRA typed the words, EAM 3533.

"EAM NO. 3533 TACAMO TO ALABAMA."

"NCA FINAL CONFIRMATION RECEIVED."

"REPEAT,   NCA   FINAL   CONFIRMATION RECEIVED."

After a full second, the sentences

"LAUNCH AUTHENTICATED—OPERATOR A?"

"LAUNCH AUTHENTICATED—OPERATOR B?"

appeared in tandem, blinking on and off.

HYDRA tapped the pound sign symbol twice, hit the return key, tapped the pound sign symbol twice again, then hit the return key again. Next, he stood up from his chair and walked to Drew's console. Standing in front of his sunken corpse, he simultaneously turned Drew's authentication key with his right hand while aiming a handheld remote control at Bruning's key, causing it to twist in its lock at the same time as Drews's, releasing Emergency Action Message 3533 over the E-6A's VLF transmitter to the USS *Alabama* below.

☆ ☆ ☆

"Level at five five—" began the XO, suddenly interrupted by an incessant ringing tone which was an octave higher than the alarm used for the ELF.

"Emergency Action Message received over VLF," uttered Kiefer, trying to control his voice. His gut told him this was no longer any drill.

Captain Parker shot a worried glance at the XO; first the ELF goes dead, then the laser, now this. Something was wrong.

"Captain, we've got problems," Kiefer announced, handing Parker a copy of HYDRA's launch order with a shaking hand.

Parker grabbed the message printout, reading it in shock.

Z031552ZMAR

COMPARTMENTALIZED   TOP   SECRET*** NUCFLASH *** NUCFLASH *** NUCFLASH ***

FM: TACAMO

TO: SUB NO. 731

INFO: ERCS

//TOOOOOO//

1. NCA AUTHORIZATION APPROVED FOR EAM NO. 3533 TACAMO TO ALABAMA

"Jesus Christ! They've launched the Emergency Rocket System!" Parker blurted out.

Parker knew that NUCFLASH was a prearranged code signifying an exoatmospheric nuclear detonation had already taken place resulting in a total shutdown of the NCA's Wimex communications network, leaving only the Minimum Essential Emergency Communications Network (MEECN) in operation. Besides six VLF transmitters with antenna towers higher than 1,000 feet, MEECN includes the TACAMO, Looking Glass, Kneecap, plus the Emergency Rocket Communications System, (ERCS) consisting of eight unarmed Minuteman missiles stationed in silos at Whiteman Air Force Base. Instead of possessing the usual nuclear warheads it was designed to carry, each of the eight ballistic missiles contained a small, powerful radio transmitter. After the Wimex system had collapsed, an Air Force general would still be able to transmit an order from his flying command post, launching all eight of the ERCS rockets, which, in turn, would transmit the proper EAMs to the remaining strategic forces.

"Mr. Lesar," Parker told the XO, "get out your key."

Captain Parker and his XO both walked over to a bright red box with a pair of matching keyholes, and simultaneously inserted their keys, opening the box. Lesar extracted a hard copy of the most recent nuclear weapons plan for the Alabama, handing it to Captain Parker. Parker rifled through the pages, finding EAM 3533 TACAMO TO ALABAMA almost immediately.

"It's in here," Parker uttered in horror.

"Captain, what do we do now?" asked a nervous XO.

"I'm sure as hell not going to fire off a missile until we check this thing out. Raise number two periscope," he told his second-in-command. Even though the *Alabama* was sailing at fifty-five foot depth, the top of its conning tower hovered only ten feet below the surface of the Atlantic, allowing Captain Parker to raise the UHF, VHF and HF antennas attached to his number-two periscope in a matter of seconds. The UHF antenna was designed to receive regular radio transmissions from overhead SSIX satellites used by Fleet Communication in Norfolk; the HF (high frequency) antenna to receive any Link 11 or Link 14 broadcast over the Navy Tactical Data System (NTDS) from any nearby vessel in the area; and the VHF to receive broadcasts over the Joint Tactical Information Distribution System (JTIDS), a joint service communications system.

"Captain, listen to this," Kiefer gasped, yanking his headset from his head, handing it to Parker. Parker took it and was about to put it on when he heard the noise.

"What is this?"

"It's Link 11," Kiefer stuttered.

"Try 14," ordered Parker, handing back the headset.

Kiefer switched a knob on his console switching the radio to Link 14 frequency, NTDS.

"Jesus!" Kiefer exclaimed, jerking his headset away from his ear. Parker could hear the interference over the JTIDS band from where he stood.

"What about SSIX?" demanded Parker.

"Nothing."

"Nothing on UHF?"

Kiefer desperately flipped a toggle switch. "Confirmed, sir. Nothing on UHF."

"Is it even on the air?"

"Negative. We're not getting any signal at all, SSIX's off the air."

Captain Parker turned to his XO. Every detail of Kiefer's report matched the predicted effects of a high-altitude electromagnetic pulse (EMP) resulting from an exoatmospheric nuclear detonation. A nuclear weapon detonated above an altitude of forty kilometers would release a burst of gamma radiation equivalent to tens of thousands of bolts of lightning which, in turn, would knock the electrons off all the surrounding air molecules in a region between twenty-kilometers and forty-kilometers in altitude. Not only is EMP thousands of times more powerful than an average lightning bolt, it's ten thousand times shorter in duration, giving any conductor exposed to it almost no time to be shielded from its force by built-in protective devices, known as "surge protectors" to the layman.

All exposed antennas would collect the resulting radio energy, converting it into currents, then conduct that energy into the electronics of their respective radio transmitters, causing them to instantly explode. Terrestrial communications cables would be immediately affected by violent distortions in the earth's magnetic field, causing them to develop their own destructive voltages, like the armature of a giant generator. The voltages would race through the lines, destroying remaining telephone switching networks. X-rays from a nuclear burst in space would neutralize satellites at distances far greater than the ranges of the radius of the burst's explosive force.

Because the effects of EMP vary as the frequency of radio waves increase, Captain Parker knew the effects of an exoatmospheric nuclear detonation would affect different bands in different ways. High frequency broadcasts from satellites would be largely unaffected, if the satellites themselves had survived, and if they had not, the *Alabama's* communications system wouldn't pick up any interference, which it hadn't; UHF and HF, on the other hand, with their long skywave paths through the lower ionosphere are the most vulnerable, explaining the blast of interference Kiefer picked up on the Link 11 and Link 14 Communications bands. VLF and ELF frequencies, from the bottom of the ionosphere would hardly be affected at all, assuming that either the ELF antenna in northern Michigan, or the Navy's six land-based VLF antennas, or the TACAMO had managed to survive a surprise attack, which, Captain Parker knew, was also highly unlikely, explaining both the abrupt cutoff of the ELF and the lack of further communication from the TACAMO.

Hovering at only fifty-five feet below the ocean's surface, the *Alabama* had suddenly become a prime target for a Russian second strike.

"Diving Officer," Parker called, "rig the ship for dive!"

"OOH-GAH! OOH-GAH!" blasted over the public address system, followed by a recording of the words, "DIVE! DIVE!"

The diving officer opened the *Alabama's* ballast tanks, blasting their trapped air out into the sea.

"Sail's under."

"Submerge the ship to four zero zero feet," ordered Parker, snapping the periscope's control grips up.

"Mr. Mitchell, Mr. Nolan," spoke Parker into his boom

microphone, calling two of the Alabama's launch control operators," report to my cabin immediately."

Chapter 60

Special Agent Larry Palmer took a quick glance out the window at the traffic on Maryland State Highway 235 beneath him, then rechecked the controls of the single-engine Cessna-182 RG he was flying towards Patuxent Naval Air Test Center. Palmer was one of two hundred FBI agents who were trained as pilots, specializing in tracking spies in the greater Washington area at night on lights-out flights in the high-winged 182-RG. Upon receipt of a telex sent by the SIOC to the FBI hangar at Andrews Air Force Base regarding the whereabouts of Naval Air Reserve Lieutenant Jack Gereke, Palmer took off in the first available aircraft for Pax River.

Agent Palmer was under no illusion as to the importance of his orders; when he caught sight of the words "FEMA Level 1 Alert" in the heading, he immediately knew it involved nuclear terrorism. The FAA controller's announcement to all aircraft aloft which occurred after the first few minutes he'd been in the air only further emphasized his fears that a nuclear accident either had happened already or was about to happen. And even though Palmer was only ten miles from the 5,500-acre air base, the Cessna's radar screen was quiet; not a single plane was in the air within its fifty-mile radius. Palmer caught visual ID on the base's tower and spoke into his headset, "Pax River, this is FEMA zero one zero one, squawk one two zero six and ident."

"FEMA zero one zero one, squawking one two zero six," answered the nervous base controller, reversing the standard tower-pilot conversation.

Inside Pax River tower, the controller, who had been expressly forbidden to issue any additional instructions, silently watched the tiny Cessna approach the main runway parallel to Cedar Point Road, perform a smooth landing, and continue to taxi towards a semi-circle of jeeps waiting at the intersection with Taxiway C.

Palmer followed the jeep caravan across the short taxiway, turned left, entered the FAIRECON FOUR Hangar and turned off his engine. Looking out his cockpit, he saw a very worried Air Force General accompanied by several intelligence officers.

"Agent Palmer?" someone asked.

Chapter 61

A single unmarked sedan raced through the sidestreets of Kansas City's Country Club Plaza shopping center, veering off Wornall Road and lumbering into a covered parking lot over Houston's Restaurant. New agent Susie McKittrick cursed out loud to herself as she circled the uneven parking deck, winding around the maze of concrete columns looking for Apartment 4B, belonging to Lieutenant Gereke of the Naval Air Reserve.

McKittrick still hadn't recovered from the crash meeting called by the Special-Agent-in-Charge of the Kansas City field office who, after announcing that a FEMA Level 1 Alert had just gone into effect, had then parceled out each agent's assignment. McKittrick was handed a copy of a telex from the SIOC, listing Gereke's age, rank, address, plus a fax enlargement of his most recent photo ID at the Pentagon. The message in the telex was clear: Lieutenant Jack Gereke was supposed to have reported to Pax River Naval Base earlier that day and should not be home, but check just in case.

In case of what? thought McKittrick to herself when she found the door. What if Gereke's sitting in his living room holding a twelve-gauge on his lap? She quickly put the thought out of her mind, when she saw the building agent standing in front of the door, holding a key chain in her hand. McKittrick got out of her car, quickly adopting the official look she had seen other agents use on assignment.

"Hi, I'm Julie Bliss," the apartment agent introduced herself, holding out her hand. "You must be the one who called."

"That's correct. Thanks for coming," McKittrick fumbled in her purse, then extracted her ID and showed it to the rental agent.

"Oh, I know it's you. You have the same voice as on the telephone," Bliss cheerfully replied.

"Yes, ma'am. Ah, look, I'll knock first, but if Mr. Gereke's not home my orders are to enter his apartment immediately. I have a special warrant with me from the Foreign Intelligence Surveillance Court in Washington to back this up."

Bliss nodded, then her expression clouded over. "Is Jack in some kind of trouble?"

"Probably not. This is just a routine check by the base," McKittrick repeated the well-rehearsed official line.

"Oh."

Agent McKittrick began pounding on the door and shouted "Lieutenant Gereke! Lieutenant Gereke, this is the FBI! Are you in there?" After repeating the same sequence twice with no response, she drew her gun, surprising Bliss. After motioning for her to hand her the key, she waved Bliss away.

In one fluid motion McKittrick put the key in the lock, turned it, and entered the room just as she'd been trained to do at the FBI Academy in Quantico, Virginia. The apartment was dark, blinds lowered, and the air had a faintly peculiar smell. McKittrick felt her skin crawl from the base of her spine to the top of her scalp. Her guts told her that Gereke was dead. With her gun in the air she crept along the wall towards the bedroom door, swung around in a crouch, seeing nothing but the unmade bed. The smell was stronger. Gereke was in the bathroom.

McKittrick swallowed hard, turned on the bathroom light

with a shaking hand, then ripped back the shower curtain, finding a large plastic lawn bag laid out in the bathtub. McKittrick gulped hard again, fumbling in her pants pocket for the fax photo ID, then dropped it on the bath mat as she leaned forward towards the bag. With a tear streaming down her face, she tore a hole at one end with her fingernails, revealing Gereke's head. A moment later she rushed to the toilet, flipped up the lid and threw up.

Chapter 62

Once inside his cabin, Captain Parker retook the measure of the other three men who had come with him. He'd known Lesar, the XO, for over a decade, and had been on patrol with him in three oceans. Mitchell, the senior launch control officer, was just a kid fresh out of the Naval Academy, only twenty-four years old. Nolan, the senior weapons officer in his thirties, who wore a moustache, had been through endless Battle Stations Missile drills and immediately realized what had happened the moment he entered the Captain's cabin.

Of the three links in the nuclear triad, only the SSBNs possessed neither permissive action links on their warheads nor special release mechanisms on their launch controls. Nolan knew all it really took to launch a nuclear ballistic missile from an SSBN was four officers agreeing to pull four switches at the same time. If the same four men believed a nuclear strike were in the best interests of the United States, they even had the capability to order a launch before ever receiving an authenticated emergency action message. Thus, due to the almost unlimited power invested in these four, any one of them could officially refuse to go along with the group — the only example of legalized mutiny in the United States Navy.

The reason Nolan knew something was horribly wrong was simple. If it had been a drill, in addition to himself, Captain Parker, the XO, Mitchell and would have all remained at their posts.

Captain Parker unfolded the copy of EAM 3533 and spread it on the small table in sight of the three other officers.

"Gentlemen, we have just received an authenticated and valid order to execute our portion of the Single Integrated Operating Plan."

"What's happened?" interjected Mitchell. "What are you saying? This isn't a drill? Captain Parker, what does this mean?"

Lesar glanced nervously at Nolan, while Captain Parker continued in a monotone, purposely devoid of all emotion.

"The order was transmitted to us by the TACAMO via the Emergency Rocket Communications System, implying the United States has already been attacked. A short time before this was transmitted the ELF went dead. I subsequently asked Lieutenant Kiefer to contact Fleet Command over OSCAR, but he informed me that it, too, was off the air. After receiving the EAM, I, again, ordered Lieutenant Kiefer to attempt to contact Norfolk over SSIX and check Link 11 and 14 bands for any local broadcasts.

"Lieutenant Kiefer failed to receive anything whatsoever over SSIX, ULF or TACAMO frequencies, and only picked up loud interference on Link 11 and Link 14."

"Jesus," whispered Nolan. "EMP."

"Maybe it's EMP, Lieutenant Nolan. And maybe it's not," Parker replied. "As of right now we don't have a shred of actual proof that a single bomb has gone off."

"What else could it be?" Mitchell asked.

"Sabotage," replied Lesar.

"*Sabotage? How?* How could someone, why would someone send a valid EAM then turn off all our communications? It's impossible!" Mitchell shouted.

"Lieutenant Nolan?" asked the Captain.

"We've been given a ninety-minute window for a good reason — it's our job to decide whether this order is valid or not. I say we send up a messenger buoy requesting confirmation then resurface. If we don't hear anything from Fleet Command after that, we've got a problem."

"XO?" asked the Captain.

"Fine with me."

"Mr. Mitchell?"

"What choice do I have?"

Captain Parker ignored Mitchell's remark.

"Mr. Lesar, how much time do we have left?"

"Approximately seventy-three minutes, Captain."

"We'll set the buoy with a thirty-minute time-delay. I don't see what else I can do."

Parker looked at the others: they all knew if World War III had actually broken out, the risk of a Russian satellite detecting the buoy's location would be remote, since, more than likely, all the communications to the Russians' command centers would be down.

"Very well, then. Let's return to our positions."

As Parker and Lesar returned to the control room silent crew members watched them pass by, the same look of fear etched on every face.

"Lieutenant Kiefer," Parker spoke, "draft a message to the Fleet Command for transmission via messenger buoy asking them to confirm EAM 3533."

"Yes, sir."

"Prepare messenger buoy for ejection," Parker ordered over the intercom.

In the upper level of the *Alabama's* aft compartment a crew member loaded a UHF satellite messenger buoy into the signal ejector, waiting for the loud clicking before he shut the door and armed the unit.

"Launch signal buoy," announced the XO, while Parker

pressed the button on the control panel.

Twenty seconds later, a baseball-bat sized buoy burst out of the ejector tube and bubbled fifty-five feet to the surface of the Atlantic, floating invisibly in the gloom.

Chapter 63

"FBI SIOC Director Myers, Channel 7…FBI SIOC Director Myers, Channel 7," simultaneously echoed over the public address systems at NORAD, SAC, the NMCC, the White House, and every other command center which was online. On each side of Myers's picture were displayed the radars of Kansas City and Minneapolis Air Traffic Control Centers, their electronic sweeps rotating around empty fields.

"This is FBI Director Myers. I have an important announcement to make," Myers spoke clearly, directly facing the portable video camera.

"The body of Naval Air Reserve Lieutenant Jack Gereke has just been found at his home in Kansas City. Lieutenant Gereke had orders to report for duty today to VQ-4 Squadron at Patuxent Naval Air Test Center for a maintenance flight on the TACAMO E-6A. I have just received a report from that same base that someone else masquerading as Gereke arrived at the base and departed at 3:01 p.m. on Aircraft No. 63918.

"Assistant Director Woodring has already departed this office for Andrews Air Force Base in an attempt to intercept this same aircraft."

☆ ☆ ☆

The FBI Director's remarks brought all activity in the Crisis Center of the National Military Command Center to an abrupt halt, as each member of Joint Planning and Execution Committee was struck by the enormity of Saleh's scheme.

"The subs! He's shut down one of the subs!" blurted out the lieutenant-colonel.

Admiral Alexander glanced at the two banks of blinking green lights representing the Atlantic and Pacific fleets, then punched an extension automatically connecting him to Atlantic Fleet Communications in Norfolk.

"This is Admiral Alexander, standby for an *en clair* message to the Atlantic Fleet."

General Howard Webb, Chief of Staff, Air Force, grabbed a telephone, shouting at the operator. "Connect me to Pax River Tower! Now!"

The room went silent as the rest of the staff members waited to hear Webb's report.

"… this is General Webb at the Pentagon…Gen-er-al Webb. Right. Where is TACAMO 63918? …What do you mean, 'you don't know'? Where is it? …It's not on your radar? …*It's what?* …Is it out of range or not? …Then give me his last known location, goddammit!" Webb grabbed the nearest pencil and paper and spoke aloud as he wrote, "tanker rendezvous at 33° 12'N, 77° 35'W thirty minutes ago."

"How do we find that plane?" Shelton asked his staff.

"Ask the Russians!" suggested the lieutenant-colonel.

Shelton grabbed the telephone, connecting him to the White House Situation Room.

"Let me speak to the President."

"Get me Langley Air Force Base!" barked General Webb.

Alexander punched a second extension, connecting him to the Navy Flag Plot Room and spoke quickly into his telephone, "I want a position report on every SSBN and every SSN and every carrier in the Atlantic Fleet and the distance between each in minutes."

☆ ☆ ☆

"Andrews Tower to Huey Zero One Zero One. Andrews Tower to Huey Zero One Zero One."

"Zero One Zero One, over," replied the FBI pilot sitting next to Woodring.

"We need following data on your passenger: height, weight, suit size, and shoe size."

"Roger, just a minute."

"What's this all about?" shouted Woodring

"They need the sizes for your flight suit — you can't go up like that — "

"Like what?"

"In your clothes! You've gotta wear a flight suit!"

"Andrews Tower to Huey Zero One Zero One, come in please."

"Just a sec', Andrews," replied the pilot turning to Woodring.

"Alright. Alright. Alright. Six feet, a hundred seventy-five pounds, forty-two long and eleven B."

The pilot repeated the information to Andrews Tower, who repeated it back for confirmation.

"Roger Huey Zero One Zero One. Please instruct passenger to be undressed for arrival. Repeat undressed."

☆ ☆ ☆

At Atlantic Fleet Communications in Norfolk an astonished officer took Admiral Alexander's message off the computer terminal — there was no need to decrypt it; Alexander had sent it *en clair.* Reading it with a shaking hand, the officer handed it to the yeoman stationed across the room and ordered him to send it to SSBNs 733, 726, 630, 727, 729, 619, 659, 656, and 731, i.e., the entire Atlantic Fleet.

As he entered the message from CINCLANT into his computer the yeoman's eyes widened in shock.

Z151732ZMAR

COMPARTMENTALIZED TOP SECRET

FM: COMSUBLANT

TO: USS OHIO, USS GEORGIA, USS GEO. W. CARVER, USS NEVADA, USS JOHN C. CALHOUN, USS MICHIGAN, USS WILL ROGERS, USS ANDREW JACKSON, USS ALABAMA.

A: *** BROKEN ARROW *** Z151504Z

B: *** POLE VAULT *** Z1515432Z

1. ASSUME LOCATOR EMERGENCY IMMEDIATELY IN EFFECT UNDER SITUATION DULL SWORD.

2. TRANSMIT FOLLOWING SENTENCE CONTINUOUSLY OVER VLF, UHF, OSCAR, AND SHF UNTIL NOTIFIED TO STOP EN CLAIR, REPEAT, EN CLAIR:

3. THE QUICK BROWN FOX JUMPS OVER THE LAZY DOG.

The yeoman tried to control his fingers as he typed; he knew the sequence, there was no way he'd ever forget it: BROKEN ARROW, accept no further EAMS except for POLE VAULT; POLE VAULT, rebroadcast all subsequent EAMS to NCA; DULL SWORD, continuously confirm your location to NCA until further notice, i.e., one or more of the confirmations just received for BROKEN ARROW and POLE VAULT is fraudulent.

DULL SWORD was a double-edged disaster whose only two outcomes were both negative, no matter which prevailed. If there were no Trojan Horse in the Wimex system and no members of the sub fleet were incommunicado, the position of the entire Atlantic SSBN fleet would still be revealed by the continuous "locator" transmissions from each sub. On the other hand, if one or more of the subs failed to transmit DULL SWORD's locator message, revealing there actually was a Trojan Horse in the Wimex system and that, in addition, one or more of the subs was the victim of onboard computer sabotage, then there was an ever more serious problem: the risk of a false EAM being successfully transmitted to the sabotaged boat.

☆ ☆ ☆

Major Rick Wyand had just opened the door to his temporary quarters inside the National Guard residence building at Andrews Air Force Base, when two MPs, one holding a flight helmet and a pair of boots, the other holding Wyand's "poopy suit", appeared at his door.

"Major Wyand?"

"Yes, sir?"

"You're to put these on immediately and come with us. Orders from base Command."

Wyand blinked. He was a member of the Maryland Air National Guard, 113th Fighter Wing, not the Strategic Air Command.

"Is this a drill?"

"No, sir! General's orders are for you to suit up immediately."

In a daze Wyand donned his flight suit, boarded the MP's jeep and was driven pell-mell to the unit's hangar where he was met by a pair of Air Force Intelligence officers who flashed their IDs in his face.

"Major Wyand?"

"Yes?"

"I'm Captain Barnett, Air Force Intelligence."

Barnett's partner failed to identify himself; in the background a half-dressed ground crew raced across the tarmac towards the hangar.

"We have just received a National Security Intelligence Decision Directive from the Director of the Federal Bureau of Investigation — "

"*You what?*" interrupted Wyand. He was a second year

associate in a D.C. law firm, and from what little national security law he was familiar with, he knew that NSIDD's were issued by the President, not the FBI.

"We may ask you to shoot down one of our own aircraft," added the second man with no name.

"NSIDD's come from the President!" cried Wyand.

"Not in a FEMA Level-1 Alert, Major," corrected Barnett. "And, frankly, Major Wyand, we don't have any more time to discuss the legality of this order with you!"

The whine of a Pratt & Whitney turbofan jet engine abruptly ended the discussion, when a Huey HH-1H swung in a dramatic arc over the hangar building and descended over the runway, hovering in the air, rocking back and forth on its skids. Ground crew members arrived, holding a pair of coveralls and matching boots, and a man wearing only a pair of boxer shorts leapt out the Huey's door, hitting the ground hard. He flashed his badge at the ground crewmen who nodded, held up the pair of coveralls, and helped him dress himself right there on the spot.

"That's your new boss!" shouted the nameless plainclothesman. "He's with the FBI! You're under his command now!"

Another crewman unfolded a yellow stepladder beneath the F-16's open cockpit, helping Woodring into the rear copilot seat. Pulling his helmet over his head, Wyand ran towards the plane and clambered up the ladder just before the cockpit snapped shut. The tower controller's voice was already blaring over the intercom inside.

"Cherokee Zero One Zero One, cleared for takeoff. Cherokee Zero One Zero One cleared for takeoff."

☆ ☆ ☆

Outside the White House large numbers of Secret Service agents mixed with additional FPS bluejackets in commando gear were running across the south lawn towards a large, unmarked, black Chinook jerkily waddling on its skids right above the earth, while other plainclothesmen leapt out the Chinook's hatches holding loaded Uzi automatics in their hands.

An unarmed passenger in civilian clothes disembarked the portside hatch and was immediately led to the waiting jeep, which raced away towards the Old Executive Office Building. Upon his arrival outside the door to Room 208, the visitor was quickly frisked by a team of techs with metal wands who nodded their OK to a pair of Secret Service agents, who, in turn, allowed the guest to enter. Once inside, the visitor released his grip on the briefcase he was holding while two more techs passed their wands across it several times before handing it back.

"Alexi, you already know the identity of everyone here, I'm sure," National Security Advisor McDowell spoke without a hint of sarcasm.

Russian Ambassador Prince Aleksander Sokolinsky merely nodded in response.

All faces at the table intently examined the razor-thin Russian nobleman, wondering if he would be willing to cooperate.

"We need your help."

Chapter 64

Stepping around the five dead crew members, HYDRA unsnapped the 33-bullet ammunition clip on the Glock, double-checking to be sure it wasn't empty, since the Model 18 cycles ammunition at 1,200 RPM, twice as fast as the Heckler & Koch MP5. But HYDRA was an experienced operator, he'd only expended twelve bullets on five targets, leaving him more than enough to take care of the pair of computer techs stationed aft before he would have to reload.

Unlike the Boeing 707 passenger plane upon which it is

based, the E-6A's hull is compartmentalized, so neither the computer operators aft nor the second crew asleep in their bunks nor the flight crew forward had heard any shots or had any idea the communications crew was already dead. Letting himself through the partition door, HYDRA passed the IBM mainframe, walking twenty feet along the corridor until he reached the pair of techs, one of whom barely had time to glance up before he was shot in the chest along with his partner.

HYDRA sprinted back along the corridor, shoving open the door to the communications room, when he caught sight of a figure standing in the door opposite. A member of the sleeping second shift had awaken to go to the bathroom and was just about to pass into the communications area. HYDRA fell in a crouch and, supporting his gun hand with his left arm, fired three rounds into his victim's chest who fell backwards, crashing into the bunk beds. Before the remaining members of the second shift could analyze what had happened, HYDRA dashed across the communications area and entered the bunk room, firing methodically at the man in each bed. Some died still asleep, while others were cut down with their hands on their bunk belts, struggling to free themselves.

HYDRA ejected the Glock's empty ammunition clip, grabbed another one from his flight suit pocket, and slammed it into his gun, while he ran through the empty lounge towards the cockpit. Now only four crew members were left: the pilot, copilot, navigator and flight engineer, all of whom had their backs to him. With his left hand HYDRA pulled open the flimsy cockpit door, firing from left to right in controlled bursts of three shots each. HYDRA moved quickly and unstrapped the pilot from his seat, dragging his corpse out the cockpit into the lounge where he left it on the floor. Still flying on autopilot, the 350,000-pound Boeing eerily maintained its course, a ghost-ship seemingly unperturbed by its sudden lack of crew.

Returning to the pilot's seat, HYDRA strapped himself in and donned the dead man's headset. He first set the civilian VHF transceiver, then the automatic direction finder, to 118.3 megahertz, the frequency he'd agreed upon with the Iraqis.

HYDRA waited a full half-minute before he heard it, a single one-second-long tone, barely strong enough to activate the TACAMO's automatic direction finder. He checked the compass needle. The TACAMO was set on a course going almost due east at 095, ninety-five degrees, while the Iraqi submarine was almost 175° straight south. He slowly turned the autopilot's compass knob to realign the 707's heading in the direction of the sub, set the vertical speed knob to a descent rate of 2,000 feet per minute with a new cruising altitude of 10,000 feet, giving him a fifteen minute interval to gather up his equipment.

After he had unstrapped himself from the pilot's seat, HYDRA jogged aft through the fuselage to the communications compartment where he'd thrown his heavy jacket behind the console. He knelt over it on the floor, tearing the lining completely away. From the jacket's remnants he extracted the lightweight Navy T-10 parachute with life jacket and day/night flare, fixed-blade knife with a web belt, two grey-colored swim fins, man-overboard ACR personal strobe, and ICOM Model M-15 handheld miniature waterproof VHF transceiver he'd purchased in New York. He stripped off his coveralls, tossing them over Bacon's corpse, then sat on the floor, pulling the rubber pants of the dry suit up over his legs until his feet fit firmly in the attached latex booties. Leaving the top part of the suit unfastened and dangling from the back of his waist, he gathered up the rest of the equipment and went aft past the computer room to the TACAMO's storage compartments located directly over the backup VLF power supply.

Punching open all the overhead compartments, HYDRA rifled through the contents of each, tossing what he didn't need on the floor beside him, until he found the inflatable life rafts. Sorting through them, he selected the smallest of the lot, then tested its CO2 cartridge to check its pressure. Satisfied, he struggled into the top half of the dry suit, strapped the web belt holding the knife on his leg, checked to see if it was tight, then pulled the life jacket over his wet suit. Next, he fastened on the parachute so the waistband was free of turns and twists and the ripcord handle was positioned on his right.

As the 707 lost altitude it encountered turbulence, and more than once HYDRA had to grasp the nearest object to keep from being pitched forward. Steadying himself against the VLF power supply, he attempted to perform a last-minute check of his parachute. He first rechecked the release assembly, making sure his canopy wasn't protruding and that the ripcord handle was truly in place, then rechecked the reserve chute in the same manner. His watch now indicated he had less than a minute to return to the cabin.

Gathering up the inflatable life raft, HYDRA walked quickly forward, returning to the cockpit, where he stood over the pilot's seat and reset the airplane's rate-of-climb knob to zero, putting it into altitude hold mode at 10,000 feet.

The next step was to slow the plane down, he couldn't very well jump out of a craft moving at over 500 miles per hour, so HYDRA pulled the flap and gear handles down, then dialed in 120 mph on the speed command control next to the autopilot. The 707 was still on autopilot, and with its flaps and gears down it would continue flying at 120 miles per hour at a level of 10,000 feet until it ran out of fuel, which would be several hours after his departure.

Leaning over the dead flight engineer's console, HYDRA turned the manual pressure controller to the "Full Decrease" position in order to depressurize the cabin, reducing the 8.6-pounds-per-square-inch differential to zero. Swallowing hard to keep his ears from popping, HYDRA knelt down on the cockpit floor and removed the $2^{1}/_{2}$- by $2^{1}/_{2}$-foot panel, creating an open hole which led to the equipment and electrical access door on the bottom of the aircraft's fuselage. Throwing the life raft down the tunnel before him, HYDRA dropped three feet into the cold air of the aircraft's lower floor. Pushing the life raft in front of him, he crawled past the PV-20 autopilot control and rows of generator relays, keeping his head below the rows of multicolored flight control cables running overhead. Finally reaching the E & E access door, he strapped in the life raft, then rotated the circular handle ninety degrees, and pulled the door panel up and inward, instantly filling his nostrils with a blast of fresh ocean air and revealing a gray sea marked with white caps rushing by below.

Positioning himself so that he was facing aft, HYDRA knelt into a crouch on the door's rim, and shoved himself out, immediately straightening his legs once he was out to guide his body away from the fuselage above. The Boeing roared past, disappearing into the gloom.

With both hands tightly clasped over his reserve parachute, HYDRA began to count out loud, "One thousand, two thousand, three thousand, four — " until he was interrupted by the sudden opening of the canopy. Grasping the risers, he thrust them apart, then threw his head back to find his suspension lines were twisted. Reaching behind his neck, he jerked the risers away from his body and kicked his legs in the direction opposite the twist. Straightening out the lines had consumed several precious seconds, barely giving HYDRA enough time to remove his waist band and loosen the left side of his reserve chute in order to put on his fins. Once his fins were on, he set the quick release box to the unlocked position, removed the safety clip, and removed the safety covers of the Capewell releases.

Now only a hundred feet above the frigid ocean, he moved his fingers over the Capewells, waiting until just before he plunged into the water to yank down the left release and press the quick release box to free himself from the leg straps and harness. The T-10 lay flattened on the water's surface, its gores withered up like a dying flower. Quickly surfacing, HYDRA swam towards its apex, trying not to gulp sea water as he gathered up the parachute with his hands as he went, not daring to leave it floating on the sea.

Breathing heavily, HYDRA unstrapped the inflatable raft from his life jacket, activated its CO_2 cartridge, let it explode open, and clambered aboard. Lying on his back, he extracted the ICOM radio from his life jacket, turned it on, and immediately began transmitting in Morse code on Marine Band Channel 21, his prearranged frequency with the Iraqis.

Chapter 65

As the first of the nine submarines in the Atlantic Fleet transmitted its locator message over a broad range of frequencies, some of the transmissions were captured by a low-earth-orbit Russian electronic surveillance satellite (EORSAT), *Kosmos* 1908. Continuing on its orbit around the earth, the *Kosmos* 1908 picked up a sideband radio signal from the nearest *Iskra* communications satellite in geostationary orbit above it, telling the *Kosmos* it was in range and activating its transmitter. The *Iskra* satellite in turn downlinked the transmission from the *Kosmos* to a ground station in Tyuratam where it was automatically forwarded it to the Electronic Intelligence (ELINT) Division of the Main Intelligence Directorate of the Russian General Staff (GRU) located at Khodinka Central Airfield inside Moscow.

Three seconds later, a bewildered technician tore a hard copy from a printer, rushing it to the office of Major General Vasiliy Monisov, the night duty officer, who was half-asleep at his desk.

"What is it?" growled Monisov, rubbing his eyes.

"It's from an American SSBN, but I don't understand why it's not encoded," replied the technician, handing Monisov the message.

THE QUICK BROWN FOX JUMPS OVER THE LAZY DOG. SSBN 727.

The blood drained from Monisov's face, as he immediately realized the transmission's implications, implications unknown to the technician in front of him.

"When did you get this? *When?*" shouted Monisov.

"Just now. I brought it to you right after — "

The telephone rang and Monisov grabbed the receiver, ignoring the frightened technician.

"The same message? ...When did we get it? ...What submarine? ...No! Keep calling me!" he ordered, slamming down the receiver and grabbing another in its place.

☆ ☆ ☆

In addition to the construction of over seventy-five different underground command posts within an eighty-mile radius of Moscow, each hardened against the effects of a direct nuclear attack, the Russian military has installed a communications system known as *Kazbek*, linking not only the various command centers, but also connecting the residences, dachas, and vehicles of key officials to be contacted in a nuclear emergency to those commands. In addition, all officials connected to the *Kazbek* network were accompanied twenty-four hours a day by a liaison officer of the general staff, sometimes called a *Shurika*. During a surprise attack the *Shurika* would aid the relevant official to transmit the official launch codes using his nuclear suitcase.

After receiving almost simultaneous calls from Major General Monisov, *Shurikas* in different parts of Moscow awoke Lieutenant General Yegor Shumeyko, Monisov's superior officer; Pavel S. Grachev, Minister of Defense; Viktor Dubynin, Chief of the General Staff; Dimitriy Zhukov, Commander-in-Chief, Strategic Rocket Forces; and Boris Yeltsin; President of the Russian Federation. Monisov's last call was to Vice-Admiral Nikolay Volkov, the night-duty commander of the Russian Navy.

After Volkov hung up his telephone, he rushed to a nearby cryptography room, sat down in front of a locked computer terminal, inserted his key, and entered the password to bring up a full menu of transmissions which Volkov already knew by heart. Next, he typed a two-numbered code, automatically selecting the option which would alert the Russian Navy's entire Atlantic Submarine fleet over ELF.

"Transmission received SSBN 733, the *Nevada*," echoed throughout the GRU facility at Khodinka as additional staff members, many half-dressed, rushed across the floor to their empty seats.

"Transmission received SSBN 656, the *George Washington Carver*."

"*Kosmos* 1904 passing over U.S. East Coast in sixty seconds. *Kosmos* 1904 passing over U.S. East Coast in sixty seconds," a second operator's voice announced.

Kosmos 1904, called a RORSAT, was a radar ocean reconnaissance satellite in low earth orbit designed specifically for maritime surveillance, while *Kosmos* 1908, its companion, was an electronic surveillance (ELINT) bird, designed to detect electromagnetic transmissions originating from oceangoing vessels. Both *Kosmos* 1904 and 1908 rebroadcast these observations over the *Iskra* communications satellite network which was downlinked to an earth station in Tyuratam and connected to the Kremlin by buried cable.

"Monisov," the GRU lieutenant general answered his phone. His caller was Admiral Ivan Ilyushenko, Commander of the Russian Navy. "Yes, Admiral, we'll have the new set of coordinates in less than a minute…Yes, sir."

Monisov's staff had already begun the process of elimination, matching the coordinates of the transmissions received over the EORSAT with the thermal images detected by its companion satellite, the RORSAT. They were hoping to single out an isolated white patch amidst a "sea" of green, giving them the location of the one submarine which failed to respond to the locator request. Meanwhile analysts informed Monisov that radar ocean surveillance satellites operating over both the Atlantic and Pacific Oceans confirmed the existence of seventeen American SSBNs, hovering right beneath the water's surface, all menacingly poised for a preliminary strike against the Russian Confederation.

Chapter 66

A not-widely-advertised-fact is that in addition to its land-line circuit, which runs from Washington to London, Copenhagen, Stockholm, Helsinki and Moscow via cable, undersea cable and microwave relay, the Washington-Moscow hot line also possesses two satellite circuits. In the 1980s an earth station was erected at Fort Detrick, Maryland with the capability of receiving signals from Russian *Molniya* satellites, uplinked to a Russian transmitter located in Vladimir. At the same time, the Russians built an Intelsat ground terminal in Moscow to downlink signals from Intelsat's Etam, West Virginia transmitter. Terminals exist in the NMCC at the Pentagon and the former Office of the General Secretary of the Soviet Communist Party in the Kremlin. Initially, the second satellite circuits were conceived as merely a backup for the hotline's duplex teletype, until analysts on both sides realized they were underutilizing the satellites' transponder bandwidth and decided first to add facsimile for charts and maps and, later, video for full teleconferencing between the two commands.

Except for quarterly test broadcasts, the teleconferencing option of the hot line had never been used. But upon the arrival of Aleksander Sokolinsky at the White House, President Clinton instructed an aide to send a teletype message to the Kremlin, requesting an immediate teleconference between both countries' NCAs. Almost instantaneously, a television picture, which was focused on a large conference table in the Kremlin's Situation Room, appeared on Display Screen 3, showing harried civilians leafing through stacks of papers and officers in uniform rushing to their seats, all sharing the same grim, determined look. Their bustle was transmitted clearly over the linkup's audio channel, giving everyone in Room 208 an eerie feeling as they overheard several whispered Russian conversations. One by one each Russian took his seat, leaving only the head of the table unoccupied. Then, to a man, they all stood up as Boris Yeltsin entered the room, took his place, and motioned to them to return to their seats.

"Mr. President," Clinton began, "due to the time constraints involved I will be brief. I assume that by now you have already been alerted to the fact that our entire SSBN fleet has just surfaced." Clinton paused, receiving only a curt nod of acknowledgment from President Yeltsin.

"Unfortunately, I was forced to take this drastic step because we have very good evidence that an individual aboard one of the TACAMO planes is a terrorist, masquerading as an American technician. We also believe that this individual has managed to steal the NCA authentication codes.

"We have also lost all contact with our military's satellites, and as a result, no longer have any means of receiving communication from our own submarine fleet."

After a brief pause, during which the Russian interpreter finished his almost simultaneous translation of President Clinton's remarks, all hell broke loose on the Russian side. Four-star generals began quarreling with civilian advisors, while Yeltsin went into an immediate huddle with the two men nearest him, Defense Minister Pavel Grachev and First Deputy Secretary to the Security Council, Lieutenant-General Valeriy Manilov. Lieutenant-General Manilov broke the silence by speaking in clear British-accented English.

"What do you want from us?"

"General Manilov, we'd like you to decrypt the transmissions from *Kosmos* 1904 and *Kosmos* 1908 and uplink them over both the *Molniya* and *Iskra* birds," quickly replied Clinton's national security advisor, J. Mark McDowell.

While the Russian interpreter was finishing translating McDowell's request to him, with a quick wave of his hand Yeltsin summoned his assistant, Victor Ilyushin, speaking first with him, then Lieutenant-General Manilov, who, in turn, gave the Russians' answer.

"We consent to your request on three conditions: first, from here on out you transact all further orders to your forces *en clair*; second, you reveal today's code groups for all active nuclear forces; and third, you grant us a ten-year moratorium on all principal and interest payments of the Confederation's debts to the United States."

"Mr. President!" objected Maddox, the chief of staff.

"I accept," Clinton responded, no longer caring what his advisors thought. No nuke was going off on his watch, period.

☆ ☆ ☆

While general Ernest Hueter sat at his desk his eyes transfixed on NORAD's empty screens, telephones rang all around him, their lines jammed with calls from hundreds of no-longer functioning listening stations.

"General? General Hueter?"

Hueter snapped out of his reverie; an adjutant was standing next to him holding a telephone handset in his hand.

"It's Director Daniels in Washington. Something about downlinking a couple of Russian birds."

Hueter grabbed the telephone and was immediately informed that the Russians had agreed to downlink unencrypted transmissions from *Kosmos* 1904 and *Kosmos* 1908 to a still functioning Intelsat civilian earth station.

Chapter 67

"Cherokee Zero One Zero One, patching through Pax River tower, standby."

"Standing by."

"Cherokee Flight Leader, this is controller Epps at Pax River. Aircraft six three nine one eight departed this base approximately 3:00 p.m. local time this afternoon. Pilot indicated he would maintain cruising speed of four-four-zero knots at flight level four-zero-zero flying in an easterly direction, before reversing course for rendezvous with tanker at three-three-one-two degrees north seven-seven-three-five degrees west."

"Roger Pax River, please estimate subject aircraft's present position and course," requested Wyand.

"Based on his flight plan, six three nine one eight's present location is three-six-three-six degrees north, seven-five-five-zero degrees west, heading two-two-five."

"Roger."

Wyand entered the E-6A's estimated location into F-16's tactical electronic warfare system, silently cursing to himself when he received the answer. The TACAMO was over 300 miles distant, 10 minutes away from possible initial radio contact and 12 minutes from maximum range of the AIM-120 AMRAAM radar-homing missile under his wings.

"Mr. Woodring," Wyand announced over the intercom, "we've got a problem."

☆ ☆ ☆

"EORSAT on Screen Two," a clerk announced in the NMCC.

Admiral Alexander turned in his seat. Display Screen Two was solid blue, save for the single word EORSAT, the acronym for the Russian ELINT ocean reconnaissance satellite, glowing in the upper right-hand corner.

"Navy Flag Plot on Screen One."

A computer rendering of the twenty-five-foot-tall wall map in the Navy Flag Plot Room appeared on Screen One, showing the locations of every SSBN, SSN, and aircraft carrier in the Atlantic Fleet.

"First confirmation incoming."

On Screen Two the acronym LANTCOM began to flash on and off, while the following telex message was rebroadcast via Russian satellite:

"THE QUICK BROWN FOX JUMPS OVER THE LAZY DOG. SSBN 733."

The master of the *Nevada* had just signalled via UHF that he had received a highly unusual request from Fleet Communications in Norfolk to identify himself *en clair*.

Next, the blinking green light on the Navy Flag Plot on Screen One corresponding to the *Nevada* changed from blinking green to solid blue.

"THE QUICK BROWN FOX JUMPS OVER THE LAZY DOG. SSBN 727."

The *Michigan*, Alexander thought to himself.

"THE QUICK BROWN FOX JUMPS OVER THE LAZY DOG. SSBN 630."

Almost immediately a second light on the Navy Flag Plot, representing the *John C. Calhoun*, switched from flashing green to solid blue.

"RORSAT on Screen Five," an operator spoke over the public address system at NORAD, announcing the linkup with the Russian ocean radar reconnaissance satellite network.

General Ernest Hueter and every technician in the NORAD operations pit watched Display Screen Five come alive over an electronic map of the western Atlantic Ocean, instantly revealing a fast-moving radar blip representing the F-16 flying east across the Atlantic towards the more slowly moving blip of the E-6A.

"General?" An aide, leaning over his shoulder, whispered to Ernest Hueter, CINCNORAD. "We're getting a faint Morse transmission on EORSAT about 157.25 megahertz. You want to take a look at this?" The aide handed Hueter a copy of HYDRA's transmission, deciphered from the Morse.

"What the hell is it?" Hueter exclaimed, furrowing his brow.

"It's not a distress signal. We couldn't figure out what it was," explained the aide.

☆ ☆ ☆

"There it is!" exclaimed Admiral Alexander, watching the RORSAT display at the NMCC.

"Sixth incoming confirmation," blared over the public address system.

"THE QUICK BROWN FOX JUMPS OVER THE LAZY DOG. SSBN 729."

The *Georgia's* blinking green light changed to blue on Screen One, but Alexander ignored it and grabbed his telephone, punching the extension connecting him to the White House Situation Room.

"Situation Room, Maddox speaking," replied the President's chief of staff.

"We've located the TACAMO! What do you want to do about it?"

"Just a minute."

"Eighth confirmation incoming."

"THE QUICK BROWN FOX JUMPS OVER THE LAZY DOG. SSBN 659." The *Will Rogers*.

"Kansas City ARTCC reports no activity over Whiteman Air Force Base. Repeat, Kansas City ARTCC reports no activity over Whiteman Air Force Base," echoed over the NMCC's public address system.

"What's happened to the *Alabama*?" someone shouted.

"Radio them back!" Alexander yelled.

"We did!"

"Well, radio them again, damnit!"

"Sir, you have a call from NORAD," an operator's voice broke in on the line.

"What do they want?" Alexander barked, then he saw it on the NORAD screen — a VHF emergency distress radar beacon had just been picked up by the Russian ELINT bird, and was rapidly blinking on and off. But the TACAMO hadn't crashed, its symbol was still moving in a straight line directly across the ocean!

"Shit! He's in the water!" Alexander cursed under his breath, then double-checked the Flag Plot on Screen One.

The *Alabama* was on routine patrol, sailing towards the Arctic Circle. Its last known location was at 63N 30W in the Denmark Straight, near the wreck of the HMS *Hood* which had been sunk by a German U-boat in 1941. The nearest carrier group was thousands of miles away and the nearest attack submarine was eight hundred miles distant; the only ASW assets available anywhere nearby were a squadron of P-3C Orions stationed at Naval Air Station Keflavik on Iceland's west coast. Alexander picked up a second telephone, speaking without introduction to an aide.

"Prepare a telex for Admiral Frewin at Keflavik telling him to use whatever ASW assets he has to locate and sink an unnamed submarine — last location 63 North 30 West."

"Yes sir."

☆ ☆ ☆

"Cherokee Flight Leader, Cherokee Flight Leader."

"Roger, tower, this is Flight Leader."

"Target is at three-six-two-four degrees north seven-five-three-five degrees west, speed one-zero-four knots."

"*104 knots?*" repeated Woodring over the F-16's intercom, wondering why the TACAMO's speed was so low.

"Cherokee Flight Leader," Langley tower interrupted.

"Roger."

"Russian bird's ID'd a second target, broadcasting on one-five-seven-two-five megahertz, three-six-five-five degrees north seven-five-four-six degrees west, approximately twenty-five miles north-northwest of aircraft."

"That's him!" shouted Woodring.

"Mr. Woodring," replied the pilot, "I think I should remind you our visibility's going to be close to zero."

"You just get me there, major. We're going to find him."

☆ ☆ ☆

Admiral Alexander's order to sink the USS *Alabama* was instantly retransmitted by Keflavik Naval Air Station Command to a lone P-3C Orion, flying routine patrol off Iceland's west coast. Its entire crew had just been transferred to Keflavik from Moffett Field NAS outside San Francisco, where they had all been members of antisubmarine warfare (ASW) Squadron VP-19.

Alerted by the aircraft's navigator-communicator, Skip Allen, that they had just received a set of encrypted orders from the Keflavik Command, the P-3C's pilot, Patrol Plane Commander Curtis Roland, and his second-in-command, Lieutenant Tom Engle, were stunned while Allen read them aloud over the intercom.

"We are to proceed to 63 North 30 West at once, locate unknown submarine, and await order to destroy it while transmitting entire operation to NAS Command *en clair*."

"What the frigging hell?" Roland blurted out. "Are you out

of your fucking mind?"

"You want to read it, Commander, you're welcome to come back and take a look yourself."

In exasperation, Roland turned to his copilot, Engle, while unstrapping himself from his seat.

"Tom, you take over for a sec. I'm going back there and find out what's going on."

The third pilot, Jerry Christenberry, who was seated between and somewhat to the rear of Engle and Roland, removed his handset and unstrapped his seatbelt to allow Roland to pass by.

Nav-Comm Allen was stationed six feet aft behind a partition, seated in front of a console filled with navigation and radio equipment and a teletype on his left. Roland tore the message from his hand, reading it in silence.

"Very funny. 'Sink a submarine whose last known location is at 63N 30W. All further communications to be *en clair*.'" Roland's sense of humor vanished.

"Radio command back and request for confirmation. And ask for the name of who's sending this and by what authority."

"Whatever," sighed Allen and quickly typed Roland's request on his keyboard, encrypted it, then transmitted it over VHF.

While Roland stood waiting with one hand resting on the metal bulkhead, the teletype responded almost immediately. Roland watched it roll out the printer and tore it off.

Z151656ZMAR

COMPARTMENTALIZED TOP SECRET

NUCFLASHNUCFLASH***NUCFLASH***

FM: KEFLAVIK NAS COM

TO: P-3C 64

1. TRANSMIT ENTIRE OPERATION INCLUDING

ALL FURTHER COMMUNICATIONS FROM YOU TO US EN CLAIR REPEAT EN CLAIR.

2. ORDER Z1516442Z MAR CONFIRMED REPEAT ORDER Z151644Z MAR CONFIRMED.

ADMIRAL FREWIN.

"Jesus!" Roland gasped.

"Unidentified target RORSAT Screen Five," blared over NORAD's public address system.

The pair of radar operators monitoring the RORSAT birds had picked up a new target fifty miles southeast of HYDRA's VHF transmitter, which, at first, might have been surface interference, but then revealed itself as a man-made object by virtue of its straight-line movement.

"Target painted Screen Five. ID UK Zero Two." Unknown Object Zero Two was making a beeline towards the VHF beacon, which was labeled UK-01 on the same screen.

"Bearing one-five-seven, speed 5 knots. UK Zero Two ETA UK Zero One in ten minutes."

"Unidentified target EORSAT Screen Two matching position UK Zero Two on Screen Five, transmitting single tone on 118.3 megahertz."

"Cherokee Flight Leader."

"Roger, this is Flight Leader."

"Third target's just been ID'd by both satellite recon and signals, broadcasting sixty-second intermittent tone on one-one-eight-three megahertz, bearing one-five-seven, speed ten knots, approximately fifty miles from aircraft and less than one mile from second target."

"Roger," Wyand replied, immediately entering the second

frequency into his automatic direction finder.

"They've come to pick him up!" Woodring exclaimed.

"Not if I can help it," muttered Wyand, setting his APG-70 pulse-doppler radar on maximum range of 80 nautical miles.

Almost immediately, the APG-70 picked up the TACAMO's transponder code, marking the target on the screen with a fresh velocity vector and altitude reading.

☆ ☆ ☆

"Radar contact on aircraft. No V.I.D. Target's steady at 105 knots at 10,000 feet," Wyand's voice echoed throughout the NMCC.

☆ ☆ ☆

In the White House Situation Room, President Clinton and his staff sat frozen to their seats, watching the two radar blips on the display screen converge.

"Fifty west of target," Wyand updated them.

In less than two minutes he'd be within range of HYDRA and the TACAMO.

☆ ☆ ☆

Wyand popped beneath the cloud cover at 20,000 feet. His altimeter showed he was descending rapidly, and his cockpit was surrounded by a sea of gray.

"Forty west of target."

With his thumb Wyand switched the button on the stick from DESIGNATE to DOGFIGHT, arming the AMRAAM's radar.

"Lock thirty miles, 10,000, and fire."

The twelve-foot-long missile shot towards the TACAMO at Mach 4, transiting the thirty-mile distance between the F-16 and its target in less than a minute. Woodring felt his ears pop violently; as they broke through the cloud cover, the AMRAAM smashed into the TACAMO's right wing, blowing it clear off, and the 707 cartwheeled into the ocean directly before them with a silent, fiery splash.

"Target down," Wyand uttered, resetting the APG to DOWNLOOK.

"I see it!" Woodring yelled. "There it is! To the right!"

There it was, bobbing amidst the roiling whitecaps, a white one-man life raft.

"V.I.D. UK Zero One," responded Wyand, slowing his throttle.

A pinpoint of light flashed forty degrees to starboard. Someone was operating a man-overboard emergency beacon, unwittingly revealing his position.

Wyand jinked the F-16 to the right, flying only two hundred feet above the deck directly towards the rubber raft, when the conning tower broke the surface. He released the arm switch, pressed the throttle back and opened up his M61A1 20mm gun, firing in a straight line leading directly to the raft and submarine. HYDRA was already in the water halfway between the raft and the sub, a tiny wake behind his moving form. Bullets spat into the water, stitching diagonally across the raft, ripping into the back of HYDRA's Goretex dry suit, and ricocheting off the hull of the submarine, killing a pair of sailors in the tower.

Roaring past the targets, Wyand executed a high-G roll to reacquire the submarine, flipping his battle computer to "combat radar". Leveling out at an altitude of 600 feet, Wyand retraced the path over the cold Atlantic, his APG-70 radar indicating he had target lock. Wyand pressed the trigger, releasing a single Harpoon subsonic antiship missile. The Harpoon fell to 100 feet and skimmed above the whitecaps, its radar homing guidance systems fixed on the Foxtrot's giant metal hull. It slammed into the conning tower, tearing it totally from the hull with its 488-pound charge, leaving the Iraqi submarine helpless in the water, before it rolled over and sank.

☆ ☆ ☆

"…General Robert Shelton on Channel 7, General Robert Shelton on Channel 7," an announcer warned over the public address system of the White House Situation Room. A second later Shelton's face filled the screen, the chaos of the NMCC's Crisis Management Room in the background.

"Mr. President, with the receipt of positive confirmations from all seventeen other SSBNs which are presently afloat, and after several repeated efforts to contact it, we have failed to receive any reply whatsoever from SSBN 731, the *Alabama*."

In the Situation Room a bright halogen spotlight automatically snapped on, illuminating the Commander in Chief's haggard face. Bill Clinton, the president whom one general had publicly dismissed as a pot-smoking draft-dodging womanizer, was now faced with the most important military decision of his career. Failure could mean death for millions, turning him overnight into the political pariah of the century.

"I thought the *Alabama* had confirmed receipt of the EAM for BROKEN ARROW and POLE VAULT! Now you're telling me it's incommunicado! Which is it? You think HYDRA's already released an authenticated EAM to that sub or not?"

"Mr. President, I'm sorry, but at this point, I have no way of knowing what orders the *Alabama* may or may not have received from the TACAMO. All I know is what I just told you."

Adjacent to the display screen showing General Shelton was an electronic situation map, one showing the sector of the Atlantic containing the last known location of the *Alabama* at 63N 30W.

"Mr. President?" prompted J. Mark McDowell, the national security advisor. President Clinton nodded, giving McDowell the floor. The national security advisor's face was, in turn, illuminated by a halogen spot.

"General Shelton, just for a second here, let's assume the worst has happened. How long is the time window for the *Alabama* to launch its ICBMs?"

"The captain has ninety minutes to act on a valid order."

"Do the Russians know about what time the TACAMO lost speed and dropped altitude?"

"Yes, about fifteen minutes ago."

"So, if we are to assume that the reason the TACAMO's lost altitude and speed is because HYDRA's bailed out of it, and that he's issued a valid EAM to the *Alabama* right before bailing out, we now have less than seventy-five minutes left, am I correct?"

"Correct."

"Let's also assume for a moment that Captain Parker will wait to almost the last minute to launch, making every attempt he can that he has a valid order. What antisubmarine assets will be in range of the *Alabama* in the next seventy-five minutes?"

"The only thing we've got is a lone P-3C Orion patrol aircraft that will be within detection range ten minutes from now. The nearest SSN, the *Providence*, is over 800 miles away, the *Enterprise* carrier group is over 2,500 miles away, neither of which gives us enough time to do anything but rely totally on the P-3."

"Mr. President?" interrupted Lieutenant-General Manilov.

"Yes?"

"We would like to see the *Alabama's* target list immediately if this is possible, since it is only reasonable to assume that the majority, if not all of the targets lie inside the Russian confederation."

"Mr. President!" General Turner, CINC-SAC, began to object, but Clinton cut him off.

"Mr. President!" shouted Admiral Alexander at the NMCC.

"Mr. President!" protested National Security Advisor McDowell.

"Print it out now, Dick! We don't have time for debate here. Before this thing's over we may need the Russians' help to sink this thing!"

☆ ☆ ☆

Turner picked up his telephone, punching the extension for his second-in-command.

"Charlie, bring up the SIOP 7 options for SSBN 731."

Moments later the following display filled a separate screen at every command center, revealing to all participants for the first time what would happen if the USS *Alabama* were to unleash its full complement of Trident II ballistic missiles.

SIOP 7
EAM 3533
PAGE ONE

FM: NCA
TO: SSBN 731

*** HAMMERCUT DECLARED *** HAMMERCUT DECLARED ***
HAMMERCUT DECLARED ***

MISSILE NO. 1   MISSILE NO. 2

WARHEAD NO. 1   WARHEAD NO. 1
TARGET: ALEKSEYEVKA AF   TARGET: SMORGON'
COORDINATES: 49 14N 140 11E   COORDINATES: 54 36N 026 23E

WARHEAD NO. 2   WARHEAD NO. 2
TARGET: VOTKINSK   TARGET: SOL'TSY AF
COORDINATES: 57 03N 053 59E   COORDINATES: 58 09N 030 20E

WARHEAD NO. 3
TARGET: DROVYANAYA
COORDINATES: 51 26N 113 03E

WARHEAD NO. 3
TARGET: TROITSK
COORDINATES: 54 05N 060 40E

WARHEAD NO. 4
TARGET: SKALA-PODOL'SKAYA
COORDINATES: 48 51N 026 09E

WARHEAD NO. 4
TARGET: VENTSPILS
COORDINATES: 57 24N 021 31E

WARHEAD NO. 5
TARGET: SHERMETYEVO
COORDINATES: 55 54N 037 20E

WARHEAD NO. 5
TARGET: ENERGODAR
COORDINATES: 47 30N 034 28E

WARHEAD NO. 6
TARGET: TATISHCHEVO
COORDINATES: 51 42N 045 36E

WARHEAD NO. 6
TARGET: ZAPADNAYA LITSA
COORDINATES: 69 25N 032 30E

WARHEAD NO. 7
TARGET: GLADKAYA
COORDINATES: 56 22N 092 26E

WARHEAD NO. 7
TARGET: PAVLOGRAD
COORDINATES: 47 00N 035 03E

WARHEAD NO. 8
TARGET: KALUGA
COORDINATES: 52 05N 041 00E

WARHEAD NO. 8
TARGET: GUSEV
COORDINATES: 54 44N 022 03E

☆ ☆ ☆

The same display screen in each command center silently scrolled through all twelve pages of Emergency Action Message 3533, listing a total of 192 different cities, towns, and military bases targeted inside the Russian confederation. In the now silent American command rooms not a single participant had the least doubt that, if it was executed, EAM 3533 would result in an eventual full-scale nuclear exchange with a furious Russian military.

☆ ☆ ☆

Chaos broke out for the second time in the Russians' Situation Room with Yeltsin's advisors arguing quite audibly amongst themselves. President Yeltsin, ignoring the others, now huddled with General Manilov and Yevgeniy Primakov, the head of the Foreign Intelligence Service, the successor organization to the old KGB. The three Russians nodded their heads in agreement, then Yeltsin glanced around the table, frowning at the spectacle his advisors were making.

"Silence! Silence!" Yeltsin ordered, bringing the meeting back to order.

"Mr. President?" spoke Primakov.

"Who's that?" Clinton demanded in a whispered aside to J. Mark McDowell.

"Yevgeniy Primakov, head of the FIS — the old KGB."

"President Yeltsin is quite worried that your armed forces will be unable to successfully prevent the *Alabama* from carrying out her mission, if, in fact, she has received a valid order from the TACAMO. I think you as a politician can understand, especially after seeing the target list General Turner has just shown us, that it would be impossible for the Russian people not to retaliate immediately to an attack of this magnitude, whether intentional or no. In order for us to preclude this chain of events from occurring I think we are going to have to be much more frank with each other."

"What's he getting at?" Clinton whispered.

"Just wait," McDowell replied.

"Mr. President? Do I have your full attention?"

"Yes. Yes. Go on."

"As I was saying, I think both sides are going to have to reach an understanding, almost immediately, regarding the intentions of the *Alabama*. What if this terrorist has succeeded? What if he has convinced the captain to launch his missiles, all twenty-four of them? What do you think the captain will do if he detects sonobuoys being dropped around his submarine?"

President Clinton glanced at the display screens on either side of the Russians, noticing the mute faces on his generals at

SAC, NORAD, the NMCC.

"What would President Yeltsin like us to do?" Clinton replied sotto voce.

Primakov turned to Yeltsin, who was listening to a simultaneous translation of his remarks with a small headset in his right ear. Yeltsin nodded once.

"Mr. President, we'd like you to release the DOOMSDAY codes for the *Alabama*."

"The what?"

"Mr. President!" objected General Turner at SAC.

"Mr. President!" interrupted General Shelton at the NMCC.

"Mr. President!" Lincoln Daniels simultaneously exclaimed in Room 208.

Clinton ignored their protests, he was already engaged in a furious whispered conference with J. Mark McDowell.

☆ ☆ ☆

While the President was whispering feverishly to his national security advisor, Mark Pruitt, a computer operator on night duty at the AT&T toll switching station in downtown Manhattan, was startled by the ringing of an artificial bell emanating from his control console.

"ANI failure 202T. ANI failure 202T," a computerized voice repeated.

Pruitt sighed. One of the 911 Emergency calling modes had just lost its Automated Number Identification compatibility, something relatively easy to fix. Then the bell went off again.

"Voice network failure, PSAP 1004 Section K. Voice network failure, PSAP 1004 Section K. ANI failure 202T. ANI failure 202T."

Pruitt furrowed his brow. The entire 911 system for lower Manhattan was collapsing. Before he could even initiate a test, the bell rang out a third time.

"All circuits to PSAP 1005 are down. All circuits to PSAP 1005 are down. ANI failure 202T. ANI failure 202T. Voice network failure, PSAP 1004 Section K. Voice network failure, PSAP 1004 Section K."

Pruitt was madly entering test commands into his keyboard, trying to locate the problem, when the automatic warning bell ominously rang yet a fourth time.

"All PSAP circuits are down. All PSAP circuits are down."

Several lights were blinking red on the electronic switching control center map above him, when a klaxon-like buzzing tone, much louder than the previous warning bell tones, almost jolted Pruitt from his seat.

"4ESS 54 is going down. 4ESS 54 is going down."

The toll switch was going into a fault and recovery routine: the entire switching station was shutting down. Pruitt typed even more furiously at his keyboard, ordering the system to tell him what part of it had failed, when the klaxon-like buzzer sounded a second time.

"4ESS 54 is back up. 4ESS 54 is back up."

Pruitt leaned back in his chair, his eyes focusing on the electronic map. The system was still in disarray and hundreds of lights were now blinking on and off; the last announcement was obviously wrong, the switch couldn't possibly be back in service.

The buzzer inexplicably blared a third time.

"4ESS 54 is going down. 4ESS 54 is going down."

☆ ☆ ☆

In a different kind of war room behind a large glass window pane, Don Halpin overlooked the AT&T Network Operations Center (NOC) in Bedminster, New Jersey. Two stories of the huge diamond-shaped telephone company complex were devoted to a twenty-foot-high wall containing seventy-two video display screens, each monitoring a different portion of AT&T's entire long distance network. Similar to the operations pits at SAC and NORAD, a team of technicians was present in the NOC twenty-four hours a day, seated at their consoles to insure AT&T's automated switching center was operating smoothly.

When Halpin glanced up at the video wall, he noticed a dot had appeared on the map of the continental United States in its center. The video screen for Switching Center 54 was radiating red-and-blue lines; the switching center in lower Manhattan had gone down, and calls were being rerouted to other nearby stations. Halpin wasn't particularly upset; the system had been purposely designed to handle just such occurrences, and the software would instantly detour Switching Center 54's calls somewhere else.

Exactly five minutes later, the NOC's computer updated itself, refreshing all seventy-two video displays. Halpin looked out his window. Several network managers were speaking animatedly on the phone. Switching Center 54 had just been joined by Centers 72, 31, and 88, located respectively in Washington, D.C., Omaha, and Denver. Red-and-blue lines radiated from each, while now four dots blinked on and off on the map. Halpin was about to leave his office for the operations floor when his extension rang.

"Halpin."

It was Lorraine Kipp, area technician for the Atlantic states.

"We've got a problem."

"I know. I've seen the board."

"This is worse. I don't think you want to wait for the next update."

Halpin was silent.

"The whole East Coast is out."

"It's what?"

"The whole East Coast is down. I've got thirty switching stations on the blink with a new one going down every ten seconds!"

"Just a minute." Halpin put Kipp on hold and grabbed another receiver, automatically patching him through to NESAC, AT&T's Network Switching Assistance Center in Lyle, Illinois. The techs at NESAC handled the problems beyond the capacities of the staff at NOC.

"Keith Kintigh please. This is Halpin at NOC. We've got an emergency here."

"Hold on a minute, please and I'll get him," replied the operator.

While Halpin hung on the line, the screens on the video display wall updated themselves. Status maps were lit with over fifty red-and-blue starbursts flashing on and off, while another set of screens representing the status of 800-number service, microwave relay towers, coaxial cables, and satellite earth stations were also blinking on and off. The visual effect was dazzling, like a light show at a discotheque, and Halpin found the display impossible not to watch. Every operator on the floor was in a frenzy, fielding several calls at once, desperately trying to reroute fallen trunk lines to switching centers still in operation only to have the substitute center subsequently collapse. The whole network was out of control.

"*Hello? Hello?*" Halpin desperately repeated into his receiver, then froze in his seat.

The line had just gone dead.

He knew the connection to NESAC didn't go through the switching network, it ran over one of AT&T's own private long distance lines. Automatically checking the monitor in the upper left-hand corner of the display wall, Halpin found it was blinking madly on and off. AT&T's own high-priority intracompany communication system had just crashed. Next Halpin checked the adjacent screen for the military's

WWMCCS network. It was blinking, too.

☆ ☆ ☆

General Manilov leaned close to Boris Yeltsin and whispered something in his ear, while Yeltsin maintained a somber expression. It was obvious the U.S. military didn't entirely trust their own Commander in Chief.

"*Bozhe moi!*" someone shouted. My God!

Boris Yeltsin's eyes automatically went to the display screen. It was blank. The Americans had just gone off the air!

"Surprise attack!" exploded Grachev. "They're planning an attack!"

"Get the Americans on the teletype!" Manilov shouted. Around him, generals were grabbing their telephones, and issuing orders to the Russian military to go to full alert.

"It's dead!" shouted Ilyushin, tapping helplessly at the keys.

☆ ☆ ☆

Simultaneously at Room 208, NORAD, SAC, and the NMCC, all display screens went blank, all telephones were dead, and all telecommunications circuits turned off. Suddenly every command center was isolated from its counterparts, each no longer being able to communicate with its respective forces in the field.

☆ ☆ ☆

"Range to target?" PPC Roland asked over the intercom.

"Five miles," replied Allen, the navigator.

Aft of the helicopter, a crewman shoved an MK-77 passive sonobuoy into one of four diagonal tubes, jutting from the helicopter's deck, then bent over and sealed the lid, automatically activating an indicator on Roland's console.

"Releasing first sonobuoy," Roland announced, pulling up

the first of four yellow levers to his right.

Roland rolled the P-3 into a turn, coming right at 173 degrees, trying not to think about the implications of what he was doing, the words "Destroy unidentified submarine" repeating over and over in his mind.

"Load second sonobuoy," he ordered, hearing his own words as if he were in a dream.

Nuclear war. Holocaust. Armageddon. It couldn't be happening — he had just talked to the controller on the radio for God sakes!

"Curt? Curt? The second sonobuoy's ready!" Engle, the copilot, reminded him.

Roland automatically pulled the second yellow lever.

"Releasing second sonobuoy."

"No target ID'd on Sonobuoy 1…Repeat, no target ID on Sonobuoy 1," announced the sensor operator, sitting amidships.

Roland winced. The unnamed submarine was no longer at 63N 30W, which would make finding it a lot more difficult. He knew he would need at least two, preferably three contacts to defeat the target before his Tacco would be able to locate and track it, but the P-3's supply of sonobuoys was limited, he couldn't drop them endlessly all across the ocean. A submarine could travel at 25 to 30 knots at top speed, giving the target a new detection radius of 1,200 square miles every sixty minutes; while the P-3 could only hope to cover 400 square miles per hour, leaving Roland at a hopeless disadvantage. Of course, besides the sonobuoys the P-3 possessed a pair of additional detection devices: forward-looking infrared scanners (FLIRs) and MADs, magnetic anomaly detectors. The FLIRs could identify variations in heat between the surrounding ocean and the body of a submarine, while the magnetic anomaly detectors looked for variations in the earth's magnetic field caused by large masses of metal. Unfortunately, the latter two sensors' ranges were both less than a few square miles, forcing PPC Roland to rely on his sonobuoys during a general search like the one in which he was presently engaged.

☆ ☆ ☆

"No target ID'd on Sonobuoy 2," the SENSO's voice blared throughout the Russians' Situation Room, followed immediately by a translation of the American operator's remarks.

"It's a trap!" Grachev protested. "They haven't found it because they have no intention of finding it! They're just stalling us, so we can't issue a retaliatory launch!"

Yeltsin remained silent with his arms crossed over his chest, his face drawn tight with tension, while an adjutant entered the room and hurriedly spoke into the ear of Lieutenant-General Manilov.

"All the telecommunications lines to the U.S. are down!"

"*Nu tak chto!*" snorted Yevgeniy Primakov, "our satellites still are functioning. Radio our embassy and tell them to tell Sokolinsky to get the codes!"

"No target ID'd on Sonobuoy 3," blared over the public address system.

"Load active sonobuoy now," Roland's voice replied.

An active sonobuoy would begin transmitting the moment it hit the water, sending out a loud and audible sonar ping to any submarine within its seven-mile range.

☆ ☆ ☆

Thirty minutes after the UHF satellite messenger buoy had been launched from the *Alabama*, a timer went off inside the unit, activating a whip antenna which automatically extended three feet in the air, transmitting Captain Parker's message to Fleet Communications to *Kosmos* 1908, the Russians' low-earth-orbit electronic surveillance satellite. The message only took five seconds to transmit, and after it was sent, the buoy automatically sank to the ocean bottom. The nearest *Iskra* communications satellite dutifully transmitted the messenger buoy's encrypted broadcast to a ground station in Tyuratam where it was decrypted and automatically forwarded it to the Situation Room in the Kremlin. There an aide ripped it off the teletype and rushed a copy to Lieutenant-General Manilov.

"My God! It's been sent! We're going to be attacked!"

Chapter 68

Aboard the USS *Alabama* three sonarmen sat in cushioned chairs under a dim blue light, their faces glued to an eight-foot-long bank of cathode-ray tube displays. Behind them a supervisor sat on a stool, holding an intercom in his right hand. The *Alabama* had just slowed to a speed of eight knots, when the sonar operator monitoring the BQR-23 towed array saw several of the three rows of green lines in his sonar display flash white.

"Sierra One contact, bearing two-two-zero."

"What the hell?" the supervisor gasped, his eyes riveted to the screen.

"Sierra One contact bearing two-three-zero," intoned the operator, trying to control his voice.

"Conn, sonar," the supervisor spoke into his intercom, "we've got a contact bearing two-four-zero."

"What's the speed?" asked Captain Parker.

"Sierra One, now bearing two-three-five, range one-zero-five-hundred yards at thirty-one knots," spoke the first technician.

"Computer shows Sierra One contact as Victor III-class *Submarine No. 7*," added the first technician.

The supervisor was stunned. He hadn't seen a Russian attack submarine along the Atlantic coast in months, now his operator was telling him they were being stalked by a Victor III whose usual duty was to escort Russian SSBNs near the Russian coasts thousands of miles away!

"What is it?" demanded Parker over the intercom.

"It's, it's a Victor III," stuttered the supervisor.

"Come again."

"A Victor III, *Submarine No. 7.*"

"Sierra Two contact, bearing zero-five-zero," interrupted the second operator. "Speed three zero knots."

"Conn! Sierra Two at zero-five-zero!" repeated the frantic supervisor over the intercom.

Parker felt his blood run cold. The *Alabama's* BQQ-6 sonar couldn't estimate the attacking subs' range much farther out than ten miles, but their torpedo range was up to twenty miles, possibly already putting the *Alabama* and its crew at risk. Any questions he now had over the validity of the EAM had vanished, he was already under attack by a Russian wolf pack and would have to maneuver his way out to survive.

"Computer shows Sierra Two's a Tango-class, *Submarine No. 15.*"

"Let's get out of here!" Parker ordered, speaking to his OOD, Stuart Morse. "Course south at ten knots."

"Helm, all ahead two thirds," barked Morse to the helmsman.

"Sierra One bearing two-one-zero," reported the sonar supervisor. "Sierra Two also maintaining bearing, now zero-four-five."

"Right twenty degrees rudder, steady course south."

"Sierra Two changing course, bearing now zero-seven-five, maintaining three zero knots and still out of range," announced the supervisor, then adding, "Sierra One also changing course, bearing now one-eight-five, still out of range."

In the red light of the control room Captain Parker mopped

his brow with his sleeve, the Russian attack subs were still criss-crossing their section of the ocean, which meant they hadn't located the *Alabama* on their sonars yet.

Chapter 69

A piercing ringing sound jolted several crypto clerks out of their seats in a basement room of the Russian Embassy on 16th Street in Washington. This certain bell, which had already rung once before that same day, signified an incoming message of the highest priority from the Kremlin. It was addressed to the senior intelligence officer, Sergey Skorinov, with instructions for Skorinov to decode it himself.

Skorinov was quickly summoned from his office and brought to the communications room, where he signed a receipt for the telex, then, in a highly unusual manner extracted a one-time code pad from his pocket and proceeded to decipher his orders on the spot. The clerks watched as Skorinov's face went white and his hands began to shake. The message, in English, was brutally simple:

PROCEED IMMEDIATELY ROOM 208 OLD EXECU-TIVE OFFICE BUILDING AND INFORM AMBASSADOR SOKOLINSKY WE HAVE JUST INTER-CEPTED ENCRYPTED CONFIRMATION REQUEST FROM AMERICAN SSBN NO. 731 USS ALABAMA RE EMERGENCY ACTION MESSAGE 3533 SIOP 7 FROM NCA TO SSBN 731 STOP HAVE SOKOLINSKY INFORM PRESIDENT CLINTON WE DEMAND IMMEDIATE RELEASE OF DOOMSDAY CODES FOR SSBN 731 OR WE WILL ASSUME LAUNCH ON WARNING STATUS IN NEXT TEN MINUTES STOP WE WILL ALLOW YOU PRECISELY NO LESS THAN 5 (FIVE) MINUTES TO REACH ROOM 208 STOP.

PRIMAKOV

Skorinov madly patted down his pockets searching for his

car keys, then burst out the door, taking the stairwell to the parking lot. The embassy was between M & L Streets, only five blocks from the Old Executive Office Building on 17th and G. Flashing his ID at the sentry in the lot and yelling at him to open the gate, Skorinov ran pell-mell towards his car, an old Mercury Monterey, ripping open the door and slamming his foot on the accelerator. Honking his horn madly and barely missing the slowly moving gate, Skorinov flew past the sentry and roared out the drive into traffic on 17th Street.

Reaching under his seat, he grasped an emergency red flashing beacon, slapped it on his dash, then punched the Monterey's emergency blinkers and proceeded to run every light between L Street and Pennsylvania Avenue. Skorinov slammed to a halt at the West Executive Avenue vehicle gate between the West Wing of the White House and the rear of the Old Executive Office Building. His sudden arrival alarmed the uniformed Secret Service sentries on duty, who ran out of their hut and pointed their automatics at his windshield.

"Get out of the car!" yelled one, dragging Skorinov by the arm, flipping him against the windshield.

"Who are you? What do you think you're doing?"

"I must see Ambassador Sokolinsky!" Skorinov pleaded, as the agent fished his wallet from his back pocket.

"Gary, this guy's Russian! He's with the FIS!"

"Please! Read this! I have no time!" Skorinov begged, reaching for his shirt pocket.

"Hold it!" snapped the agent. "Easy. I'll take that."

The agent grabbed Primakov's telex and quickly read it.

"Shit! We've got problems. Keep him there, I've gotta call Burnett." Depressing the button on his walkie-talkie the agent contacted the acting duty chief of the Secret Service Uniform Division.

"Cal, this is Mark outside. I got a Mister Skorinov here from the Russian Embassy who wants to see his Ambassador in Room 208 — ...Yes, sir. Yes, sir. Yes — " Mark turned to his partner. "Get in the car! Now!"

"What about the gate?"

"Fuck the gate! We're taking him to the east door now!"

Shoving Skorinov back in his car, the first agent took the wheel as his companion jumped in the passenger door, sandwiching a frightened Skorinov between them. They raced the short distance along the rear of the Old Executive Office Building on West Executive Avenue, skidding to a stop across the security entrance. As if by magic a tow truck appeared behind them and a pair of grim-faced uniform agents leaping out its doors and attaching a lift to the underside of Skorinov's car. A team of dogs burst out the security entrance, straining at their leashes, barking at Skorinov as he stepped out the door and sniffing all around the Mercury for a hidden bomb.

"What are they doing?" cried Skorinov, watching his car being towed away.

"Let's worry about that later!" snapped the sentry, grabbing his right arm and frogmarching him to the main door while he was screaming into his walkie-talkie.

"Sergey Skorinov?" asked a plainclothesman inside the entrance. Behind him stood a crowd of thirty gun-toting Secret Service, FPS, and Marine guards.

"Yes?"

"Follow me!"

A squad of six agents detached itself from the throng, fully surrounding Skorinov and his handler. Not trusting the elevator, they ran up a stairwell, exiting on the second floor and dashed towards the heavily guarded entrance to Room 208. The combination lock had already been released, allowing Skorinov to enter the crisis center without delay.

"*Sergey?*" whispered Ambassador Sokolinsky.

Saying nothing, Skorinov handed Prince Sokolinsky the

telex from the Kremlin.

"My God...it's happened," uttered Sokolinsky in shock.

President Clinton reeled back in his chair as if he had received a physical blow, and J. Mark McDowell leapt from his seat, snatching the cable from Sokolinsky's hands, instantly scanning its contents.

"The codes! Mr. President! The codes! You've got to release the codes or we'll all be destroyed!"

Skorinov cast a desperate glance towards Sokolinsky, but the Ambassador's eyes were riveted on Bill Clinton.

"Let's go," the young president ordered, grabbing Sokolinsky by the arm.

"Mr. President!"

"Mr. President!"

"Mr. President!"

But Bill Clinton was already outside the door, shouting orders to a phalanx of uniformed and plainclothes Secret Service agents.

Chapter 70

Captain Parker stood peering at the *Alabama's* electronic chart table, a four-foot-square CRT wired directly into the submarine's new central processor. The courses of the two Russian SSNs were expressed by blue lines, the *Alabama's* a red line. If the sonar reports were correct, the *Alabama* was now heading in the opposite direction of the two Russian submarines, so that the two sides were separating at almost fifty knots per hour. Already more than ten miles distant, the Russian subs would be be out of torpedo range in another fifteen minutes. Temporarily out of range, Parker thought to himself, knowing the moment he gave the order to fire his SLBMs he would also automatically be giving away the *Alabama's* location.

☆ ☆ ☆

Flying out of the West Executive Avenue vehicle gate with sirens blaring, a high-speed motorcade bearing President Clinton, Sergey Skorinov and J. Mark McDowell raced past Lafayette Park towards the Russian Embassy. Motorcycle outriders sped ahead of dark sedans, halting cross traffic at the intersections of Pennsylvania Avenue, H, I, and K Streets, allowing the caravan to proceed nonstop through the Embassy's open eight-foot-high iron gates.

The parking lot was filled with Russian FIS plainclothesmen, shouting into walkie-talkies and uniformed sentries holding automatic weapons. Sharpshooters bearing high-powered rifles stood openly in the urn-balustered balconies, their eyes sweeping back and forth. A crew of Secret Service shoved the President out of his limousine, forming a human shield around him and following him to the door. Skorinov led the way inside, directing them along a corridor to the nearest stairwell which they took to the communications room, while Skorinov shouted at the pair of sentries to unlock the door.

The small staff of crypto clerks inside couldn't believe their eyes; Skorinov was with the President of the United States!

"Prepare to transmit!" Skorinov shouted, further frightening them.

A Secret Service agent slammed a briefcase on a nearby desk, ripped open his shirt, snapped a keychain off his neck, immediately unlatched both locks and flipped open the lid, grabbing a small cassette filled with strong, plastic CD-ROM disks. He extracted one of the disks from the cassette and inserted it into a slot on the other side of the briefcase. Tapping madly on a miniature keyboard, the agent entered the word DOOMSDAY, followed by alphanumeric term SSBN 731. The small display screen on the briefcase's lid blinked once, filling with twenty-four 10-digit numbers, the DOOMSDAY codes for each of the USS *Alabama's* Trident II ballistic missiles.

"Missile Number One," spoke the agent without any further explanation, "Zero-Eight-Four-Zero-Three-Four-Nine-Seven-Eight-Eight.

"Repeat: Zero-Eight-Four-Zero-Three-Four-Nine-Seven-Eight-Eight."

One of the Russian code clerks entered the digits into his console as Skorinov double-checked him, then muttered the order for it to be transmitted to the Kremlin.

"Missile Number Two," the agent intoned, "Zero-Seven-Three-Seven-Five-Three-Three-Nine-Seven-Six.

"Repeat. Zero-Seven-Three-Seven-Five-Three-Three-Nine-Seven-Six."

"Missile Number Three: Three-Eight-Four-One-Four-One-Eight-Nine-One-Three.

"Repeat. Three-Eight-Four-One-Four-One-Eight-Nine-One-Three."

On the floor of the GRU early warning facility at Khodinka Central Airfield, a frantic operative entered the digits into his console, causing the DOOMSDAY codes for the USS *Alabama's* third Trident missile to scroll across a large display screen. Other technicians plotted the azimuths of each of the *Alabama's* twenty-four ballistic missiles, transmitting the results as soon as they were computed to a large electronic map of the Russian Confederation, while Major General Monisov shouted instructions over his telephone to the ground station at Tyuratam, demanding that every satellite aloft be made available for an imminent transmission.

☆ ☆ ☆

After receiving orders from the Kremlin, strategic bases throughout Russia switched to launch-on-warning status: Strategic Rocket Forces ICBM silos dotted along the Trans-Siberia Railway opened their hatches; pilots of Tu-16 Badger, Tu-22 Blinder, Tu-22M Backfire and Tu-95 and -145 Bear bombers belonging to the 4th, 24th, 30th, 36th and 46th Air Armies were ordered to take off and proceed towards their pre-assigned targets; and four SSBNs belonging to the Russian Navy which were already on alert under the Arctic Ice Cap, the North Atlantic, Western Pacific, and Southern Atlantic slowed their speed and checked their arming circuits in anticipation of a final launch order.

☆ ☆ ☆

In the communications room of the Russian Embassy in Washington, President Clinton sat alone in a chair, his eyes staring into space. By inserting a couple of hundred lines of code, a mere computer programmer had effectively stripped him of his command, forced him into a bunker, and left him unable to contact his forces.

☆ ☆ ☆

"4ESS 54 is back up. 4ESS 54 is back up."

At the AT&T toll switching situation in downtown Manhattan, Mark Pruitt almost jumped out of his seat. The toll switch was back up; display screens showing the status of the station's various networks indicated that each was suddenly back in full operation.

☆ ☆ ☆

At the AT&T Network Operations Center in Bedminster, New Jersey, Don Halpin watched the spider web of blinking red-and-blue lines begin to recede, starburst by starburst, until, in a matter of less than ten seconds, AT&T's entire long-distance network appeared to have been completely restored.

Halpin stared dumbstruck at the bank of seventy-two television monitors as the room was filled with the sound of ringing telephones.

From his glassed-in command cubicle General Ernest Hueter watched Display Screens Two and Five go blank. The transmissions from NORAD's last remaining sensors, the Russians' ocean ELINT and radar reconnaissance satellites, had just ceased.

"RORSAT is down."

"EORSAT is down."

"The Russians have disconnected us!"

Before Hueter could react, Display Screen Two came alive again, this time revealing the original sector map for NORAD's own PAVE PAWS radar. Inexplicably, sectors 2 and 8 began flashing on and off, soon to be followed by sectors 5 and 6, and finally, sector 7.

"PAVE PAWS has resumed transmission," answered a startled technician.

"Repeat, PAVE PAWS is back on the air."

Hueter's jaw dropped in shock. A second display screen showing one over-the-horizon radars had just lit up.

"OTH-B Sector 4 is up. OTH-B Sector 4 is up."

A third screen began blinking off and on.

"OTH-B Sector 6 is up. OTH-B Sector 6 is back on the air."

On the operations floor previously silent telephones rang all at once along with several others in Hueter's office.

"CINC-NORAD," Hueter replied in a daze, watching the screens light up one after another. It was General Ford at Sunnyvale. NRO's Big Blue Cube had reacquired contact with its fleet of satellites. Out his window Hueter watched the display for DSPS WEST come alive.

"DSPS WEST is on the air. DSPS WEST is up."

"BMEWS Thule has resumed transmission. BMEWS Thule — "

Hueter punched a second extension, instantly connecting him to Carter Marshall, Director of the Defense Special Missile and Aeronautics Center (DEFSMAC) at Ft. Meade, when the screen for DSPS EAST resumed transmission, showing the unmistakable tracks of hundreds of Russian planes heading inexorably for the United States.

"My God!" Hueter gasped. "It's war!"

☆ ☆ ☆

Warning klaxons sounded in the operations room of the Strategic Air Command: with the restoration of telephone service previously isolated base commanders began calling for their orders; ground stations were reporting squadrons of Russian bombers heading towards the Arctic; and commanders of Scott, Grand Forks and Whiteman Air Bases were demanding updates on the status of their false EAMS.

In his cubicle, General Dick Turner, seeing the chaos in the other command centers reflected in the teleconferencing screens, immediately reached for the gold telephone hoping to get a response from the other end.

"Argus Control."

"Get me General Ford!"

☆ ☆ ☆

In the parking lot at the Russian Embassy, an alert Secret Service agent answered the radiotelephone inside President Clinton's limousine, gripping it more and more tightly as he listened to his caller, the Director of the Secret Service.

"Right!" he answered, slamming the handset back in place. He let himself out of the car, walking in a deliberate fashion towards the door, where he was stopped by a pair of uniformed Russian sentries.

"Call from Mrs. Clinton for the President."

The sentries shrugged, letting him pass. Sprinting along the corridor, he found the stairwell and bounded down the three flights to the communications room, where he met a second set of sentries who waved him through.

"Mr. President," whispered his visitor. "Can I have a word with you for a moment?"

☆ ☆ ☆

"We have to countermand! We have to send the codes!" the CINC-SAC's voice blared over the public address system at the NRO's Satellite Central Facility in Sunnyvale, California.

"We can't!" objected Haywood Ford. "We've already tried! Saleh's cut us off! We can only watch!"

☆ ☆ ☆

"Jesus!" uttered Turner, "we've been set up."

☆ ☆ ☆

"Sonarroom, give me status of contacts Sierra One and Two," requested Captain Parker aboard the *Alabama*.

"Negative, Captain. We've lost them. They must be out of range."

"Well, Mr. Lesar? Are you ready?"

"Yes, sir," replied the XO.

"Alright, XO, update fire control systems."

"Yes, sir."

Lesar took a seat and began typing on a console connected to the sub's MK-2, MOD 7 Ships Inertial Navigation System to determine the *Alabama's* exact location in order to properly program the MK-98 FCS fire control system.

"Sound general quarters! Lieutenant Morse ascend to launch depth!" Parker told the OOD.

"Helm, ascend to launch depth!" Morse repeated to the helmsman.

Taking a seat next to Lesar, Captain Parker turned on his launch panel while he spoke in his microphone.

"Man Battle Stations Missile, begin countdown!"

☆ ☆ ☆

President Clinton's limousine careened to a halt outside the rear entrance of the Old Executive Office Building; Secret Service agents holding weapons in their hands flew out its doors, guarding the Chief Executive as he was ushered inside by a phalanx of uniformed personnel.

Chief of staff Maddox intercepted him in the corridor, yelling above the crowd, "The Russians are in the air! It's a disaster!"

"Out of the way!" shouted an agent at a bystander.

"Move it! Move it!"

The combination doors were already unlocked, and Clinton and his aides swept past the security detail into Room 208.

One look at the displays caused the President to stop dead in his tracks: hundreds of blinking arcs representing Russian long-range bombers filled one; enlargements of open missile silos and surfaced SLBMs filled another; while teleconferencing channels connecting Room 208 to NMCC, SAC, NORAD, DEFSMAC revealed command centers collapsing into chaos: generals were futilely issuing orders to skeptical units which had previously been stood down under Operation BROKEN ARROW. Saleh's Trojan Horse had inadvertently succeeded in decapitating all the nuclear forces of the United States; Emergency Action Messages were being rejected en masse, only to be rerouted to SAC as required under Situation POLE VAULT.

"Firecontrol teams report," Captain Parker ordered.

"Tubes One and Two are ready," reported Nolan.

"Weapons status?"

"Weapons ready."

"Sonarroom report."

"No contacts, Captain."

Valves hissed in the background as its hovering system brought the *Alabama* to a final stop.

"Lieutenant Nolan, open Missile Tube One."

A much louder hissing sound broke the silence as Nolan forced air into the first missile tube to equalize its pressure with the sea pressure outside in order to facilitate a launch.

"Pressure in Missile Tube One adjusted," reported Nolan.

"XO, verify SINS location."

"SINS location is six-five three-five four-one north three-one one-nine two-eight west. Repeat: six-five three-five four-one north three-one one-nine two-eight west."

"Launch control officer, verify SINS location."

"SINS location verified," replied a nervous Lieutenant Mitchell, knowing he was about to die.

"Fire control officer, verify targets."

"Verifying Missile Number One targets now, Captain," reported the fire control officer.

"Warhead Number One coordinates: four-nine one-four north, one-four-zero one-one east.

"Repeat: four-nine one-four north, one-four-zero one-one east.

"Warhead Number Two coordinates: five-seven zero-three north,zero-five-three five-nine east.

"Repeat: five-seven zero-three north, zero-five-three five-nine east."

☆ ☆ ☆

"Transient! Transient!"

The noise caused by the opening of the *Alabama's* missile hatches had alerted the sensor operator inside P-3C Orion.

The tactical action officer immediately checked his screen: sonobuoys numbers 49 and 50 showed a weak signal at the far reaches of their combined range.

"Weak transient ID'd on buoys four-nine and five-zero!" the Tacco informed PPC Roland.

"Plot it! Plot it!" Roland ordered.

"I don't know if I can — there's not much signal!"

☆ ☆ ☆

"Warhead Number Eight Coordinates: five-two zero-five north, zero-four-one zero-zero east.

"Repeat: five-two zero-five north, zero-four-one zero-zero east."

"XO, prepare to launch!" uttered Captain Parker.

In the *Alabama's* control room, Parker and Lcsar each removed a single key from his breast pocket, while officers Mitchell and Nolan also each did the same at his respective post. Parker swung out the portable seat under the panel and sat next to Lesar.

"Insert key!"

Both captain and XO inserted their keys in the direct unlock mechanism. Nolan and Mitchell followed suit.

"Key turn!"

In the control room a slight pneumatic hiss preceded the opening of two control panels, each containing twenty-four bright red plastic switches.

In the Orion, the tactical display scope blinked on and off, its screen filled with a mixture of half-circles and jagged lines set in a background of interference. The Orion's UYS-2 processor was working overtime, trying to get a fix on the *Alabama*. Finally, two full small circles intersected by the circumference of a large circle, each with a single dot in its center, appeared on the Tacco's screen. In a split second the UYS-2 connected up the dots, and the Tacco grabbed his hand-held microphone.

"Target plotted! Range fifty-seven-thousand yards, bearing zero-five-five, no number yet for speed!"

"*What?*"

"I show no speed for tar — "

"*No!*" screamed Roland. "*No!*"

"Arm Missile Tube Number One."

Captain Parker and Lesar each flipped separate toggle switches beneath the first row of red buttons, activating a flashing red light. Lieutenants Mitchell and Nolan performed the same task at their control panels. Missile No. 1, a 34-foot-long, 70,000-pound Trident D-5 was now fully armed.

"Fire Missile Number One!"

All four officers punched the flashing red buttons at once, leaving the four switches depressed in the panel. The Trident's steam ignition system ignited and its dome-shaped shell blew off, propelling the missile out the tube and upwards through the water.

"Transient! Transient!"

"My God!"

"Holy Jesus! They've fired!"

"Range to target! Range to target!"

"Fifty-one thousand yards! Still out of range!"

☆ ☆ ☆

The missile's launch caused the Ocean Early Warning West satellite display screen in the GRU's ELINT Operations room to flare white, instantly attracting the attention of several operators on the floor.

"Launch V.I.D. on OEWS WEST! Launch V.I.D. on OEWS WEST!"

"Location is six-five three-five four-two north three-one one-nine two-seven east. Repeat: six-five three-five four-two north three-one one-nine two-seven east."

Major General Vasiliy Monisov immediately picked up his telephone, connecting him to the Situation Room in the Kremlin.

"We have a launch!"

☆ ☆ ☆

"The Americans have attacked!" gasped Lieutenant-General Manilov in the Situation Room. "They've launched!"

Turning to Boris Yeltsin, Viktor Dubynin, Chief of the general staff, exploded "How can you sit there? We have to counterattack!"

"We have twelve minutes until the first warhead hits!" added Grachev.

Yeltsin nodded, turning his gaze back to the bank of display screens in front of him.

Speaking from the center screen was Dimitriy Zhukov, Commander-in-Chief of the Strategic Rocket Forces, the division of the Russian Army which controlled the nation's ICBM bases.

"Missiles at Kostroma, Tatishevo and Kartaly, ready to fire."

Russian SS-17, SS-18, SS-20, and SS-24 ICBMs containing powerful VHF/UHF transmitters similar in function to America's Emergency Rocket Communications Systems missiles had been programmed with the DOOMSDAY codes for the *Alabama's* SLBMs and were about to be launched in order to intercept the incoming American SLBM.

"Missiles at Dumbarovskiy, Gladkaya, and Imeni Gastello, ready to fire," Zhukov announced next. Three more bases.

"Missile acquired by OEWS WEST 2," echoed a loudspeaker, connected to Khodinka. "Plotting azimuth now."

"How do we know this isn't just a ruse?" whispered Yevgeniy Primakov.

Yeltsin grunted in derision, then blinked at the sight in front of him. The teleconferencing connection with the United States had been restored; display screens were again filled with the simultaneous activity at SAC, NORAD, the NMCC, and Room 208.

"The Americans!" uttered Manilov.

"Lieutenant Nolan, open Missile tube two."

"Missile Tube Two is open."

"XO, verify SINS location."

"SINS location is unchanged."

"Launch control officer, verify SINS location."

"SINS location verified."

"Fire control officer, verify targets."

"Verifying Missile Number Two targets: Warhead Number One coordinates: five-four three-six north, zero-two-six two-three east."

"Range to target! Range to target!"

"Forty-three thousand yards!"

"Fire torpedo!" PPC Roland screamed into his headset.

"Torpedo away!"

☆ ☆ ☆

"Repeat: five-four three-six — "

"Conn, sonar! Torpedo in the water! Bearing three-two-zero!"

One of the sonar technicians ripped off his headset. "My God, it's a Mark 48!"

"It's one of ours!" gasped the supervisor.

"Helm! Left full rudder!"

"Conn, sonar! Torpedo in the water!"

"Flood the MOSS tube!" ordered Parker.

"It's a Mark 48!"

"*It's what?*"

"We're being fired on by our own men!"

☆ ☆ ☆

The Trident had shot beyond the range of Ocean Early Warning Satellite West; rows of technicians in the GRU ELINT Operations room were tensely awaiting to reacquire its flight path on a ground radar. Major-General Monisov sat in his office, his eyes glued to the displays, when the buzzer sounded.

"Missile reacquired via Olenegorski Hen House radar." Olenegorski was the distant radar ground station closest to Iceland and would be the first to reacquire the D-5 after it jettisoned its third stage rocket and "went ballistic."

"Second confirmation Olenegorski phased array radar."

Monisov heaved a sigh of relief; the phased array had confirmed the launch directly after the Hen House radar just as he expected.

"Second confirmation Olenegor — " the operator's voice halted in mid-sentence as the others saw it on the screen.

"Azimuth is two-nine-five *west!* Repeat: azimuth is two-nine-five *west!*"

"It's headed for the United States!" Monisov uttered aloud. He lurched towards a special telephone, automatically connecting him to the earth station at Tyuratam.

"The missile's headed in the opposite direction! Realign *Kosmos* 1904 west fifteen degrees now!"

"We can only move five degrees every three minutes!" warned the official.

"*Do it! Do it!*"

☆ ☆ ☆

"Missile acquired BMEWS Flyingdales!" announced the operator in charge of the Ballistic Missile Early Warning Systems at NORAD ten seconds later.

"Missile now acquired BMEWS Thule!"

"Missile now acquired PARCS." The perimeter acquisition attack radar at Grand Forks had just confirmed the two BMEWS sitings.

"Azimuth is two-nine-five southwest — "

"*It's what?*" General Turner exploded.

Stunned operators on the floors of NORAD, SAC and NRO rechecked their displays. At NORAD General Hueter punched an extension, connecting him directly to the analyst who was receiving the BMEWS report.

"What's going on? That azimuth is for the United States!"

"Sir, I just double-checked it with Thule and they're getting the same thing!"

"He's reprogrammed the missiles!" cried General Shelton.

"What's the target? What's the target?" shouted Turner.

"New azimuth now two-nine-four five-five zero-four."

What's the goddamned target?

☆ ☆ ☆

"It's headed for the United States!" uttered Manilov.

"And you idiots wanted me to counterattack!" mused Yeltsin, taking a sip from his flask, then turning to watch the display showing GRU ELINT Operations Room.

"*Kosmos* 1904's rockets firing for second adjustment of five degrees," blared the speaker. "Estimated adjustment time: one hundred eighty seconds."

☆ ☆ ☆

"Azimuth is constant at two-nine-four five-five zero-four. Estimated target one-zero-five west four-one north — "

In every American command center a dotted glowing line shot across a map of North America, showing the warhead's final destination.

"That's Cheyenne!"

"Warren Air Force Base! It's gonna hit the missile base!"

"Everything is down! We can't countermand!"

"Go commercial! Try the FEMA network!"

Operators at NORAD and SAC madly scrambled to patch themselves into any local TV, radio and overhead satellite transmission networks which possessed the capability of broadcasting once high-frequency UHF bandwidth in order to relay the DOOMSDAY codes to the incoming warhead.

☆ ☆ ☆

"*Kosmos* 1904's rockets firing for third adjustment of five degrees. Estimated adjustment time: one hundred eighty seconds."

"Azimuth constant: two-nine-four five-five zero-six. Estimated time to target three hundred sixty-two seconds."

☆ ☆ ☆

"Looking Glass! Looking Glass! Countermand!" screamed General Turner.

"The computer won't take the codes!"

"Try them again, goddamnit! Where are we on commercial?"

"Patch to KCTP unsuccessful; computer refuses to log on. Patch to SBS-1 unsuccessful; computer refuses to log on. Patch to SATCOM-2 unsuccessful; computer refuses to log on."

"Call the operator, goddammit! Fuck the computer!"

"We don't get anything!"

"*You what?*"

☆ ☆ ☆

"We can't get the operator! Phones won't dial it!"

"First reentry vehicle has departed bus," announced a GRU technician. The Trident's bus had released the first of eight multiple independently targeted reentry vehicles (MIRVs).

"Twenty-four seconds remaining until full satellite realignment."

"Second reentry vehicle has departed bus. Azimuth RV One; two-nine-four five-five three-two."

"Third reentry vehicle departing bus. Azmuth RV Two: two-nine-four five-five zero-five. Ten seconds remaining until satellite realignment."

Major General Manisov sat frozen in his chair; he knew if *Kosmos* 1904's rockets failed to reorient the satellite on schedule, the SLBM's eight independent warheads would detonate over their new targets, plunging the United States into a nuclear war with his own country, since the American public would never accept the attack as a mere accident.

"Fourth reentry vehicle departing bus. Azimuth RV Three:two-nine-four five-five five-two. Realignment in five seconds, four, three, two, one, zero."

"Issue codes to countermand!" Monisov ordered into his microphone.

☆ ☆ ☆

"Warhead One time to target: one-hundred-ninety seconds," echoed amidst the chaos of the American command centers.

"Warhead Five has departed bus. Warhead Two time to target: two-hundred-eight seconds."

"New azimuths Warheads One, Two, Three and Four target: Warren AFB MX fields Q & A and Minuteman G & K."

In Room 208 hardly anyone noticed the reappearance of the Kremlin Situation Room on Display Screen 3, until a camera brought President Yeltsin's face into full view.

"Pres-i-dent Clinton! Pres-i-dent Clinton!" shouted the voice of Victor Ilyushin over the air.

"Warhead One time to target: one hundred seconds."

"Pres-i-dent Clinton! *Do you hear me?*"

"Warhead Eight has departed bus. New azimuths Warheads Five, Six, and Seven — "

Clinton slapped a button with his hand, reducing the audio from all displays except Screen 3 to a minimum.

"President Clinton. This is Victor Ilyushin in Moscow. President Yeltsin wants you to know we have just sent the DOOMSDAY codes over *Kosmos* 1904."

On the display a beaming Boris Yeltsin raised a flask in the air, smiled, then took a gulp.

"Good luck!" Yeltsin belched in a thick accent.

☆ ☆ ☆

The first warhead hit first, plunging over one hundred feet into the earth between two silos in the "Q" MX missile field just northwest of Cheyenne. The second was a direct hit, crashing through the 20-foot-thick concrete hatch of a silo in the "A" MX-missile field, completely destroying everything inside. Riveting harmlessly into the earth, Warheads Three and Four both just missed their target silos in Minuteman-missile fields "G" and "K" across the state line in southwestern Nebraska. Warheads Five, Six, Seven and Eight rained down in quick succession, all four also missing their targets by several feet in MX fields "S" and "A" and Minuteman fields "F" and "J".

EPILOGUE

The man who called himself Edwin D. Bailey sat strapped in the same chair where Harry Volz had been, facing the same blank, mirrored wall Volz had faced. An operator sat next to him, making preliminary observation of the subject's respiration, blood pressure, and heart rate.

Behind the one-way glass, David Woodring, still wearing his flight suit, sat in the control room next to a pair of operators in swivel chairs. A duplicate set of pens danced across two rolls of paper.

"What is your name?"

"Bailey...Edwin D. Bailey."

"That's good. Was your breakfast good today?"

"Yes, very good."

"Will you be telling me the truth today?"

"Yes."

Woodring grabbed a microphone and pressed a switch to talk.

"Run through the resume."

Without a hitch, the interrogator continued.

"When did you join the Army?"

"June, 1972."

"What day?"

"The 24th."

"Enrolled what unit?"

"4th Airborne Training Battalion, Fort Benning."

"Where were you posted after that?"

"82nd Airborne, 3rd Brigade."

"What next?"

"Returned to the Special Warfare Center — "

"Next?"

"I went into the field."

"Where?"

"All over. Cuba, the base. Panama, Honduras — "

"After that?"

"I joined Special Forces."

"Which group?"

"The 5th."

"What next?"

"What do you mean?"

"What did you do next?"

"Do I have to answer this?"

"Yes."

"I joined Blue Light."

"Please repeat that."

"I joined Blue Light."

The control room operator shot Woodring a glance and touched the responding chart with his finger, indicating to Woodring a pattern of jagged sine waves which showed the subject had continually been dissimulating.

"Good. Are you afraid I might ask you something you would prefer not to discuss?"

"I want to see a lawyer."

The interrogator paused, switched off his microphone and looked to Woodring for directions. Woodring merely nodded for him to continue.

"As we've told you earlier, the law allows us to hold you for twenty-four hours without advice of counsel. Now I'm going to repeat the question: Are you afraid I might ask you something you would prefer not to discuss?"

"Look, I have immunity — you can't do this to me, I'm one

of you guys."

"Who granted you immunity?"

"Axe. Keith Axe. Ask him."

"Keith Axe is dead."

"Then ask Daniels. Ask somebody else. I don't know. Ask one of Axe's people."

"Director Daniels has been fired."

"He's what?"

"Lincoln Daniels no longer works at the CIA. He can't help you."

"He's been fired? By who?"

"By the President."

"That's impossible! Look, I don't know what you guys think you're doing, but I want to see my lawyer."

"Mr. Bailey, like we told you, we'll let you see your lawyer, but, first, we just want you to answer a few questions.

"Why is it impossible for Director Daniels to have been fired?"

"Why don't you ask him? Look, I told you, I'm a Fed, one of you guys. I don't have to answer this shit. You don't have anything on me and I demand to have my attorney present!"

☆ ☆ ☆

It was the barking dog that made him look out the window. *It was near midnight, but he was wide awake, standing on the edge of the world. The V-20 was off Islamorada in the Keys, the engine cut, floating to the mother ship. A line fell from the deck, followed by a cargo net.* His hearing was shot, but he knew they had their engines on, he knew who parked on the street. *The rail was cold and slippery; the V-20 had left them there on the ship, some World War II rust bucket with refitted diesels.* The crickets had stopped; *the dropoff point was off Bahia Honda; he later found out the boat's name was Leda. The Swan. Two .50-calibers*

*on deck with 40mm cannons fore and aft. The decoy boat,
buzzing like a mosquito, ran in circles and was lit up like a jack-
o-lantern.*

One of them had just lit a cigarette which meant they
didn't care if he could see them. He saw three cars out the
window — there would probably be more men outside, but he
didn't want to look.

☆ ☆ ☆

"Do you know Harry Volz?"

"Who?"

"Volz. Harry Volz."

"Volz?"

"That's right. Volz."

"Never heard of him."

Woodring felt a tap on his shoulder. The operator was
pointing to the charts — the subject's stress levels were going
through the roof.

"Do you know Charles Colman?"

"No!"

"Who gave you, Volz and Colman the order to shoot the
senator?"

"No one! I don't know! I don't know what you're talking
about — "

Woodring raised his right hand in the air index-finger outstretched and made a chopping action. The operator next to
him flipped a switch.

"Police! Police! Keep your hands up! Police!"

"Hey, Charlie, look at this! There's an armory over here!"

"Hey! You don't have a warrant for that!"

"Come on, Lieutenant, we're on your team."

"Lieutenant, there's enough fake IDs in here for twenty guys!"

"Where did you get that?"

"Get what, Ed?"

"Get that tape? How did you get that?"

"What tape?"

"The tape! The tape I just heard!"

"*Police! Police! Keep your hands up! Police!*"

"*Hey, Charlie, look at this! There's an armory over here!*"

"*Hey! You don't have a warrant for that!*"

"*Come on, Lieutenant, we're on your team.*"

"*Lieutenant, there's enough fake IDs in here for twenty guys!*"

"*What's that?*"

"*Lieutenant, let's be reasonable about this, we haven't done anything wrong — the Feds'll vouch for us.*"

"*I don't know who you are, Mister, but you're full of shit.*"

"No! No! Turn it off! No!"

"Who gave you the order to shoot the senator?"

"I don't know. I have no idea."

"Who ran BUNCIN?"

"I don't know! I'm telling you, I'm a Fed! I'm on contract!"

"What do you guys want? I have a deal! What do you want?"

"What deal, Ed?"

"I can't. I can't. I can't tell you — you should already know — "

For the third time Woodring motioned to the operator to play the tape.

"*FBI! Open up!*"

"*Don't shoot. We're cops!*"

"*Jesus.*"

"*Thank God, you guys ar — *"

"*Shut the fuck up!*"

"*He's got the book!*"

"*Shutup Bartel!*"

"*What book?*"

"*Inspector Rainey, I'm afraid you're going to have to hand over any evidence you may have gathered here, today, including this man's appointment book.*"

"*Are you crazy? These men are about to kill Senator Edward Kennedy! This here's the floor plan of his hotel!*"

Lanier and Mendoza escorted Inspector Rainey into the control booth; Rainey froze beside the glass when he saw the man in the chair behind the glass.

"You're sure?" demanded Woodring.

"Oh yeah. He's the one, alright."

Woodring depressed the switch on the microphone. "Show him the picture."

The interrogator reached into an envelope, extracted an $8^1/_2$-by 11-inch black-and-white photograph of the real Edwin D. Bailey and set it in front of the subject.

"Do you recognize this man?"

"Fuck you! You can't do anything to me! I've got a deal!"

Woodring punched a button on his console, murmured a few words into his headset, then punched a second switch.

"Who gave Axe the deal?" asked the interrogator.

"Fuck you! Fuck off!"

"Who did Axe work for?"

"Who was it?"

"You don't have anything, do you? What do you guys know? Nothing!"

The interrogator touched a switch on his console, dousing the lights.

"Hey? What're you doing? What's going on?"

A small movie screen descended from the ceiling ten feet from Bailey's chair. Without introduction, a camera showed a group shot of several men in their early twenties wearing Special Forces uniforms, standing in an open field. It remained on the screen for five full seconds.

"Who are these people? I don't have to look at this!"

An officer was next. He was in full-dress uniform, standing at attention.

The operator seated next to Woodring checked his chart, then shook his head.

"Is he using countermeasures?" whispered Woodring.

"No."

The third photograph was a second officer whom Bailey had never met.

"He just closed his eyes," whispered the floor operator over the intercom.

"He what?"

"His eyes are closed!"

Woodring turned to Rainey, handing him the microphone.

"Remember me? It's me, Lieutenant Rainey."

When he opened his eyes, Colonel Morrell's picture filled the screen, and in the control room, the needle flew off the chart.

☆ ☆ ☆

He went in with the brigade at dawn, made them fan out from the LZ on the shore, when the FAR arrived and sank the Rio Escondido, hit a B-26 from Happy Valley then sank the Houston, taking the rest of their supplies. By nightfall, they were still in a tight perimeter on the beach, firing their last bullets.

In the morning under the clouds and haze San Roman called

them together telling them it was all over. Then all eyes shifted to
him, the single white face in the lot. The driver in the second car
put out his cigarette and picked up a microphone. All three
cars were identical: same make, same model, same color. *No*
escape plan had been officially approved, even though the coastal
highway would take them right into the Escambray Mountains.
He found that out later during a training course at Leavenworth.

The next day Somoza's B-26s appeared at first light, only to be
torn to shreds by a pair of FAR T-33s. The Cuban ground troops
just stayed in their positions, pouring fire onto them. Some of the
men went mad and rushed arms akimbo into the water until they
were cut down. Others ran into it, holding their weapons at their
hips, cursing Castro and his men.

The dog barked again. They had left the cars all at once and
were on the sidewalk. The rifle was in the closet. He opened
the door, got it out, sat on the bed and put it in his mouth.

Death by
FIRE

For more copies of this thrilling book,
see your bookstore or call day or night,
toll free 1 800/444-2524